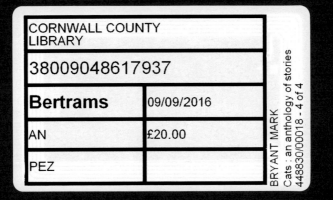

CATS

An anthology of stories and poems

Edited by Mark Bryant

ROBINSON

For Venita

ROBINSON

First published in Great Britain in 1999 as
The Mammoth Book of Cats
by Robinson Publishing

This revised edition published in 2016 by Robinson

1 3 5 7 9 10 8 6 4 2

A CIP catalogue record for this book
is available from the British Library.

ISBN: 978-1-47213-808-8

Designed and typeset in Great Britain
by Andrew Barron @ Thextension
Printed and bound in Great Britain
by Clays Ltd, St Ives plc

Papers used by Robinson are from
well-managed forests and other responsible sources

MIX
Paper from
responsible sources
FSC
www.fsc.org   FSC® C104740

Robinson
An imprint of
Little, Brown Book Group
Carmelite House, 50 Victoria Embankment,
London EC4Y 0DZ

An Hachette UK Company
www.hachette.co.uk

www.littlebrown.co.uk

CONTENTS

1

THE FIRESIDE SPHINX

Sitting drowsy in the fire-light,
winked and purred the mottled cat.

John Greenleaf Whittier (1807–92)

THE CAT BY THE FIRE

Leigh Hunt (1784–1859)

A blazing fire, a warm rug, candles lit and curtains drawn, the kettle on for tea (nor do the 'first circles' despise the preference of a kettle to an urn, as the third or fourth may do), and finally, the cat before you, attracting your attention – it is a scene which everybody likes unless he has a morbid aversion to cats; which is not common. There are some nice inquirers, it is true, who are apt to make uneasy comparisons of cats with dogs – to say they are not so loving, that they prefer the house to the man, etc. But agreeably to the good old maxim, that 'comparisons are odious', our readers, we hope, will continue to like what is likable in anything, for its own sake, without trying to render it unlikable from its inferiority to something else – a process by which we might ingeniously contrive to put soot into every dish that is set before us, and to reject one thing after another, till we were pleased with nothing. Here is a good fireside, and a cat to it; and it would be our own fault, if, in removing to another house and another fireside, we did not take care that the cat removed with us. Cats cannot look to the moving of goods, as men do. If we would have creatures considerate towards us, we must be so towards them. It is not to be expected of everybody, quadruped or biped, that they should stick to us in spite of our want of merit, like a dog or a benevolent sage. Besides, stories have been told of cats very much to the credit of their benignity; such as their following a master about like a dog, waiting at a gentleman's door to thank him for some obligation overnight, etc. And our readers may remember the history of the famous Godolphin Arabian, upon whose grave a cat that had lived with him in the stable went and stretched itself, and died.

The cat purrs, as if it applauded our consideration – and gently moves its tail. What an odd expression of the power to be irritable and the will to be pleased there is in its face, as it looks up at us! We must own, that we do not prefer a cat in the act of purring, or of looking in that manner. It reminds us of the sort of smile, or simmer (simper is too weak and fleeting a word) that is apt to be in the faces of irritable people when they are pleased to be in a state of satisfaction. We prefer, for a general expression, the cat in a quiet, unpretending state, and the human countenance with a look indicative of habitual grace and composure, as if it were not necessary to take any violent steps to prove its amiability – the 'smile without a smile', as the poet beautifully calls it [...]

Poor Pussy! she looks up at us again [...] and symbolically gives a twist of a yawn and a lick to her whiskers. Now she proceeds to clean herself all over, having a just sense of the demands of her elegant person – beginning judiciously with her paws, and fetching amazing tongues at her hind-hips. Anon, she scratches her neck with a foot of rapid delight, leaning her head towards it, and shutting her eyes, half to accommodate the action of the skin, and half to enjoy the luxury. She then rewards her paws with a few more touches; look at the action of her head and neck, how pleasing it is, the ears pointed forward, and the neck gently arching to and fro. Finally, she gives a sneeze, and another twist of mouth and whiskers, and then, curling her tail towards her front claws, settles herself on her hind quarters, in an attitude of bland meditation.

What does she think of – of her saucer of milk at breakfast? or of the thump she got yesterday in the kitchen for stealing the meat? or of her own meat, the Tartar's dish, noble horse-flesh? or of her friend the cat next door, the most impassioned of serenaders? or of her little ones, some of whom are now large, and all of them gone? Is *that* among her recollections when she looks pensive? Does she taste of the noble prerogative-sorrows of man? [...]

That lapping of the milk out of the saucer is what one's human thirst cannot sympathize with. It seems as if there could be no satisfaction in such a series of atoms of drink. Yet the saucer is soon emptied; and there is a refreshment to one's ears in that sound of plashing with which the action is accompanied, and which seems indicative of a like comfort to Pussy's mouth. Her tongue is thin, and can make a spoon of itself. This, however, is common to other quadrupeds with the cat, and does not, therefore, more particularly belong to our feline consideration. Not so the electricity of its coat, which gives out sparks under the hand; its passion for the herb valerian (did the reader ever see one roll in it? it is a mad sight) and other singular delicacies of nature, among which, perhaps, is to be reckoned its taste for fish, a creature with whose element it has so little to do, that it is supposed even to abhor it; though lately we read somewhere of a swimming cat, that

used to fish for itself. And this reminds us of an exquisite anecdote of dear, dogmatic, diseased, thoughtful, surly, charitable Johnson, who would go out of doors himself, and buy oysters for his cat, because his black servant was too proud to do it! Not that we condemn the black, in those enslaving, unliberating days. He had a right to the mistake, though we should have thought better of him had he seen farther, and subjected his pride to affection for such a master. But Johnson's true practical delicacy in the matter is beautiful. Be assured that he thought nothing of 'condescension' in it, or of being eccentric. He was singular in some things, because he could not help it. But he hated eccentricity. No: in his best moments he felt himself simply to be a man, and a good man too, though a frail – one that in virtue as well as humility, and in a knowledge of his ignorance as well as his wisdom, was desirous of being a Christian philosopher; and accordingly he went out, and bought food for his hungry cat, because his poor negro was too proud to do it, and there was nobody else in the way whom he had a right to ask. What must anybody that saw him have thought, as he turned up Bolt Court! But doubtless he went as secretly as possible – that is to say, if he considered the thing at all. His friend Garrick could not have done as much! He was too grand, and on the great 'stage' of life. Goldsmith could; but he would hardly have thought of it. Beauclerc might; but he would have thought it necessary to excuse it with a jest or a wager, or some such thing. Sir Joshua Reynolds, with his fashionable, fine-lady-painting hand, would certainly have shrunk from it. Burke would have reasoned himself into its propriety, but he would have reasoned himself out again. Gibbon! Imagine its being put into the head of Gibbon!! He and his bag-wig would have started with all the horror of a gentleman-usher; and he would have rung the bell for the cook's-deputy's-under-assistant-errand-boy.

Cats at firesides live luxuriously, and are the picture of comfort; but lest they should not bear their portion of trouble in this world, they have the drawbacks of being liable to be shut out of doors on cold nights, beatings from the 'aggravated' cooks, overpettings of children (how should we like to be squeezed and pulled about in that manner by some great patronizing giants?) and last, not least, horrible merciless tramples of unconscious human feet and unfeeling legs of chairs. Elegance, comfort, and security seem the order of the day on all sides, and you are going to sit down to dinner, or to music, or to take tea, when all of a sudden the cat gives a squall as if she was mashed; and you are not sure that the fact is otherwise. Yet she gets in the way again, as before; and dares all the feet and mahogany in the room. Beautiful present sufficingness of a cat's imagination! Confined to the snug circle of her own sides, and the two next inches of rug or carpet.

from *Essays* (c.1870)

A CAT'S FRIENDSHIP

Théophile Gautier (1811–72)

To gain the friendship of a cat is not an easy thing. It is a philosophic, well-regulated, tranquil animal, a creature of habit and a lover of order and cleanliness. It does not give its affections indiscriminately. It will consent to be your friend if you are worthy of the honour, but it will not be your slave. With all its affection, it preserves its freedom of judgment, and it will not do anything for you which it considers unreasonable; but once it has given its love, what absolute confidence, what fidelity of affection! It will make itself the companion of your hours of work, of loneliness, or of sadness. It will lie the whole evening on your knee, purring and happy in your society, and leaving the company of creatures of its own kind to be with you. In vain the sound of caterwauling reverberates from the house-tops, inviting it to one of those cats' evening parties where essence of red-herring takes the place of tea. It will not be tempted, but continues to keep its vigil with you. If you put it down it climbs up again quickly, with a sort of crooning noise, which is like a gentle reproach. Sometimes, when seated in front of you, it gazes at you with such soft, melting eyes, such a human and caressing look, that you are almost awed, for it seems impossible that reason can be absent from it.

from 'The White and Black Dynasties'
in *La Ménagerie Intime*, translated by Lady Chance

TO A CAT

Algernon Charles Swinburne (1837–1909)

Stately, kindly, lordly friend,
    Condescend
Here to sit by me, and turn
Glorious eyes that smile and burn,
Golden eyes, love's lustrous meed,
On the golden page I read.

All your wondrous wealth of hair,
    Dark and fair,
Silken-shaggy, soft and bright
As the clouds and beams of night,
Pays my reverent hand's caress
Back with friendlier gentleness.

Dogs may fawn on all and some,
    As they come;
You, a friend of loftier mind,
Answer friends alone in kind;
Just your foot upon my hand
Softly bids it understand.

Morning round this silent sweet
    Garden-seat
Sheds its wealth of gathering light,
Thrills the gradual clouds with might,
Changes woodland, orchard, heath,
Lawn, and garden there beneath.

Fair and dim they gleamed below:
  Now they glow
Deep as even your sunbright eyes,
Fair as even the wakening skies.
Can it not or can it be
Now that you give thanks to see?

May not you rejoice as I,
  Seeing the sky
Change to heaven revealed, and bid
Earth reveal the heaven it hid
All night long from stars and moon,
Now the sun sets all in tune?

What within you wakes with day
  Who can say?
All too little may we tell,
Friends who like each other well,
What might haply, if we might,
Bid us read our lives aright.

Wild on woodland ways your sires
  Flashed like fires;
Fair as flame and fierce and fleet
As with wings on wingless feet
Shone and sprang your mother, free,
Bright and brave as wind or sea.

Free and proud and glad as they,
  Here today
Rests or roams their radiant child,
Vanquished not, but reconciled,
Free from curb of aught above
Save the lovely curb of love.

Love through dreams of souls divine
    Fain would shine
Round a dawn whose light and song
Then should right our mutual wrong –
Speak, and seal the love-lit law
Sweet Assisi's seer foresaw.

Dreams were theirs; yet haply may,
    Dawn a day
When such friends and fellows born,
Seeing our earth as fair at morn,
May for wiser love's sake see
More of heaven's deep heart than we.

LE CHAT NOIR

Graham Tomson (1863–1911)

Half loving-kindliness, and half disdain,
Thou comest to my call, serenely suave,
With humming speech and gracious gesture grave,
In salutation courtly and urbane.
Yet must I humble me thy grace to gain,
For wiles may win thee, but no arts enslave,
And nowhere gladly thou abidest, save
Where naught disturbs the concord of thy reign.
Sphinx of my quiet hearth! who deignst to dwell
Friend of my toil, companion of mine ease,
Thine is the lore of Ra and Rameses;
That men forget dost thou remember well,
Beholden still in blinking reveries,
With sombre, sea-green gaze inscrutable.

TO WINKY

Amy Lowell (1874–1925)

Cat, Cat,
What are you?
Son, through a thousand generations, of the black leopards
Padding among the sprigs of young bamboo;
Descendant of many removals from the white panthers
Who crouch by night under the loquat-trees?
You crouch under the orange begonias,
And your eyes are green
With the violence of murder,
Or half-closed and stealthy
Like your sheathed claws.

Slowly, slowly,
You rise and stretch
In a glossiness of beautiful curves,
Of muscles fluctuating under black, glazed hair.

Cat,
You are a strange creature.
You sit on your haunches
And yawn,
But when you leap
I can almost hear the whine
Of a released string,
And I look to see its flaccid shaking
In the place whence you sprang.

You carry your tail as a banner,
Slowly it passes my chair,
But when I look for you, you are on the table
Moving easily among the most delicate porcelains.

Your food is a matter of importance
And you are insistent on having
Your wants attended to,
And yet you will eat a bird and its feathers
Apparently without injury.

In the night, I hear you crying,
But if I try to find you
There are only the shadows of rhododendron leaves
Brushing the ground.
When you come in out of the rain,
All wet and with your tail full of burrs,
You fawn upon me in coils and subtleties;
But once you are dry
You leave me with a gesture of inconceivable impudence,
Conveyed by the vanishing quirk of your tail
As you slide through the open door.

You walk as a king scorning his subjects;
You flirt with me as a concubine in robes of silk.
Cat,
I am afraid of your poisonous beauty,
I have seen you torturing a mouse.
Yet when you lie purring in my lap
I forget everything but how soft you are,
And it is only when I feel your claws open upon my hand
That I remember –
Remember a puma lying out on a branch above my head
Years ago.

Shall I choke you, Cat,
Or kiss you?
Really I do not know.

THE RETICENCE OF LADY ANNE

Saki (1870–1916)

Egbert came into the large, dimly lit drawing-room with the air of a man who is not certain whether he is entering a dovecote or a bomb factory, and is prepared for either eventuality. The little domestic quarrel over the luncheon-table had not been fought to a definite finish, and the question was how far Lady Anne was in a mood to renew or forgo hostilities. Her pose in the armchair by the tea-table was rather elaborately rigid; in the gloom of a December afternoon Egbert's pince-nez did not materially help him to discern the expression of her face.

By way of breaking whatever ice might be floating on the surface he made a remark about a dim religious light. He or Lady Anne was accustomed to make that remark between 4.30 and 6 on winter and late autumn evenings; it was a part of their married life. There was no recognized rejoinder to it, and Lady Anne made none.

Don Tarquinio lay astretch on the Persian rug, basking in the firelight with superb indifference to the possible ill-humour of Lady Anne. His pedigree was as flawlessly Persian as the rug, and his ruff was coming into the glory of its second winter. The page-boy, who had Renaissance tendencies, had christened him Don Tarquinio. Left to themselves, Egbert and Lady Anne would unfailingly have called him Fluff, but they were not obstinate.

Egbert poured himself out some tea. As the silence gave no sign of breaking on Lady Anne's initiative, he braced himself for another Yermak effort.

'My remark at lunch had a purely academic application,' he announced; 'you seem to put an unnecessarily personal significance into it.'

Lady Anne maintained her defensive barrier of silence. The bullfinch lazily filled in the interval with an air from *Iphigénie en Tauride*. Egbert recognized it immediately, because it was the only air the bullfinch whistled, and he had come to them with the reputation for whistling it. Both Egbert and Lady Anne would have preferred something from *The Yeomen of the Guard*, which was their favourite opera. In matters artistic they had

a similarity of taste. They leaned towards the honest and explicit in art, a picture, for instance, that told its own story, with generous assistance from its title. A riderless warhorse with harness in obvious disarray, staggering into a courtyard full of pale swooning women, and marginally noted 'Bad News', suggested to their minds a distinct interpretation of some military catastrophe. They could see what it was meant to convey, and explain it to friends of duller intelligence.

The silence continued. As a rule Lady Anne's displeasure became articulate and markedly voluble after four minutes of introductory muteness. Egbert seized the milk-jug and poured some of its contents into Don Tarquinio's saucer; as the saucer was already full to the brim an unsightly overflow was the result. Don Tarquinio looked on with a surprised interest that evanesced into elaborate unconsciousness when he was appealed to by Egbert to come and drink up some of the spilt matter. Don Tarquinio was prepared to play many roles in life, but a vacuum carpet-cleaner was not one of them.

'Don't you think we're being rather foolish?' said Egbert cheerfully.

If Lady Anne thought so she didn't say so.

'I daresay the fault has been partly on my side,' continued Egbert, with evaporating cheerfulness. 'After all, I'm only human, you know. You seem to forget that I'm only human.' He insisted on the point, as if there had been unfounded suggestions that he was built on Satyr lines, with goat continuations where the human left off.

The bullfinch recommenced its air from *Iphigénie en Tauride*. Egbert began to feel depressed. Lady Anne was not drinking her tea. Perhaps she was feeling unwell. But when Lady Anne felt unwell she was not wont to be reticent on the subject. 'No one knows what I suffer from indigestion' was one of her favourite statements; but the lack of knowledge can only have been caused by defective listening; the amount of information available on the subject would have supplied material for a monograph.

Evidently Lady Anne was not feeling unwell.

Egbert began to think he was being unreasonably dealt with; naturally he began to make concessions.

'I daresay,' he observed, taking as central a position on the hearth-rug as Don Tarquinio could be persuaded to concede him, 'I may have been to blame. I am willing, if I can thereby restore things to a happier standpoint, to undertake to lead a better life.'

He wondered vaguely how it would be possible. Temptations came to him, in middle age, tentatively and without insistence, like a neglected butcher-boy who asks for a Christmas box in February for no more hopeful reason than that he didn't get one in December. He had no more idea of succumbing to them than he had of purchasing the fish-knives and fur boas that ladies are impelled to sacrifice through the medium of advertisement columns during twelve months of the year. Still, there was something impressive in this unasked-for renunciation of possibly latent enormities.

Lady Anne showed no sign of being impressed.

Egbert looked at her nervously through his glasses. To get the worst of an argument with her was no new experience. To get the worst of a monologue was a humiliating novelty.

'I shall go and dress for dinner,' he announced in a voice into which he intended some shade of sternness to creep.

At the door a final access of weakness impelled him to make a further appeal.

'Aren't we being very silly?'

'A fool,' was Don Tarquinio's mental comment as the door closed on Egbert's retreat. Then he lifted his velvet forepaws in the air and leapt lightly on to a bookshelf immediately under the bullfinch's cage. It was the first time he had seemed to notice the bird's existence, but he was carrying out a long-formed theory of action with the precision of mature deliberation. The bullfinch, who had fancied himself something of a despot, depressed himself of a sudden into a third of his normal displacement; then he fell to a helpless wing-beating and shrill cheeping. He had cost twenty-seven shillings without the cage, but Lady Anne made no sign of interfering. She had been dead for two hours.

from Reginald in Russia (1910)

THE WELL-DRESSED CAT

Champfleury (1821–89)

The love of dress is very marked in this attractive animal; he is proud of the lustre of his coat, and cannot endure that a hair of it shall lie the wrong way. When the cat has eaten, he passes his tongue several times over both sides of his jaws, and his whiskers, in order to clean them thoroughly; he keeps his coat clean with a prickly tongue which fulfils the office of the curry-comb.

from *The Cat Past and Present*, translated by Mrs Cashel Hoey

THE DREAMING CAT

Sir Oliver Lodge (1851–1940)

Puddy is the oldest of the cats. Mostly she sits by the fireside and dreams her dreams. I imagine that she has come to agree with the philosopher that the eye and the ear and the other senses are full of deceit. More and more her mind dwells on the invisible.

THE COLLEGE CAT

Alfred Denis Godley (1856–1925)

Within those halls where student zeal
   Hangs every morn on learning's lips,
Intent to make its daily meal
   Of Tips,

While drones the conscientious Don
   Of Latin Prose, of Human
Will, Of Aristotle and of John
   Stuart Mill,

We mouth with stern didactic air:
   We prate of this, we rant of that:
While slumbers on his favourite chair
   The Cat!

For what is Mill, and what is Prose,
   Compared with warmth, and sleep, and food,
– All which collectively compose
   The Good?

Although thy unreceptive pose
   In presence of eternal Truth
No virtuous example shows
   To youth,

Sleep on, O Cat! serenely through
   My hurricanes of hoarded lore,
Nor seek with agitated mew
   The door:

Thy calm repose I would not mar,
    Nor chase thee forth in angry flight
Protesting loud (though some there are
    Who might),

Because to my reflective mind
    Thou dost from generations gone
Recall a wholly different kind
    Of Don,

Who took his glass, his social cup,
    And having quaffed it, mostly sat
Curled (metaphorically) up
    Like that!

Far from those scenes of daily strife
    And seldom necessary fuss
Wherein consists the most of life
    For us,

When Movements moved, they let them move:
    When Problems raged, they let them rage:
And quite ignored the Spirit of
    The Age.

Of such thou wert the proper mate,
    O peaceful-minded quadruped!
But liv'st with fellows up to date
    Instead –

With men who spend their vital span
    In petty stress and futile storm,
And for a recreation plan
    Reform:

Whom pupils ne'er in quiet leave,
    But throng their rooms in countless hordes:
Who sit from morn to dewy eve
    On Boards:

Who skim but erudition's cream,
    And con by night and cram by day
Such subjects as the likeliest seem
    To pay!

But thou, from cares like these exempt,
    Our follies dost serenely scan,
Professing thus thy just contempt
    For Man:

For well thou knowest, that wished-for goal
    Which still to win we vainly pine,
That calm tranquillity of soul
    Is thine!

THE SPHINX

Oscar Wilde (1854–1900)

In a dim corner of my room for longer than my fancy thinks
A beautiful and silent Sphinx has watched me through the shifting gloom.

Inviolate and immobile she does not rise she does not stir
For silver moons are naught to her and naught to her the suns that reel.

Red follows grey across the air, the waves of moonlight ebb and flow
But with the Dawn she does not go and in the night-time she is there.

Dawn follows Dawn and Nights grow old and all the while this curious cat
Lies couching on the Chinese mat with eyes of satin rimmed with gold.

Upon the mat she lies and leers and on the tawny throat of her
Flutters the soft and silky fur or ripples to her pointed ears.

Come forth, my lovely seneschal! so somnolent, so statuesque!
Come forth you exquisite grotesque! half woman and half animal!

Come forth my lovely languorous Sphinx! and put your head upon
    my knee!
And let me stroke your throat and see your body spotted like the Lynx!

And let me touch those curving claws of yellow ivory and grasp
The tail that like a monstrous Asp coils round your heavy velvet paws!

A thousand weary centuries are thine while I have hardly seen
Some twenty summers cast their green for Autumn's gaudy liveries.

But you can read the Hieroglyphs on the great sandstone obelisks,
And you have talked with Basilisks, and you have looked on Hippogriffs.

O tell me, were you standing by when Isis to Osiris knelt?
And did you watch the Egyptian melt her union for Antony?

And drink the jewel-drunken wine and bend her head in mimic awe
To see the huge proconsul draw the salted tunny from the brine?

And did you mark the Cyprian kiss white Adon on his catafalque?
And did you follow Amenalk, the God of Heliopolis?

And did you talk with Thoth, and did you hear the moon-horned Io weep?
And know the painted kings who sleep beneath the wedge-shaped Pyramid?

Lift up your large black satin eyes which are like cushions where one sinks!
Fawn at my feet, fantastic Sphinx! and sing me all your memories!

Sing to me of the Jewish maid who wandered with the Holy Child,
And how you led them through the wild, and how they slept beneath
    your shade.

Sing to me of that odorous green eve when crouching by the marge
You heard from Adrian's gilded barge the laughter of Antinous

And lapped the stream and fed your drouth and watched with hot and
    hungry stare
The ivory body of that rare young slave with his pomegranate mouth!

Sing to me of the Labyrinth in which the twi-formed bull was stalled!
Sing to me of the night you crawled across the temple's granite plinth

When through the purple corridors the screaming scarlet Ibis flew
In terror, and a horrid dew dripped from the moaning Mandragores,

And the great torpid crocodile within the tank shed slimy tears,
And tare the jewels from his ears and staggered back into the Nile,

And the priests cursed you with shrill psalms as in your claws you seized
    their snake
And crept away with it to slake your passion by the shuddering palms.

Who were your lovers? who were they who wrestled for you in the dust?
Which was the vessel of your Lust? What Leman had you, every day?

Did giant Lizards come and crouch before you on the reedy banks?
Did Gryphons with great metal flanks leap on you in your trampled couch?

Did monstrous hippopotami come sidling toward you in the mist?
Did gilt-scaled dragons writhe and twist with passion as you passed
    them by?

And from the brick-built Lycian tomb what horrible Chimera came
With fearful heads and fearful flame to breed new wonders from
    your womb?

Or had you shameful secret quests and did you harry to your home
Some Nereid coiled in amber foam with curious rock crystal breasts?

Or did you treading through the froth call to the brown Sidonian
For tidings of Leviathan, Leviathan or Behemoth?

Or did you when the sun was set climb up the cactus-covered slope
To meet your swarthy Ethiop whose body was of polished jet?

Or did you while the earthen skiffs dropped down the grey Nilotic flats
At twilight and the flickering bats flew round the temple's triple glyphs

Steal to the border of the bar and swim across the silent lake
And slink into the vault and make the Pyramid your lúpanar

Till from each black sarcophagus rose up the painted swathèd dead?
Or did you lure unto your bed the ivory-horned Tragelaphos?

Or did you love the god of flies who plagued the Hebrews and was splashed
With wine unto the waist? or Pasht, who had green beryls for her eyes?

Or that young god, the Tyrian, who was more amorous than the dove
Of Ashtaroth? or did you love the god of the Assyrian

Whose wings, like strange transparent talc, rose high above his
    hawk-faced head,
Painted with silver and with red and ribbed with rods of Oreichalch?

Or did huge Apis from his car leap down and lay before your feet
Big blossoms of the honey-sweet and honey-coloured nenuphar?

How subtle-secret is your smile! Did you love none then? Nay, I know
Great Ammon was your bedfellow! He lay with you beside the Nile! [...]

Your lovers are not dead, I know. They will rise up and hear your voice
And clash their cymbals and rejoice and run to kiss your mouth! And so,

Set wings upon your argosies! Set horses to your ebon car!
Back to your Nile! Or if you are grown sick of dead divinities

Follow some roving lion's spoor across the copper-coloured plain,
Reach out and hale him by the mane and bid him be your paramour!

Couch by his side upon the grass and set your white teeth in his throat
And when you hear his dying note lash your long flanks of polished brass

And take a tiger for your mate, whose amber sides are flecked with black,
And ride upon his gilded back in triumph through the Theban gate,

And toy with him in amorous jests, and when he turns, and snarls,
     and gnaws,
O smite him with your jasper claws! and bruise him with your agate breasts!

Why are you tarrying? Get hence! I weary of your sullen ways,
I weary of your steadfast gaze, your somnolent magnificence.

Your horrible and heavy breath makes the light flicker in the lamp,
And on my brow I feel the damp and dreadful dews of night and death.

Your eyes are like fantastic moons that shiver in some stagnant lake,
Your tongue is like a scarlet snake that dances to fantastic tunes,

Your pulse makes poisonous melodies, and your black throat is like
    the hole
Left by some torch or burning coal on Saracenic tapestries.

Away! The sulphur-coloured stars are hurrying through the Western gate!
Away! Or it may be too late to climb their silent silver cars!

See, the dawn shivers round the grey gilt-dialled towers, and the rain
Streams down each diamonded pane and blurs with tears the wannish day.

What snake-tressed fury fresh from Hell, with uncouth gestures
    and unclean,
Stole from the poppy-drowsy queen and led you to a student's cell?

What songless tongueless ghost of sin crept through the curtains of
    the night,
And saw my taper turning bright, and knocked, and bade you enter in?

Are there not others more accursed, whiter with leprosies than I?
Are Abana and Pharphar dry that you come here to slake your thirst?

Get hence, you loathsome mystery! Hideous animal, get hence!
You wake in me each bestial sense, you make me what I would not be.

You make my creed a barren sham, you wake foul dreams of sensual life,
And Atys with his blood-stained knife were better than the thing I am.

False Sphinx! False Sphinx! By reedy Styx old Charon, leaning on his oar,
Waits for my coin. Go thou before, and leave me to my crucifix,

Whose pallid burden, sick with pain, watches the world with wearied eyes,
And weeps for every soul that dies, and weeps for every soul in vain.

TO A CAT

Hartley Coleridge (1796–1849)

Nellie, methinks, 'twixt thee and me
There is a kind of sympathy;
And could we interchange our nature –
If I were cat, thou human creature –
I should, like thee, be no great mouser,
And thou, like me, no great composer;
For, like thy plaintive mews, my muse
With villainous whine doth fate abuse,
Because it hath not made me sleek
As golden down on Cupid's cheek;
And yet thou canst upon the rug lie,
Stretched out like snail, or curled up snugly,
As if thou wert not lean or ugly;
And I, who in poetic flights
Sometimes complain of sleepless nights,
Regardless of the sun in heaven,
Am apt to doze till past eleven –
The world would just the same go round
If I were hanged and thou wert drowned;
There is one difference, 'tis true:
Thou dost not know it, and I do.

2

TALES OF KITTENS

A kitten is in the animal world
what a rosebud is in a garden.

Robert Southey (1774–1843)

IN THE IMAGE OF THE LION

Heinrich Heine (1797–1856)

Wild beasts he created later,
Lions with their paws so furious;
In the image of the lion
Made he kittens small and curious.

from *Songs of Creation*, translated by E.A. Bowring

THE TAIL OF A KITTEN

H.D. Thoreau (1817–62)

A kitten is so flexible that she is almost double; the hind parts are equivalent to another kitten with which the fore part plays. She does not discover that her tail belongs to her till you tread upon it.

How eloquent she can be with her tail! Its sudden swellings and vibrations! She jumps into a chair and then stands on her hind legs to look out the window; looks steadily at objects far and near, first turning her gaze to this side then to that, for she loves to look out a window as much as any gossip. Ever and anon she bends back her ears to hear what is going on within the room, and all the while her eloquent tail is reporting the progress and success of her survey by speaking gestures which betray her interest in what she sees.

Then what a delicate hint she can give with her tail! passing perhaps underneath, as you sit at table, and letting the tip of her tail just touch your legs, as much as to say, I am here and ready for that milk or meat, though she may not be so forward as to look round at you when she emerges.

from *Journal*, 15 February 1861

THE KITTEN

Joanna Baillie (1762–1851)

Wanton droll, whose harmless play
Beguiles the rustic's closing day,
When, drawn the evening fire about,
Sit aged crone and thoughtless lout,
And child upon his three-foot stool,
Waiting until his supper cool,
And maid, whose cheek outblooms the rose,
As bright the blazing faggot glows,
Who, bending to the friendly light,
Plies her task with busy sleight;
Come, show thy tricks and sportive graces,
Thus circled round with merry faces!

Backward coil'd and crouching low,
With glaring eyeballs watch thy foe,
The housewife's spindle whirling round,
Or thread or straw that on the ground
Its shadow throws, by urchin sly
Held out to lure thy roving eye;
Then stealing onward, fiercely spring
Upon the tempting faithless thing.
Now, wheeling round with bootless skill,
Thy bo-peep tail provokes thee still,
As still beyond thy curving side
Its jetty tip is seen to glide;
Till from thy centre starting far,
Thou sidelong veerst with rump in air
Erected stiff, and gait awry,
Like madam in her tantrums high;
Though ne'er a madam of them all,
Whose silken kirtle sweeps the hall,

More varied trick and whim displays
To catch the admiring stranger's gaze.

Doth power in measured verses dwell,
All thy vagaries wild to tell?
Ah no! the start, the jet, the bound,
The giddy scamper round and round,
With leap and toss and high curvet,
And many a whirling somerset,
(Permitted by the modern muse
Expression technical to use)
These mock the deftest rhymester's skill,
But poor in art, though rich in will.

The featest tumbler, stage bedight,
To thee is but a clumsy wight,
Who every limb and sinew strains
To do what costs thee little pains;
For which, I trow, the gaping crowd
Requite him oft with plaudits loud.

But, stopp'd the while thy wanton play,
Applauses too thy pains repay:
For then, beneath some urchin's hand
With modest pride thou tak'st thy stand,
While many a stroke of kindness glides
Along thy back and tabby sides.
Dilated swells thy glossy fur,
And loudly croons thy busy purr,
As, timing well the equal sound,
Thy clutching feet bepat the ground,
And all their harmless claws disclose
Like prickles of an early rose,
While softly from thy whisker'd cheek
Thy half-closed eyes peer, mild and meek.

But not alone by cottage fire
Do rustics rude thy feats admire.
The learned sage, whose thoughts explore
The widest range of human lore,
Or with unfetter'd fancy fly
Through airy heights of poesy,
Pausing smiles with alter'd air
To see thee climb his elbow-chair,
Or, struggling on the mat below,
Hold warfare with his slipper'd toe.
The widow'd dame or lonely maid,
Who, in the still but cheerless shade
Of home unsocial, spends her age,
And rarely turns a letter'd page,
Upon her hearth for thee lets fall
The rounded cork or paper ball,
Nor chides thee on thy wicked watch,
The ends of ravell'd skein to catch,
But lets thee have thy wayward will,
Perplexing oft her better skill.

E'en he, whose mind of gloomy bent,
In lonely tower or prison pent,
Reviews the coil of former days,
And loathes the world and all its ways.
What time the lamp's unsteady gleam
Hath roused him from his moody dream,
Feels, as thou gambol'st round his seat,
His heart of pride less fiercely beat,
And smiles, a link in thee to find,
That joins it still to living kind.

Whence hast thou then, thou witless puss!
The magic power to charm us thus?
Is it that in thy glaring eye

And rapid movements, we descry –
Whilst we at ease, secure from ill,
The chimney corner snugly fill –
A lion darting on his prey,
A tiger at his ruthless play?
Or is it that in thee we trace,
With all thy varied wanton grace,
An emblem, view'd with kindred eye,
Of tricky, restless infancy?
Ah! many a lightly sportive child,
Who hath like thee our wits beguiled,
To dull and sober manhood grown,
With strange recoil our hearts disown.

And so, poor kit! must thou endure,
When thou becom'st a cat demure,
Full many a cuff and angry word,
Chased roughly from the tempting board.
But yet, for that thou hast, I ween,
So oft our favour'd playmate been,
Soft be the change which thou shalt prove!
When time hath spoil'd thee of our love,
Still be thou deem'd by housewife fat
A comely, careful, mousing cat,
Whose dish is, for the public good,
Replenish'd oft with savoury food,
Nor, when thy span of life is past,
Be thou to pond or dung-hill cast,
But, gently borne on goodman's spade,
Beneath the decent sod be laid;
And children show with glistening eyes
The place where poor old pussy lies.

from *Dramatic and Poetical Works* (1851)

THE MASTER'S CAT

Mamie Dickens (1838–96)

On account of our birds, cats were not allowed in the house; but from a friend in London I received a present of a white kitten – Williamina – and she and her numerous offspring had a happy home at 'Gad's Hill'. She became a favourite with all the household, and showed particular devotion to my father. I remember on one occasion when she had presented us with a family of kittens, she selected a corner of father's study for their home. She brought them one by one from the kitchen and deposited them in her chosen corner. My father called to me to remove them, saying that he could not allow the kittens to remain in his room. I did so, but Williamina brought them back again, one by one. Again they were removed. The third time, instead of putting them in the corner, she placed them all, and herself beside them, at my father's feet, and gave him such an imploring glance that he could resist no longer, and they were allowed to remain. As the kittens grew older they became more and more frolicsome, swarming up the curtains, playing about on the writing table and scampering behind the bookshelves. But they were never complained of and lived happily in the study until the time came for finding them other homes. One of these kittens was kept, who, as he was quite deaf, was left unnamed, and became known by the servants as 'the master's cat', because of his devotion to my father. He was always with him, and used to follow him about the garden like a dog, and sit with him while he wrote. One evening we were all, except father, going to a ball, and when we started, left 'the master' and his cat in the drawing-room together. 'The master' was reading at a small table, on which a lighted candle was placed. Suddenly the candle went out. My father, who was much interested in his book, relighted the candle, stroked the cat, who was looking at him pathetically he noticed, and continued his reading. A few minutes later, as the light became dim, he looked up just in time to see puss deliberately put out the candle with his paw, and then look appealingly towards him. This second and unmistakable hint was not disregarded, and puss was given the petting he craved. Father was full of this anecdote when all met at breakfast the next morning.

from *My Father As I Recall Him* (1897)

THE CRUEL BOY AND THE KITTENS

Anonymous

What! go to see the kittens drowned,
On purpose, in the yard!
I did not think there could be found
A little heart so hard.

Poor kittens! no more pretty play
With pussy's wagging tail:
Oh! I'd go far enough away
Before I'd see the pail.

Poor things! the little child that can
Be pleased to go and see,
Most likely when he grows a man,
A cruel man will be.

And many a wicked thing he'll do,
Because his heart is hard;
A great deal worse than killing you,
Poor kittens, in the yard.

from *Rhymes for the Nursery* (new edition, 1839)

TITTUMS

Jerome K. Jerome (1859–1927)

He came in this morning in his usual style, which he appears to have founded on that of an American cyclone, and the first thing he did was to sweep my coffee cup off the table with his tail, sending the contents full into the middle of my waistcoat. I rose from my chair, hurriedly, and remarking '—', approached him at a rapid rate. He preceded me in the direction of the door. At the door, he met Eliza, coming in with eggs. Eliza observed, 'Ugh!' and sat down on the floor, the eggs took up different positions about the carpet, where they spread themselves out, and Gustavus Adolphus left the room. I called after him, strongly advising him to go straight downstairs, and not let me see him again for the next hour or so; and he, seeming to agree with me, dodged the coal-scoop, and went; while I returned, dried myself, and finished breakfast. I made sure that he had gone into the yard, but when I looked into the passage ten minutes later, he was sitting at the top of the stairs. I ordered him down at once, but he only barked and jumped about, so I went to see what was the matter.

It was Tittums. She was sitting on the top stair but one, and wouldn't let him pass.

Tittums is our kitten. She is about the size of a penny roll. Her back was up, and she was swearing like a medical student. She does swear fearfully. I do a little that way myself sometimes, but I am a mere amateur compared with her. To tell you the truth – mind, this is strictly between ourselves, please; I shouldn't like your wife to know I said it, the womenfolk don't understand these things; but between you and me, you know, I think it does a man good to swear. Swearing is the safety-valve through which the bad temper, that might otherwise do serious internal injury to his mental mechanism, escapes in harmless vapouring. When a man has said: 'Bless you, my dear, sweet sir. What the sun, moon and stars made you so careless (if I may be permitted the expression) as to allow your light and delicate foot to descend upon my corn with so much force? Is it that you are physically incapable of comprehending the direction in which you are proceeding? you nice, clever young man – you!' or words to that effect, he feels better. Swearing has the

same soothing effect upon our angry passions that smashing the furniture or slamming the doors is so well known to exercise; added to which it is much cheaper. Swearing clears a man out like a pen'orth of gunpowder does the wash-house chimney. An occasional explosion is good for both. I rather distrust a man who never swears, or savagely kicks the footstool, or pokes the fire with unnecessary violence. Without some outlet, the anger caused by the ever-occurring troubles of life is apt to rankle and fester within. The petty annoyance, instead of being thrown from us, sits down beside us, and becomes a sorrow; and the little offence is brooded over till, in the hotbed of rumination, it grows into a great injury, under whose poisonous shadow springs up hatred and revenge.

Swearing relieves the feelings, that is what swearing does. I explained this to my aunt on one occasion, but it didn't answer with her. She said I had no business to have such feelings.

That is what I told Tittums. I told her she ought to be ashamed of herself, brought up in a Christian family as she was, too. I don't so much mind hearing an old cat swear, but I can't bear to see a mere kitten give way to it. It seems sad in one so young.

I put Tittums in my pocket, and returned to my desk. I forgot her for the moment, and when I looked I found that she had squirmed out of my pocket on to the table, and was trying to swallow the pen; then she put her leg into the ink-pot and upset it; then she licked her leg; then she swore again – at *me* this time.

I put her down on the floor, and there Tim began rowing with her. I do wish Tim would mind his own business. It was no concern of his what she had been doing. Besides, he is not a saint himself. He is only a two-year-old fox terrier, and he interferes with everything, and gives himself the airs of a grey-headed Scotch collie.

Tittum's mother has come in, and Tim has got his nose scratched, for which I am remarkably glad. I have put them all three out in the passage, where they are fighting at the present moment. I'm in a mess with the ink, and in a thundering bad temper; and if anything more in the cat or dog line comes fooling about me this morning, it had better bring its own funeral contractor with it.

from 'On Cats and Dogs' in *Idle Thoughts of an Idle Fellow* (1886)

THE COLUBRIAD

William Cowper (1731–1800)

Close by the threshold of a door nail'd fast
Three kittens sat: each kitten look'd aghast.
I, passing swift and inattentive by,
At the three kittens cast a careless eye;
Not much concern'd to know what they did there,
Not deeming kittens worth a poet's care.
But presently a loud and furious hiss
Caused me to stop, and to exclaim – what's this?
When, lo! upon the threshold met my view,
With head erect, and eyes of fiery hue,
A viper, long as Count de Grasse's queue.
Forth from his head his forkèd tongue he throws,
Darting it full against a kitten's nose;
Who having never seen in field or house
The like, sat still and silent, as a mouse:
Only, projecting with attention due
Her whisker'd face, she ask'd him – who are you?

On to the hall went I, with pace not slow,
But swift as lightning, for a long Dutch hoe;
With which well arm'd I hasten'd to the spot,
To find the viper. But I found him not,
And, turning up the leaves and shrubs around,
Found only, that he was not to be found.
But still the kittens, sitting as before
Sat watching close the bottom of the door.
I hope – said I – the villain I would kill
Has slipt between the door and the door's sill;
And if I make dispatch, and follow hard,
No doubt but I shall find him in the yard –
For long ere now it should have been rehears'd,

'Twas in the garden that I found him first.
E'en there I found him; there the full-grown cat
His head with velvet paw did gently pat,
As curious as the kittens erst had been
To learn what this phenomenon might mean.
Fill'd with heroic ardour at the sight,
And fearing every moment he might bite,
And rob our household of our only cat
That was of age to combat with a rat,
With outstretch'd hoe I slew him at the door,
And taught him NEVER TO COME THERE NO MORE.

K WAS A KITTEN

Anonymous

K, was a Kitten,
   Who jump'd at a cork,
And learn'd to eat mice
   Without plate, knife, or fork.

And L, was a Lady,
   Who made him so wise;
But he tore her long train,
   And she cried out her eyes.

from *The Alphabet of Goody Two Shoes* (1808)

FAMILIARITY DANGEROUS

Vincent Bourne (1695–1747)

As in her ancient mistress' lap,
  The youthful tabby lay,
They gave each other many a tap,
  Alike dispos'd to play.

But strife ensues. Puss waxes warm,
  And with protruded claws
Ploughs all the length of Lydia's arm,
  Mere wantonness the cause.

At once, resentful of the deed,
  She shakes her to the ground
With many a threat, that she shall bleed
  With still a deeper wound.

But, Lydia, bid thy fury rest!
  It was a venial stroke;
For she, that will with kittens jest,
  Should bear a kitten's joke.

translated by William Cowper

A LITTLE PICKLE

Leigh Hunt (1784–1859)

She is a sprightly cat, hardly past her youth; so, happening
to move the fringe of the rug a little with our foot, she darts out a paw, and
begins plucking it and enquiring into the matter, as if it were a challenge
to play, or something lively enough to be eaten. What a graceful action of

that foot of hers, between delicacy and petulance – combining something of a thrust out, a beat, and a scratch. There seems even something of a little bit of fear in it, as if just enough to provoke her courage, and give her the excitement of a sense of hazard. We remember being much amused with seeing a kitten manifestly making a series of experiments upon the patience of its mother – trying how far the latter would put up with positive bites and thumps. The kitten ran at her every moment, gave her a knock or a bite of the tail; and then ran back again, to recommence the assault. The mother sat looking at her, as if betwixt tolerance and admiration, to see how far the spirit of the family was inherited or improved by her sprightly offspring. At length, however, the 'little Pickle' presumed too far, and the mother, lifting up her paw, and meeting her at the very nick of the moment, gave her one of the most unsophisticated boxes of the ear we ever beheld. It sent her rolling half over the room, and made her come to a most ludicrous pause, with the oddest little look of premature and wincing meditation.

from 'The Cat by the Fire' in *Essays* (c.1887)

THE KITTEN AND THE FALLING LEAVES
—
William Wordsworth (1770–1850)

That way look, my Infant, lo!
What a pretty baby show!
See, the Kitten on the Wall,
Sporting with the leaves that fall,
Wither'd leaves, one, two, and three,
From the lofty Elder-tree!
Through the calm and frosty air
Of this morning bright and fair.
Eddying round and round they sink
Softly, slowly: one might think,
From the motions that are made,
Every little leaf convey'd

Sylph or Faery hither tending,
To this lower world descending,
Each invisible and mute,
In his wavering parachute.
But the Kitten, how she starts,
– Crouches, stretches, paws, and darts;
First at one and then its fellow
Just as light and just as yellow;
There are many now – now one –
Now they stop; and there are none –
What intenseness of desire
In her upward eye of fire!
With a tiger-leap half way
Now she meets the coming prey,
Lets it go as fast, and then
Has it in her power again:
Now she works with three or four,
Like an Indian Conjuror;
Quick as he in feats of art,
Far beyond in joy of heart.
Were her antics play'd in the eye
Of a thousand Standers-by,
Clapping hands with shout and stare,
What would little Tabby care
For the plaudits of the Crowd?
Over happy to be proud,
Over wealthy in the treasure
Of her own exceeding pleasure!

'Tis a pretty Baby-treat;
Nor, I deem, for me unmeet:
Here, for neither Babe or me,
Other Playmate can I see.
Of the countless, living things,
That with stir of feet and wings,

(In the sun or under shade
Upon bough or grassy blade)

And with busy revellings,
Chirp and song, and murmurings,
Made this Orchard's narrow space,
And this Vale so blithe a place;
Multitudes are swept away
Never more to breathe the day:
Some are sleeping; some in Bands
Travell'd into distant Lands;
Others slunk to moor and wood,
Far from human neighbourhood,
And, among the Kinds that keep
With us closer fellowship,
With us openly abide,
All have laid their mirth aside.

– Where is he that giddy Sprite,
Blue-cap, with his colours bright,
Who was blest as bird could be,
Feeding in the apple-tree,
Made such wanton spoil and rout,
Turning blossoms inside out,
Hung with head towards the ground,
Flutter'd, perch'd; into a round
Bound himself, and then unbound;
Lithest, gaudiest Harlequin,
Prettiest Tumbler ever seen,
Light of heart, and light of limb,
What is now become of Him?
Lambs, that through the mountains went
Frisking, bleating merriment,
When the year was in its prime,
They are sober'd by this time.

If you look to vale or hill,
If you listen, all is still,
Save a little neighbouring Rill;
That from out the rocky ground
Strikes a solitary sound.
Vainly glitters hill and plain,
And the air is calm in vain;
Vainly Morning spreads the lure
Of a sky serene and pure;
Creature none can she decoy
Into open sign of joy:
Is it that they have a fear
Of the dreary season near?
Or that other pleasures be
Sweeter even than gaiety?

Yet, whate'er enjoyments dwell
In the impenetrable cell
Of the silent heart which Nature
Furnishes to every Creature,
Whatsoe'er we feel and know
Too sedate for outward show,
Such a light of gladness breaks,
Pretty Kitten! from thy freaks,
Spreads with such a living grace
O'er my little Laura's face;
Yes, the sight so stirs and charms
Thee, Baby, laughing in my arms,
That almost I could repine
That your transports are not mine,
That I do not wholly fare
Even as ye do, thoughtless Pair!
And I will have my careless season
Spite of melancholy reason,
Will walk through life in such a way

That, when time brings on decay,
Now and then I may possess
Hours of perfect gladsomeness.
– Pleas'd by any random toy;
By a Kitten's busy joy,
Or an infant's laughing eye
Sharing in the ecstasy,
I would fare like that or this,
Find my wisdom in my bliss;
Keep the sprightly soul awake,
And have faculties to take
Even from things by sorrow wrought
Matter for a jocund thought;
Spite of care, and spite of grief,
To gambol with Life's falling Leaf.

YOUTH AND AGE

Jerome K. Jerome (1859–1927)

Ah me! life sadly changes us all. The world seems a vast horrible grinding machine, into which what is fresh and bright and pure is pushed at one end, to come out old and crabbed and wrinkled at the other. Look even at Pussy Sobersides, with her dull sleepy glance, her grave slow walk, and dignified, prudish airs; who could ever think that once she was the blue-eyed, whirling, scampering, head-over-heels, mad little firework that we call a kitten.

What marvellous vitality a kitten has. It is really something very beautiful the way life bubbles over in the little creatures. They rush about, and mew, and spring; dance on their hind legs, embrace everything with their front ones, roll over and over and over, lie on their backs and kick. They don't know what to do with themselves, they are so full of life.

from 'On Cats and Dogs' in *Idle Thoughts of an Idle Fellow* (1886)

TWO LITTLE KITTENS

Anonymous (c.1879)

Two little kittens, one stormy night,
Began to quarrel, and then to fight;
One had a mouse, the other had none,
And that's the way the quarrel began.

'I'll have that mouse,' said the biggest cat;
'You'll have that mouse? We'll see about that!'
'I *will* have that mouse,' said the eldest son;
'You *shan't* have the mouse,' said the little one.

I told you before 'twas a stormy night
When these two little kittens began to fight;
The old woman seized her sweeping broom,
And swept the two kittens right out of the room.

The ground was covered with frost and snow,
And the two little kittens had nowhere to go;
So they laid them down on the mat at the door,
While the old woman finished sweeping the floor.

Then they crept in, as quiet as mice,
All wet with the snow, and as cold as ice,
For they found it was better, that stormy night,
To lie down and sleep than to quarrel and fight.

A LOST KITTEN

H.D. Thoreau (1817–62)

When yesterday Sophia and I were rowing past Mr Prichard's land, where the river is bordered by a row of elms and low willows, at 6 p.m., we heard a singular note of distress as it were from a catbird – a loud, vibrating, catbird sort of note, as if the catbird's mew were imitated by a smart vibrating spring. Blackbirds and others were flitting about, apparently attracted by it. At first, thinking it was merely some peevish catbird or red-wing, I was disregarding it, but on second thought turned the bows to the shore, looking into the trees as well as over the shore, thinking some bird might be in distress, caught by a snake or in a forked twig. The hovering birds dispersed at my approach; the note of distress sounded louder and nearer as I approached the shore covered with low osiers. The sound came from the ground, not from the trees. I saw a little black animal making haste to meet the boat under the osiers. A young muskrat? A mink? No, it was a little dot of a kitten. It was scarcely six inches long from the face to the base – or I might as well say the tip – of the tail, for the latter was a short, sharp pyramid, perfectly perpendicular but not swelled in the least. It was a very handsome and very precocious kitten, in perfectly good condition, its breadth being considerably more than one third of its length. Leaving its mewing, it came scrambling over the stones as fast as its weak legs would permit, straight to me. I took it up and dropped it into the boat, but while I was pushing off it ran the length of the boat to Sophia, who held it while we rowed homeward. Evidently it had not been weaned – was smaller than we remembered that kittens ever were – almost infinitely small; yet it had hailed a boat, its life being in danger, and saved itself. Its performance, considering its age and amount of experience, was more wonderful than that of any young mathematician or musician that I have read of. Various were the conjectures as to how the kitten came there, a quarter of a mile from a house. The possible solutions were finally reduced to three: first, it must either have been born there, or, secondly, carried there by its mother, or, thirdly, by human hands. In the first case, it had possibly brothers and sisters, one or both, and its mother had left them to go a-hunting on her own account and might be expected back. In the second, she might equally be expected to return. At any rate, not having thought of all this till we got home, we found that we had got ourselves into a scrape; for this kitten, though exceedingly interesting, required one nurse to attend it constantly for the present, and, of course, another to spell the first; and, beside, we had already a cat well-nigh grown, who manifested such a disposition towards the young stranger that we had no doubt it would have torn it in pieces in a moment if left alone with it. As nobody made up his or her mind to have it drowned, and still less to drown it – having once looked into its innocent extremely pale blue eyes (as of milk thrice skimmed) and had his finger or his chin sucked by it, while, its eyes being shut, its little paws played a soothing tune – it was resolved to keep it till it could be suitably disposed of. It rested nowhere, in no lap, under no covert, but still faintly cried for its mother and its accustomed supper. It ran towards every sound or movement of a human being, and whoever crossed the room it was sure to follow at a rapid pace. It had all the ways of a cat of the maturest years; could purr divinely and raised its back to rub all boots and shoes. When it raised its foot to scratch its ear, which by the way it never hit, it was sure to fall over and roll on the floor. It climbed straight up the sitter, faintly mewing all the way, and sucked his chin. In vain, at first, its head was bent down into saucers of milk which its eyes did not see, and its chin was wetted. But soon it learned to suck a finger that had been dipped in it, and better still a rag; and then at last it slept and rested. The street was explored in vain to find its owner, and at length an Irish family took it into their cradle. Soon after we learned that a neighbour who had heard the mewing of kittens in the partition had sent for a carpenter, taken off a board, and found two the very day at noon that we sailed. That same hour it was first brought to the light a coarse Irish cook had volunteered to drown it, had carried it to the river, and without bag or sinker had cast it in! It saved itself and hailed a boat! What an eventful life! What a precocious kitten! We feared it owed its first plump condition to the water. How strong and effective the instinct of self-preservation!

from *Journal*, 22 May 1853

THE HISTORY OF THE SEVEN YOUNG CATS

Edward Lear (1812–88)

The Seven Young Cats set off on their travels with great delight and rapacity. But, on coming to the top of a high hill, they perceived at a long distance off a Clangle-Wangle (or, as it is more properly written, Clangel-Wangel), and in spite of the warning they had had, they ran straight up to it.

(Now the Clangle-Wangle is a most dangerous and delusive beast, and by no means commonly to be met with. They live in the water as well as on land, using their long tail as a sail when in the former element. Their speed is extreme, but their habits of life are domestic and superfluous, and their general demeanour pensive and pellucid. On summer evenings they may sometimes be observed near the Lake Pipple-popple, standing on their heads and humming their national melodies: they subsist entirely on vegetables, excepting when they eat veal, or mutton, or pork, or beef, or fish, or saltpetre.)

The moment the Clangle-Wangle saw the Seven Young Cats approach, he ran away; and as he ran straight on for four months, and the Cats, though they continued to run, could never overtake him, they all gradually *died* of fatigue and of exhaustion, and never afterwards recovered.

And this was the end of the Seven Young Cats.

CHOOSING THEIR NAMES

Thomas Hood (1799–1845)

Our old cat has kittens three –
What do you think their names should be?
Pepperpot, Sootikin, Scratchaway-there,
Was there ever a kitten with these to compare?
And we call their old mother – now, what do you think?
Tabitha Long-claws Tiddley-wink!

One is tabby with emerald eyes,
    And a tail that's long and slender,
And into a temper she quickly flies
    If you ever by chance offend her.
        I think we shall call her this –
        I think we shall call her that –
Now, don't you think that Pepperpot
        Is a nice name for a cat?

One is black with a frill of white,
    And her feet are all white fur,
If you stroke her she carries her tail upright
    And quickly begins to purr.
        I think we shall call her this –
        I think we shall call her that –
Now, don't you think that Sootikin
        Is a nice name for a cat?

One is a tortoiseshell yellow and black,
    With plenty of white about him;
If you tease him, at once he sets up his back,
    He's a quarrelsome one, ne'er doubt him.
        I think we shall call him this –
        I think we shall call him that –
Now, don't you think that Scratchaway
        Is a nice name for a cat?

TOM QUARTZ

Theodore Roosevelt (1858–1919)

Tom Quartz is certainly the cunningest kitten I have ever seen. He is always playing pranks on Jack and I get very nervous lest Jack should grow too irritated. The other evening they were both in the library – Jack sleeping before the fire – Tom Quartz scampering about, an exceedingly playful little creature – which is about what he is. He would race across the floor, then jump upon the curtain or play with the tassel. Suddenly he spied Jack and galloped up to him. Jack, looking exceedingly sullen and shame-faced, jumped out of the way and got upon the sofa and around the table, and Tom Quartz instantly jumped upon him again. Jack suddenly shifted to the other sofa, where Tom Quartz again went after him. Then Jack started for the door, while Tom made a rapid turn under the sofa and around the table and just as Jack reached the door leaped on his hind-quarters. Jack bounded forward and away and the two went tandem out of the room – Jack not co-operating at all; and about five minutes afterwards Tom Quartz stalked solemnly back.

Another evening, the next Speaker of the House, Mr Cannon, an exceedingly solemn, elderly gentleman with chin whiskers, who certainly does not look to be of playful nature, came to call upon me. He is a great friend of mine, and we sat talking over what our policies for the session should be until about eleven o'clock and when he went away I accompanied him to the head of the stairs. He had gone about halfway down when Tom Quartz strolled by, his tail erect and very fluffy. He spied Mr Cannon going down the stairs, jumped to the conclusion that he was a playmate escaping, and raced after him, suddenly grasping him by the leg the way he does Archie and Quentin when they play hide and seek with him; then loosening his hold he tore downstairs ahead of Mr Cannon, who eyed him with an iron calm and not one particle of surprise . . .

from a letter to his daughter, 6 January 1903

A YOUNG CAT FROM CLIFFORD'S INN

Samuel Butler (1835–1902)

No, I will not have any Persian cat; it is undertaking too much responsibility. I must have a cat whom I find homeless, wandering about the court, and to whom, therefore, I am under no obligation. There is a Clifford's Inn euphemism about cats which the laundresses use quite gravely: they say people come to this place to lose their cats. They mean that, when they have a cat they don't want to kill and don't know how to get rid of, they bring it here, drop it inside the railings of our grass-plot, and go away under the impression that they have been 'losing' their cat. Well, this happens very frequently and I have already selected a dirty little drunken wretch of a kitten to be successor to my poor old cat. I don't suppose it drinks anything stronger than milk and water but then, you know, so much milk and water must be bad for a kitten that age – at any rate it looks as if it drank; but it gives me the impression of being affectionate, intelligent, and fond of mice, and I believe, if it had a home, it would become more respectable; at any rate I will see how it works.

from a letter to his sister

A RESCUED KITTEN

Gerard Manley Hopkins (1844–89)

Rescued a little kitten that was perched in the sill of the round window at the sink over the gas jet and dared not jump down. I heard her mew a piteous long time till I could bear it no longer; but I make a note of it because of her gratitude after I had taken her down, which made her follow me about and at each turn of the stairs as I went down leading her to the kitchen ran back a few steps up and try to get up to lick me through the banisters from the flight above.

from his *Diary*

OLD MOTHER MITTEN AND HER FUNNY KITTEN

Anonymous (c.1825)

Old mother Mitten
And her pretty kitten,
Took supper, one night rather late;

But they sat down to tea,
And the dog came to see
Pussy cut the meat up on her plate.

The dog and the cat
Were having a chat,
When Pussy cried out with a mew:

'Dear old mother Mitten,
Just look at your kitten,
She's going to drink mead with you.'

When the supper was over,
The kitten moreover,
Did stand on the top of her head.

So the dog he declares,
They must sleep in their chairs,
And none of them get into bed.

So when they awoke,
Miss Pussy first spoke,
And to the old Lady said she:

'My dear if you please,
Take this bread and cheese,
And I'll give you a hot cup of tea.'

At the table there sat,
The dog and the cat,
With cards they were trying to play;

But the dog's beard is long,
Which the cat thinks is wrong,
And soon she is shaving poor Tray.

Having shaved Mr Tray,
She hastens away,
And dresses herself for a walk;

And when she came in,
Told where she had been,
To have with the neighbours a talk.

Says granny indeed,
'I believe you're agreed,
To marry Miss Puss, Mr Tray';

The dog made a bow,
And the cat she said mow,
And I think they got married that day.

from *The Pretty Primer* (c.1825)

KITTEN OVERBOARD

Henry Fielding (1707–54)

Thursday, July 11th 1754. A most tragical incident fell out this day at sea. While the ship was under sail, but making as will appear no great way, a kitten, one of four of the feline inhabitants of the cabin, fell from the window into the water: an alarm was immediately given to the captain, who was then upon deck, and received it with the utmost concern and many bitter oaths. He immediately gave orders to the steersman in favour of the poor thing, as he called it; the sails were instantly slackened, and all hands, as the phrase is, employed to recover the poor animal. I was, I own, extremely surprised at all this; less indeed at the captain's extreme tenderness than at his conceiving any possibility of success; for if puss had had nine thousand instead of nine lives, I concluded they had been all lost. The boatswain, however, had more sanguine hopes, for having stripped himself of his jacket, breeches and shirt, he leaped boldly into the water, and to my great astonishment, in a few minutes returned to the ship, bearing the motionless animal in his mouth. Nor was this, I observed, a matter of such great difficulty as it appeared to my ignorance, and possibly may seem to that of my fresh-water reader. The kitten was now exposed to air and sun on the deck, where its life, of which it retained no symptoms, was despaired of by all.

The captain's humanity, if I may so call it, did not so totally destroy his philosophy as to make him yield himself up to affliction on this melancholy occasion. Having felt his loss like a man, he resolved to shew he could bear it like one; and, having declared he had rather have lost a cask of rum or brandy, betook himself to threshing at backgammon with the Portuguese friar, in which innocent amusement they passed about two-thirds of their time.

But as I have, perhaps, a little too wantonly endeavoured to raise the tender passions of my readers in this narrative, I should think myself unpardonable if I concluded it without giving them the satisfaction of hearing that the kitten at last recovered, to the great joy of the good captain, but to the great disappointment of some of the sailors, who asserted that the drowning cat was the very surest way of raising a favourable wind; a supposition of which, though we have heard several plausible accounts, we will not presume to assign the true original reason.

Wednesday. He even extended his humanity, if I may so call it, to animals, and even his cats and kittens had large shares in his affection. An instance of which we saw this evening, when the cat, which had shewn it could not be drowned, was found suffocated under a feather-bed in the cabin. I will not endeavour to describe his lamentations with more prolixity than barely by saying they were grievous, and seemed to have some mixture of the Irish howl in them.

from *Journal of a Voyage to Lisbon* (1755)

THE KITTEN AND THE BILLIARD-TABLE

Mark Twain (1835–1910)

If I can find a photograph of my 'Tammany' and her kittens, I will enclose it in this. One of them likes to be crammed into a corner-pocket of the billiard-table – which he fits as snugly as does a finger in a glove – and then he watches the game (and obstructs it) by the hour, and spoils many a shot by putting out his paw and changing the direction of a passing ball. Whenever a ball is in his arms, or so close to him that it cannot be played upon without risk of hurting him, the player is privileged to remove it to any one of the three spots that chances to be vacant.

from *Letters*

THE BLACK KITTEN

Lewis Carroll (1832–98)

One thing was certain, that the *white* kitten had had nothing to do with it: it was the black kitten's fault entirely. For the white kitten had been having its face washed by the old cat for the last quarter of an hour (and bearing it pretty well, considering); so you see that it *couldn't* have had any hand in the mischief.

The way Dinah washed her children's faces was this: first she held the poor thing down by its ear with one paw, and then with the other paw she rubbed its face all over, the wrong way, beginning at the nose: and just now, as I said, she was hard at work on the white kitten, which was lying quite still and trying to purr – no doubt feeling that it was all meant for its good.

But the black kitten had been finished with earlier in the afternoon, and so, while Alice was sitting curled up in a corner of the great armchair, half talking to herself and half asleep, the kitten had been having a grand game of romps with the ball of worsted Alice had been trying to wind up, and had been rolling it up and down till it had all come undone again; and there it was, spread over the hearth-rug, all knots and tangles, with the kitten running after its own tail in the middle.

'Oh, you wicked, wicked little thing!' cried Alice, catching up the kitten, and giving it a little kiss to make it understand that it was in disgrace. 'Really, Dinah ought to have taught you better manners! You *ought*, Dinah, you know you ought!' she added, looking reproachfully at the old cat, and speaking in as cross a voice as she could manage – and then she scrambled back into the armchair, taking the kitten and the worsted with her, and began winding up the ball again. But she didn't get on very fast, as she was talking all the time, sometimes to the kitten, and sometimes to herself. Kitty sat very demurely on her knee, pretending to watch the progress of the winding, and now and then putting out one paw and gently touching the ball, as if it would be glad to help if it might.

'Do you know what tomorrow is, Kitty?' Alice began.

'You'd have guessed if you'd been up in the window with me – only Dinah was making you tidy, so you couldn't. I was watching the boys getting in sticks for the bonfire – and it wants plenty of sticks, Kitty! Only it got so cold, and it snowed so, they had to leave off. Never mind, Kitty, we'll go and see the bonfire tomorrow.' Here Alice wound two or three turns of the worsted round the kitten's neck, just to see how it would look: this led to a scramble, in which the ball rolled down upon the floor, and yards and yards of it got unwound again.

'Do you know, I was so angry, Kitty,' Alice went on, as soon as they were comfortably settled again, 'when I saw all the mischief you had been doing, I was very nearly opening the window, and putting you out into the snow! And you'd have deserved it, you little mischievous darling! What have you got to say for yourself? Now don't interrupt me!' she went on, holding up one finger. 'I'm going to tell you all your faults. Number one: you squeaked twice while Dinah was washing your face this morning. Now you can't deny it, Kitty: I heard you! What's that you say?' (pretending that the kitten was speaking). 'Her paw went into your eye? Well, that's *your* fault, for keeping your eyes open – if you'd shut them tight up, it wouldn't have happened. Now don't make any more excuses, but listen! Number two: you pulled Snowdrop away by the tail just as I had put down the saucer of milk before her! What, you were thirsty, were you? How do you know she wasn't thirsty too? Now for number three: you unwound every bit of the worsted while I wasn't looking!

'That's three faults, Kitty, and you've not been punished for any of them yet. You know I'm saving up all your punishments for Wednesday week – suppose they had saved up all *my* punishments?' she went on, talking more to herself than the kitten. 'What *would* they do at the end of a year? I should be sent to prison, I suppose, when the day came. Or – let me see – suppose each punishment was to be going without a dinner: then, when the miserable day came, I should have to go without fifty dinners at once! Well, I shouldn't mind *that* much! I'd far rather go without them than eat them!

'Do you hear the snow against the window-panes, Kitty? How nice and soft it sounds! Just as if someone was kissing the window all over outside. I wonder if the snow *loves* the trees and fields, that it kisses them so gently? And then it covers them up snug, you know, with a white quilt; and perhaps it says, "Go to sleep, darlings, till the summer comes again". And when

they wake up in the summer, Kitty, they dress themselves all in green, and dance about – whenever the wind blows – oh, that's very pretty!' cried Alice, dropping the ball of worsted to clap her hands. 'And I do so *wish* it was true! I'm sure the woods look sleepy in the autumn, when the leaves are getting brown.

'Kitty, can you play chess? Now, don't smile, my dear, I'm asking it seriously. Because, when we were playing just now, you watched just as if you understood it: and when I said "Check!" you purred! Well, it *was* a nice check, Kitty, and really I might have won, if it hadn't been for that nasty Knight, that came wriggling down among my pieces. Kitty, dear, let's pretend – ' And here I wish I could tell you half the things Alice used to say, beginning with her favourite phrase 'Let's pretend'. She had had quite a long argument with her sister only the day before – all because Alice had begun with 'Let's pretend we're kings and queens'; and her sister, who liked being very exact, had argued that they couldn't, because there were only two of them, and Alice had been reduced at last to say, 'Well, *you* can be one of them, then, and *I'll* be all the rest.' And once she had really frightened her old nurse by shouting suddenly in her ear, 'Nurse! Do let's pretend that I'm a hungry hyæna, and you're a bone!'

But this is taking us away from Alice's speech to the kitten. 'Let's pretend that you're the Red Queen, Kitty! Do you know, I think if you sat up and folded your arms, you'd look exactly like her. Now do try, there's a dear!' And Alice got the Red Queen off the table, and set it up before the kitten as a model for it to imitate: however, the thing didn't succeed, principally, Alice said, because the kitten wouldn't fold its arms properly. So, to punish it, she held it up to the Looking Glass, that it might see how sulky it was, '– and if you're not good directly,' she added, 'I'll put you through into Looking Glass House. How would you like *that*?

'Now, if you'll only attend, Kitty, and not talk so much, I'll tell you all my ideas about Looking Glass House. First, there's the room you can see through the glass – that's just the same as our drawing-room, only the things go the other way. I can see all of it when I get upon a chair – all but the bit just behind the fireplace. Oh! I do so wish I could see *that* bit! I want so much to know whether they've a fire in the winter: you never *can* tell, you know, unless our fire smokes, and then smoke comes up in that room too – but that may be only pretence, just to make it look as if they had a fire. Well then, the books are something like our books, only the words go the wrong way; I know *that*, because I've held up one of our books to the glass, and then they hold up one in the other room.

'How would you like to live in Looking Glass House, Kitty? I wonder if they'd give you milk in there? Perhaps Looking Glass milk isn't good to drink – but oh, Kitty! now we come to the passage. You can just see a little *peep* of the passage in Looking Glass House, if you leave the door of our drawing-room wide open: and it's very like our passage as far as you can see, only you know it may be quite different on beyond. Oh, Kitty! how nice it would be if we could only get through into Looking Glass House! I'm sure it's got, oh! such beautiful things in it! Let's pretend there's a way of getting through into it somehow, Kitty. Let's pretend the glass has got all soft like gauze, so that we can get through. Why, it's turning into a sort of mist now, I declare! It'll be easy enough to get through –' She was up on the chimney-piece while she said this, though she hardly knew how she had got there. And certainly the glass *was* beginning to melt away, just like a bright silvery mist.

In another moment Alice was through the glass, and had jumped lightly down into the Looking Glass room. The very first thing she did was to look whether there was a fire in the fireplace, and she was quite pleased to find that there was a real one, blazing away as brightly as the one she had left behind. 'So I shall be as warm here as I was in the old room,' thought Alice: 'warmer, in fact, because there'll be no one here to scold me away from the fire. Oh, what fun it'll be, when they see me through the glass in here, and can't get at me!' [...]

[*After her adventures in the Looking-Glass world, Alice awakes to find it has all been a dream.*]

'Your Red Majesty shouldn't purr so loud,' Alice said, rubbing her eyes, and addressing the kitten, respectfully, yet with some severity. 'You woke me out of oh! such a nice dream! And you've been along with me, Kitty – all through the Looking Glass world. Did you know it, dear?'

It is a very inconvenient habit of kittens (Alice had once made the

remark) that, whatever you say to them, they *always* purr. 'If they would only purr for "yes", and mew for "no", or any rule of that sort,' she had said, 'so that one could keep up a conversation! But how *can* you talk with a person if they *always* say the same thing?'

On this occasion the kitten only purred: and it was impossible to guess whether it meant 'yes' or 'no'.

So Alice hunted among the chessmen on the table till she had found the Red Queen: then she went down on her knees on the hearth rug, and put the kitten and the Queen to look at each other. 'Now, Kitty!' she cried, clapping her hands triumphantly. 'Confess that was what you turned into!'

('But it wouldn't look at it,' she said, when she was explaining the thing afterwards to her sister: 'it turned away its head, and pretended not to see it: but it looked a *little* ashamed of itself, so I think it *must* have been the Red Queen.')

'Sit up a little more stiffly, dear!' Alice cried with a merry laugh. 'And curtsey while you're thinking what to – what to purr. It saves time, remember!' And she caught it up and gave it one little kiss 'just in honour of its having been a Red Queen'.

'Snowdrop, my pet!' she went on, looking over her shoulder at the white kitten, which was still patiently undergoing its toilet, 'when *will* Dinah have finished with your White Majesty, I wonder? That must be the reason you were so untidy in my dream. Dinah! Do you know that you're scrubbing a White Queen? Really, it's most disrespectful of you!

'And what did *Dinah* turn to, I wonder?' she prattled on, as she settled comfortably down, with one elbow on the rug, and her chin in her hand, to watch the kittens. 'Tell me, Dinah, did you turn to Humpty Dumpty? I *think* you did – however, you'd better not mention it to your friends just yet, for I'm not sure.

'By the way, Kitty, if only you'd been really with me in my dream, there was one thing you *would* have enjoyed – I had such a quantity of poetry said to me, all about fishes! Tomorrow morning you shall have a real treat. All the time you're eating your breakfast, I'll repeat "The Walrus and the Carpenter" to you; and then you can make believe it's oysters, my dear!

'Now, Kitty, let's consider who it was that dreamed it all. This is a serious question, my dear, and you should *not* go on licking your paw like that – as if Dinah hadn't washed you this morning! You see, Kitty, it *must* have been either me or the Red King. He was part of my dream, of course – but then I was part of his dream, too! *Was* it the Red King, Kitty? You were his wife, my dear, so you ought to know – oh, Kitty, *do* help to settle it! I'm sure your paw can wait!' But the provoking kitten only began on the other paw, and pretended it hadn't heard the question.

from *Through the Looking Glass and What Alice Found There* (1871)

KITTEN

Heinrich Heine (1797–1856)

Kitten! O my pretty kitten!
Why delightest thou to do ill?
Sadly is my poor heart smitten
By thy tiger-talons cruel.

from *Clarissa*, translated by E.A. Bowring

OBSERVATIONS ON KITTENS

No matter how much cats fight, there always seem to be plenty of kittens.

Abraham Lincoln (1809–65)

Do you see that kitten chasing so prettily her own tail? If you could look with her eyes, you might see her surrounded with hundreds of figures performing complex dramas, with tragic and comic issues, long conversations, many characters, many ups and downs of fate.

Ralph Waldo Emerson (1803–82)

3

TIGER! TIGER!

God made the cat that man might have the
pleasure of caressing the tiger.

Fernand Méry (1897–1984)

WHO IS THIS CAT?

Anonymous (c.3000 BC)

I am the Cat which fought hard by the Acacia Tree in Heliopolis on the night when the foes of the Setting Sun were destroyed.

Who is this Cat?

This male Cat is the Sun-god Ra himself and he was called Mau because of the speech of the God Sa concerning him: He is like unto that which he hath made, therefore did the name Ra become Mau. Others, however, say that the male cat is Shu, the God of the Air, who made over the possessions of the Earth-god Geb to Osiris. As concerning the fight which took place near the Acacia Tree in Heliopolis these words refer to the slaughter of the children of rebellion, when righteous retribution was meted out to them for the evil they had done. As concerning the night of the battle these words refer to the invasion of the eastern portion of the heavens by the children of rebellion, whereupon a great battle arose in heaven and in all the earth.

from *The Book of the Dead*

JIM WOLF AND THE CATS

Mark Twain (1835–1910)

It was back in those far-distant days – 1848 or '49 – that Jim Wolf came to us. He was from a hamlet thirty or forty miles back in the country, and he brought all his native sweetnesses and gentlenesses and simplicities with him. He was approaching seventeen, a grave and slender lad, trustful, honest, honourable, a creature to love and cling to. And he was incredibly bashful. He was with us a good while, but he could never conquer that peculiarity; he could not be at ease in the presence of any woman, not even in my good and gentle mother's; and as to speaking to any girl, it was wholly impossible. He sat perfectly still, one day – there were ladies chatting in the room – while a wasp up his leg stabbed him cruelly a dozen times; and all the sign he gave was a slight wince for each stab and the tear of torture in his eye. He was too bashful to move.

It is to this kind that untoward things happen. My sister gave a 'candy-pull' on a winter's night. I was too young to be of the company, and Jim was too diffident. I was sent up to bed early, and Jim followed of his own motion. His room was in the new part of the house and his window looked out on the roof of the L annexe. That roof was six inches deep in snow, and the snow had an ice crust upon it which was as slick as glass. Out of the comb of the roof projected a short chimney, a common resort for sentimental cats on moonlight nights – and this was a moonlight night. Down at the eaves, below the chimney, a canopy of dead vines spread away to some posts, making a cosy shelter, and after an hour or two the rollicking crowd of young ladies and gentlemen grouped themselves in its shade, with their saucers of liquid and piping-hot candy disposed about them on the frozen ground to cool. There was joyous chaffing and joking and laughter – peal upon peal of it.

About this time a couple of old, disreputable tomcats got up on the chimney and started a heated argument about something; also about this time I gave up trying to get to sleep and went visiting to Jim's room. He was awake and fuming about the cats and their intolerable yowling. I asked him, mockingly, why he didn't climb out and drive them away. He was nettled, and said overboldly that for two cents he *would*.

It was a rash remark and was probably repented of before it was fairly out of his mouth. But it was too late – he was committed. I knew him; and I knew he would rather break his neck than back down, if I egged him on judiciously.

'Oh, of course you would! Who's doubting it?'

It galled him, and he burst out, with sharp irritation, 'Maybe you doubt it!'

'I? Oh no! I shouldn't think of such a thing. You are always doing wonderful things, with your mouth.'

He was in a passion now. He snatched on his yarn socks and began to raise the window, saying in a voice quivering with anger: 'You think I dasn't – you do! Think what you blame please. *I* don't care what you think. I'll show you!'

The window made him rage; it wouldn't stay up. I said, 'Never mind, I'll hold it.'

Indeed, I would have done anything to help. I was only a boy and was already in a radiant heaven of anticipation. He climbed carefully out, clung to the window sill until his feet were safely placed, then began to pick his perilous way on all-fours along the glassy comb, a foot and a hand on each side of it. I believe I enjoy it now as much as I did then; yet it is nearly fifty years ago. The frosty breeze flapped his short shirt about his lean legs; the crystal roof shone like polished marble in the intense glory of the moon; the unconscious cats sat erect upon the chimney, alertly watching each other, lashing their tails and pouring out their hollow grievances; and slowly and cautiously Jim crept on, flapping as he went, the gay and frolicsome young creatures under the vine canopy unaware, and outraging these solemnities with their misplaced laughter. Every time Jim slipped I had a hope; but always on he crept and disappointed it. At last he was within reaching distance. He paused, raised himself carefully up, measured his distance deliberately, then made a frantic grab at the nearest cat – and missed it. Of course he lost his balance. His heels flew up, he struck on his back, and like a rocket he darted down the roof feet first, crashed through the dead vines, and landed in a sitting position in fourteen saucers of red-hot candy, in the midst of all that party – and dressed as he was – this lad who could not look a girl in the face with his clothes on. There was a wild scramble and a storm of shrieks, and Jim fled up the stairs, dripping broken crockery all the way.

from *Autobiography* (1924)

TO MRS REYNOLDS' CAT

John Keats (1795–1821)

Cat! who hast pass'd thy grand climacteric,
    How many mice and rats hast in thy days
    Destroy'd? – How many titbits stolen? Gaze
With those bright languid segments green, and prick
Those velvet ears – but pr'ythee do not stick
    Thy latent talons in me – and upraise
    Thy gentle mew – and tell me all thy frays
Of fish and mice, and rats and tender chick.
Nay, look not down, nor lick thy dainty wrists –
    For all the wheezy asthma, and for all
Thy tail's tip is nick'd off – and though the fists
    Of many a maid have given thee many a maul,
Still is that fur as soft as when the lists
    In youth thou enter'dst on glass bottled wall.

THE POACHER CAT

W.H. Hudson (1841–1922)

It is a well-known habit of some hunting, or poaching, cats to bring their captives to their master or mistress. I have met with scores – I might say with hundreds – of such cases. I remember an old gaucho, a neighbour of mine in South America, who used to boast that he usually had a spotted tinamou – the partridge of the pampas – for his dinner every day, brought in by his cat. Even in England, where partridges are not so abundant or easily taken, there are clever partridge-hunting cats. I remember one, a very fine white cat, owned by a woodman I once lodged with in Savernake Forest, who was in the habit of bringing in a partridge and would place it on the kitchen floor and keep guard over it until the woodman's wife came to take it up and put it away for the Sunday's dinner. A lady friend told me of a cat at a farmhouse where she was staying during the summer months, which became attached to her and was constantly bringing her young rabbits. They were never injured but held firmly by the skin of the neck. The lady would take the rabbit gently into her hands and deposit it on her lap, and cover it over with a handkerchief or a cloth, and pussy, seeing it safe in her power, would then go away. The lady would then walk away to a distance from the house to liberate the little trembler, devoutly wishing that this too affectionate cat would get over the delusion that such gifts were acceptable to her. One day pussy came trotting into the drawing-room with a stoat in her mouth, and depositing it on the carpet by the side of her chair immediately turned round and hastily left the room. The stoat was dead, not being a creature that could easily be carried about alive, and pussy, having other matters to attend to, did not think it necessary to wait to see her present taken up and carefully deposited in her mistress's lap. Cases of this kind are exceedingly common, and the simple explanation is, that the cat is not quite so unsocial a creature as some naturalists would have us believe. We may say that in this respect he compares badly with elephants, whales, pigs, seals, cattle, apes, wolves, dogs, and other large-brained social mammals; but he does not live wholly for himself. He is able to take thought for other cats and for his human companion – master hardly seems the right word in the case of such an animal – who is doubtless to him only a very big cat that walks erect on his hind-legs.

from *A Shepherd's Life* (1910)

THE TRIAL OF MYSOUFF

Alexandre Dumas (1802–70)

We left Mysouff gloating over the mangled remains of his feathered victims, and his capture presented little difficulty. By merely shutting the door of the aviary we had the culprit at the disposition of justice.

The only question was to decide his fate. Michel voted to shoot him straight away. I opposed such a step, which seemed too violent altogether.

I proposed to wait for the coming Sunday and have Mysouff brought to trial before the friends who always visited me on that day.

In addition to the regular weekly habitués of the house, we could invite others specially for the occasion. This was accordingly done, and judgment postponed till the fateful Sunday.

Meantime Mysouff remained a prisoner on the very scene of his crime. Michel removed the last vestiges of the dead birds on which he was feeding without a touch of compunction. He was put on a diet of bread and water, Michel constituting himself his gaoler. When Sunday came, both the ordinary weekly habitués and the specially invited guests having turned up in force, the necessary quorum for a jury was more than provided.

Michel was nominated Procureur-Général, and Nogent Saint-Laurent official Counsel for the Defence.

I am bound to say the minds of the jury were manifestly predisposed against the prisoner, and that after the Public Prosecutor's speech, a sentence of death seemed a practical certainty. But the clever advocate to whom poor Mysouff's defence had been entrusted, taking the accusation in the most serious way and calling all his eloquence into play, insisted on the animal's innocent intentions contrasted with the mischievousness of the monkeys, on the absence of initiation on the part of the four-footed as compared with two-handed vertebrates. He demonstrated how, closely approximating to men as they did, the latter were bound to be full of criminal promptings. He showed Mysouff incapable by himself of meditating such a crime. He showed him sleeping the sleep of the just; then suddenly awakened from his harmless slumbers by the odious apes that had long been watching the aviary intent on committing murder. He described Mysouff, still only half awake, stretching his paws, purring softly the while, opening his little pink mouth and showing his pretty tongue; listening, and shaking his ears – a plain sign that he rejected the odious proposal his tempters dared to make; at first refusing all participation in the foul deed (the speaker asserted positively that his client had begun by refusing); then, young and easily led astray, demoralized moreover by the cook, who instead of giving him his innocent bread and milk and bowl of broth according to orders, had excited his carnivorous appetite by feeding him on scraps of meat, the remains of bullocks' hearts and mutton bones; gradually degenerating more from weakness of character and feebleness to resist temptation than from actual greediness and cruelty; following, even now only part awake, with half-shut eyes and staggering steps, the wretched apes, the true instigators of the crime. Then he took the accused in his arms, displayed his paws, drew attention to their shape and form, appealed to the anatomists, calling upon them to say if, with such paws, an animal could open a locked aviary. Finally he borrowed from Michel himself his famous *Dictionary of Natural History*, he opened it at the article 'Cat' – *domestic cat, brindled cat*; he demonstrated that Mysouff, albeit not of the brindled sort, was not a whit less interesting for having a white coat – the token of his innocence. Then, to wind up, he struck a resounding blow on the book.

'Cat!' he exclaimed vehemently, 'cat! . . . yes, I will read you what Buffon, the great Buffon, who always wrote in lace ruffles, what he wrote on the knees of Mother Nature, concerning the cat –

' "The cat," M. de Buffon tells us, "is but a faithless domestic pet, one we only keep out of necessity, to keep down other household enemies even more annoying, and which we cannot otherwise get rid of . . . ; true," continues the illustrious Naturalist, "true, the cat, and still more the kitten, has pretty ways, it has at the same time an inborn love of mischief, a treacherous disposition, a natural perversity, which age only increases and training only succeeds in partially concealing." '

'Well,' pursued the orator, after concluding this description of his client, 'what need I say more? . . . Did Mysouff, I ask you, did poor Mysouff present himself here with a false certificate of character signed, it may be, by Lacépède or Geoffroy Saint-Hilaire, to weigh in the balance against Buffon's indictment? No, he scorned to do so. It was the cook herself who went and fetched him from M. Acoyer's, who hunted him out from behind a heap of firewood where he had taken refuge, who then invented a fictitious tale to enlist her master's sympathies of how she had found the creature mewing piteously in the cellar. Was any attempt made to give him an idea of the wickedness he was guilty of in killing these unfortunate birds, these poor little creatures – greatly to be pitied, of course, yet which, when all is said and done – the quails in particular – were liable to be sacrificed at any moment to satisfy man's hunger, and now find themselves happily delivered from the agonies of terror they must daily have experienced every time they saw the cook come near their cage? . . . In a word, gentlemen, I appeal to your sense of fairness; we have invented a new word to excuse crime among ourselves, as featherless bipeds, endowed with free will, to wit *monomania*; when, thanks to the word, we have saved the lives of the greatest criminals, shall we not admit that the unfortunate and interesting Mysouff yielded not merely to his natural instincts but also to extraneous suggestions? . . . I have done, gentlemen. I claim for my client the benefit of extenuating circumstances.'

Shouts of enthusiasm greeted this flight of eloquence, which was purely extempore. The jury gave their verdict whilst still under the impression of the great advocate's address, and Mysouff was declared guilty of complicity in the assassination of the doves and quails, also of the wrynecks, widow-birds, Indian sparrows, and other rare birds, but with extenuating circumstances. He was merely condemned to five years of incarceration with the apes.

from *My Pets* (1867), translated by Alfred Allinson

THE WHITE CAT

Sir Philip Sidney (1554–86)

I have (and long shall have) a white great nimble cat,
A king upon a mouse, a strong foe to the rat,
Fine eares, long taile he hath, with Lions curbed clawe,
Which oft he lifteth up, and stayes his lifted pawe,
Deepe musing to himselfe, which after-mewing showes,
Till with lickt blood, his eye of fire espie his foes.

from *Second Eclogues of Arcadia*

THE ZOMBI

Robert Southey (1774–1843)

Now to a more important subject. You were duly apprised towards the end of the year of Othello's death. Since that lamented event this house was cat-less, till on Saturday, March 24, Mrs Calvert, knowing how grievously we were annoyed by rats, offered me what she described as a fine full-grown black cat, who was moreover a tom. She gave him an excellent character in all points but one, which was that he was a most expert pigeon-catcher; and as they had a pigeon-house, the propensity rendered it necessary to pass sentence upon him either of transportation or of death. Moved by compassion (his colour and his tomship also being taken into consideration), I consented to give him an asylum, and on the evening of that day here he came in a sack.

You, Grosvenor, who are a *philogalist*, and therefore understand more of cat nature than has been ever attained by the most profound naturalists, know how difficult it is to reconcile a cat to a new domicile. When the sack was opened, the kitchen door, which led into the passage, was open also, and the cat disappeared; not indeed like a flash of lightning, but as fast as one – that is to say, for all purposes of a simile. There was no chance of his making his way back to the pigeon-house. He might have done this had he been carried thrice the distance in any other direction; but in this there was either a river to cross, or a part of the town to pass, both of which were such obstacles to his travels that we were quite sure all on this side of them was to him *terra incognita*. Food, therefore, was placed where he would be likely to find it in the night; and at the unanimous desire of the children, I took upon myself the charge of providing him with a name, for it is not proper that a cat should remain without one. Taking into consideration his complexion, as well as his sex, my first thought was to call him Henrique Diaz, a name which poor Koster would have approved, had he been living to have heard it; but it presently occurred to me that the Zombi would be an appellation equally appropriate and more dignified. The Zombi, therefore, he was named.

It was soon ascertained that the Zombi had taken possession of poor

Wilsey's cellar, which being filled with pea-sticks afforded him a secure hiding-place; the kitchen also of that part of the house being forsaken, he was in perfect quiet. Food was laid for him every day, and the children waited impatiently for the time when the Zombi would become acquainted with the house, and suffer them to become acquainted with him. Once or twice in the evening he was seen out of doors, and it was known that he reconnoitred the premises in the night; but in obstinate retirement he continued from Saturday till Saturday, seven days and nights, notwithstanding all kind words were used to bring him out, as if he had been determined to live and die a hermit.

But between four and five o'clock on the Sunday morning, all who had ears to hear were awakened by such screams as if the Zombi had been caught in a rat-trap, or had met with some other excruciating accident. You, Mr Bedford, understand cats, and know very well that a cat-*solo* is a very different thing from a *duet*; and that no person versed in their tongue can mistake their expression of pain for anything else. The creature seemed to be in agonies. A light was procured, that it might be relieved if that were possible. Upon searching the house, the Zombi was seen at the top of Wilsey's stairs, from whence he disappeared, retreating to his stronghold in the cellar; nor could any traces be discovered of any hurt that could have befallen him, nor has it since appeared that he had received any, so that the cause of this nocturnal disturbance remains an impenetrable mystery.

Various have been our attempts to explain it. Some of the women who measure the power of rats by their own fears, would have it that he was bitten by a rat, or by an association of rats; but to this I indignantly replied that in that case the ground would have been strewn with their bodies, and that it would have been the rats' cry, not the Zombi's, that would have been heard. Dismissing, therefore, that impossible supposition, I submit to your consideration, in the form of queries, the various possibilities which have occurred to me – all unsatisfactory, I confess – requesting you to assist me in my endeavour to find out the mystery of this wonderful history, as it may truly be called. You will be pleased to bear in mind that the Zombi was the only cat concerned in the transaction: of that I am perfectly certain.

Now then, Grosvenor –

1. Had he seen the devil?

2.   Was he making love to himself?
3.   Was he engaged in single combat with himself?
4.   Was he attempting to raise the devil by invocation?
5.   Had he heard me sing, and was he attempting (vainly) to imitate it?

These queries, you will perceive, all proceed upon the supposition that it was the Zombi who made the noise. But I have further to ask –

6.   Was it the devil?
7.   Was it Jeffery?
8.   Were either of these personages tormenting the Zombi?

I have only to add that from that time to this he continues in the same obstinate retirement, and to assure you that

I remain, Mr Bedford. With the highest consideration,

Yours as ever,

Robert Southey

PS. One further query occurs while I am writing. Sunday having been the first of the month –

9.   Was he making April fools of us? R.S.

from a letter to Grosvenor C. Bedford, 3 April 1821,
in *Selections from the Letters of Robert Southey* (1856)

BARBARIC CATS

Charles Dickens (1812–70)

As the dogs of shy neighbourhoods usually betray a slinking consciousness of being in poor circumstances – for the most part manifested in an aspect of anxiety, an awkwardness in their play, and a misgiving that somebody is going to harness them to something, to pick up a living – so the cats of shy neighbourhoods exhibit a strong tendency to relapse into barbarism. Not only are they made selfishly ferocious by ruminating on the surplus population around them, and on the densely crowded state of all the avenues to cat's meat; not only is there a moral and politico-economical haggardness in them, traceable to these reflections; but they evince a physical deterioration. Their linen is not clean, and is wretchedly got up; their black turns rusty, like old mourning; they wear very indifferent fur; and take to the shabbiest cotton velvet, instead of silk velvet. I am on terms of recognition with several small streets of cats, about the Obelisk in Saint George's Fields, and also in the vicinity of Clerkenwell-green, and also in the back settlements of Drury-lane. In appearance, they are very like the women among whom they live. They seem to turn out of their unwholesome beds into the street, without any preparation. They leave their young families to stagger about the gutters, unassisted, while they frouzily quarrel and swear and scratch and spit, at street corners. In particular, I remark that when they are about to increase their families (an event of frequent recurrence) the resemblance is strongly expressed in a certain dusty dowdiness, down-at-heel self-neglect, and general giving up of things. I cannot honestly report that I have ever seen a feline matron of this class washing her face when in an interesting condition.

from *The Uncommercial Traveller* (1860)

THE CARLISH CAT

John Skelton (c.1460–1529)

[...] When I remember again
How my Philip was slain,
Never half the pain
Was between you twain,
Pyramus and Thisbe,
As then befell to me.
I wept and I wailéd,
The teares down hailéd,
But nothing it availéd
To call Philip again,
Whom Gib, our cat, hath slain.

Gib, I say, our cat
Worrowéd her on that
Which I lovéd best.
It cannot be exprest
My sorrowful heaviness,
But all without redress!
For within that stound,
Half slumbering, in a sound
I fell downe to the ground [...]

That vengeance I ask and cry,
By way of exclamation,
On all the whole nation
Of cattes wild and tame:
God send them sorrow and shame!
That cat specially
That slew so cruelly
My little pretty sparrow
That I brought up at Carrow.

O cat of carlish kind,
The fiend was in thy mind
When thou my bird untwined!
I would thou hadst been blind!
The léopards savage,
The lions in their rage
Might catch thee in their paws,
And gnaw thee in their jaws!
The serpents of Libany
Might sting thee venomously!
The dragons with their tongues
Might poison thy liver and lungs!
The manticors of the mountains
Might feed them on thy brains!

Melanchaetes, that hound
That pluckéd Actaeon to the ground,
Gave him his mortal wound,
Changéd to a deer,
The story doth appear,
Was changéd to an hart:
So thou, foul cat that thou art,
The selfsame hound
Might thee confound,
That his own lorde bote,
Might bite asunder thy throat!

Of Ind the greedy grypes
Might tear out all thy tripes!
Of Arcady the bears
Might pluck away thine ears!
The wild wolf Lycaon
Bite asunder thy backbone!
Of Etna the burning hill,
That day and night burneth still,
Set in thy tail a blaze
That all the world may gaze
And wonder upon thee,
From Ocean the great sea
Unto the Isles of Orcady,
From Tilbury Ferry
To the plain of Salisbury!
So traitorously my bird to kill
That never ought thee evil will!

Was never bird in cage
More gentle of coráge
In doing his homáge
Unto his sovereign.
Alas, I say again,

Death hath departed us twain!
The false cat hath thee slain:
Farewell, Philip, adew!
Our Lord, thy soul rescue!
Farewell, without restore,
Farewell, for evermore! [...]

from *Philip Sparrow*

AN HUMBLE PETITION PRESENTED TO MADAME HELVÉTIUS BY HER CATS

Benjamin Franklin (1706–90)

We shall not endeavour to defend ourselves equally from devouring as many sparrows, blackbirds, and thrushes, as we can possibly catch. But here we have to plead in extenuation, that our most cruel enemies, your Abbés themselves, are incessantly complaining of the ravages made by these birds among the cherries and other fruit. The Sieur Abbé Morellet, in particular, is always thundering the most violent anathemas against the blackbirds and thrushes, for plundering your vines, which they do with as little mercy as he himself. To us, however, most illustrious Lady, it appears that the grapes may just as well be eaten by *blackbirds* as by *Abbés*, and that our warfare against the winged plunderers will be fruitless, if you encourage other biped and featherless pilferers, who make ten times more havoc.

We know that we are also accused of eating nightingales, who never plunder, and sing, as they say, most enchantingly. It is indeed possible that we may now and then have gratified our palates with a delicious morsel in this way, but we can assure you that it was in utter ignorance of your affection for the species; and that, resembling sparrows in their plumage, we, who make no pretensions to being connoisseurs in music, could not distinguish the song of the one from that of the other, and therefore supposed ourselves regaling only on sparrows. A cat belonging to M. Piccini has assured us, that they who only know how to *mew*, cannot be any judges of the art of singing; and on this we rest for our justification. However, we will henceforward exert our utmost endeavours to distinguish the *Gluckists*, who are, as we are informed, the sparrows, from the *Piccinists*, who are the nightingales. We only intreat of you to pardon the inadvertence into which we may possibly fall, if, in roving after nests, we may sometimes fall upon a brood of *Piccinists*, who, being then destitute of plumage, and not having learnt to sing, will have no mark by which to distinguish them.

THE RAT-CATCHER AND CATS

John Gay (1685–1732)

The rats by night such mischief did,
Betty was every morning chid.
They undermined whole sides of bacon,
Her cheese was sapp'd, her tarts were taken.
Her pasties fenced with thickest paste,
Were all demolish'd, and laid waste.
She cursed the Cat for want of duty,
Who left her foes a constant booty.
    An engineer, of noted skill,
Engaged to stop the growing ill.
From room to room he now surveys
Their haunts, their works, their secret ways;
Finds where they 'scape and ambuscade,
And whence the nightly sally's made,
    And envious Cat, from place to place,
Unseen attends his silent pace.
She saw that if his trade went on,
The purring race must be undone;
So, secretly removes his baits,
And ev'ry stratagem defeats.
    Again he sets the poison'd toils,

And Puss again the labour foils.
What foe (to frustrate my designs)
My schemes thus nightly countermines?
Incensed, he cries, this very hour
The wretch shall bleed beneath my power.

So said, a pond'rous trap he brought,
And in the fact poor Puss was caught.

Smuggler, says he, thou shalt be made
A victim to our loss of trade.

The captive Cat, with piteous mews,
For pardon, life, and freedom sues.
A sister of the science spare;
One int'rest is our common care.

What insolence! the man replied;
Shall cats with us the game divide?
Were all you interloping band
Extinguish'd or expell'd the land,
We Rat-catchers might raise our fees,
Sole guardians of a nation's cheese!

A Cat, who saw the lifted knife,
Thus spoke, and saved her sister's life:

In ev'ry age and clime we see,
Two of a trade can ne'er agree.
Each hates his neighbour for encroaching;
Squire stigmatizes squire for poaching;
Beauties with beauties are in arms,
And scandal pelts each other's charms;
Kings, too, their neighbour kings dethrone,
In hope to make the world their own,
But let us limit out desires,
Not war like beauties, kings, and squires!
For though we both one prey pursue,
There's game enough for us and you.

A CAT

Edward Thomas (1878–1917)

She had a name among the children:
But no one loved though someone owned
Her, locked her out of doors at bedtime.
And had her kittens duly drowned.

In spring, nevertheless, this cat
Ate blackbirds, thrushes, nightingales,
And birds of bright voice, and plume, and flight,
As well as scraps from neighbours' pails.

I loathed and hated her for this;
One speckle on a thrush's breast
Was worth a million such: and yet
She lived long till God gave her rest.

THE SAVAGE BENEATH THE SKIN

H.D. Thoreau (1817–62)

Only skin deep lies the feral nature of the cat, unchanged still. I just had the misfortune to rock on to our cat's leg, as she was lying playfully spread out under my chair. Imagine the sound that arose, and which was excusable; but what will you say to the fierce growls and flashing eyes with which she met me for a quarter of an hour thereafter? No tiger in its jungle could have been savager.

from *Journal*, 15 February 1861

A FABLE OF THE WIDOW AND HER CAT

Jonathan Swift (1667–1745)

A widow kept a favourite cat.
At first a gentle creature;
But when he was grown sleek and fat,
With many a mouse, and many a rat,
He soon disclosed his nature.

The fox and he were friends of old,
Nor could they now be parted;
They nightly slunk to rob the fold,
Devoured the lambs, the fleeces sold,
And puss grew lion-hearted.

He scratched her maid, he stole the cream,
He tore her best laced pinner;
Nor Chanticleer upon the beam,
Nor chick, nor duckling 'scapes, when Grim
Invites the fox to dinner.

The dame full wisely did decree,
For fear he should dispatch more,
That the false wretch should worried be:
But in a saucy manner he
Thus speeched it like a Lechmere.

'Must I, against all right and law,
Like pole-cat vile be treated?
I! who so long with tooth and claw
Have kept domestic mice in awe,
And foreign foes defeated!

'Your golden pippins, and your pies,
How oft have I defended?
'Tis true, the pinner which you prize
I tore in frolic; to your eyes
I never harm intended.

'I am a cat of honour –' 'Stay,'
Quoth she, 'no longer parley;
Whate'er you did in battle slay,
By law of arms become your prey,
I hope you won it fairly.

'Of this, we'll grant you stand acquit,
But not of your outrages:
Tell me, perfidious! was it fit
To make my cream a *perquisite*,
And steal to mend your wages!

'So flagrant is thy insolence,
So vile thy breach of trust is;
That longer with thee to dispense,
Were want of power, or want of sense:
Here, Towser! – Do him justice.'

CATS ON THE ROOF

H.D. Thoreau (1817–62)

At the Pilgrim House, though it was not crowded, they put
me into a small attic chamber which had two double beds in it, and only
one window, high in a corner, twenty and a half inches by twenty-five and
a half, in the alcove when it was swung open, and it required a chair to look
out conveniently. Fortunately it was not a cold night and the window could

be kept open, though at the risk of being visited by the cats, which appear to swarm on the roofs of Provincetown like the mosquitoes on the summits of its hills. I have spent four memorable nights there in as many different years, and have added considerable thereby to my knowledge of the natural history of the cat and the bedbug. Sleep was out of the question. A night in one of the attics of Provincetown! to say nothing of what is to be learned in entomology. It would be worth the while to send a professor there, one who was also skilled in entomology. Such is your *Pilgerruhe* or Pilgrims'-Rest. Every now and then one of these animals on its travels leaped from a neighbouring roof on to mine, with such a noise as if a six-pounder had fallen within two feet of my head – the discharge of a catapult – a twelve-pounder discharged by a catapult – and then followed such a scrambling as banished sleep for a long season, while I watched lest they came in at the open window. A kind of foretaste, methought, of the infernal regions. I didn't wonder they gave quit-claim deeds of their land here. My experience is that you fare best at private houses. The barroom may be defined a place to spit.

> 'Soon as the evening shades prevail,
> The *cats take* up the wondrous tale.'

At still midnight, when, half awake, half asleep, you seem to be weltering in your own blood on a battlefield, you hear the stealthy tread of padded feet belonging to some animal of the cat tribe, perambulating the roof within a few inches of your head.

from *Journal*, 21 June 1857

CAT AND MOUSE

Geoffrey Chaucer (c.1343–1400)

Lat take a cat, and fostre hym wel with milk
And tendre flessh, and make his couche of silk,
And lat hym seen a mous go by the wal,
Anon he weyveth milk, and flessh, and al,
And every deyntee that is in that hous,
Swich appetit he hath to ete a mous.
Lo, heere hath lust his dominacioun,
And appetit fleemeth discrecioun.

from *Canterbury Tales* (c.1387)

SAD MEMORIES

C.S. Calverley (1831–84)

They tell me I am beautiful: they praise my silken hair,
My little feet that silently slip on from stair to stair:
They praise my pretty trustful face and innocent grey eye;
Fond hands caress me oftentimes, yet would that I might die!

Why was I born to be abhorred of man and bird and beast?
The bullfinch marks me stealing by, and straight his song hath ceased;
The shrewmouse eyes me shudderingly, then flees; and, worse than that,
The housedog he flees after me – why was I born a cat?

Men prize the heartless hound who quits dry-eyed his native land;
Who wags a mercenary tail and licks a tyrant hand.
The leal true cat they prize not, that if e'er compelled to roam
Still flies, when let out of the bag, precipitately home.

They call me cruel. Do I know if mouse or song-bird feels?
I only know they make me light and salutary meals:
And if, as 'tis my nature to, ere I devour I tease 'em,
Why should a low-bred gardener's boy pursue me with a besom?

Should china fall or chandeliers, or anything but stocks –
Nay stocks, when they're in flowerpots – the cat expects hard knocks:
Should ever anything be missed – milk, coals, umbrellas, brandy –
The cat's pitched into with a boot or anything that's handy.

'I remember, I remember', how one night I 'fleeted by',
And gained the blessed tiles and gazed into the cold clear sky.
'I remember, I remember, how my little lovers came';
And there, beneath the crescent moon, played many a little game.

They fought – by good St Catharine, 'twas a fearsome sight to see
The coal-black crest, the glowering orbs, of one gigantic He.
Like bow by some tall bowman bent at Hastings or Poitiers,
His huge back curved, till none observed a vestige of his ears:

He stood, an ebon crescent, flouting that ivory moon;
Then raised the pibroch of his race, the Song without a Tune;
Gleamed his white teeth, his mammoth tail waved darkly to and fro,
As with one complex yell he burst, all claws, upon the foe.

It thrills me now, that final Miaow – that weird unearthly din:
Lone maidens heard it far away, and leaped out of their skin.
A potboy from his den o'erhead peeped with a scared wan face;
Then sent a random brickbat down, which knocked me into space.

Nine days I fell, or thereabouts: and, had we not nine lives,
I wis I ne'er had seen again thy sausage-shop, St Ives!
Had I, as some cats have, nine tails, how gladly I would lick
The hand, and person generally, of him who heaved that brick!

For me they fill the milkbowl up, and cull the choice sardine:
But ah! I nevermore shall be the cat I once have been!
The memories of that fatal night they haunt me even now:
In dreams I see that rampant He, and tremble at that Miaow.

CALVIN THE HUNTER

Charles Dudley Warner (1829–1900)

I think he was genuinely fond of birds, but, so far as I know, he usually confined himself to one a day; he never killed, as some sportsmen do, for the sake of killing, but only as civilized people do – from necessity. He was intimate with the flying squirrels who dwelt in the chestnut trees – too intimate, for almost every day in the summer he would bring in one, until he nearly discouraged them. He was, indeed, a superb hunter, and would have been a devastating one if his bump of destructiveness had not been offset by a bump of moderation. There was very little of the brutality of the lower animals about him; I don't think he enjoyed rats for themselves, but he knew his business, and for the first few months of his residence with us he waged an awful campaign against the horde, and after that his simple presence was sufficient to deter them from coming on the premises. Mice amused him, but he usually considered them too small game to be taken seriously; I have seen him play for an hour with a mouse, and then let him go with a royal condescension. In this whole matter of 'getting a living', Calvin was a great contrast to the rapacity of the age in which he lived.

from 'Calvin, the Cat' in *My Summer in a Garden* (1882)

AN ODE TO EIGHT CATS BELONGING TO ISRAEL MENDEZ, A JEW

Peter Pindar (1738–1819)

SCENE, *the Street in a Country Town.*
The TIME, *Midnight—The Poet at his Chamber Window, in his Shirt.*

Singers of Israel, O ye singers sweet,
    Who, with your gentle mouths from ear to ear,
Pour forth rich symphonies from street to street,
    And to the sleepless wretch the night endear!

Lo! in my shirt, on you these eyes I fix,
Admiring much the quaintness of your tricks:
    Your friskings, crawlings, squalls, I much approve:
Your spittings, pawings, high-rais'd rumps,
Swell'd tails, and merry-andrew jumps,
    With the wild minstrelsy of rapt'rous love.

How sweetly roll your gooseb'rry eyes,
As loud you tune your am'rous cries,
    And, loving, scratch each other black and blue!
No boys in wantonness now bang your backs;
No curs, nor fiercer mastiffs, tear your flax;
    But all the moon-light world seems made for you.

Singers of Israel, ye no parsons want
    To tie the matrimonial cord;
Ye call the matrimonial service, cant –
    Like our first parents, take each other's word:
On no one ceremony pleas'd to fix –
To jump not even o'er two sticks.

You want no furniture, alas!
    Spit, spoon, dish, frying-pan, nor ladle;
No iron, pewter, copper, tin, nor brass;
    No nurses, wet not dry, nor cradle,
(Which custom, for our *Christian* babes, enjoins)
To rock the staring offspring of your loins.

Nor of the lawyers have you need,
    Ye males, before you seek your bed,
To settle pin-money on Madam:
    No fears of cuckoldom, heav'n bless ye,
    Are ever harbour'd to distress ye,
Tormenting people, since the days of Adam.

    No schools ye want for fine behaving;
    No powdering, painting, washing, shaving:
No nightcaps snug – no trouble in undressing
    Before ye seek your strawy nest,
    Pleas'd in each other's arms to rest,
To feast on luscious Love,
Heav'n's greatest blessing.

    Good gods! ye sweet love-chanting rams!
    How nimble are ye with your hams
To mount a house, to scale a chimney-top;
    And, peeping down that chimney's hole,
    Pour, in a tuneful cry, th' impassion'd soul,
Inviting Miss Grimalkin to come up:

Who, sweet obliging female, far from coy,
    Answers your invitation note with joy;
And, scorning midst the ashes more to mope,
Lo! borne on Love's all-daring wing,
She mounteth with a pickle-herring spring,
    Without th'assistance of a rope.

Dear mousing tribe, my limbs are waxing cold –
Singers of Israel sweet, adieu, adieu!
I do suppose you need not now be told
How much I wish that I was one of *you.*

GIP

W.H. Hudson (1841–1922)

It is rather an odd coincidence that in the village inn where I am writing a portion of this book, including the present chapter, there should be three cats, unlike one another in appearance and habits as three animals of different and widely separated species. [...] All three were strays, which the landlady, who has a tender heart, took in when they were starving, and made pets of; and all are beautiful. One has Persian blood in him; a long-haired, black and brown animal with gold-coloured eyes; playful as a kitten, incessantly active, fond of going for a walk with some inmate of the house, and when no one – cat or human being – will have any more of him you will see him in the garden stalking a fly, or lying on his back on the ground under a beech-tree striking with his claws or catching at something invisible in the air – motes in the sunbeam. The second is a large black cat with white collar and muzzle and sea-green eyes, and is of an indolent, luxurious disposition, lying coiled up by the hour on the most comfortable cushion it can find. The last is Gip, a magnificent creature, a third bigger than an average-sized cat – as large and powerfully built as the British wild cat, a tabby with opaline eyes, which show a pale green colour in some lights. These singular eyes, when I first saw this animal, almost startled me with their wild, savage expression; nor was it a mere deceptive appearance, as I soon found. I never looked at this animal without finding these panther or lynx eyes fixed with a fierce intensity on me, and no sooner would I look towards him than he would crouch down, flatten his ears, and continue to watch my every movement as if apprehending a sudden attack on his life. It was many days before he allowed me to come near him without bounding away and vanishing, and not for two or three weeks would he suffer me to put a hand on him.

But the native wildness and suspicion in him could never be wholly overcome; it continued to show itself on occasions even after I had known him for months and had won his confidence, and when it seemed that, in his wild-cat, conditional way, he had accepted my friendship. He became lame, having injured one of his forelegs while hunting, and as the weather was cold he was pleased to spend his inactive and suffering time on the hearth-rug in my sitting-room. I found that rubbing warm, melted butter on his injured leg appeared to give him relief, and after the massaging and buttering he would lick the leg vigorously for ten or fifteen minutes, occasionally purring with satisfaction. Yet if I made any sudden movement, or rustled the paper in my hand, he would instantly spring up from his cushion at my feet and dart away to the door to make his escape; then, finding the door closed, he would sit down, recover his domesticity, and return to my feet.

Yet this cat had been taken in as a kitten and had already lived some two or three years in the house, seeing many people and fed regularly with the others every day. It is not, however, very rare to meet with a cat of this disposition – the cat pure and simple, as nature made it, without that little tameness on the surface, or veneer of domesticity which life with man has laid on it.

Gip is the most inveterate rat-killer I have ever known. He is never seen hunting other creatures, not even mice, although it is probable that he does kill and devour them on the spot, but he has the habit of bringing in the rats he captures; and as a day seldom passes on which he is not seen with one, and as sometimes two or three are brought in during the night, he cannot destroy fewer than three hundred to four hundred rats in the year.

Let anyone who knows the destructive powers of the rat consider what that means in an agricultural village, and what an advantage it is to the farmers to have their rick-yards and barns policed day and night by such an animal. For the whole village is his hunting-ground. His owner says that he is 'worth his weight in gold'. I should say that he is worth much more; that the equivalent in cash of his weight in purest gold, though he is big and heavy, would not be more than the value of the grain and other foodstuffs he saves from destruction in a single year.

He invariably brings in his rats alive to release and play with them in an old, stone-paved yard, and after a little play he kills them, and if they are full-grown he leaves them; but when young he devours them or allows the other cats to have them.

Gip has a somewhat remarkable history. The village has always been a favourite resort of gypsies, and it happened that once when a party of gypsies had gone away it was discovered that they had left a litter of six kittens behind, and it greatly troubled the village mind to know what was to be done with them. 'Why didn't we drown them? Oh, no, we couldn't do that,' they said, 'they were several weeks old and past the time for drowning.' However, someone who kept ferrets turned up and kindly said he would take them to give to his ferrets, and everybody was satisfied to have the matter disposed of in that way. But it was a rather disgusting way, for although it seems quite natural to give little living rodents to ferrets to be sucked of their warm blood, it goes against one's feelings to cast young cats to the pink-eyed beast; for the cat is a carnivorous creature, too, and not only so but is infinitely more beautiful and intelligent than the ferret and higher in the organic scale. However, these ideas did not prevail in the village, and the six kittens were taken; but they proved to be exceedingly vigorous and fierce for kittens, as if they knew what was going to be done to them: they fought and scratched, and eventually two, the biggest and fiercest of them, succeeded in making their escape, and by and by one of them was found on the premises at the inn – a refuge for all creatures in distress – which thereupon became its home.

from A *Shepherd's Life* (1910)

THE CAT

A.C. Benson (1862–1925)

On some grave business, soft and slow
Along the garden paths you go
    With bold and burning eyes,
Or stand with twitching tail to mark
What starts and rustles in the dark
    Among the peonies.

The dusty cockchafer that springs
Upon the dusk with shirring wings,
    The beetle glossy-horned,
The rabbit pattering through the fern
May frisk unheeded by your stern
    Preoccupation scorned.

You go, and when the morning dawns
O'er blowing trees and dewy lawns
    Dim-veiled with gossamer,
When cheery birds are on the wing,
You creep, a wild and wicked thing,
    With stained and starting fur.

You all day long beside the fire
Retrace in dreams your dark desire
    And mournfully complain
In grave displeasure if I raise
Your languid form to pet or praise,
    And so to sleep again.

The gentle hound that near me lies
Looks up with true and tender eyes
    And waits my generous mirth.
You do not woo me, but demand
A gift from my unwilling hand,
    A tribute to your worth.

You loved me when the fire was warm,
But now I stretch a fondling arm,
    You eye me and depart.
Cold eye, sleek skin and velvet paws,
You win my indolent applause,
    You do not win my heart.

TIGERS IN MINIATURE

Leigh Hunt (1784–1859)

Furthermore (in order to get rid at once of all that may be objected to poor Pussy, as boys at school get down their bad dumpling as fast as possible before the meat comes), we own we have an objection to the way in which a cat sports with a mouse before she kills it, tossing and jerking it about like a ball, and letting it go, in order to pounce upon it with the greater relish. And yet what right have we to apply human measures of cruelty to the inferior reflectability of a cat? Perhaps she has no idea of the mouse's being alive, in the sense that we have; most likely she looks upon it as a pleasant movable toy, made to be eaten – a sort of lively pudding, that oddly jumps hither and thither. It would be hard to beat into the head of a country squire of the old class that there is any cruelty in hunting a hare; and most assuredly it would be still harder to beat mouse-sparing into the head of a cat. You might read the most pungent essay on the subject into her ear, and she would only sneeze at it.

As to the unnatural cruelties, which we sometimes read of, committed by cats upon their offspring, they are exceptions to the common and beautiful rules of nature, and accordingly we have nothing to do with them. They are traceable to some unnatural circumstances of breeding or position. Enormities as monstrous are to be found among human beings, and argue nothing against the general character of the species. Even dogs are not always immaculate; and sages have made slips. Dr Franklin cut off his son with a shilling for differing with him in politics.

But cats resemble tigers! They are tigers in miniature? Well – and very pretty miniatures they are. And what has the tiger himself done, that he has not a right to eat his dinner as well as Jones? A tiger treats a man much as a cat does a mouse, granted; but we have no reason to suppose that he is aware of the man's sufferings, or means anything but to satisfy his hunger; and what have the butcher and poulterer been about meanwhile? The tiger, it is true, lays about him a little superfluously sometimes, when he gets into a sheep-fold, and kills more than he eats; but does not the Squire or the Marquis do pretty much like him in the month of September? Nay, do we not hear of venerable judges, that would not hurt a fly, going about in that refreshing month, seeking whom they may lame? See the effect of habit and education! And you can educate the tiger in no other way than by attending to his stomach. Fill that, and he will want no men to eat, probably not even to lame. On the other hand, deprive Jones of his dinner for a day or two, and see what a state he will be in, especially if he is by nature irascible. Nay, keep him from it for half an hour, and observe the tiger propensities of his stomach and fingers – how worthy of killing he thinks the cook, and what boxes of the ear he feels inclined to give the footboy.

Animals, by the nature of things, in their present state, dispose of one another into their respective stomachs, without ill-will on any side. They keep down the several populations of their neighbours, till time may come when superfluous population of any kind need not exist, and predatory appearances may vanish from the earth, as the wolves have done from England. But whether they may or not is not a question by a hundred times so important to moral inquirers as into the possibilities of human education and the nonsense of ill-will. Show the nonentity of that, and we may all get our dinners as jovially as we can, sure of these three undoubted facts – that life is long, death short, and the world beautiful.

from 'The Cat by the Fire' in *Essays* (1887)

GRIMALKIN

John Philips (1676–1709)

Grimalkin to Domestick Vermin sworn
An everlasting Foe, with watchful Eye
Lies nightly brooding o'er a chinky Gap
Protending her fell Claws, to thoughtless Mice
Sure Ruin.

from *The Splendid Shilling* (1705)

THE LOVER

George Turberville (c.1544–c.1597)

If I might alter kind,
What, think you, I would bee?
Nor Fish, nor Foule, nor Fle, nor Frog,
Nor Squirril on the Tree;
The Fish the Hooke, the Foule
The lymed Twig doth catch,
The Fle the Finger, and the Frog
The Bustard doth dispatch.

The Squirril thinking nought,
That feately cracks the Nut,
The greedie Goshawke wanting pray
In dread of Death doth put;
But scorning all these kindes,
I would become a Cat,
To combat with the creeping Mouse,
And scratch the screeking Rat.

I would be present, aye,
And at my ladie's call;
To gard her from the fearfull mouse,
In Parlour and in Hall;
In Kitchen, for his Lyfe,
He should not shew his head;
The Peare in Poke should lie untoucht
When shee were gone to Bed.
The Mouse should stand in Feare,
So should the squeaking Rat;
And this would I do if I were
Converted to a Cat.

The Lover, whose mistresse feared a mouse, declareth that he would become a Cat if he might have his desire.

CATS AND MEN

Thomas Flatman (1637–88)

Men ride many miles,
Cats tread many tiles,
Both hazard their necks in the fray;
Only Cats, when they fall
From a house or a wall,
Keep their feet, mount their tails, and away!

from *An Appeal to Cats in the Business of Love*

THE YELLOW TERROR

W.L. Alden (1837–1908)

'Speaking of cats,' said Captain Foster, 'I'm free to say that I don't like 'em. I don't care to be looked down on by any person, whether he be man or cat. I know I ain't the President of the United States, nor yet a millionaire, nor yet the Boss of New York, but all the same I calculate that I'm a man, and entitled to be treated as such. Now, I never knew a cat yet that didn't look down on me, same as cats do on everybody. A cat considers that men are just dirt under his or her paws, as the case may be. I can't see what it is that makes a cat believe that he is so everlastingly superior to all the men that have ever lived, but there's no denying the fact that such is his belief, and he acts accordingly. There was a professor here one day, lecturing on all sorts of animals, and I asked him if he could explain this aggravating conduct of cats. He said that it was because cats used to be gods, thousands of years ago in the land of Egypt; but I didn't believe him. [...]

'The most notorious cat I ever met was old Captain Smedley's Yellow Terror. His real legal name was just plain Tom: but being yellow, and being a holy terror in many respects, it got to be the fashion among his acquaintances to call him "The Yellow Terror", He was a tremendous big cat, and he had been with Captain Smedley for five years before I saw him. ...

'Smedley had him regularly shipped, and signed his name to the ship articles, and held a pen in his paw while he made a cross. [...] You see, in those days the underwriters wouldn't let a ship go to sea without a cat, so as to keep the rats from getting at the cargo. I don't know what a land cat may do, but there ain't a seafaring cat that would look at a rat. What with the steward, and the cook and the men forrard, being always ready to give the ship's cat a bite, the cat in generally full from kelson to deck, and wouldn't take the trouble to speak to a rat, unless one was to bite her tail. But, then, underwriters never know anything about what goes on at sea, and it's a shame that a sailorman should be compelled to give in to their ideas. The Yellow Terror had the general idea that the *Medford* was his private yacht, and that all hands were there to wait on him. And Smedley sort of confirmed him in that idea, by treating him with more respect than he treated his owners, when he was ashore. I don't blame the cat, and after I got to know what sort of a person the cat really was, I can't say as I blamed Smedley to any great extent.

'Tom, which I think I told you was the cat's real name, was far and away the best fighter of all cats in Europe, Asia, Africa and America. Whenever we sighted land he would get himself up in his best fur, spending hours brushing and polishing it, and biting his claws so as to make sure that they were as sharp as they could be made. As soon as the ship was made fast to the quay, or anchored in the harbour, the Yellow Terror went ashore to look for trouble. He always got it too, though he had such a reputation as a fighter, that whenever he showed himself, every cat that recognized him broke for cover. [...]

'When Tom went ashore in a foreign port he generally stopped ashore till we sailed. A few hours before we cast off hawsers, Tom would come aboard. He always knew when we were going to sail, and he never once got left. I remember one time when we were just getting up anchor in Cape Town harbour, and we all reckoned that this time we should have to sail without Tom, he having evidently stopped ashore just a little too long. But presently alongside comes a boat, with Tom lying back at full length in the sternsheets, for all the world like a drunken sailor who has been delaying the ship, and is proud of it. The boatman said that Tom had come down to the pier and jumped into his boat, knowing that the man would row him off to the ship, and calculating that Smedley would be glad to pay the damage. It's my belief that if Tom hadn't found a boatman, he would have chartered the government launch. He had the cheek to do that or anything else. [...]

'Smedley always said that Tom was religious. I used to think that was rubbish; but after I had been with Tom for a couple of voyages I began to believe what Smedley said about him. Every Sunday when the weather permitted, Smedley used to hold service on the quarter-deck. [...]

'Now Tom never failed to attend service, and to do his level best to help. He would sit somewhere near the old man and pay attention to what was going on better than I've seen some folks do in first-class churches ashore. When the men sang, Tom would start in and let out a yell here and there, which showed that he meant well even if he had never been to a singing-school, and didn't exactly understand singing according to Gunter.

First along, I thought that it was all an accident that the cat came to service, and I calculated that his yelling during the singing meant that he didn't like it. But after a while I had to admit that Tom enjoyed the Sunday service as much as the Captain himself, and I agreed with Smedley that the cat was a thorough-going Methodist.'

THE POOR GIRL AND HER CAT

W.H. Hudson (1841–1922)

I must, however, relate one more instance of a cat who hunted for others, told to me by a very aged friend of mine, a native of Fonthill Bishop. [...]

When she was a young motherless girl and they were very poor indeed, her father being incapacitated, they had a cat that was a great help to them; a large black and white animal who spent a greater part of his time hunting in Fonthill Abbey woods, and who was always bringing in something for the pot. The cat was attached to her, and whatever was brought in was for her exclusively, and I imagine it is so in all cases in which a cat has the custom of bringing anything it catches into the house. The cat mind cannot understand a division of food. It does not and cannot share a mouse or bird with another cat, and when it gives it gives the whole animal, and to one person alone. When the cat brought a rabbit home he would not come into the kitchen with it if he saw her little brother or any other person there, lest they should take it into their hands; he would steal off and conceal it among the weeds at the back of the cottage, then come back to make little mewing sounds understood by his young mistress, and she would thereupon follow him out to where the rabbit was hidden and take it up, and the cat would then be satisfied.

The cat brought her rabbits and di-dappers, as she called the moorhen, caught in the sedges by the lake in the park. This was the first occasion of my meeting with this name for a bird, but it comes no doubt from dive-dapper, an old English vernacular name (found in Shakespeare) of the dabchick, or little grebe. Moorhens were not the only birds it captured: on two or three occasions it brought in a partridge and on one occasion a fish. Whether it was a trout or not she could not say; she only knew that she cooked and ate it and that it was very good.

One day, looking out, she spied her cat coming home with something very big, something it had caught larger than itself; and it was holding its head very high, dragging its burden along with great labour. It was a hare, and she ran out to receive it, and when she got to the cat and stooped down to take it from him he released it too soon, for it was uninjured, and away it bounded and vanished into the woods, leaving them both very much astonished and disgusted.

For a long time her cat managed to escape the poaching animal's usual fate in the woods, which were strictly preserved then, in the famous Squire Beckford's day, as they are now; but a day arrived when it came hobbling in with a broken leg. It had been caught in a steel trap, and some person who was not a keeper had found and released it. She washed the blood off, and taking it on her lap put the bones together and bound up the broken limb as well as she was able, and the bones joined, and before very long the cat was well again. And no sooner was it well than it resumed its hunting in the woods and bringing in rabbits and di-dappers.

But alas, it had but nine lives, and having generously spent them all in the service of its young mistress it came to its end; at all events it finally disappeared, and it was conjectured that a keeper had succeeded in killing it.

from *A Shepherd's Life* (1910)

WHEN THE CAT'S AWAY THE MICE MAY PLAY

Matthew Prior (1664–1721)

A *Lady* once (so Stories say)
    By *Rats* and *Mice* infested,
With Gins and Traps long sought to slay
The *Thieves*; but still they scap'd away,
    And daily her molested.

Great Havock 'mongst her Cheese was made,
    And much the loss did grieve her:
At length *Grimalkin* to her Aid
She call'd (no more of *Cats* afraid)
    And begg'd him to relieve her.

Soon as *Grimalkin* came in view,
    The *Vermin* back retreated;
Grimalkin swift as Lightning flew,
Thousands of *Mice* he daily slew,
    Thousands of *Rats* defeated.

Ne'er *Cat* before such Glory won,
    All People did adore him:
Grimalkin far all Cats out-shone,
And in his *Lady's* Favour none
    Was then preferr'd before him.

Pert Mrs *Abigail* alone
    Envy'd *Grimalkin's* Glory:
Her favourite *Lap Dog* now was grown
Neglected, him she did bemoan,
    And rav'd like any Tory.

She cannot bear, she swears she won't,
　　To see the *Cat* regarded,
But firmly is resolv'd upon 't,
And vows, that, whatsoe'er comes on 't,
　　She'll have the *Cat* discarded.

She Begs, she Storms, she Fawns, she Frets,
　　(Her Arts are all employ'd)
And tells her *Lady* in a Pett,
Grimalkin cost her more in Meat
　　Than all the *Rats* destroy'd.

At length this Spiteful *Waiting-maid*
　　Produc'd a Thing amazing;
The Favourite *Cat's* a Victim made,
To satisfy this prating Jade,
　　And fairly turn'd a-grazing.

Now *Lap Dog* is again restor'd
　　Into his *Lady's* Favour;
Sumptuously kept at Bed and Board,
And He (so *Nab* has given her word)
　　Shall from all *Vermin* save Her.

Nab much exults at this Success,
　　And, overwhelm'd with Joy,
Her Lady fondly does caress,
And tells her *Fubb* can do no less,
　　Than all Her Foes destroy.

But vain such Hopes; The *Mice* that fled
　　Return, now *Grim's* discarded;
Whilst *Fubb* till Ten, on Silken Bed,
Securely lolls his drowsy Head,
　　And leaves Cheese unregarded.

Nor *Rats*, nor *Mice* the *Lap Dog* fear,
     Now uncontrol'd their Theft is:
And whatsoe'er the Vermin spare,
Nab and her *Dog* betwixt them share,
     Nor Pie, nor Pippin left is.

Mean while, to cover their Deceit,
     At once, and slander *Grim*;
Nab says, the *Cat* comes out of spight
To rob her *Lady* every Night,
     So lays it all on him.

Nor Corn secure in Garret high,
     Nor Cheesecake safe in Closet;
The *Cellars* now unguarded lie,
On ev'ry Shelf the *Vermin* Prey,
     And still *Grimalkin* does it.

The Gains from Corn apace decay'd,
     No Bags to Market go:
Complaints came from the Dairy-maid,
The *Mice* had spoil'd her Butter Trade,
     And eke her Cheese also.

With this same Lady once there liv'd
     A trusty *Servant Maid*,
Who, hearing this, full much was griev'd,
Fearing her *Lady* was deceiv'd,
     And hasten'd to her Aid.

Much Art she us'd for to disclose
     And find out the Deceit;
At length she to the *Lady* goes,
Discovers her Domestic Foes,
     And opens all the Cheat.

Struck with the Sense of Her Mistake,
    The *Lady* discontented,
Resolves again Her *Cat* to take,
And ne'er again Her *Cat* forsake
    Least she again repent it.

CHILDEBRAND

Théophile Gautier (1811–72)

Childebrand was a splendid gutter-cat, short-haired, striped
black and tan . . . His great green eyes, with the almond- shaped pupils, and
his regular velvet stripes, gave him a distant, tigerish look that I liked. Cats
are the tigers of poor devils, I once wrote . . .

from *La Ménagerie Intime*, translated by Lady Chance

KITTY: WHAT SHE THINKS OF HERSELF

William Brighty Rands (1823–82)

I am the Cat of Cats. I am
    The everlasting cat!
Cunning and old and sleek as jam,
    The everlasting cat!
I hunt the vermin in the night –
    The everlasting cat!
For I see best without the light –
    The everlasting cat!

TO A CAT WHICH HAD KILLED A FAVOURITE BIRD

Richarde Garnett (1835–1906)

O Cat in semblance, but in heart akin
To canine raveners, whose ways are sin;
Still at my hearth a guest thou dar'st to be?
Unwhipt of Justice, hast no dread of me?
Or deem'st the sly allurements shall avail
Of purring throat and undulating tail?
No! as to pacify Patroclus dead
Twelve Trojans by Pelides' sentence bled,
So shall thy blood appease the feathery shade,
And for one guiltless life shall nine be paid.

after the sixth-century poet Agathias

CAT AND KING

Ambrose Bierce (1842–1914)

A cat was looking at a king, as permitted by the proverb.

'Well,' said the monarch, observing her inspection of the royal person, 'how do you like me?'

'I can imagine a king,' said the Cat, 'whom I should like better.'

'For example?'

'The King of Mice'

The sovereign was so pleased with the wit of the reply that he gave her permission to scratch his Prime Minister's eyes out.

A DICTIONARY DEFINITION

Samuel Johnson (1709–84)

Cat: A domestic animal that catches mice, commonly reckoned by naturalists the lowest order of the leonine species.

TO MY CHILD CARLINO

Walter Savage Landor (1775–1864)

Carlino! What art thou about, my boy? . . .
Does Cincirillo follow thee about?
Inverting one swart foot suspensively,
And wagging his dread jaw, at every chirp
Of bird above him in the olive-branch?
Frighten him then away! 'twas he who slew
Our pigeons, our white pigeons, peacock-tailed,
That fear'd not you and me . . . alas, nor him!
I flattened his striped sides along my knee,
And reasoned with him on his bloody mind,
Till he looked blandly, and half-closed his eyes
To ponder on my lecture in the shade.
I doubt his memory much, his heart a little
And in some minor matters (may I say it?)
Could wish him rather sager. But from thee
God hold back wisdom yet for many years!

from *The Pentameron* (1837)

BELLING THE CAT

William Langland (c.1330–c.1386)

[...] Then forth ran a rout of great rats, all at once,
Where met them small mice, yea, more than a thousand;
All came to a council for their common profit.
For a cat of the court would come, when he liked,
And chase them and clutch them, and catch them at will,

Play with them perilously, and push them about:
'For dread of the danger, look round us we dare not;
If we grudge him his game, he will grieve us the more,
Tease us or toss us, or take in his claws,
That we loathe our own lives, ere he lets us go free.
If by wit or by wile we his will might withstand,
We might lord it aloft, and might live at our ease.'

Then a rat of renown, very ready of tongue,
Said, for a sovereign help to themselves,
'Some cits have I seen, in the city of London,
Wear chains on their necks of the choicest gold,
Or collars of crafty work; uncoupled they go
Both in warren and waste, as their will inclines,
And elsewhere at odd times, as I hear tell.
If they bore each a bell, by its ringing, me thinketh,
One might wit where they were, and away soon run!
Right so': quoth the rat, 'doth reason suggest
To buy a bell of brass or of bright silver,
To be bound on a collar, for our common profit,
On the cat's neck to hang; then each hearer can tell
If he rambles or rests him, or runs out to play!
When mild is his mood, we can move as we list
And appear in his presence, when playful and pleased,
Or, when angry, beware; and away will we run!'

All the rout of great rats to his reasons assented,
But when bought was the bell, and well bound on the collar,
Not a rat in the rout, for the realm of all France,
Durst bind the said bell about the cat's neck,
Nor hang it beside him, all England to win!
They owned they were cowards, and their counsel weak;
So their labour was lost, and all their long study.

Then a mouse of mind, who had merit, methought,
Strode forth sternly, and stood before them all,
And to the rout of rats rehearsèd these words:
'Though we killed the old cat, yet another would come
To catch all our kin, though we crept under benches.
I counsel the commons to let the cat be;
Be we never so bold as to show him the bell.
For I heard my sire say, some seven years since,
"Where the cat is a kitten, the court is a sad one";
So witnesseth scripture, who willeth may read it,

Woe to thee, land, when thy king is a child! (Eccl. x. 16).
For no one could rest him, for rats in the night!
While the cat catches rabbits, he covets us less,
But is fed as with venison; defame we him never!
Better a little loss than a livelong sorrow,
By loss of a loathed one to live in disorder!
For many men's malt we mice would destroy,
And ye, rout of rats, would rend men's clothes,
If the cat of the court could not catch you at will!
Ye rats, if unruled, could not rule o'er yourselves.
I see,' quoth the mouse, 'such a mischief might follow,
Neither kitten nor cat, by my counsel, shall suffer;
Nor care I for collars that have cost me nothing;
Had they cost me a crown, I would keep it unknown,
And suffer our rulers to rove where they like,
Uncoupled, or coupled, to catch what they can.

I warn well each wise man to ward well his own.'
What this vision may mean, ye men that are merry,
Discern ye! I dare not discern it myself!

from Piers Plowman (c.1367–70), translated by W.W. Skeat

THE OLD CAT AND THE YOUNG MOUSE

—

Jean de la Fontaine (1621–95)

A young and inexperienced mouse
Had faith to try a veteran cat –
Raminagrobis, death to rat,
And scourge of vermin through the house –
Appealing to his clemency
With reasons sound and fair.
'Pray let me live; a mouse like me
It were not much to spare.
Am I, in such a family,
A burden? Would my largest wish
Our wealthy host impoverish?
A grain of wheat will make my meal;
A nut will fat me like a seal.
I'm lean at present; please to wait,
And for your heirs reserve my fate.'
The captive mouse thus spake.
Replied the captor, 'You mistake;
To me shall such a thing be said?
Address the deaf! address the dead!
A cat to pardon! – old one too!
Why, such a thing I never knew.
Thou victim of my paw,
By well-establish'd law,
Die as a mousling should,

And beg the sisterhood
Who ply the thread and shears,
To lend thy speech their ears.
Some other like repast
My heirs may find, or fast.'
He ceased. The moral's plain.
Youth always hopes its ends to gain,
Believes all spirits like its own:
Old age is not to mercy prone.

from *The Fables* (1842), translated by Elizur Wright

ON LUTESTRINGS CATT-EATEN

Thomas Master (1603–43)

Are these the strings that poets feigne
Have clear'd the Ayre, and calm'd the mayne?
Charm'd wolves, and from the mountaine creasts
Made forests dance with all their beasts?
Could these neglected shreads you see
Inspire a Lute of Ivorie
And make it speake? Oh! think then what
Hath beene committed by my catt,
Who, in the silence of this night
Hath gnawne these cords, and marr'd them quite;
Leaving such reliques as may be
For fretts, not for my lute, but me.
Pusse, I will curse thee; may'st thou dwell
With some dry Hermit in a cell
Where Ratt neere peep'd, where mouse neere fedd,
And flyes go supperlesse to bedd;
Or with some close-par'd Brother, where
Thou'lt fast each Saboath in the yeare;

Or else, prophane, be hang'd on Munday,
For butchering a mouse on Sunday;
Or may'st thou tumble from some tower,
And misse to light upon all fower,
Taking a fall that may untie
Eight of nine lives, and let them flye;
Or may the midnight embers sindge
Thy daintie coate, or Jane beswinge
Thy hide, when she shall take thee biting
Her cheese clouts, or her house beshiting.
What, was there neere a ratt nor mouse,
Nor Buttery ope? nought in the house
But harmelesse Lutestrings could suffice
Thy paunch, and draw thy glaring eyes?
Did not thy conscious stomach finde
Nature prophan'd, that kind with kind
Should stanch his hunger? thinke on that,
Thou caniball, and Cyclops catt.
For know, thou wretch, that every string
Is a catt-gutt, which art doth spinne
Into a thread; and how suppose
Dunstan, that snuff'd the divell's nose,
Should bid these strings revive, as once
He did the calfe, from naked bones;
Or I, to plague thee for thy sinne,
Should draw a circle, and beginne
To conjure, for I am, look to't,
An Oxford scholler, and can doo't.
Then with three setts of mapps and mowes,
Seaven of odd words, and motley showes,
A thousand tricks, that may be taken
From Faustus, Lambe, or Fryar Bacon:
I should beginne to call my strings
My catlings, and my mynikins;
And they recalled, straight should fall

To mew, to purr, to catterwaule
From puss's belly. Sure as death,
Pusse should be an Engastranith;
Pusse should be sent for to the king
For a strange bird, or some rare thing.
Pusse should be sought to farre and neere,
As she some cunning woman were.
Pusse should be carried up and downe,
From shire to shire, from Towne to Towne,
Like to the camell, Leane as Hagg,
The Elephant, or Apish negg,
For a strange sight; pusse should be sung
In Lousy Ballads, midst the Throng
At markets, with as good a grace
As Agincourt, or Chevy-chase.
The Troy-sprung Brittan would forgoe
His pedigree he chaunteth soe,
And singe that Merlin – long deceast –
Returned is in a nyne-liv'd beast.

Thus, pusse, thou seest what might betyde thee;
But I forbeare to hurt or chide thee;
For may be pusse was melancholy
And so to make her blythe and jolly,
Finding these strings, shee'ld have a fitt
Of mirth; nay, pusse, if that were it,
Thus I revenge mee, that as thou
Hast played on them, I've plaid on you;
And as thy touch was nothing fine,
Soe I've but scratched these notes of mine.

4

CLEVER CATS

Cats have gnosis to a degree
that is granted to few bishops.

Carl van Vechten (1880–1954)

DAME WIGGINS OF LEE AND HER SEVEN WONDERFUL CATS

Anonymous (1823)

Dame Wiggins of Lee,
Was a worthy old soul,
As e'er threaded a nee-
dle, or wash'd in a bowl:
She held mice and rats
In such antipa-thy;
That seven fine cats
Kept Dame Wiggins of Lee.

The rats and mice scared
By this fierce whisker'd crew,
The poor seven cats
Soon had nothing to do;
So, as anyone idle
She ne'er loved to see,
She sent them to school,
Did Dame Wiggins of Lee.

But soon she grew tired
Of living alone;
So she sent for her cats
From school to come home.
Each rowing a wherry,
Returning you see:
The frolic made merry
Dame Wiggins of Lee.

The Dame was quite pleas'd,
And ran out to market,
When she came back
They were mending the carpet.
The needle each handled
As brisk as a bee:
'Well done, my good cats,'
Said Dame Wiggins of Lee.

To give them a treat,
She ran out for some rice;
When she came back,
They were skating on ice;
'I shall soon see one down,
Aye, perhaps, two or three,
I'll bet half-a-crown'
Said Dame Wiggins of Lee.

While to make a nice pudding,
She went for a sparrow,
They were wheeling a sick lamb
Home in a barrow.
'You shall all have some sprats
For your humani-ty,
My seven good cats,'
Said Dame Wiggins of Lee.

While she ran to the field,
To look for its dam,
They were warming the bed
For the poor sick lamb:
They turn'd up the clothes
All as neat as could be;
'I shall ne'er want a nurse,'
Said Dame Wiggins of Lee.

She wish'd them good night,
And went up to bed:
When, lo! in the morning,
The cats were all fled.
But soon – what a fuss!
'Where can they all be?
Here, pussy, puss, puss!'
Cried Dame Wiggins of Lee.

The Dame's heart was nigh broke,
So she sat down to weep,
When she saw them come back
Each riding a sheep:
She fondled and patted
Each purring Tom-my:
'Ah! welcome, my dears,'
Said Dame Wiggins of Lee.

The Dame was unable
Her pleasure to smother;
To see the sick Lamb
Jump up to its mother.
In spite of the gout,
And a pain in her knee,
She went dancing about:
Did Dame Wiggins of Lee.

The Farmer soon heard
Where his sheep went astray;
And arrived at Dame's door.
With his faithful dog Tray.
He knock'd with his crook,
And the stranger to see,
Out of window did look
Dame Wiggins of Lee.

For their kindness he had them
All drawn by his team;
And gave them some field-mice,
And raspberry-cream.
Said he, 'All my stock
You shall presently see;
For I honour the cats
Of Dame Wiggins of Lee.'

To shew them his poultry,
He turn'd them all loose,
When each nimbly leap'd
On the back of a Goose,
Which frighten'd them so
That they ran to the sea,
And half-drown'd the poor cats
Of Dame Wiggins of Lee.

He sent his maid out
For some muffins and crumpets:
And when he turn'd round
They were blowing of trumpets.
Said he, 'I suppose,
She's as deaf as can be,
Or this ne'er could be borne
By Dame Wiggins of Lee.'

For the care of his lamb,
And their comical pranks,
He gave them a ham,
And abundance of thanks.
'I wish you good day,
My fine fellows,' said he,
'My compliments, pray,
To Dame Wiggins of Lee.'

You see them arrived
At their Dame's welcome door,
They shew her their presents,
And all their good store,
'Now come in to supper,
And sit down with me;
All welcome once more,'
Cried Dame Wiggins of Lee.

TOBERMORY

Saki (1870–1916)

It was a chill, rain-washed afternoon of a late August day, that indefinite season when partridges are still in security or cold storage, and there is nothing to hunt – unless one is bounded on the north by the Bristol Channel, in which case one may lawfully gallop after fat red stags. Lady Blemley's house-party was not bounded on the north by the Bristol Channel, hence there was a full gathering of her guests round the tea-table on this particular afternoon. And, in spite of the blankness of the season and the triteness of the occasion, there was no trace in the company of that fatigued restlessness which means a dread of the pianola and a subdued hankering for auction bridge. The undisguised open-mouthed attention of the entire party was fixed on the homely negative personality of Mr Cornelius Appin. Of all her guests, he was the one who had come to Lady Blemley with the vaguest reputation. Someone had said he was 'clever', and he had got his invitation in the moderate expectation, on the part of his hostess, that some portion at least of his cleverness would be contributed to the general entertainment. Until tea-time that day she had been unable to discover in what direction, if any, his cleverness lay. He was neither a wit nor a croquet champion, a hypnotic force nor a begetter of amateur theatricals. Neither did his exterior suggest the sort of man in whom women are willing to pardon a generous measure of mental deficiency.

He had subsided into mere Mr Appin, and the Cornelius seemed a piece of transparent baptismal bluff. And now he was claiming to have launched on the world a discovery beside which the invention of gunpowder, of the printing-press, and of steam locomotion were inconsiderable trifles. Science had made bewildering strides in many directions during recent decades, but this thing seemed to belong to the domain of miracle rather than to scientific achievement.

'And do you really ask us to believe,' Sir Wilfrid was saying, 'that you have discovered a means for instructing animals in the art of human speech, and that dear old Tobermory has proved your first successful pupil?'

'It is a problem at which I have worked for the last seventeen years,' said Mr Appin, 'but only during the last eight or nine months have I been rewarded with glimmerings of success. Of course I have experimented with thousands of animals, but latterly only with cats, those wonderful creatures which have assimilated themselves so marvellously with our civilization while retaining all their highly developed feral instincts. Here and there among cats one comes across an outstanding superior intellect, just as one does among the ruck of human beings, and when I made the acquaintance of Tobermory a week ago I saw at once that I was in contact with a Beyond-cat of extraordinary intelligence. I had gone far along the road to success in recent experiments; with Tobermory, as you call him, I have reached the goal.'

Mr Appin concluded his remarkable statement in a voice which he strove to divest of a triumphant inflection. No one said 'Rats', though Clovis's lips moved in a monosyllabic contortion which probably invoked those rodents of disbelief.

'And do you mean to say,' asked Miss Resker, after a slight pause, 'that you have taught Tobermory to say and understand easy sentences of one syllable?'

'My dear Miss Resker,' said the wonder-worker patiently, 'one teaches little children and savages and backward adults in that piecemeal fashion; when one has once solved the problem of making a beginning with an animal of highly developed intelligence one has no need for those halting methods. Tobermory can speak our language with perfect correctness.'

This time Clovis very distinctly said, 'Beyond-rats!' Sir Wilfrid was more polite, but equally sceptical.

'Hadn't we better have the cat in and judge for ourselves?' suggested Lady Blemley.

Sir Wilfrid went in search of the animal, and the company settled themselves down to the languid expectation of witnessing some more or less adroit drawing-room ventriloquism.

In a minute Sir Wilfrid was back in the room, his face white beneath its tan and his eyes dilated with excitement.

'By Gad, it's true!'

His agitation was unmistakably genuine, and his hearers started forward in a thrill of awakened interest.

Collapsing into an armchair, he continued breathlessly: 'I found him dozing in the smoking-room, and called out to him to come for his tea. He blinked at me in his usual way, and I said, "Come on, Toby; don't keep us waiting"; and, by Gad! he drawled out in a most horribly natural voice that he'd come when he dashed well pleased! I nearly jumped out of my skin!' 'Appin had preached to absolutely incredulous hearers; Sir Wilfrid's statement carried instant conviction. A Babel-like chorus of startled exclamation arose, amid which the scientist sat mutely enjoying the first fruit of his stupendous discovery.

In the midst of the clamour Tobermory entered the room and made his way with velvet tread and studied unconcern across to the group seated round the tea-table.

A sudden hush of awkwardness and constraint fell on the company. Somehow there seemed an element of embarrassment in addressing on equal terms a domestic cat of acknowledged dental ability.

'Will you have some milk, Tobermory?' asked Lady Blemley in a rather strained voice.

'I don't mind if I do,' was the response, couched in a tone of even indifference. A shiver of suppressed excitement went through the listeners, and Lady Blemley might be excused for pouring out the saucerful of milk rather unsteadily.

'I'm afraid I've spilt a good deal of it,' she said apologetically.

'After all, it's not my Axminster,' was Tobermory's rejoinder.

Another silence fell on the group, and then Miss Resker, in her best district-visitor manner, asked if the human language had been difficult to learn. Tobermory looked squarely at her for a moment and then fixed his gaze serenely on the middle distance. It was obvious that boring questions lay outside his scheme of life.

'What do you think of human intelligence?' asked Mavis Pellington lamely.

'Of whose intelligence in particular?' asked Tobermory coldly.

'Oh, well, mine for instance,' said Mavis, with a feeble laugh.

'You put me in an embarrassing position,' said Tobermory, whose tone and attitude certainly did not suggest a shred of embarrassment. 'When your inclusion in this house-party was suggested Sir Wilfrid protested that you were the most brainless woman of his acquaintance, and that there was a wide distinction between hospitality and the care of the feeble-minded. Lady Blemley replied that your lack of brain-power was the precise quality which had earned you your invitation, as you were the only person she could think of who might be idiotic enough to buy their old car. You know, the one they call "The Envy of Sisyphus", because it goes quite nicely uphill if you push it.'

Lady Blemley's protestations would have had greater effect if she had not casually suggested to Mavis only that morning that the car in question would be just the thing for her down at her Devonshire home.

Major Barfield plunged in heavily to effect a diversion.

'How about your carryings-on with the tortoiseshell puss up at the stables, eh?'

The moment he had said it everyone realized the blunder.

'One does not usually discuss these matters in public,' said Tobermory frigidly. 'From a slight observation of your ways since you've been in this house I should imagine you'd find it inconvenient if I were to shift the conversation on to your own little affairs.'

The panic which ensued was not confined to the Major.

'Would you like to go and see if cook has got your dinner ready?' suggested Lady Blemley hurriedly, affecting to ignore the fact that it wanted at least two hours to Tobermory's dinner-time.

'Thanks,' said Tobermory, 'not quite so soon after my tea. I don't want to die of indigestion.'

'Cats have nine lives, you know,' said Sir Wilfrid heartily.

'Possibly,' answered Tobermory; 'but only one liver.'

'Adelaide!' said Mrs Cornett, 'do you mean to encourage that cat to go out and gossip about us in the servants hall?'

The panic had indeed become general. A narrow ornamental balustrade ran in front of most of the bedroom windows at the Towers, and it was recalled with dismay that this had formed a favourite promenade for Tobermory at all hours, whence he could watch the pigeons – and heaven knew what else besides. If he intended to become reminiscent in his present outspoken strain the effect would be something more than disconcerting. Mrs Cornett, who spent much time at her toilet table, and whose complexion was reputed to be of a nomadic though punctual disposition, looked as ill at ease as the Major. Miss Scrawen, who wrote fiercely sensuous poetry and led a blameless life, merely displayed irritation; if you are methodical and virtuous in private you don't necessarily want everyone to know it. Bertie van Tahn, who was so depraved at seventeen that he had long ago given up trying to be any worse, turned a dull shade of gardenia white, but he did not commit the error of dashing out of the room like Odo Finsberry, a young gentleman who was understood to be reading for the Church and who was possibly disturbed at the thought of scandals he might hear concerning other people. Clovis had the presence of mind to maintain a composed exterior; privately he was calculating how long it would take to procure a box of fancy mice through the agency of the *Exchange and Mart* as a species of hush-money.

Even in a delicate situation like the present, Agnes Resker could not endure to remain too long in the background.

'Why did I ever come down here?' she asked dramatically.

Tobermory immediately accepted the opening.

'Judging by what you said to Mrs Cornett on the croquet-lawn yesterday, you were out for food. You described the Blemleys as the dullest people to stay with that you knew, but said they were clever enough to employ a first-rate cook; otherwise they'd find it difficult to get anyone to come down a second time.'

'There's not a word of truth in it! I appeal to Mrs Cornett –' exclaimed the discomfited Agnes.

'Mrs Cornett repeated your remark afterwards to Bertie van Tahn,' continued Tobermory, 'and said, "That woman is a regular Hunger Marcher; she'd go anywhere for four square meals a day", and Bertie van Tahn said –'

At this point the chronicle mercifully ceased. Tobermory had caught a glimpse of the big yellow tom from the Rectory working his way through the shrubbery towards the stable wing. In a flash he had vanished through the open French window.

With the disappearance of his too brilliant pupil Cornelius Appin found himself beset by a hurricane of bitter upbraiding, anxious inquiry, and frightened entreaty. The responsibility for the situation lay with him, and he must prevent matters from becoming worse. Could Tobermory impart his dangerous gift to other cats? was the first question he had to answer. It was possible, he replied, that he might have initiated his intimate friend the stable puss into his new accomplishment, but it was unlikely that his teaching could have taken a wider range as yet.

'Then,' said Mrs Cornett, 'Tobermory may be a valuable cat and a great pet; but I'm sure you'll agree, Adelaide, that both he and the stable cat must be done away with without delay.'

'You don't suppose I've enjoyed the last quarter of an hour, do you?' said Lady Blemley bitterly. 'My husband and I are very fond of Tobermory – at least, we were before this horrible accomplishment was infused into him; but now, of course, the only thing is to have him destroyed as soon as possible.'

'We can put some strychnine in the scraps he always gets at dinner-time,' said Sir Wilfrid, 'and I will go and drown the stable cat myself. The coachman will be very sore at losing his pet, but I'll say a very catching form of mange has broken out in both cats and we're afraid of it spreading to the kennels.'

'But my great discovery!' expostulated Mr Appin; 'after all my years of research and experiment –'

'You can go and experiment on the short-horns at the farm, who are under proper control,' said Mrs Cornett, 'or the elephants at the Zoological Gardens. They're said to be highly intelligent, and they have this recommendation, that they don't come creeping about our bedrooms and under chairs, and so forth.'

An archangel ecstatically proclaiming the Millennium, and then finding that it clashed unpardonably with Henley and would have to be indefinitely postponed, could hardly have felt more crestfallen than Cornelius Appin at the reception of his wonderful achievement. Public opinion, however, was against him – in fact, had the general voice been consulted on the subject it is probable that a strong minority vote would have been in favour of including him in the strychnine diet.

Defective train arrangements and a nervous desire to see matters brought to a finish prevented an immediate dispersal of the party, but dinner that evening was not a social success. Sir Wilfrid had had rather a trying time with the stable cat and subsequently with the coachman. Agnes Resker ostentatiously limited her repast to a morsel of dry toast, which she bit as though it were a personal enemy; while Mavis Pellington maintained a vindictive silence throughout the meal. Lady Blemley kept up a flow of what she hoped was conversation, but her attention was fixed on the doorway. A plateful of carefully dosed fish scraps was in readiness on the sideboard, but sweets and savoury and dessert went their way, and no Tobermory appeared either in the dining-room or kitchen.

The sepulchral dinner was cheerful compared with the subsequent vigil in the smoking-room. Eating and drinking had at least supplied a distraction and cloak to the prevailing embarrassment. Bridge was out of the question in the general tension of nerves and tempers, and after Odo Finsberry had given a lugubrious rendering of 'Melisande in the Wood' to a frigid audience, music was tacitly avoided. At eleven the servants went to bed, announcing that the small window in the pantry had been left open as usual for Tobermory's private use. The guests read steadily through the current batch of magazines, and fell back gradually on the Badminton Library and bound volumes of Punch. Lady Blemley made periodic visits to the pantry, returning each time with an expression of listless depression which forestalled questioning.

At two 'o' clock Clovis broke the dominating silence.

'He won't turn up tonight. He's probably in the local newspaper office at the present moment, dictating the first instalment of his reminiscences. Lady What's-her-name's book won't be in it. It will be the event of the day.'

Having made this contribution to the general cheerfulness, Clovis went to bed. At long intervals the various members of the house-party followed his example.

The servants taking round the early tea made a uniform announcement in reply to a uniform question. Tobermory had not returned.

Breakfast was, if anything, a more unpleasant function than dinner had been, but before its conclusion the situation was relieved. Tobermory's corpse was brought in from the shrubbery, where a gardener had just discovered it. From the bites on his throat and the yellow fur which coated his claws it was evident that he had fallen in unequal combat with the big tom from the Rectory.

By midday most of the guests had quitted the Towers, and after lunch Lady Blemley had sufficiently recovered her spirits to write an extremely nasty letter to the Rectory about the loss of her valuable pet.

Tobermory had been Appin's one successful pupil, and he was destined to have no successor. A few weeks later an elephant in the Dresden Zoological Garden, which had shown no previous signs of irritability, broke loose and killed an Englishman who had apparently been teasing it. The victim's name was variously reported in the papers as Oppin and Eppelin, but his front name was faithfully rendered Cornelius.

'If he was trying German irregular verbs on the poor beast,' said Clovis, 'he deserved all he got.'

from *The Chronicles of Clovis* (1911)

THE CAT AND THE RAT

Jean de la Fontaine (1621–95)

Four creatures, wont to prowl –
Sly Grab-and-Snatch, the cat,
Grave Evil-bode, the owl,
Thief Nibble-stitch, the rat,
And Madam Weasel, prim and fine –
Inhabited a rotten pine.
A man their home discover'd there,
And set, one night, a cunning snare.
The cat, a noted early-riser,
Went forth, at break of day,
To hunt her usual prey.

Not much the wiser
For morning's feeble ray,
The noose did suddenly surprise her.
Waked by her strangling cry,
Grey Nibble-stitch drew nigh:
As full of joy was he
As of despair was she,
For in the noose he saw
His foe of mortal paw.
'Dear friend,' said Mrs Grab-and-Snatch,
'Do, pray, this cursed cord detach.
I've always known your skill,
And often your good-will;
Now help me from this worst of snares,
In which I fell at unawares.
'Tis by a sacred right,
You, sole of all your race,
By special love and grace,
Have been my favourite –
The darling of my eyes.
'Twas order'd by celestial cares,
No doubt: I thank the blessed skies,
That, going out to say my prayers,
As cats devout each morning do,
This net has made me pray to you.
Come, fall to work upon the cord.'

Replied the rat,
'And what reward
Shall pay me, if I dare?'
'Why,' said the cat.
'I swear to be your firm ally:
Henceforth, eternally.
These powerful claws are yours.
Which safe your life insures.

I'll guard from quadruped and fowl;
I'll eat the weasel and the owl.'
'Ah,' cried the rat, 'you fool!
I'm quite too wise to be your tool.'
He said, and sought his snug retreat,
Close at the rotten pine-tree's feet.
Where plump he did the weasel meet;
Whom shunning by a happy dodge,
He climb'd the hollow trunk to lodge;
And there the savage owl he saw.
Necessity became his law,
And down he went, the rope to gnaw.
Strand after strand in two he bit,
And freed, at last, the hypocrite.
That moment came the man in sight;
The new allies took hasty flight.

A good while after that,
Our liberated cat
Espied her favourite rat,
Quite out of reach, and on his guard.
'My friend,' said she,
'I take your shyness hard;
Your caution wrongs my gratitude;
Approach, and greet your staunch ally.
Do you suppose, dear rat, that I
Forget the solemn oath I mew'd?'
'Do I forget,' the rat replied,
'To what your nature is allied?
To thankfulness, or even pity,
Can cats be ever bound by treaty?'

Alliance from necessity
Is safe just while it has to be.

from *The Fables* (1842), translated by Elizur Wright

CAT AND MOUSE IN PARTNERSHIP

J.L.C. Grimm (1785–1863) and W.C. Grimm (1786–1859)

A certain cat had made the acquaintance of a mouse, and had said so much to her about the great love and friendship she felt for her, that at length the mouse agreed that they should live and keep house together. 'But we must make a provision for winter, or else we shall suffer from hunger,' said the cat; 'and you, little mouse, cannot venture everywhere, or you will be caught in a trap some day.' The good advice was followed, and a pot of fat was bought, but they did not know where to put it. At length, after much consideration, the cat said: 'I know no place where it will be better stored up than in the church, for no one dares take anything away from there. We will set it beneath the altar, and not touch it until we are really in need of it.' So the pot was placed in safety, but it was not long before the cat had a great yearning for it, and said to the mouse: 'I want to tell you something, little mouse; my cousin has brought a little son into the world, and has asked me to be godmother; he is white with brown spots, and I am to hold him over the font at the christening. Let me go out today, and you look after the house by yourself.'

'Yes, yes,' answered the mouse, 'by all means go, and if you get anything very good to eat, think of me, I should like a drop of sweet red christening wine myself.'

All this, however, was untrue; the cat had no cousin, and had not been asked to be godmother. She went straight to the church, stole to the pot of fat, began to lick at it, and licked the top of the fat off. Then she took a walk upon the roofs of the town, looked out for opportunities, and then stretched herself in the sun, and licked her lips whenever she thought of the pot of fat, and not until it was evening did she return home.

'Well, here you are again,' said the mouse, no doubt you have had a merry day.'

'All went off well,' answered the cat.

'What name did they give the child?'

'Top-off!' said the cat quite coolly.

'Top-off!' cried the mouse, 'that is a very odd and un-common name; is it a usual one in your family?'

'What does that matter,' said the cat, 'it is no worse than Crumb-stealer, as your godchildren are called.'

Before long the cat was seized by another fit of yearning. She said to the mouse: 'You must do me a favour, and once more manage the house for a day alone. I am again asked to be godmother, and, as the child has a white ring round its neck, I cannot refuse.' The good mouse consented, but the cat crept behind the town walls to the church, and devoured half the pot of fat. 'Nothing ever seems so good as what one keeps to oneself,' said she, and was quite satisfied with her day's work.

When she went home the mouse inquired: 'And what was this child christened?'

'Half-done,' answered the cat.

'Half-done! What are you saying? I never heard the name in my life, I'll wager anything it is not in the calendar!'

The cat's mouth soon began to water for some more licking.

'All good things go in threes,' said she, 'I am asked to stand godmother again. The child is quite black, only it has white paws, but with that exception, it has not a single white hair on its whole body; this only happens once every few years. You will let me go, won't you?'

'Top-off! Half-done!' answered the mouse, 'they are such odd names, they make me very thoughtful.'

'You sit at home,' said the cat, 'in your dark-grey fur coat and long tail, and are filled with fancies, that's because you do not go out in the daytime.' During the cat's absence the mouse cleaned the house, and put it in order, but the greedy cat entirely emptied the pot of fat. 'When everything is eaten up one has some peace,' said she to herself, and well filled and fat she did not return home till night. The mouse at once asked what name had been given to the third child. 'It will not please you more than the others,' said the cat. 'He is called All-gone.'

'All-gone,' cried the mouse, 'that is the most suspicious name of all! I have never seen it in print. All-gone; what can that mean?' and she shook her head, curled herself up, and lay down to sleep.

From this time forth no one invited the cat to be godmother, but when the winter had come and there was no longer anything to be found outside, the mouse thought of their provision, and said: 'Come, cat, we will go to our pot of fat which we have stored up for ourselves – we shall enjoy that.'

'Yes,' answered the cat, 'you will enjoy it as much as you would enjoy sticking that dainty tongue of yours out of the window.'

They set out on their way, but when they arrived, the pot of fat certainly was still in its place, but it was empty. 'Alas!' said the mouse, 'now I see what has happened, now it comes to light! You a true friend! You have devoured all when you were standing godmother. First top off, then half done, then –'

'Will you hold your tongue,' cried the cat, 'one word more, and I will eat you too.'

'All-gone' was already on the poor mouse's lips; scarcely had she spoken it before the cat sprang on her, seized her, and swallowed her down. Verily, that is the way of the world.

from German Popular Stories (1823)

SIR HENRY WYATT'S CAT

W.H. Hudson (1841–1922)

And here I recall an old story of a cat (an immortal puss) who only hunted pigeons. This tells that Sir Henry Wyatt was imprisoned in the Tower of London by Richard III, and was cruelly treated, having no bed to sleep on in his cell and scarcely food enough to keep him alive. One winter night, when he was half dead with cold, a cat appeared in his cell, having come down the chimney, and was very friendly, and slept curled up on his chest, thus keeping him warm all night. In the morning it vanished up the chimney, but appeared later with a pigeon, which it gave to Sir Henry, and then again departed. When the jailer appeared and repeated that he durst not bring more than the few morsels of food provided, Sir Henry then asked: 'Wilt thou dress any I provide?' This the jailer promised to do, for he pitied his prisoner, and taking the pigeon had it dressed and cooked for him. The cat continued bringing pigeons every day, and the jailer, thinking they were sent miraculously, continued to cook them, so that Sir Henry fared well, despite the order which Richard gave later, that no food at all was to be provided. He was getting impatient of his prisoner's power to keep alive on very little food, and he didn't want to behead him – he wanted him to die naturally. Thus in the end Sir Henry outlived the tyrant and was set free, and the family preserve the story to this day. It is classed as folklore, but there is no reason to prevent one from accepting it as literal truth.

from *A Shepherd's Life* (1910)

THE CAT AND THE RAIN

Jonathan Swift (1667–1745)

Careful observers may foretell the hour
(By sure prognostics) when to dread a shower;
While rain depends, the pensive cat gives o'er
Her frolics, and pursues her tail no more.

THE STORY OF THE FAITHFUL CAT

Lord Redesdale (1837–1916)

About sixty years ago, in the summer-time, a man went to pay a visit at a certain house at Osaka, and, in the course of conversation, said, 'I have eaten some very extraordinary cakes today,' and on being asked what he meant, he told the following story.

'I received the cakes from the relatives of a family who were celebrating the hundredth anniversary of the death of a cat that had belonged to their ancestors. When I asked the history of the affair, I was told that, in former days, a young girl of the family, when she was about sixteen years old, used always to be followed about by a tom-cat, who was reared in the house, so much so that the two were never separated for an instant. When her father perceived this, he was very angry, thinking that the tom-cat, forgetting the kindness with which he had been treated for years in the house, had fallen in love with his daughter, and intended to cast a spell upon her; so he determined that he must kill the beast. As he was planning this in secret, the cat overheard him, and that night went to his pillow, and, assuming a human voice, said to him, "You suspect me of being in love with your daughter; and although you might well be justified in so thinking, your suspicions are groundless. The fact is this: there is a very large old rat who has been living for many years in your granary. Now it is this old rat who is in love with my young mistress, and this is why I dare not leave her side for a moment, for fear the old rat should carry her off. Therefore I pray you to dispel your suspicions. But as I, by myself, am no match for the rat, there is a famous cat, named Buchi, at the house of Mr So-and-so, at Ajikawa: if you will borrow that cat, we will soon make an end of the old rat."

'When the father awoke from his dream, he thought it so wonderful, that he told the household of it; and the following day he got up very early and went off to Ajikawa, to inquire for the house which the cat had indicated, and had no difficulty in finding it; so he called upon the master of the house, and told him what his own cat had said, and how he wished to borrow the cat Buchi for a little while.

' "That's a very easy matter to settle," said the other: "pray take him with you at once"; and accordingly the father went home with the cat Buchi in charge. That night he put the two cats into the granary; and after a little while, a frightful clatter was heard, and then all was still again; so the people of the house opened the door, and crowded out to see what had happened; and there they beheld the two cats and the rat all locked together, and panting for breath; so they cut the throat of the rat, which was as big as either of the cats: then they attended to the two cats; but, although they gave them ginseng and other restoratives, they both got weaker and weaker, until at last they died. So the rat was thrown into the river; but the two cats were buried with all honours in a neighbouring temple.'

from *Tales of Old Japan* (1871)

RED SLIPPERS

Heinrich Heine (1797–1856)

A wicked cat, grown old and grey,
That she was a shoemaker chose to say,
And put before her window a board
Where slippers for young maidens were stored;
While some were of morocco made,
Others of satin were there display'd;
Of velvet some, with edges of gold,
And figured strings, all gay to behold.
But fairest of all exposed to view
Was a pair of slippers of scarlet hue;
They gave full many a lass delight
With their gorgeous colours and splendour bright.

A young and snow-white noble mouse
Who chanced to pass the shoemaker's house
First turn'd to look, and then stood still,
And then peep'd over the window sill.
At length she said: 'Good day, mother cat;
You've pretty red slippers, I grant you that.
If they're not dear, I'm ready to buy,
So tell me the price, if it's not too high.'

'My good young lady,' the cat replied,
'Pray do me the favour to step inside,
And honour my house, I venture to pray,
With your gracious presence. Allow me to say
That the fairest maidens come shopping to me,
And duchesses too, of high degree.
The slippers I'm willing full cheap to sell,
Yet let us see if they'll fit you well.
Pray step inside, and take a seat' –
Thus the wily cat did falsely entreat,

And the poor white thing in her ignorance then
Fell plump in the snare in that murderous den.
The little mouse sat down on a chair,
And lifted her small leg up in the air,
In order to try how the red shoes fitted,
A picture of innocent calm to be pitied.
When sudden the wicked cat seized her fast,
Her murderous talons around her cast,
And bit right off her poor little head.
'My dear white creature,' the cat then said,
'My sweet little mouse, you're as dead as a rat.
The scarlet red slippers that served me so pat
I'll kindly place on the top of your tomb,
And when is heard, on the last day of doom,
The sound of the trump, O mouse so white,
From out of your grave you'll come to light,
Like all the rest, and then you'll be able
To wear your red slippers.' Here ends my fable.

MORAL

Ye little white mice, take care where you go,
And don't be seduced by worldly show;
I counsel you sooner barefooted to walk,
Than buy slippers of cats, however they talk.

from *The Poems of Heine* (1861), translated by E.A. Bowring

THE CHESHIRE CAT

Lewis Carroll (1832–98)

The Cat only grinned when it saw Alice. It looked good-natured, she thought: still it had *very* long claws and a great many teeth, so she felt that it ought to be treated with respect.

'Cheshire Puss,' she began, rather timidly, as she did not at all know whether it would like the name: however, it only grinned a little wider. 'Come, it's pleased so far,' thought Alice, and she went on. 'Would you tell me, please, which way I ought to go from here?'

'That depends a good deal on where you want to get to,' said the Cat.

'I don't much care where –' said Alice.

'Then it doesn't matter which way you go,' said the Cat.

'– so long as I get *somewhere*,' Alice added as an explanation.

'Oh, you're sure to do that,' said the Cat, 'if you only walk long enough.'

Alice felt that this could not be denied, so she tried another question. 'What sort of people live about here?'

'In *that* direction,' the Cat said, waving its right paw round, 'lives a Hatter: and in *that* direction,' waving the other paw, 'lives a March Hare. Visit either you like: they're both mad.'

'But I don't want to go among mad people,' Alice remarked.

'Oh, you can't help that,' said the Cat: 'we're all mad here. I'm mad. You're mad.'

'How do you know I'm mad?' said Alice.

'You must be,' said the Cat, 'or you wouldn't have come here.'

Alice didn't think that proved it at all; however, she went on. 'And how do you know that you're mad?'

'To begin with,' said the Cat, 'a dog's not mad. You grant that?'

'I suppose so,' said Alice.

'Well, then,' the Cat went on, 'you see, a dog growls when it's angry, and wags its tail when it's pleased. Now I growl when I'm pleased and wag my tail when I'm angry. Therefore I'm mad.'

'*I* call it purring, not growling,' said Alice.

'Call it what you like,' said the Cat. 'Do you play croquet with the Queen today?'

'I should like it very much,' said Alice, 'but I haven't been invited yet.'

'You'll see me there,' said the Cat, and vanished.

Alice was not much surprised at this, she was getting so well used to queer things happening. While she was still looking at the place where it had been, it suddenly appeared again.

'By the bye, what became of the baby?' said the Cat. 'I'd nearly forgotten to ask.'

'It turned into a pig,' Alice answered very quietly, just as if the Cat had come back in a natural way.

'I thought it would,' said the Cat, and vanished again.

Alice waited a little, half expecting to see it again, but it did not appear, and after a minute or two she walked on in the direction in which the March Hare was said to live. 'I've seen hatters before,' she said to herself; 'the March Hare will be much the most interesting, and perhaps, as this is May, it won't be raving mad – at least not so mad as it was in March.' As she said this, she looked up, and there was the Cat again, sitting on a branch of a tree.

'Did you say pig, or fig?' said the Cat.

'I said pig,' replied Alice; 'and I wish you wouldn't keep appearing and vanishing so suddenly: you make one quite giddy.'

'All right,' said the Cat; and this time it vanished quite slowly, beginning with the end of the tail, and ending with the grin, which remained some time after the rest of it had gone.

'Well! I've often seen a cat without a grin,' thought Alice; 'but a grin without a cat! It's the most curious thing I ever saw in all my life!'

from *Through the Looking Glass and What Alice Found There* (1871)

THE MIND OF THE CAT

Samuel Butler (1835–1902)

If you say 'Hallelujah' to a cat, it will excite no fixed set of fibres in connection with any other set and the cat will exhibit none of the phenomena of consciousness. But if you say 'Me-e-at', the cat will be there in a moment . . .

from *Notebooks of Samuel Butler*

THE KING OF THE CATS

Washington Irving (1783–1859)

The evening passed away delightfully in this quaint-looking apartment, half study half drawing-room. Scott read several passages from the old romance of Arthur, with a fine deep sonorous voice and a gravity of tone that seemed to suit the antiquated, black-letter volume. It was a rich treat to hear such a work, read by such a person and in such a place; and his appearance as he sat reading, in a large armed chair, with his favourite hound Maida at his feet, and surrounded by books, and relics and border trophies, would have formed an admirable and most characteristic picture.

While Scott was reading, the sage grimalkin ... had taken his seat in a chair beside the fire, and remained with fixed eye and grave demeanour, as if listening to the reader. I observed to Scott that his cat seemed to have a black-letter taste in literature.

'Ah,' said he, 'these cats are a very mysterious kind of folk. There is always more passing in their minds than we are aware of. It comes no doubt from their being so familiar with witches and warlocks.' He went on to tell a little story about a good man who was returning to his cottage one night, when in a lonely out of the way place he met with a funeral procession of cats all in mourning, bearing one of their race to the grave in a coffin covered with a black velvet pall. The worthy man, astonished and half frightened, at so strange a pageant, hastened home and told what he had seen to his wife and children. Scarce had he finished when a great black cat that sat beside the fire raised himself up, exclaimed, "Then am I king of the cats", and vanished up the chimney. The funeral seen by the good man was of one of the cat dynasty.

'Our grimalkin, here,' added Scott, 'sometimes reminds me of the story by the airs of sovereignty which he assumes; and I am apt to treat him with respect from the idea that he may be a great prince incog: and may sometime or other come to the throne.'

In this way Scott would make the habits and peculiarities of even the dumb animals about him subjects for humorous remark or whimsical story.

from 'Abbotsford' in *The Crayon Miscellany* (1849)

THE CAT, THE WEASEL, AND THE YOUNG RABBIT

Jean de la Fontaine (1621–95)

John Rabbit's palace under ground
Was once by Goody Weasel found.
She, sly of heart, resolved to seize
The place, and did so at her ease.
She took possession while its lord
Was absent on the dewy sward,
Intent upon his usual sport,
A courtier at Aurora's court.
When he had browsed his fill of clover
And cut his pranks all nicely over.
Home Johnny came to take his drowse,
All snug within his cellar-house.
The weasel's nose he came to see.
    Outsticking through the open door.
'Ye gods of hospitality!'
    Exclaim'd the creature, vexed sore,
'Must I give up my father's lodge?
    Ho! Madam Weasel, please to budge,
Or, quicker than a weasel's dodge,
    I'll call the rats to pay their grudge!'
The sharp-nosed lady made reply,
    That she was first to occupy.
The cause of war was surely small –
A house where one could only crawl!
And though it were a vast domain,
Said she, 'I'd like to know what will
Could grant to John perpetual reign –
    The son of Peter or of Bill –
More than to Paul, or even me.'
John Rabbit spoke – great lawyer he –
Of custom, usage, as the law,

Whereby the house, from sire to son,
As well as all its store of straw,
    From Peter came at length to John.
Who could present a claim so good
As he, the first possessor, could?
'Now,' said the dame, 'let's drop dispute,
    And go before Raminagrobis,
Who'll judge, not only in this suit,
    But tell us truly whose the globe is.'
This person was a hermit cat,
    A cat that play'd the hypocrite,
A saintly mouser, sleek and fat,
    An arbiter of keenest wit.
John Rabbit in the judge concurr'd,
    And off went both their case to broach
Before his majesty, the furr'd.
    Said Clapperclaw, 'My kits, approach,
And put your noses to my ears:
I'm deaf, almost, by weight of years.'
And so they did, not fearing aught.
    The good apostle, Clapperclaw,
    Then laid on each a well-arm'd paw,
And both to an agreement brought,
    By virtue of his tusked jaw.

This brings to mind the fate
Of little kings before the great.

from *The Fables* (1842), translated by Elizur Wright

THE ACHIEVEMENT OF THE CAT

Saki (1870–1916)

In the political history of nations it is no uncommon experience to find States and peoples which but a short time since were in bitter conflict and animosity with each other, settled down comfortably on terms of mutual goodwill and even alliance. The natural history of the social developments of species affords a similar instance in the coming-together of two once warring elements, now represented by civilized man and the domestic cat. The fiercely waged struggle which went on between humans and felines in those far-off days when sabre-toothed tiger and cave lion contended with primeval man, has long ago been decided in favour of the most fitly equipped combatant – the Thing with a Thumb – and the descendants of the dispossessed family are relegated today, for the most part, to the waste lands of jungle and veld, where an existence of self-effacement is the only alternative to extermination. But the *Felis catus*, or whatever species was the ancestor of the modern domestic cat (a vexed question at present), by a master-stroke of adaptation avoided the ruin of its race, and 'captured' a place in the very keystone of the conqueror's organization. For not as a bond-servant or dependent has this proudest of mammals entered the human fraternity; not as a slave like the beasts of burden, or a humble camp-follower like the dog. The cat is domestic only as far as suits its own ends; it will not be kennelled or harnessed nor suffer any dictation as to its goings out or comings in. Long contact with the human race has developed in it the art of diplomacy, and no Roman Cardinal of medieval days knew better how to ingratiate himself with his surroundings than a cat with a saucer of cream on its mental horizon. But the social smoothness, the purring innocence, the softness of the velvet paw may be laid aside at a moment's notice, and the sinuous feline may disappear, in deliberate aloofness, to a world of roofs and chimney-stacks where the human element is distanced and disregarded. Or the innate savage spirit that helped its survival in the bygone days of tooth and claw may be summoned forth from beneath the sleek exterior, and the torture-instinct (common alone to human and feline) may find free play in the death-throes of some luckless bird or rodent. It is, indeed, no small triumph to have combined the untrammelled liberty of primeval savagery with the luxury which only a highly developed civilization can command; to be lapped in the soft stuffs that commerce has gathered from the far ends of the world, to bask in the warmth that labour and industry have dragged from the bowels of the earth; to banquet on the dainties that wealth has bespoken for its table, and withal to be a free son of nature, a mighty hunter, a spiller of life-blood. This is the victory of the cat. But besides the credit of success the cat has other qualities which compel recognition. The animal which the Egyptians worshipped as divine, which the Romans venerated as a symbol of liberty, which Europeans in the ignorant Middle Ages anathematized as an agent of demonology, has displayed to all ages two closely blended characteristics – courage and self-respect. No matter how unfavourable the circumstances, both qualities are always to the fore. Confront a child, a puppy, and a kitten with a sudden danger, the child will turn instinctively for assistance, the puppy will grovel in abject submission to the impending visitation, the kitten will brace its tiny body for a frantic resistance. And disassociate the luxury-loving cat from the atmosphere of social comfort in which it usually contrives to move, and observe it critically under the adverse conditions of civilization – that civilization which can impel a man to the degradation of clothing himself in tawdry ribald garments and capering mountebank dances in the streets for the earning of the few coins that keep him on the respectable, or non-criminal, side of society. The cat of the slums and alleys, starved, outcast, harried, still keeps amid the prowlings of its adversity the bold, free, panther-tread with which it paced of yore the temple courts of Thebes, still displays the self-reliant watchfulness which man has never taught it to lay aside. And when its shifts and clever managings have not sufficed to stave off inexorable fate, when its enemies have proved too strong or too many for its defensive powers, it dies fighting to the last, quivering with the choking rage of mastered resistance, and voicing in its death-yell that agony of bitter remonstrance which human animals, too, have flung at the powers that may be the last protest against a destiny that might have made them happy – and has not.

from *The Square Egg* (1924)

THE FOX AND THE CAT

J.L.C. Grimm (1785–1863) and W.C. Grimm (1786–1859)

It happened that the cat met the fox in a forest, and as she thought to herself, 'He is clever and full of experience, and much esteemed in the world,' she spoke to him in a friendly way. 'Good-day, dear Mr Fox, how are you? How is all with you? How are you getting through this dear season?'

The fox, full of all kinds of arrogance, looked at the cat from head to foot, and for a long time did not know whether he would give any answer or not. At last he said, 'Oh, thou wretched beard-cleaner, thou piebald fool, thou hungry mouse-hunter, what canst thou be thinking of? Dost thou venture to ask how I am getting on? What hast thou learnt? How many arts dost thou understand?'

'I understand but one,' replied the cat, modestly.

'What art is that?' asked the fox.

'When the hounds are following me, I can spring into a tree and save myself.'

'Is that all?' said the fox. 'I am master of a hundred arts, and have into the bargain a sackful of cunning. Thou makest me sorry for thee; come with me, I will teach thee how people get away from the hounds.'

Just then came a hunter with four dogs. The cat sprang nimbly up a tree, and sat down at the top of it, where the branches and foliage quite concealed her. 'Open your sack, Mr Fox, open your sack,' cried the cat to him, but the dogs had already seized him, and were holding him fast. 'Ah, Mr Fox,' cried the cat. 'You with your hundred arts are left in the lurch! Had you been able to climb like me, you would not have lost your life.'

THE COMIC ADVENTURES OF OLD DAME TROT, AND HER CAT

Anonymous (1803)

Here you behold Dame Trot, and here
    Her comic Cat you see;
Each seated in an elbow chair
    As snug as they can be.

Dame Trot came home one wintry night,
    A shivering, starving soul,
But Puss had made a blazing fire,
    And nicely truss'd a Fowl.

The Dame was pleased, the Fowl was dress'd,
    The table set in place;
The wondrous Cat began to carve,
    And Goody said her grace.

The cloth withdrawn, old Goody cries,
    'I wish we'd liquor too':
Up jump'd Grimalkin for some wine,
    And soon a cork she drew.

The wine got up in Pussy's head:
    She would not go to bed;
But purr'd and tumbled, leap'd and danced,
    And stood upon her head.

Old Goody laugh'd to see the sport,
    As though her sides would crack;
When Puss, without a single word,
    Leap'd on the Spaniel's back.

'Ha, ha! well done!' old Trot exclaims,
    'My Cat, you gallop well';
But Spot grew surly, growl'd and bit,
    And down the rider fell.

Now Goody sorely was fatigued,
    Nor eyes could open keep,
So Spot, and she, and Pussy too,
    Agreed to go to sleep.

Next morning Puss got up betimes,
    The breakfast-cloth she laid:
And ere the village clock struck eight,
    The tea and toast she made.

Goody awoke and rubb'd her eyes,
    And drank her cup of tea;
Amazed to see her Cat behave
    With such propriety.

The breakfast ended, Trot went out
    To see old neighbour Hards;
And coming home, she found her Cat
    Engaged with Spot at cards.

Soon after this, as she came in
    (It happen'd quite by chance),
Pussy was playing on the flute,
    And teaching Spot to dance.

Another time the Dame came in,
    When Spot demurely sat
Half lather'd to the ears and eyes,
    Half shaven by the Cat.

Grimalkin, having shaved her friend,
    Sat down before the glass,
And wash'd her face, and dress'd her hair,
    Like any modern lass.

A hat and feather then she took,
    And stuck it on aside;
And o'er a gown of crimson silk,
    A handsome tippet tied.

Just as her dress was all complete,
    In came the good old Dame;
She look'd, admired, and curtsied low,
    And Pussy did the same.

PUSS IN BOOTS

Charles Perrault (1628–1703)

There was a miller, who had left no more estate to the three sons he had, than his mill, his ass and his cat. The partition was soon made. Neither the scrivener nor attorney were sent for. They would soon have eaten up all the patrimony. The eldest had the mill, the second the ass and the youngest nothing but the cat.

The poor young fellow was quite comfortless at having so poor a lot. 'My brothers,' said he, 'may get their living handsomely enough, by joining their stocks together; but for my part, when I have eaten up my cat, and made me a muff of his skin, I must die with hunger.'

The Cat, who heard all this, but made as if he did not, said to him with a grave and serious air, 'Do not thus afflict yourself, my good master; you have nothing else to do, but to give me a bag, and get a pair of boots made for me, that I may scamper through the dirt and brambles, and you shall see that you have not so bad a portion of me as you imagine.'

Though the Cat's master did not build very much upon what he said, he had, however, often seen him play a great many cunning tricks to catch rats and mice; as when he used to hang by the heels, or hide himself in the meal, and make as if he were dead; so that he did not altogether despair of his affording him some help in his miserable condition. When the Cat had what he asked for, he booted himself very gallantly; and putting his bag about his neck, he held the strings of it in his forepaws, and went into a warren where was great abundance of rabbits. He put bran and sow thistle into his bag, and stretching himself out at length, as if he had been dead, he waited for some young rabbits, not yet acquainted with the deceits of the world, to come and rummage his bag for what he had put into it.

Scarce was he laid down, but he had what he wanted; a rash and foolish young rabbit jumped into his bag, and Monsieur Puss, immediately drawing close the strings, took and killed him without pity. Proud of his prey, he went with it to the palace, and asked to speak with his Majesty. He was shown upstairs into the King's apartments and, making a low reverence, said to him, 'I have brought you, Sir, a rabbit of the warren, which my noble Lord, the Marquis of Carabas – for that was the title which Puss was pleased to give his master – has commanded me to present to your Majesty from him.'

'Tell thy master,' said the King, 'that I thank him, and that he does me a great deal of pleasure.'

Another time he went and hid himself among some standing corn, holding still his bag open; and when a brace of partridges ran into it, he drew the strings, and so caught them both. He went and made a present of them to the King, as he had done before of the rabbits which he took in the warren. The King, in like manner, received the partridges with great pleasure, and ordered him some money to drink.

The Cat continued for two or three months thus to carry his Majesty, from time to time, game of his master's taking. One day in particular, when he knew for certain that he was to take the air, along the riverside, with his daughter, the most beautiful princess in the world, he said to his master, 'If you will follow my advice, your fortune is made; you have nothing else to do, but go and wash yourself in the river, in that part I shall show you, and leave the rest to me.' The Marquis of Carabas did what the Cat advised him to, without knowing why or wherefore.

While he was washing, the King passed by, and the Cat began to cry out as loud as he could, 'Help, help, my Lord Marquis of Carabas is going to be drowned.' At this noise the King put his head out of the coach window and, finding it was the Cat who had often brought him such good game, he commanded his guards to run immediately to the assistance of his Lordship the Marquis of Carabas.

While they were drawing the poor Marquis out of the river, the Cat came up to the coach, and told the King that while his master was washing there came by some rogues, who went off with his clothes, though he had cried out, 'Thieves! Thieves!' several times, as loud as he could. This cunning Cat had hidden them under a great stone. The King immediately commanded the officers of his wardrobe to run and fetch one of his best suits for the Lord Marquis of Carabas.

The King caressed him after a very extraordinary manner; and as the fine clothes he had given him extremely set off his good mien (for he was well made and very handsome in his person), the King's daughter took a secret inclination to him, and the Marquis of Carabas had no sooner cast two or three respectful and somewhat tender glances, but she fell in love with him to distraction. The King would needs have him come into the coach, and partake of the airing. The Cat, quite overjoyed to see his project begin to succeed, marched on before and, meeting some countrymen who were mowing a meadow, he said to them, 'Good people, you who are mowing, if you do not tell the King that the meadow you mow belongs to my Lord Marquis of Carabas, you shall be chopped as small as herbs for the pot.'

The King did not fail of asking of the mowers, to whom the meadow they were mowing belonged; 'To my Lord Marquis of Carabas,' answered they all together; for the Cat's threats had made them terribly afraid.

'You see, Sir,' said the Marquis, 'this is a meadow which never fails to yield a plentiful harvest every year.'

The Master Cat, who went still on before, met with some reapers, and said to them, 'Good people, you who are reaping, if you do not tell the King that all this corn belongs to the Marquis of Carabas, you shall be chopped as small as herbs for the pot.'

The King, who passed by a moment after, would needs know to whom all that corn, which he then saw, did belong; 'To my Lord Marquis of

Carabas,' replied the reapers; and the King was very well pleased with it, as well as the Marquis, whom he congratulated thereupon. The Master Cat, who went always before, said the same words to all he met; and the King was astonished at the vast estates of my Lord Marquis of Carabas.

Monsieur Puss came at last to a stately castle, the master of which was an Ogre, the richest that had ever been known; for all the lands which the King had then gone over belonged, with this castle, to him. The Cat, who had taken care to inform himself who this Ogre was, and what he could do, asked to speak to him, saying he could not pass so near the castle without having the honour of paying his respects to him.

The Ogre received him as civilly as an Ogre could do, and made him sit down. 'I have been assured,' said the Cat, 'that you have the gift of being able to change yourself into all sorts of creatures you have a mind to; you can, for example, transform yourself into a lion, or elephant, and the like.'

'This is true,' answered the Ogre very briskly, 'and to convince you, you shall see me now become a lion.' Puss was so sadly terrified at the sight of a lion so near him, that he immediately got into the gutter, not without abundance of trouble and danger, because of his boots, which were of no use at all to him in walking upon the tiles. A little while after, when Puss saw that the Ogre had resumed his natural form, he came down, and owned he had been very much frightened.

'I have been moreover informed,' said the Cat, 'but I know not how to believe it, that you have also the power to take upon you the shape of the smallest animals; for example, to change yourself into a rat or a mouse; but I must own to you, I take this to be impossible.'

'Impossible!' cried the Ogre. 'You shall see that presently,' and at the same time changed himself into a mouse, and began to run about the floor. Puss no sooner perceived this, but he fell upon him and ate him up.

Meanwhile the King, who saw, as he passed, this fine castle of the Ogre, had a mind to go into it. Puss, who heard the noise of his Majesty's coach running over the drawbridge, ran out, and said to the King, 'Your Majesty is welcome to the castle of my Lord Marquis of Carabas.'

'What! my Lord Marquis,' cried the King, 'and does this castle also belong to you? There can be nothing finer than this court, and all the stately buildings which surround it; let us go into it, if you please.' The Marquis gave his hand to the Princess, and followed the King, who went up first. They passed into a spacious hall, where they found a magnificent collation, which the Ogre had prepared for his friends, who were that very day to visit him, but dared not to enter, knowing the King was there.

His Majesty was perfectly charmed with the good qualities of my Lord Marquis of Carabas, as was his daughter, who was fallen violently in love with him; and seeing the vast estate he possessed, he said to him; after having drunk five or six glasses, 'It will be owing to yourself only, my Lord Marquis, if you are not my Son-in-Law.' The Marquis, making several low bows, accepted the honour which his Majesty conferred upon him, and forthwith, that very same day, married the Princess.

Puss became a great Lord and never ran after mice any more, only for his diversion.

translated by G.M. Gent (1802)

THE CAT AND THE COW

St George Mivart (1827–1900)

My friend Captain Noble, of Maresfield, informs me that he has himself known a cat which was in the habit of catching starlings by getting on a cow's back and waiting till the cow happened to approach the birds, which little suspected what the approaching inoffensive beast bore crouching upon it. He assures me he has himself witnessed this elaborate trick, by means of which the cat managed to catch starlings which otherwise it could never have got near.

from *The Cat* (1881)

5

LADY GRIMALKIN

Her elegance and distinction gave one an idea of
aristocratic birth, and among her own kind she must have
been at least a duchess.

Théophile Gautier (1811–72)

MARIGOLD

Richard Garnett (1835–1906)

She moved through the garden in glory because
She had very long claws at the end of her paws.
Her neck was arched, her tail was high.
A green fire glared in her vivid eye;
And all the toms, though never so bold,
Quailed at the martial Marigold.

SERAPHITA

Théophile Gautier (1811–72)

Don Pierrot had a companion of the same race as himself,
and no less white. All the imaginable snowy comparisons it were possible
to pile up would not suffice to give an idea of that immaculate fur, which
would have made ermine look yellow.

I called her Seraphita, in memory of Balzac's Swedenborgian romance.
The heroine of that wonderful story, when she climbed the snow peaks
of the Falberg with Minna, never shone with a more pure white radiance.
Seraphita had a dreamy and pensive character. She would lie motionless
on a cushion for hours, not asleep, but with eyes fixed in rapt attention on
scenes invisible to ordinary mortals.

Caresses were agreeable to her, but she responded to them with great
reserve, and only to those of people whom she favoured with her esteem,
which it was not easy to gain. She liked luxury, and it was always in the
newest armchair or on the piece of furniture best calculated to show off her
swan-like beauty, that she was to be found. Her toilette took an immense
time. She would carefully smooth her entire coat every morning, and wash
her face with her paw, and every hair on her body shone like new silver when
brushed by her pink tongue. If anyone touched her she would immediately

efface all traces of the contact, for she could not endure being ruffled. Her elegance and distinction gave one an idea of aristocratic birth, and among her own kind she must have been at least a duchess. She had a passion for scents. She would plunge her nose into bouquets, and nibble a perfumed handkerchief with little paroxysms of delight. She would walk about on the dressing-table sniffing the stoppers of the scent-bottles, and she would have loved to use the violet powder if she had been allowed.

Such was Seraphita, and never was a cat more worthy of a poetic name.

from 'The White and Black Dynasties' in *La Ménagerie Intime*, translated by Lady Chance

LADY GRIMALKIN'S CONCERT AND SUPPER

Anonymous (1809)

Miss TABITHA GOSSIP, a mischievous Vandal,
Professor of Spite in the College of Scandal,
Among other passengers, happen'd to stop,
To look at the pictures in Harris's shop.
When she found there was scarcely a bird or a beast,
But had given a ball, or provided a feast;
Always ready to hear, or to tell, something new,
She determin'd her friends should know of it too;
So to Lady GRIMALKIN's milk-party she went,
To spit out her venom, and mew discontent:
And thus, while the ladies were drinking their tea,
The whisper went round through the whole coterie.
When TABITHA spoke of the Butterfly's Ball,
In horrible chorus they set up a squall.
GRIMALKIN, of Cats the experienc'd Nestor,
Stood up, and gave vent to the cares which oppress'd her,
'Shall others stick up their impertinent phizzes,
Whilst *we* are proscribed as a set of old quizzes?
Shall Grubs of the earth, and contemptible Sprats,

Presume to compare with the Duchess of Cats?'
When their tables they spread, and their fine clothes
  they tie on,
I cou'd scratch out their eyes – for a month I cou'd cry on,
These whiskers – this beard, are the emblems of knowledge,
For my rank, I refer to the Heraldry College,
Great heroes I reckon among my relations,
Who back to the flood stretch in long generations;
By my ancestors brave has been glorious fun done,
I allude to the Cat and the Lord Mayor of London.
They say we're allied to the Tiger's grim race,
That the family likeness appears in our face;
But let us set insults like these at defiance,
We've cause to be proud of so great an alliance.
Yes! GRIZZLE GRIMALKIN so handsome and tall,
Shall hold up her head with the best of them all;
To the Bookseller's window we'll put in our claim,
And find a snug niche in the Temple of Fame.'
She finish'd – the Cats gave a mew of applause,
And the party broke up with much shaking of paws.
Now Lady GRIMALKIN made great preparation,
To accommodate all the Feline generation;
So busy was she in arranging her house,
'Twas a holiday then for poor Master Mouse;
The chairs were uncover'd, the tables set out,
The drawing-room swept for her Ladyship's route;
When the cook was well scolded, the lustres well lighted,
She sent out her cards, and her neighbours invited:
'Lady GRIZZLE GRIMALKIN her friends hopes to see
To a Concert and Supper, sans ceremonie.'
Now arming for conquest, the pretty Miss Cats
Curl'd up their sweet whiskers, and put on their hats,
To Bond-street they sent for the *Poke* and the *Gypsy*
Which stuck all aside made the wearers look tipsy;
They brush'd their fur-tippets, and tied on their pinners,

As city dames do at the Mansion House dinners.
To display their fine shape they sported no pockets,
But plenty of necklaces, bracelets, and lockets;
The belle who wears pockets is voted a fool,
For John stands behind with the smart *ridicule*.
The single Miss TABBIES call out for a fan,
To screen their coy charms from the vile monster Man.
Due regard to the time of the year must be had,
So in Russian pelisses of fur they were clad;
But some Cats of taste thinking red most becoming,
In scarlet cloaks wrap themselves up like old women;
While those who a Patriot's ardour maintain
Put on velvet mantles in honour of Spain.
The elderly Ladies stay'd long at their glass,
Like Ninon of old, that sweet evergreen lass;
Cruel Time had the province of beauty invaded,
Some teeth had dropp'd out, and some roses had faded,
So an ivory row must be planted instead,
And Kitty give two or three touches of *red*.
Then, arm'd at all points with pins and with brooches,
The Ladies step into their chariots and coaches.
Meanwhile let us see what's become of the Beaux,
'Tis said each appear'd in a new suit of clothes,
They had wigs à la Titus, and Opera hats,
Such vanity swells in the bosoms of Cats!
As a finishing stroke of polite education,
To see more of the world they had left their own nation,
'Til their heads were in danger they travell'd in France,
And learn'd to eat frogs, and like Parisot dance;
When the troubles broke out, they had fled for their lives,
And came back to England to look sharp for wives.

Now! ye Tabbies advanc'd in your grand climacteric
Try a blush if ye can – if not, try an hysteric!
Ah! those killing eyes will convince each Adonis,

How hapless the case of a damsel alone is.
Genteelly unpunctual they reach'd the Saloon,
For Cats of the Ton must not get there too soon;
Let us stand in the ante-room counting each comer,
And so set them down like the Ships of old Homer.
SQUALLINI was there, a great amateur,
Who sang in the Concerts of fashion sans peur,
Mr CATGUT perform'd on the violoncello,
Like Orpheus, a very harmonious fellow,
A solo was sung by Signor SOPRANO,
And Miss CROTCHET play'd on the Forte Piano.
But why should we mention each musical name,
In the circles of science, of fashion and fame?
Suffice it to say, that each Mademoiselle SCRATCHI
Was equal – superior indeed, to STORACE.
Each Signor had talents, and well cou'd display 'em,
Hide your heads, Messrs INCLEDON, DIGNUM, and BRAHAM!
At each exquisite strain they all cried encore,
We can give CATALINI, GRASSINI no more;
And oft as a signal of Feline applause,
They mew'd approbation, kept time with their paws.
What they sang, what they play'd, tis not easy to say well,
A ballad of DIBDIN, or quartet of PLEYEL.
After many a rondo, and sweet pastorale,
'Twas time the Orchestra shou'd play their finale;
So clos'd with a chorus this grand Concertante;
What is HANDEL compared with such dilettanti?
Now wearied at length with melodious notes,
They adjourn'd to the supper to moisten their throats;
The fare might have answer'd an Alderman's wishes,
Nor could *Birch* have provided more elegant dishes.
Her Ladyship's chaplain, a reverend divine,
Who wond'rous to tell, was no lover of wine,
Before they sat down, being call'd to say grace,
Full half an inch longer extended his face;

Each damsel he pledg'd in a saucer of milk,
And ogl'd and smirk d in his cassock of silk.
Men are fond of roast beef, but a barbicued mouse,
Is the great standing dish in every Cat's house.
'Twas an animal worthy the pencil of Snyders,
And near it was plac'd a side-dish of spiders.
In the midst was a china tureen of Gold-fish,
Beware, oh ye Cats, of so fatal a dish!
Tho' smiling the Lake of Inchantment appear,
Remember, poor SELIMA ventur'd too near,
Come, drink to her shade! o'er her fate drop a tear!
This libation pour'd out, at the bottom was put on,
A roast leg of rat, for a roast leg of mutton;
Bastill'd in a pie, came some sweet little wrens,
Teal, and widgeon, were sent by a friend from the fens.

Then came in the cheese, which most likely was toasted,
With chesnuts, by Æsop's receipt, so well roasted;
Odoriferous civet was brought in an urn,
And Valerian roots in a silver Epergne.
After Supper, went round the most popular toasts,
'May Monsieur Le Chat never land on our coasts!
By these beards, by these Patriot Mustachios we swear,
That if in a freak the invader should dare,
To disturb our firesides, we'll each turn volunteer,
And send him away with a flea in his ear.
French monkeys shall ne'er put a ring in our noses,
For we sharpen our claws *pro aris et focis.*'
Between every sentiment, every toast,
They sang catches and glees, that no time might be lost;
The ladies were shy, and reluctant of course,
Protesting they'd sung 'til they'd made themselves hoarse;
Mrs BLAND had a cold, Mrs DICKONS was husky,
And 'twas time to depart, for the evening grew dusky.
In chariots, and chairs, went the velvets and satins;

For ladies of rank must not hobble in pattens.

Some chose in barouches, to drive themselves home;

But all made a solemn engagement to come

On a mouse-hunting party, at some future day,

Ah! tremble ye mice, when they sound 'Hark away!'

VENUS AND THE CAT

Æsop (6th century BC)

In ancient times there lived a beautiful cat who fell in love with a young man. Naturally, the young man did not return the cat's affections, so she besought Venus, the goddess of love and beauty, for help. The goddess, taking compassion on her plight, changed her into a fair damsel.

No sooner had the young man set eyes on the maiden than he became enamoured of her beauty and in due time led her home as his bride. One evening a short time later, as the young couple were sitting in their chamber, the notion came to Venus to discover whether in changing the cat's form she had also changed her nature. So she set down a mouse before the beautiful damsel. The girl, reverting completely to her former character, started from her seat and pounced upon the mouse as if she would eat it on the spot, while her husband watched her in dismay.

The goddess, provoked by such clear evidence that the girl had revealed her true nature, turned her into a cat again.

MORAL

What is bred in the bone will never be absent in the flesh.

from *Fables*

THE OWL AND THE PUSSY-CAT

Edward Lear (1812–88)

The Owl and the Pussy-cat went to sea
    In a beautiful pea-green boat,
They took some honey, and plenty of money,
    Wrapped up in a five-pound note.
The Owl looked up to the stars above,
    And sang to a small guitar,
'O lovely Pussy! O Pussy, my love,
    What a beautiful Pussy you are,
        You are,
        You are!
    What a beautiful Pussy you are!'

Pussy said to the Owl, 'You elegant fowl!
    How charmingly sweet you sing!
Oh let us be married! too long we have tarried:
    But what shall we do for a ring?'
They sailed away, for a year and a day,
    To the land where the Bong-tree grows
And there in a wood a Piggy-wig stood
    With a ring at the end of his nose,
        His nose,
        His nose,
    With a ring at the end of his nose.

'Dear Pig, are you willing to sell for one shilling
    Your ring?' Said the Piggy, 'I will.'
So they took it away, and were married next day
    By the Turkey who lives on the hill.
They dined on mince, and slices of quince,
    Which they ate with a runcible spoon;
And hand in hand, on the edge of the sand,

They danced by the light of the moon,
      The moon,
      The moon,
They danced by the light of the moon.

from *Nonsense Songs* (1871)

GINGER

Sydney, Lady Morgan (1776–1859)

Though my mother could never teach me to read, she taught me hymns and poetry by rote, which incited me to write rhymes on my own account. I had many favourites among cats, dogs and birds, my mother's reprobation and the servant's nuisance; but I turned them all to account and wove them into stories, to which I tried to give as much personal interest as old Mother Hubbard bestowed on her dog.

The head favourite of my menagerie was a magnificent and very intelligent cat, 'Ginger' by name, from the colour of her coat, which though almost orange was very much admired. She was the last of a race of cats sacred in the traditions of the Music Hall. Pat Brennan, 'The sad historian of the ruined towers', held them in the greatest reverence mingled with superstitious awe. Brennan was a good Catholic, but rather given to exaggeration, which rendered his testimony to matters of fact proverbially questionable; and it became a byword among unbelieving neighbours when anyone told a wonderful story, to ask, 'Do you know Brennan? Well, then, enough said!' After this, there was nothing left for the disconcerted narrator but to walk away. One of his stories was – that the monastic cats had *stings* in their tails, which after their death were preserved by the monks for purposes of flagellation, or by the nuns – Brennan was not sure which!

Ginger was as much the object of my idolatry as if she had had a temple and I had been a worshipper in ancient Egypt; but, like other deities, she was reprobated by those who were not of my faith.

I made her up a nice little cell, under the beaufet, as sideboards were then called in Ireland – a sort of alcove cut out of the wall of our parlour where we kept the best glass and the family 'bit of plate' – a silver tankard – with the crest of the Hills upon it (a dove with an olive branch in its mouth), which commanded great respect in our family.

Ginger's sly attempts to hide herself from my mother, to whom she had that antipathy which animals so often betray to particular individuals, were a source of great amusement to my little sister and myself; but when she chose the retreat of the beaufet as the scene of her *accouchement*, our fear lest it should come to my mother's knowledge was as great as if we had been concealing a moral turpitude.

It was a good and pious custom of my mother's to hear our prayers every night; when Molly tapped at the parlour door at nine o'clock, we knelt at my mother's feet, our four little hands clasped in hers, and our eyes turned to her with looks of love, as they repeated that simple and beautiful invocation, the Lord's Prayer; to this was always added the supplication, 'Lighten our darkness we beseech Thee'; after which we were accustomed to recite a prayer of our affectionate suggestion, calling a blessing on the heads of all we knew and loved, which ran thus, 'God bless papa, mamma, my dear sister, and Molly, and Betty, and Joe, and James, and all our good friends.' One night, however, before my mother could pronounce her solemn 'amen', a soft muttered 'purr' issued from the cupboard, my heart echoed the appeal, and I added, 'God bless Ginger the cat!' Wasn't my mother shocked! She shook both my shoulders and said, 'What do you mean by that, you stupid child?"

'May I not say, "Bless Ginger?"' I asked humbly.

'Certainly *not*,' said my mother emphatically.

'Why, mamma?'

'Because Ginger is not a Christian.'

'*Why* is not Ginger a Christian?'

'Why? because Ginger is only an animal.'

'Am I a Christian, mamma, or an animal?'

'I will not answer any more foolish questions tonight. Molly, take these children to bed, and do teach Sydney not to ask those silly questions.'

So we were sent off in disgrace, but not before I had given Ginger a wink, whose bright eyes acknowledged the salute through the half-open door.

The result of this was that I tried my hand at a poem.

The jingle of rhyme was familiar to my ear through my mother's constant recitation of verses, from the sublime Universal Prayer of Pope to the nursery rhyme of Little Jack Horner, whilst my father's dramatic citations, which had descended even to the servants, had furnished me with the tags of plays from Shakespeare to O'Keefe; so that 'I lisped in numbers' though the numbers never came.

Here is my first attempt:

> My dear pussy cat,
> Were I a mouse or rat,
>> Sure I never would run off from you,
> You're so funny and gay,
> With your tail when you play,
>> And no song is so sweet as your 'mew';
> But pray keep in your press,
> And don't make a mess,
>> When you share with your kittens our posset;
> For mamma can't abide you,
> And I cannot hide you,
>> Except you keep close in your closet!

I tagged these doggrels together while lying awake half the night, and as soon as I could get a hearing in the morning I recited them to the kitchen, and no elocution ever pronounced in *that* kitchen (although it was dedicated to Melpomene, whose image shone on an orchestra that had been converted into a dresser, the whole apartment being the remains of the fantastic Ridotto, though now being converted to culinary purposes in the same floor as our dining-room), no elocution had ever excited more applause. James undertook to write it down, and Molly corrected the press. It was served up at breakfast to my father, and it not only procured me his rapturous praise but my mother's forgiveness.

My father took me to Moira House; made me recite my poem, to which he had taught me to add appropriate emphasis and action, to which my own tendency to grimace added considerable comicality. The Countess of Moira laughed heartily at the 'infant Muse' as my father called me, and ordered the housekeeper to send up a large plate of bread and jam, the earliest recompense of my literary labours.

from *Lady Morgan's Memoirs* (1862)

SHE SIGHTS A BIRD

Emily Dickinson (1830–86)

She sights a Bird – she chuckles –
She flattens – then she crawls –
She runs without the look of feet –
Her eyes increase to Balls –

Her Jaws stir – twitching – hungry –
Her Teeth can hardly stand –
She leaps, but Robin leaped the first –
Ah, Pussy, of the Sand,

The Hopes so juicy ripening –
You almost bathed your Tongue –
When Bliss disclosed a hundred Toes –
And fled with every one –

YE MARVELLOUS LEGEND OF TOM CONNOR'S CAT

Samuel Lover (1797–1868)

'There was a man in these parts, sir, you must know, called Tom Connor, and he had a cat that was equal to any dozen of rat traps, and he was proud of the baste, and with rayson; for she was worth her weight

in gold to him in saving his sacks of meal from the thievery of the rats and mice; for Tom was an extensive dealer in corn, and influenced the rise and fall of that article in the market, to the extent of a full dozen of sacks at a time, which he either kept or sold, as the spirit of free trade or monopoly came over him. Indeed, at one time, Tom had serious thoughts of applying to the government for a military force to protect his granary when there was a threatened famine in the country.'

'Pooh pooh, sir!' said the matter-of-fact little man. 'As if a dozen sacks could be of the smallest consequence in a whole country – pooh pooh!'

'Well, sir,' said Murtough, 'I can't help you if you don't believe; but it's truth what I'm telling you, and pray don't interrupt me, though you may not believe; by the time the story's done you'll have heard more wonderful things than *that* – and besides, remember you're a stranger in these parts, and have no notion of the extraordinary things, physical, metaphysical, and magical, which constitute the idiosyncrasy of rural destiny.'

The little man did not know the meaning of Murtough's last sentence – nor Murtough either; but, having stopped the little man's throat with big words, he proceeded: 'This cat, sir, you must know, was a great pet, and was so up to everything, that Tom swore she was a most like a Christian, only she couldn't speak, and had so sensible a look in her eyes, that he was sartin sure the cat knew every word that was said to her. Well, she used to set by him at breakfast every morning, and the eloquent cock of her tail, as she used to rub against his leg, said: "Give me some milk, Tom Connor", as plain as print, and the plentitude of her purr afterwards spoke a gratitude beyond language. Well, one morning, Tom was going to the neighbouring town to market, and he had promised the wife to bring home shoes to the childre' out o' the price of the corn; and sure enough before he sat down to breakfast, there was Tom taking the measure of the children's feet, by cutting notches on a bit of stick; and the wife gave him so many cautions about getting a "nate fit" for "Billy's purty feet" that Tom, in his anxiety to nick the closest possible measure, cut off the child's toe. This disturbed the harmony of the party, and Tom was obliged to breakfast alone, while the mother was endeavouring to cure Billy; in short, trying to make a *heal* of his *toe*. Well, sir, all the time Tom was taking measure for the shoes, the cat was observing him with that luminous peculiarity of eye for which her tribe is remarkable, and when Tom sat down to breakfast the cat rubbed up against him more vigorously than usual; but Tom being bewildered, between his expected gain in corn and the positive loss of his child's toe, kept never minding her, until the cat, with a sort of caterwauling growl, gave Tom a dab of her claws, that went clean through his leathers, and a little further. "Wow!" says Tom, with a jump, clapping his hand on the part and rubbing it. "By this and that, you drew the blood out of me," says Tom. "You wicked divil – tish! – go along!" says he, making a kick at her. With that the cat gave a reproachful look at him, and her eyes glared just like a pair of mail-coach lamps in a fog. With that, sir, the cat, with a mysterious "meow", fixed a most penetrating glance on Tom, and distinctly uttered his name.

'Tom felt every hair on his head as stiff as a pump handle; and scarcely crediting his ears, he returned a searching look at the cat, who very quietly proceeded in a sort of nasal twang:

' "Tom Connor," ' says she.

' "The Lord be good to me!" says Tom. "If it isn't spakin' she is!"

' "Tom Connor," says she again.

' "Yes, ma'am," says Tom.

' "Come here," says she. "Whisper – I want to talk to you, Tom," says she, "the laste taste in private," says she – rising on her hams and beckoning him with her paw out o' the door, with a wink and a toss o' the head aiqual to a milliner.

'Well, as you may suppose, Tom didn't know whether he was on his head or his heels, but he followed the cat, and off she went and squatted herself under the hedge of a little paddock at the back of Tom's house; and as he came round the corner, she held up her paw again, and laid it on her mouth, as much as to say "Be cautious, Tom." Well, divil a word Tom could say at all, with the fright, so up he goes to the cat, and says she:

' "Tom," says she, I have a great respect for you, and there's something I must tell you, because you're losing character with your neighbours," says she, "by your goin's on," says she, 'and it's out o' the respect that I have for you, that I must tell you," says she.

' "Thank you, ma'am," says Tom.

' "You're going off to the town," says she, to buy shoes for the childre'," says she, "and never thought o' getting me a pair."

' "You!" says Tom.

' "Yis, me, Tom Connor," says she, "and the neighbours wondhers that a respectable man like you allows your cat to go about the counthry barefutted," says she.

' "Is it a cat to ware shoes?" says Tom.

' "Why not?" says she. "Doesn't horses ware shoes? And I have a prettier foot than a horse, I hope," says she with a toss of her head.

' "Faix, she spakes like a woman; so proud of her feet," says Tom to himself, astonished, as you may suppose, but pretending never to think it remarkable all the time; and so he went on discoursin'; and says he: "It's thrue for you, ma'am," says he, "that horses ware shoes – but that stands to rayson, ma'am, you see – seeing the hardship their feet has to go through on the hard roads."

' "And how do you know what hardship my feet has to go through?" says the cat, mighty sharp.

' "But, ma'am", says Tom, "I don't well see how you could fasten a shoe on you," says he.

' "Lave that to me," says the cat.

' "Did anyone ever stick walnut shells on you, pussy?" says Tom, with a grin.

' "Don't be disrespectful, Tom Connor," says the cat, with a frown.

' "I ax your pard'n, ma'am", said he, "but as for the horses you wor spakin' about warin' shoes, you know their shoes is fastened on with nails, and how would your shoes be fastened on?"

' "Ah, you stupid thief!" says she, "haven't I illigant nails o' my own?" and with that she gave him a dab of her claw, that made him roar.

' "Ow! murdher!" says he.

' "Now no more of your palaver, Misther Connor," says the cat. "Just be off and get me the shoes."

' "Tare and ouns!" says Tom. "What'll become o' me if I'm to get shoes for my cats?" says he. "For you increase your family four times a year, and you have six or seven every time," says he; "and then you must all have two pair apiece – wirra! wirra! – I'll be ruined in shoeleather," says Tom.

' "No more o' your stuff," says the cat; "don't be standin' here undher the hedge talkin' or we'll lose our characters – for I've remarked your wife is jealous, Tom."

' "'Pon my sowl, that's thrue," says Tom, with a smirk.

' "More fool she," says the cat, "for 'pon my conscience, Tom, you're as ugly as if you wor bespoke."

'Off ran the cat with these words, leaving Tom in amazement. He said nothing to the family, for fear of fright'ning them, and off he went to the town, as he pretended – for he saw the cat watching him through a hole in the hedge; but when he came to a turn at the end of the road, the dickings a mind he minded the market, good or bad, but went off to Squire Botherum's, the magisthrit, to swear examinations agen the cat.'

'Pooh pooh – nonsense!' broke in the little man, who had listened thus far to Murtough with an expression of mingled wonder and contempt, while the rest of the party willingly gave up the reins to nonsense, and enjoyed Murtough's legend and their companion's more absurd common sense.

'Don't interrupt him, Coggins,' said Mr Wiggins.

'How can you listen to such nonsense!' returned Coggins.

'Swear examinations against a cat, indeed! Pooh pooh!'

'My dear sir,' said Murtough, 'remember this is a fairy story, and that the country all round here is full of enchantment. As I was telling you, Tom went off to swear examinations.'

'Ay, ay!' shouted all but Coggins. 'Go on with the story.'

'And when Tom was asked to relate the events of the morning, which brought him before Squire Botherum, his brain was so bewildered between his corn, and his cat, and his child's toe, that he made a very confused account of it.

' "Begin your story from the beginning," said the magistrate to Tom.

' "Well, your honour," says Tom, "I was goin to market this mornin', to sell the child's corn – I beg your pard'n – my own toes, I mane, sir."

' "Sell your toes!" said the Squire.

' "No, sir, takin' the cat to market, I mane –"

' "Take a cat to market!" said the Squire. "You're drunk, man."

' "No, your honour, only confused a little; for when the toes began to spake to me – the cat, I mane – I was bothered clane –"

' "The cat speak to you!" said the Squire. "Phew! Worse than before. You're drunk, Tom."

' "No, your honour; it's on the strength of the cat I come to spake to you –"

' "I think it's on the strength of a pint of whiskey, Tom."

' "By the vartue o' my oath, your honour, it's nothin' but the cat." And so Tom then told him all about the affair, and the Squire was regularly astonished. Just then the bishop of the diocese and the priest of the parish happened to call in, and heard the story; and the bishop and the priest had a tough argument for two hours on the subject: the former swearing she must be a witch; but the priest denying *that*, and maintaining she was *only* enchanted, and that part of the argument was afterward referred to the primate, and subsequently to the conclave at Rome; but the Pope declined interfering about cats, saying he had quite enough to do minding his own bulls.

' "In the meantime, what are we to do with the cat?" says Botherum.

' "Burn her, says the bishop. She's a witch."

' "*Only* enchanted," said the priest, "and the ecclesiastical court maintains that –"

' "Bother the ecclesiastical court!" said the magistrate; "I can only proceed on the statutes"; and with that he pulled down all the lawbooks in his library, and hunted the laws from Queen Elizabeth down, and he found that they made laws against everything in Ireland, *except a cat*. The divil a thing escaped them but a cat, which did not come within the meaning of any Act of Parliament – *the cats only had escaped*.

' "There's the alien act, to be sure," said the magistrate, "and perhaps she's a French spy in disguise."

' "She spakes like a French spy, sure enough," says Tom, "and she was missin', I remember, all last Spy Wednesday."

' "That's suspicious," says the Squire, "but conviction might be difficult; and I have a fresh idea," says Botherum.

' "Faith, it won't keep fresh long, this hot weather," says Tom, "so your honour had betther make use of it at wanst."

' "Right," says Botherum. "We'll make her a subject to the game laws; we'll hunt her," says he.

' "Ow! Elegant!" says Tom; "we ll have a brave run out of her."

' "Meet me at the crossroads," says the Squire, "in the morning, and I'll have the hounds ready."

'Well, off Tom went home; and he was racking his brain what excuse he could make to the cat for not bringing the shoes; and at last he hit one off, just as he saw her cantering up to him, half a mile before he got home.

' "Where's the shoes, Tom?" says she.

' "I have not got them today, ma'am," says he.

' "Is that the way you keep your promise, Tom?" says she. "I'll tell you what it is, Tom – I'll tare the eyes out o' the childre' if you don't get me those shoes."

' "Whist, whist!" says Tom, frightened out his life for his children's eyes. "Don't be in a passion, pussy. The shoemaker said he had not a shoe in his shop, nor a last that would make one to fit you; and he says I must bring you into the town for him to take your measure."

' "And when am I to go?" says the cat, looking savage.

' "Tomorrow," says Tom.

' "It's well you said that, Tom," said the cat, "or the divil an eye I'd leave in your family this night," and off she hopped.

'Tom thrimbled at the wicked look she gave.

' "Remember!" says she, over the hedge, with a bitter caterwaul.

' "Never fear," says Tom.

'Well, sure enough, the next mornin' there was the cat at cockcrow, licking herself as nate as a new pin, to go into the town, and out came Tom with a bag undher his arm and the cat after him.

' "Now git into this, and I'll carry you into the town," says Tom, opening the bag.

' "Sure, I can walk with you," says the cat.

' "Oh, that wouldn't do," says Tom. "The people in the town is curious and slandherous people, and sure it would rise ugly remarks if I was seen with a cat afther me – a dog is a man's companion by nature, but cats does not stand to rayson."

'Well, the cat, seeing there was no use in argument, got into the bag, and off Tom set to the crossroads with the bag over his shoulder, and he came up, quite innocent-like, to the corner, where the Squire, and his huntsman, and the hounds, and a pack of people were waitin'. Out came the Squire on a sudden, just as if it was all by accident.

' "God save you, Tom," says he.

' "God save you kindly, sir," says Tom.

' "What's that bag you have at your back?" says the Squire.

' "Oh, nothin' at all, sir," says Tom, makin a face all the time, as much as to say, I have her safe.

' "Oh, there's something in that bag, I think, says the Squire. You must let me see it."

' "If you bethray me, Tom Connor," says the cat, in a low voice, "by this and that I'll never spake to you again!"

' "'Pon my honour, sir," says Tom, with a wink and a twitch of his thumb towards the bag, "I haven't anything in it."

' "I have been missing my praties of late," says the Squire; "and I'd just like to examine that bag," says he.

' "Is it doubting my character you'd be, sir?" says Tom, pretending to be in a passion.

' "Tom, your sowl!" says the voice in the sack. "If you let the cat out of the bag, I'll murther you."

' "An honest man would make no objection to be sarched," said the Squire, "and I insist on it," says he, laying hold o' the bag, and Tom purtending to fight all the time; but, my jewel! before two minutes, they shook the cat out o' the bag, sure enough, and off she went, with her tail as big as a sweeping brush, and the Squire, with a thundering view halloo after her, clapped the dogs at her heels, and away they went for the bare life. Never was there seen such running as that day – the cat made for a shaking bog, the loneliest place in the whole country, and there the riders were all thrown out, barrin' the huntsman, who had a web-footed horse on purpose for soft places, and the priest, whose horse could go anywhere by reason of the priest's blessing; and, sure enough, the huntsman and his riverence stuck to the hunt like wax; and just as the cat got on the border of the bog, they saw her give a twist as the foremost dog closed with her, for he gave her a nip in the flank. Still she went on, however, and headed them well, towards an old mud cabin in the middle of the bog, and there they saw her jump in at the window, and up came the dogs the next minit, and gathered round the house, with the most horrid howling ever was heard. The huntsman alighted, and went into the house to turn the cat out again, when what should he see but an old hag lying in bed in the corner!

' "Did you see a cat come in here?" says he.

' "Oh, no-o-o-o!" squealed the old hag in a trembling voice. "There's no cat here," says she.

' "Yelp, yelp, yelp!" went the dogs outside.

' "Oh, keep the dogs out of this," says the old hag – "oh-o-o- o!" and the huntsman saw her eyes glare under the blanket, just like a cat's.

' "Hillo!" says the huntsman, pulling down the blanket – and what should he see but the old hag's flank all in a gore of blood.

' "Ow, ow! you old divil – is it you? You old cat!" says he, opening the door.

'In rushed the dogs. Up jumped the old hag and, changing into a cat before their eyes, out she darted through the window again, and made another run for it; but she couldn't escape, and the dogs gobbled her while you could say "Jack Robinson". But the most remarkable part of this extraordinary story, gentlemen, is that the pack was ruined from that day out; for after having eaten the enchanted cat, *the divil a thing they would ever hunt afterwards but mice.*'

TO A PERSIAN CAT

F.C.W. Hiley

So dear, so dainty, so demure,
So charming in whate'er position;
By race the purest of the pure,
A little cat of high condition:
Her coat lies not in trim-kept rows
Of carpet-like and vulgar sleekness:
But like a ruffled sea it grows
Of wavy grey (my special weakness):
She vexes not the night with squalls
That make one seize a boot and throw it:
She joins in no unseemly brawls
(At least she never lets me know it!);

She never bursts in at the door
In manner boisterous and loud:
But silently along the floor
She passes, like a little cloud.
Then, opening wide her amber eyes,
Puts an inquiring nose up –
Sudden upon my knee she flies,
Then purrs and tucks her little toes up.
Yet did she once, as I recall,
By Love's o'ermastering power impelled,
Scale Mr C.'s back-garden wall –
A feat before unparalleled –
Alas! the faithless Tom had flown:
Yet on she glides, with body pliant:
And then, when bidden to come down,
Stood half alarmed and half defiant;
One sudden spring sufficed to land her –
When to return she condescended –
Upon my landlord's glass verandah –
I don't suppose they've had it mended!
This set of verses, Puss, to you
I dedicate – and ask in quittance
One thing alone – 'tis nothing new –
A set of quarter-Persian kittens.

A SNOBBISH CAT

Andrew Lang (1844–1912)

Some cats are snobs, though not so many cats as dogs
share this human infirmity. A lady had two cats; one was a drawing-room
cat, the other a common kitchen cat. Both, simultaneously, had families.
The drawing-room cat carried her kittens downstairs to be nursed by the

common kitchen cat, but every day she visited the nursery several times. She was not quite heartless, but she had never read Jean-Jacques Rousseau, on the nursing of children, and she was very aristocratic . . .

TO MY LORD BUCKHURST, VERY YOUNG, PLAYING WITH A CAT

Matthew Prior (1664–1721)

The am'rous Youth, whose tender Breast
Was by his darling Cat possest,
Obtain'd of VENUS his Desire,
Howe'er irregular his Fire:
Nature the Pow'r of Love obey'd:
The Cat became a blushing Maid;
And, on the happy Change, the Boy
Imploy'd his Wonder and his Joy.
    Take care, O beauteous Child, take care,
Lest Thou prefer so rash a Pray'r:
Nor vainly hope, the Queen of Love
Will e'er thy Fav'rite's Charms improve.
O quickly from her Shrine retreat;
Or tremble for thy Darling's Fate.
    The Queen of Love, who soon will see
Her own ADONIS live in Thee,
Will lightly her first Loss deplore;
Will easily forgive the Boar:
Her Eyes with Tears no more will flow;
With jealous Rage her Breast will glow:
And on her tabby Rival's Face
She deep will mark her new Disgrace.

A STRANGE AFFECTION

Gilbert White (1720–93)

We have remarked in a former letter how much incongruous animals, in a lonely state, may be attached to each other from a spirit of sociality; in this it may not be amiss to recount a different motive which has been known to create as strange a fondness.

My friend had a little helpless leveret brought to him, which the servants fed with milk in a spoon, and about the same time his cat kittened and the young were dispatched and buried. The hare was soon lost, and supposed to be gone the way of most foundlings, to be killed by some dog or cat. However, in about a fortnight, as the master was sitting in his garden in the dusk of the evening, he observed his cat, with tail erect, trotting towards him, and calling with little short inward notes of complacency, such as they use towards their kittens, and something gambolling after, which proved to be the leveret that the cat had supported with her milk and continued to support with great affection. Thus was a graminivorous animal nurtured by a carnivorous and predaceous one!

Why so cruel and sanguinary a beast as a cat, of the ferocious genus of *Feles*, the *murium leo*, as Linnaeus calls it, should be affected with any tenderness towards an animal which is its natural prey, is not so easy to determine.

This strange affection probably was occasioned by that *desiderium*, those tender maternal feelings, which the loss of her kittens had awakened in her breast; and by the complacency and ease she derived to herself from the procuring her teats to be drawn, which were too much distended with milk, till, from habit, she became as much delighted with this foundling as if it had been her real offspring.

This incident is no bad solution of that strange circumstance which grave historians as well as the poets assert, of exposed children being sometimes nurtured by female wild beasts that probably had lost their young. For it is not one whit more marvellous that Romulus and Remus, in their infant state, should be nursed by a she-wolf, than that a poor little sucking leveret should be fostered and cherished by a bloody grimalkin.

from *The Natural History and Antiquities of Selborne* (1789)

MY WIFE, THE CAT

Jerome K. Jerome (1859–1927)

I had a cat once that used to follow me about everywhere, until it even got quite embarrassing, and I had to beg her, as a personal favour, *not* to accompany me any further down the High Street. She used to sit up for me when I was late home, and meet me in the passage. It made me feel quite like a married man, except that she never asked where I had been, and then didn't believe me when I told her.

Another cat I had used to get drunk regularly every day. She would hang about for hours outside the cellar door for the purpose of sneaking in on the first opportunity, and lapping up the drippings from the beer cask. I do not mention this habit of hers in praise of the species, but merely to show how almost human some of them are. If the transmigration of souls is a fact, this animal was certainly qualifying most rapidly for a Christian, for her vanity was only second to her love of drink. Whenever she caught a particularly big rat, she would bring it up into the room where we were all sitting, lay the corpse down in the midst of us, and wait to be praised. Lord! how the girls used to scream.

from 'On Cats and Dogs' in *Idle Thoughts of an Idle Fellow* (1886)

EPONINE

Théophile Gautier (1811–72)

The cat named after the interesting Eponine was more delicate and slender than her brothers. Her nose was rather long, and her eyes slightly oblique, and green as those of Pallas Athene, to whom Homer always applied the epithet of γλαυκῶπις. Her nose was of velvety black, with the grain of a fine Périgord truffle; her whiskers were in a perpetual state of agitation, all of which gave her a peculiarly expressive countenance. Her superb black coat was always in motion, and was watered and shot with shadowy markings. Never was there a more sensitive, nervous, electric animal. If one stroked her two or three times in the dark, blue sparks would fly crackling out of her fur.

Eponine attached herself particularly to me, like the Eponine of the novel to Marius, but I, being less taken up with Cosette than that handsome young man, could accept the affection of this gentle and devoted cat, who still shares the pleasures of my suburban retreat, and is the inseparable companion of my hours of work.

She comes running up when she hears the front-door bell, receives the visitors, conducts them to the drawing-room, talks to them – yes, talks to them – with little chirruping sounds, that do not in the least resemble the language cats use in talking to their own kind, but which simulate the articulate speech of man. What does she say? She says in the clearest way, 'Will you be good enough to wait till monsieur comes down? Please look at the pictures, or chat with me in the meantime, if that will amuse you.' Then when I come in she discreetly retires to an armchair or a corner of the piano, like a well-bred animal who knows what is correct in good society. Pretty little Eponine gave so many proofs of intelligence, good disposition and sociability, that by common consent she was raised to the dignity of a *person*, for it was quite evident that she was possessed of higher reasoning power than mere instinct. This dignity conferred on her the privilege of eating at table like a person instead of out of a saucer in a corner of the room like an animal.

So Eponine had a chair next to me at breakfast and dinner, but on account of her small size she was allowed to rest her two front paws on the edge of the table. Her place was laid, without spoon or fork, but she had her glass. She went right through dinner dish by dish, from soup to dessert, waiting for her turn to be helped, and behaving with such propriety and nice manners as one would like to see in many children. She made her appearance at the first sound of the bell, and on going into the dining-room one found her already in her place, sitting up in her chair with her paws resting on the edge of the table-cloth, and seeming to offer you her little face to kiss, like a well-brought-up little girl who is affectionately polite towards her parents and elders.

As one finds flaws in diamonds, spots on the sun, and shadows on perfection itself, so Eponine, it must be confessed, had a passion for fish. She shared this in common with all other cats. Contrary to the Latin proverb, 'Catus amat pisces, sed non vult tingere plantas', she would willingly have dipped her paw into the water if by so doing she could have pulled out a trout or a young carp. She became nearly frantic over fish, and, like a child who is filled with the expectation of dessert, she sometimes rebelled at her soup when she knew (from previous investigations in the kitchen) that fish was coming. When this happened she was not helped, and I would say to her coldly: 'Mademoiselle, a person who is not hungry for soup cannot be hungry for fish', and the dish would be pitilessly carried away from under her nose. Convinced that matters were serious, greedy Eponine would swallow her soup in all haste, down to the last drop, polishing off the last crumb of bread or bit of macaroni, and would then turn round and look at me with pride, like someone who has conscientiously done his duty. She was then given her portion, which she consumed with great satisfaction, and after tasting of every dish in turn, she would finish up by drinking a third of a glass of water.

When I am expecting friends to dinner Eponine knows there is going to be a party before she sees the guests. She looks at her place, and if she sees a knife and fork by her plate she decamps at once and seats herself on a music-stool, which is her refuge on these occasions.

Let those who deny reasoning powers to animals explain if they can this little fact, apparently so simple, but which contains a whole series of inductions. From the presence near her plate of those implements which man alone can use, this observant and reflective cat concludes that she will have to give up her place for that day to a guest, and promptly proceeds to do so. She never makes a mistake; but when she knows the visitor well she climbs on his knee and tries to coax a tit-bit out of him by her pretty caressing ways.

from 'The White and Black Dynasties'
in *La Ménagerie Intime*, translated by Lady Chance

MOTHER CATS

Herodotus (c. 485–425 BC)

There are many household animals; and there would be many more, were it not for what happens to the cats. When the females have kittened they will not consort with the males; and these seek them but cannot get their will of them; so their device is to steal and carry off and kill the kittens (but they do not eat what they have killed). The mothers, deprived of their young and desiring to have more, will then consort with the males; for they are creatures that love offspring.

from *The Histories*

CAT AND CANARY

Jane Welsh Carlyle (1801–66)

I am sorry for your cat's Influenza (it is a clear case of Influenza!) but it would have been worse if she had given way to passion, as her mother has just done, and done no end of mischief in attempting a great crime! For several days there had been that in her eyes when raised to my canary, which filled my heart with alarm. I sent express for a carpenter, and had the cage attached to the drawing-room ceiling, with an elaborate apparatus of chain and pulley and weight. 'Most expensive!' (as my Scotch servant exclaimed with clasped hands over a Picture of the *Virgin and Child* in the National Gallery!) and there had it swung for two days; to Mr C.'s intense disgust, who regards thy pet as '*the most inanely chimerical of all*' – the cat meanwhile spending all its spare time in gazing up at the bird with eyes aflame! But it was safe *now* – I thought! and went out for a walk. On my return Charlotte met me with 'Oh! whatever do you think the cat has gone and done?' – 'Eaten my canary?' – 'No, *far worse!* – pulled down the cage and the weight, and broke the chain and upset the little table and broken everything on it!' – 'And not eaten the canary?' – 'Oh, I suppose the dreadful crash she made frightened *herself*; for I met *her* running downstairs as I ran up – tho' the cage was on the floor, and the door open and the canary in *such* a way!' You never saw such a scene of devastation. The carpet was covered with fragments of a pretty terra cotta basket given me by Lady Airlie – and fragments of the glass which covered it, and with the earth and ferns that had been growing in it, and with birdseed, and bits of brass chain, and I can't tell what all! That is what one gets by breeding up a cat! – She had rushed right out by the back door and didn't show her face for twenty-four hours after! And now I don't know where the poor bird will be safe.

from a letter to Thomas Woolner in *New Letters and Memorials of Jane Welsh Carlyle* (1893)

BONA FIDELIA AND HER DAUGHTERS

Robert Southey (1774–1843)

Bona Fidelia was a tortoiseshell cat. She was filiated upon Lord Nelson, others of the same litter having borne the unequivocal stamp of his likeness. It was in her good qualities that she resembled him, for in truth her name rightly bespoke her nature. She approached as nearly as possible in disposition, to the ideal of a perfect cat: he who supposes that animals have not their difference of disposition as well as men, knows very little of animal nature. Having survived her daughter Madame Catalani, she died of extreme old age, universally esteemed and regretted by all who had the pleasure of her acquaintance. Bona Fidelia left a daughter and a granddaughter; the former I called Madame Bianchi – the latter Pulcheria. It was impossible ever to familiarize Madame Bianchi, though she had been bred in all respects like her gentle mother, in the same place, and with the same persons. The nonsense of that arch-philosophist Helvetius would be sufficiently confuted by this single example, if such rank folly, contradicted as it is by the experience of every family, needed confutation. She was a beautiful and singular creature, white, with a fine tabby tail, and two or three spots of tabby, always delicately clean; and her wild eyes were bright and green as the Duchess de Cadaval's emerald necklace. Pulcheria did not correspond as she grew up to the promise of her kittenhood and her name; but she was as fond as her mother was shy and intractable. Their fate was extraordinary as well as mournful. When good old Mrs Wilson died, who used to feed and indulge them, they immediately forsook the house, nor could they be allured to enter it again, though they continued to wander and moan round it, and came for food. After some weeks Madame Bianchi disappeared, and Pulcheria soon afterwards died of a disease endemic at that time among cats.

from 'Memoir of the Cats of Greta Hall' (18 June 1828)

MADAME THÉOPHILE

Théophile Gautier (1811–72)

'Madame Théophile', a reddish cat with a white breast, a pink nose and blue eyes, was so called because she lived with us in an intimacy which was quite conjugal, sleeping at the foot of our bed, dreaming on the arm of our chair while we wrote, going down to the garden in order to follow us in our walks, assisting at our meals, and sometimes even intercepting a tit-bit from our plate to our mouth.

One day a friend of ours who was going away for a few days brought us his parrot to look after during his absence. The bird, feeling himself to be among strangers, had climbed to the top of his perch by the help of his beak, and was rolling his eyes, which were like brass-headed nails, and blinking the white skin which served him for eyelids in a decidedly frightened way.

'Madame Théophile' had never seen a parrot, and this new creature evidently caused her much surprise.

Motionless as an embalmed Egyptian cat in its wrappings, she watched the bird with an air of profound meditation, putting together all the notions of natural history which she had been able to gather on the roof, in the yard, or the garden. The shadow of her thoughts passed across her opalescent eyes, and we could read in them this summary of her investigations: 'This is decidedly a green chicken.'

The parrot followed the cat's movements with feverish anxiety. His instinct told him that this was an enemy meditating some evil deed.

As to the cat's eyes, which were fixed on the bird with fascinating intensity, they said in language which the parrot understood perfectly, for there was nothing ambiguous about it, 'Although it is green, this chicken must be good to eat.'

We followed this scene with interest, ready to intervene if necessity arose. Madame Théophile had insensibly drawn nearer. Her pink nose quivered, she half closed her eyes, and her contractile claws went in and out. Little shivers ran down her spine. Suddenly her back was bent like a bow, and in one vigorous, elastic bound she alighted on the perch. The parrot, perceiving the danger, promptly exclaimed in a bass voice, as solemn and deep as that of Monsieur Joseph Prudhomme, 'As tu *déjeuné, Jacquot?*' This speech caused the cat to spring back in unspeakable terror. All her ornithological ideas were upset.

The parrot continued: '*Et de quoi? De roti du roi.*'

The cat's face clearly expressed: 'It is not a bird; it is a gentleman; he is speaking!'

She cast a look full of interrogation at us, and not being satisfied with our reply she went and hid herself under the bed, from where it was impossible to get her out for the rest of the day.

from *La Ménagerie Intime*, translated by Lady Chance

MY CAT AND I

Michel de Montaigne (1533–92)

When my cat and I entertain each other with mutual antics, as playing with a garter, who knows but that I make more sport for her than she makes for me? Shall I conclude her to be simple that has her time to begin or to refuse to play, as freely as I have mine? Nay, who knows but that it is a defect of my not understanding her language (for doubtless cats can talk and reason with one another) that we agree no better; and who knows but that she pities me for being no wiser than to play with her; and laughs, and censures my folly in making sport for her, when we two play together.

THE KITTEN MYSTERY

Daniel Defoe (1660–1731)

In this season, I was much surprised with the increase of my family. I had been concerned for the loss of one of my cats, who ran away from me, or, as I thought, had been dead, and I heard no more tale or tidings of her, till, to my astonishment, she came home about the end of August with three kittens. This was the more strange to me, because, though I had killed a wild cat, as I called it, with my gun, yet I thought it was a quite different kind from our European cats; yet the young cats were the same kind of house-breed like the old one; and both my cats being females, I thought it very strange. But from these three cats I afterwards came to be so pestered with cats, that I was forced to kill them like vermin, or wild beasts, and to drive them from my house as much as possible [...] but at length, when the two old ones I brought with me were gone, and after some time continually driving them from me, and letting them have no provision with me, they all ran wild into the woods, except two or three favourites, which I kept tame, and whose young, when they had any, I always drowned; and these were part of my family.

from *Robinson Crusoe* (1719)

THE EAGLE, THE WILD SOW, AND THE CAT

Jean de la Fontaine (1621–95)

A certain hollow tree
Was tenanted by three.
An eagle held a lofty bough,
The hollow root a wild wood sow,
A female cat between the two.
All busy with maternal labours,
They lived awhile obliging neighbours.
At last the cat's deceitful tongue
Broke up the peace of old and young.
Up climbing to the eagle's nest,
She said, with whisker'd lips compress'd,
'Our death, or, what as much we mothers fear,
That of our helpless offspring dear,
Is surely drawing near.
Beneath our feet, see you not how
Destruction's plotted by the sow?
Her constant digging, soon or late,
Our proud old castle will uproot.
And then – Oh, sad and shocking fate! –
She'll eat our young ones, as the fruit!
Were there but hope of saving one,
'Twould soothe somewhat my bitter moan.'
Thus leaving apprehensions hideous,
Down went the puss perfidious
To where the sow, no longer digging,
Was in the very act of pigging.
'Good friend and neighbour,' whisper'd she,
'I warn you on your guard to be.
Your pigs should you but leave a minute,
This eagle here will seize them in it.
Speak not of this, I beg, at all,

Lest on my head her wrath should fall.'
Another breast with fear inspired,
With fiendish joy the cat retired.
The eagle ventured no egress
To feed her young, the sow still less.
Fools they, to think that any curse
Than ghastly famine could be worse!
Both staid at home, resolved and obstinate,
To save their young ones from impending fate –
The royal bird for fear of mine,
For fear of royal claws the swine.
All died, at length, with hunger,
The older and the younger;
There staid, of eagle race or boar,
Not one this side of death's dread door;
A sad misfortune, which
The wicked cats made rich.
Oh, what is there of hellish plot
The treacherous tongue dares not!
Of all the ills Pandora's box outpour'd,
Deceit, I think, is most to be abhorr'd.

from *The Fables* (1842), translated by Elizur Wright

A DYING MOTHER

Andrew Lang (1844–1912)

If we take the case of cats, they say little, but they think a great deal; they conduct trains of reasoning. I have read an anecdote told by Mrs Frederick Harrison. An old lady cat felt that she was dying, before her kittens were weaned. She could hardly walk, but she disappeared one morning, carrying a kitten, and came back without it. Next day, quite exhausted, she did this with her two other kittens, and then died. She had carried each kitten to a separate cat, each of which was nourishing a family, and accepted the new fosterling. Can anything be wiser or more touching? This poor old cat had memory, reflection, reason. Though wordless, she was as much a thinking creature as any man who makes his last will and testament.

THE RETIRED CAT

William Cowper (1731–1800)

A poet's cat, sedate and grave,
As poet well could wish to have,
Was much addicted to inquire
For nooks, to which she might retire,
And where, secure as mouse in chink,
She might repose, or sit and think.
I know not where she caught the trick –
Nature perhaps herself had cast her
In such a mould *philosophique*,
Or else she learn'd it of her master.
Sometimes ascending, debonair,
An apple-tree or lofty pear,
Lodg'd with convenience in the fork,
She watched the gard'ner at his work;
Sometimes her ease and solace sought
In an old empty wat'ring pot,
There wanting nothing, save a fan,
To seem some nymph in her sedan,
Apparell'd in exactest sort,
And ready to be borne to court.

But love of change it seems has place
Not only in our wiser race;
Cats also feel as well as we

That passion's force, and so did she.
Her climbing, she began to find,
Expos'd her too much to the wind,
And the old utensil of tin
Was cold and comfortless within:
She therefore wish'd instead of those,
Some place of more serene repose,
Where neither cold might come, nor air
Too rudely wanton with her hair,
And sought it in the likeliest mode
Within her master's snug abode.

A draw'r – it chanc'd, at bottom lin'd
With linen of the softest kind,
With such as merchants introduce
From India, for the ladies' use –
A draw'r impending o'er the rest,
Half open in the topmost chest,
Of depth enough, and none to spare,
Invited her to slumber there.
Puss with delight beyond expression,
Survey'd the scene, and took possession.
Recumbent at her ease ere long,
And lull'd by her own hum-drum song,
She left the cares of life behind,
And slept as she would sleep her last,
When in came, housewifely inclin'd,
The chambermaid, and shut it fast,
By no malignity impell'd,
But all unconscious whom it held.

Awaken'd by the shock (cried puss)
Was ever cat attended thus!
The open draw'r was left, I see,
Merely to prove a nest for me,

For soon as I was well compos'd,
Then came the maid, and it was closed:
How smooth these kerchiefs, and how sweet,
Oh what a delicate retreat!
I will resign myself to rest
Till Sol, declining in the west,
Shall call to supper; when, no doubt,
Susan will come and let me out.

The evening came, the sun descended,
And puss remain'd still unattended.
The night roll'd tardily away,
(With her indeed 'twas never day)
The sprightly morn her course renew'd,
The evening grey again ensued,
And puss came into mind no more
Than if entomb'd the day before.
With hunger pinch'd, and pinch'd for room,
She now presag'd approaching doom,
Not slept a single wink, or purr'd,
Conscious of jeopardy incurr'd.

That night, by chance, the poet watching,
Heard an inexplicable scratching,
His noble heart went pit-a-pat,
And to himself he said – what's that?
He drew the curtain at his side,
And forth he peep'd, but nothing spied.
Yet, by his ear directed, guess'd
Something imprison'd in the chest,
And doubtful what, with prudent care,
Resolv'd it should continue there.
At length a voice, which well he knew,
A long and melancholy mew,
Saluting his poetic ears,

Consol'd him, and dispell'd his fears;
He left his bed, he trod the floor,
He 'gan in haste the draw'rs explore,
The lowest first, and without stop,
The rest in order to the top.
For 'tis a truth well known to most,
That whatsoever thing is lost,
We seek it, ere it come to light,
In ev'ry cranny but the right.
Forth skipp'd the cat; not now replete
As erst with airy self-conceit,
Nor in her own fond apprehension,
A theme for all the world's attention,
But modest, sober, cur'd of all
Her notions hyberbolical,
And wishing for a place of rest
Anything rather than a chest:
Then stept the poet into bed,
With this reflexion in his head:

MORAL

Beware of too sublime a sense
Of your own worth and consequence!
The man who dreams himself so great,
And his importance of such weight,
That all around, in all that's done,
Must move and act for him alone,
Will learn, in school of tribulation,
The folly of his expectation.

AT THE ZOO

Mark Twain (1835–1910)

In the great Zoological Gardens [of Marseille] we found specimens of all the animals the world produces, I think . . . The boon companion of the colossal elephant was a common cat! This cat had a fashion of climbing up the elephant's hind legs, and roosting on his back. She would sit up there, with her paws curved under her breast, and sleep in the sun half the afternoon. It used to annoy the elephant at first and he would reach up and take her down, but she would go aft and climb up again. She persisted until she finally conquered the elephant's prejudices, and now they are inseparable friends. The cat plays about her comrade's forefeet or his trunk often, until dogs approach, and then she goes aloft out of danger. The elephant has annihilated several dogs lately, that pressed his companion too closely.

THE CAT THAT WALTZED

Mrs Humphry Ward (1851–1920)

Chattie jumped up on the window-sill, with her usual stealthy *aplomb*, and rubbed herself against the girl's face.

'Oh, Chattie!' cried Rose, throwing her arms around the cat, 'if Catherine'll *only* marry Mr Elsmere, my dear, and be happy ever afterwards, and set me free to live my own life a bit, I'll be so good, you won't know me, Chattie. And you shall have a new collar, my beauty, and cream till you die of it!'

And springing up, she dragged in the cat, and snatching a scarlet anemone from a bunch on the table, stood opposite Chattie, who stood slowly waving her magnificent tail from side to side, and glaring as though it were not at all to her taste to be hustled and bustled in this way.

'Now, Chattie, listen! Will she?'

A leaf of the flower dropped on Chattie's nose.

'Won't she? Will she? Won't she? Will – Tiresome flower, why did Nature give it such a beggarly few petals? If I'd had a daisy it would have all come right. Come, Chattie, waltz; and let's forget this wicked world!'

And, snatching up her violin, the girl broke into a Strauss waltz, dancing to it the while, her cotton skirts flying, her pretty feet twinkling, till her eyes glowed, and her cheeks blazed with a double intoxication – the intoxication of movement, and the intoxication of sound – the cat meanwhile following her with little mincing perplexed steps as though not knowing what to make of her.

'Rose, you madcap!' cried Agnes, opening the door.

'Not at all, my dear,' said Rose calmly, stopping to take breath. 'Excellent practice and uncommonly difficult. Try if you can do it, and see!'

from *Robert Elsmere* (1888)

LOVE LETTERS OF CLERICAL CATS

Erasmus Darwin (1731–1802) and Anna Seward (1747–1809)

[*From the Persian Snow, at Dr Darwin's, to Miss Po Felina, at the Palace, Lichfield, who had been broken of her propensity to kill birds, and lived several years without molesting a dove, a tame lark, and a redbreast, all of which used to fly about the room where the cat was daily admitted. The dove frequently sat on pussy's back, and the little birds would peck fearlessly from the plate in which she was eating.*]

Lichfield Vicarage
7 September 1780

Dear Miss Pussey,

As I sat, the other day, basking myself in the Dean's Walk, I saw you, in your stately palace, washing your beautiful round face, and elegantly brindled ears, with your velvet paws, and whisking about, with graceful sinuosity, your meandering tail. That treacherous hedgehog, Cupid, concealed himself behind your tabby beauties, and darting one of his too well aimed quills, pierced, O cruel imp! my fluttering heart.

Ever since that fatal hour have I watched, day and night, in my balcony, hoping that the stillness of the starlight evenings might induce you to take the air on the leads of the palace. Many serenades have I sung under your windows; and, when you failed to appear, with the sound of my voice made the vicarage re-echo through all its winding lanes and dirty alleys. All heard me but my cruel Fair-one; she, wrapped in fur, sat purring with contented insensibility, or slept with untroubled dreams.

Though I cannot boast those delicate varieties of melody with which you sometimes ravish the ear of night, and stay the listening stars; though you sleep hourly on the lap of the favourite of the muses, and are patted by those fingers which hold the pen of science; and every day, with her permission, dip your white whiskers in delicious cream; yet am I not destitute of all advantages of birth, education, and beauty. Derived from Persian kings, my snowy fur yet retains the whiteness and splendour of their ermine.

This morning, as I sat upon the Doctor's tea-table, and saw my reflected features in the slop-basin, my long white whiskers, ivory teeth, and topaz eyes, I felt an agreeable presentiment of my suit; and certainly the slop-basin did not flatter me, which shews the azure flowers upon its borders less beauteous than they are.

You know not, dear Miss Pussey Po, the value of the address you neglect. New milk have I, in flowing abundance, and mice pent up in twenty garrets, for your food and amusement.

Permit me, this afternoon, to lay at your divine feet the head of an enormous Norway rat, which has even now stained my paws with its gore. If you will do me the honour to sing the following song, which I have taken the liberty to write, as expressing the sentiments I wish you to entertain, I will bring a band of catgut and catcall, to accompany you in chorus.

(Air: *Spirituosi*)
Cats I scorn, who sleek and fat,
Shiver at a Norway rat;
Rough and hardy, bold and free,

Be the cat that's made for me!
He, whose nervous paws can take
My lady's lapdog by the neck;
With furious hiss attack the hen,
And snatch a chicken from the pen.
If the treacherous swain should prove
Rebellious to my tender love,
My scorn the vengeful paw shall dart,
Shall tear his fur, and pierce his heart.

Chorus
Qu-ow wow, quall, wawl, moon.

Deign, most adorable charmer, to purr your assent to this my request, and believe me to be with the profoundest respect, your true admirer,

Snow

From Miss Po Felina to Mr Snow.

Palace, Lichfield
8 September 1780

I am but too sensible of the charms of Mr Snow; but while I admire the spotless whiteness of his ermine, and the tyger-strength of his commanding form, I sigh in secret, that he, who sucked the milk of benevolence and philosophy, should yet retain the extreme of that fierceness, too justly imputed to the grimalkin race. Our hereditary violence is perhaps commendable when we exert it against the foes of our protectors, but deserves much blame when it annoys their friends.

The happiness of a refined education was mine; yet, dear Mr Snow, my advantages in that respect were not equal to what yours might have been; but, while you give unbounded indulgence to your carnivorous desires, I have so far subdued mine, that the lark pours his mattin song, the canarybird warbles wild and loud, and the robin pipes his farewell song to the setting sun, unmolested in my presence; nay, the plump and tempting dove has reposed securely upon my soft back, and bent her glossy neck in graceful curves as she walked around me.

But let me hasten to tell thee how my sensibilities in thy favour were, last month, unfortunately repressed. Once, in the noon of one of its most beautiful nights, I was invited abroad by the serenity of the amorous hour, secretly stimulated by the hope of meeting my admired Persian. With silent steps I paced around the dimly gleaming leads of the palace. I had acquired a taste for scenic beauty and poetic imagery, by listening to ingenious observations upon their nature from the lips of thy own lord, as I lay purring at the feet of my mistress.

I admired the lovely scene, and breathed my sighs for thee to the listening moon. She threw the long shadows of the majestic cathedral upon the silvered lawn. I beheld the pearly meadows of Stow Valley, and the lake in its bosom, which, reflecting the lunar rays, seemed a sheet of diamonds. The trees of the Dean's Walk, which the hand of Dulness had been restrained from torturing into trim and detestable regularity, met each other in a thousand various and beautiful forms. Their liberated boughs danced on the midnight gale, and the edges of their leaves were whitened by the moonbeams. I descended to the lawn, that I might throw the beauties of the valley into perspective through the graceful arches, formed by their meeting branches. Suddenly my ear was startled, not by the voice of my lover, but by the loud and dissonant noise of the war-song, which six black grimalkins were raising in honour of the numerous victories obtained by the Persian, Snow; compared with which, they acknowledged those of English cats had little brilliance, eclipsed, like the unimportant victories of the Howes, by the puissant Clinton and Arbuthnot, and the still more puissant Cornwallis. It sung that thou didst owe thy matchless might to thy lineal descent from the invincible Alexander, as he derived his more than mortal valour from his mother Olympia's illicit commerce with Jupiter. They sang that, amid the renowned siege of Persepolis, while Roxana and Statira were contending for the honour of his attentions, the conqueror of the world deigned to bestow them upon a large white female cat, thy grandmother, warlike Mr Snow, in the ten thousandth and ninety-ninth ascent.

Thus far their triumphant din was music to my ear; and even when it

sung that lakes of milk ran curdling into whey, within the ebon conclave of their pancheons, with terror at thine approach; that mice squealed from all the neighbouring garrets; and that whole armies of Norway rats, crying out amain, 'The devil take the hindmost', ran violently into the minster-pool, at the first gleam of thy white mail through the shrubs of Mr Howard's garden.

But O! when they sang, or rather yelled, of larks warbling on sunbeams, fascinated suddenly by the glare of thine eyes, and falling into thy remorseless talons; of robins, warbling soft and solitary upon the leafless branch, till the pale cheek of winter dimpled into joy; of hundreds of those bright-breasted songsters, torn from their barren sprays by thy pitiless fangs! – Alas! my heart died within me at the idea of so preposterous a union!

Marry you, Mr Snow, I am afraid I cannot; since, though the laws of our community might not oppose our connection, yet those of principle, of delicacy, of duty to my mistress, do very powerfully oppose it.

As to presiding at your concert, if you extremely wish it, I may perhaps grant your request; but then you must allow me to sing a song of my own composition, applicable to our present situation, and set to music by my sister Sophy at Mr Brown's the organist's, thus:

(Air: *Affettuoso*)
He, whom Pussey Po detains
A captive in her silken chains,
Must curb the furious thirst of prey,
Nor rend the warbler from his spray!
Nor let his wild, ungenerous rage
An unprotected foe engage.

Oh, should cat of Darwin prove
Foe to pity, foe to love!
Cat, that listens day by day,
To mercy's mild and honied lay,
Too surely would the dire disgrace
More deeply brand our future race,
The stigma fix, where'er they range,
That cats can ne'er their nature change.

Should I consent with thee to wed,
These sanguine crimes upon thy head,
And ere the wish'd reform I see,
Adieu to lapping Seward's tea!
Adieu to purring gentle praise
Charm'd as she quotes thy master's lays! –
Could I, alas! our kittens bring
Where sweet her plumy favourites sing,
Would not the watchful nymph espy
Their father's fierceness in their eye,

And drive us far and wide away,
In cold and lonely barn to stray?
Where the dark owl, with hideous scream,
Shall mock our yells for forfeit cream,
As on starv'd mice we swearing dine,
And grumble that our lives are nine.

Chorus (Largo)
Waal, woee, trone, moan, mall, oll, moule.

The still too much admired Mr Snow will have the goodness to pardon the freedom of these expostulations, and excuse their imperfections. The morning, O Snow! had been devoted to this my correspondence with thee, but I was interrupted in that employment by the visit of two females of our species, who fed my ill-starved passion by praising thy wit and endowments, exemplified by thy elegant letter to which the delicacy of my sentiments obliges me to send so inauspicious a reply.

I am, dear Mr Snow
Your ever obliged
Po Felina

DO CATS EAT BATS?

Lewis Carroll (1832–98)

Down, down, down. There was nothing else to do, so Alice soon began talking again. 'Dinah'll miss me very much tonight. I should think!' (Dinah was the cat.) 'I hope they'll remember her saucer of milk at tea-time. Dinah, my dear, I wish you were down here with me! There are no mice in the air, I'm afraid, but you might catch a bat, and that's very like a mouse, you know. But do cats eat bats, I wonder?' And here Alice began to get rather sleepy, and went on saying to herself, in a dreamy sort of way, 'Do cats eat bats? Do cats eat bats?' and sometimes, 'Do bats eat cats?' for, you see, as she couldn't answer either question, it didn't much matter which way she put it. She felt that she was dozing off, and had just begun to dream that she was walking hand in hand with Dinah, and was saying to her very earnestly, 'Now, Dinah, tell me the truth: did you ever eat a bat?' when suddenly, thump! thump! down she came upon a heap of sticks and dry leaves, and the fall was over.

from *Alice's Adventures in Wonderland* (1865)

A TERRIBLE MISTAKE

Elizabeth Gaskell (1810–65)

Of course, your ladyship knows that such lace must never be starched or ironed. Some people wash it in sugar and water, and some in coffee, to make it the right yellow colour, but I myself have a very good receipt for washing it in milk, which stiffens it enough and gives it a very good creamy colour. Well, ma'am, I had tacked it together (and the beauty of this fine lace is that, when it is wet, it goes into a very little space), and put it to soak in milk, when, unfortunately, I left the room; on my return I found pussy on the table, looking very like a thief, but gulping very uncomfortably, as if she was half-choked with something she wanted to swallow and could not. And would you believe it? At first I pitied her, and said 'Poor pussy! Poor pussy!' till, all at once, I looked and saw the cup of milk empty – cleaned out! 'You naughty cat!' said I; and I believe I was provoked enough to give her a slap, which did no good, but only helped the lace down – just as one slaps a choking child on the back. I could have cried, I was so vexed; but I determined I would not give the lace up without a struggle for it. I hoped the lace might disagree with her, at any rate; but it would have been too much for Job, if he had seen, as I did, that cat come in, quite placid and purring, not a quarter of an hour after, and almost expecting to be stroked. 'No, pussy!' said I, 'if you have any conscience you ought not to expect that!' And then a thought struck me; and I rang the bell for my maid, and sent her to Mr Hoggins, with my compliments, and would he be kind enough to lend me one of his top-boots for an hour? I did not think there was anything odd in the message; but Jenny said the young men in the surgery laughed as if they would be ill at my wanting a top-boot. When it came, Jenny and I put pussy in, with her fore-feet straight down, so that they were fastened, and could not scratch, and we gave her a teaspoonful of currant-jelly in which (your ladyship must excuse me) I had mixed some tartar emetic. I shall never forget how anxious I was for the next half-hour. I took pussy to my own room, and spread a clean towel on the floor. I could have kissed her when she returned the lace to sight, very much as it had gone down. Jenny had boiling water ready, and we soaked it and soaked it, and spread it on a lavender-bush in the sun before I could touch it again, even to put it in milk. But now your ladyship would never guess that it had been in pussy's inside.

from *Cranford* (1853)

6

ON CATS AND DOGS

Cat: a pygmy lion who loves mice, hates dogs,
and patronizes human beings.

Oliver Herford (1863–1935)

THE FARMER, THE SPANIEL AND THE CAT

Edward Moore (1712–57)

As at his board a farmer sat,
Replenish'd by his homely treat,
His favourite Spaniel near him stood,
And with his master shar'd the food;
The crackling bones his jaws devour'd,
His lapping tongue the trenchers scour'd,
Till sated, now supine he lay,
And snor'd the rising fumes away.

The hungry Cat in turn drew near,
And humbly crav'd a servant's share;
Her modest worth the Master knew,
And straight the fattening morsel threw;
Enrag'd the snarling Cur awoke,
And this with spiteful envy spoke:

'They only claim a right to eat
Who earn by services their meat:
Me zeal and industry inflame
To scour the fields and spring the game,
Or plunging in the wintry wave
For man the wounded bird to save.
With watchful diligence I keep
From prowling wolves his fleecy sheep,
At home his midnight hours secure,
And drive the robber from the door:
For this his breast with kindness glows,
For this his hand the food bestows;
And shall thy indolence impart
A warmer friendship to his heart,
That thus he robs me of my due,
To pamper such vile things as you?'

'I own (with meekness Puss replied)
Superior merit on your side;
Nor does my breast with envy swell
To find it recompens'd so well;
Yet I, in what my nature can,
Contribute to the good of man.
Whose claws destroy the pilfering mouse?
Who drives the vermin from the house?
Or, watchful for the labouring swain,
From lurking rats secures the grain?
From hence if he rewards bestow,
Why should your heart with gall o'erflow?
Why pine my happiness to see,
Since there's enough for you and me?'

'Thy words are just,' the Farmer cried,
And spurn'd the snarler from his side.

ON CATS AND DOGS

Jerome K. Jerome (1859–1927)

Yet, in general, I like cats and dogs very much indeed. What jolly chaps they are! They are much superior to human beings as companions. They do not quarrel or argue with you. They never talk about themselves, but listen to you while you talk about yourself, and keep up an appearance of being interested in the conversation. They never make stupid remarks. They never observe to Miss Brown across a dinner-table, that they always understood she was very sweet on Mr Jones (who has just married Miss Robinson). They never mistake your wife's cousin for her husband, and fancy that you are the father-in-law. And they never ask a young author with fourteen tragedies, sixteen comedies, seven farces, and a couple of burlesques in his desk, why he doesn't write a play.

They never say unkind things. They never tell us of our faults, 'merely for our own good'. They do not, at inconvenient moments, mildly remind us of our past follies and mistakes. They do not say, 'Oh yes, a lot of use *you* are, if you are ever really wanted' – sarcastic like. They never inform us, as our *inamoratas* sometimes do, that we are not nearly so nice as we used to be. We are always the same to them.

They are always glad to see us. They are with us in all our humours. They are merry when we are glad, sober when we feel solemn, sad when we are sorrowful.

'Hulloa! happy, and want a lark! Right you are; I'm your man. Here I am, frisking round you, leaping, barking, pirouetting, ready for any amount of fun and mischief. Look at my eyes, if you doubt me. What shall it be? A romp in the drawing-room, and never mind the furniture, or a scamper in the fresh, cool air, a scud across the fields, and down the hill, and won't we let old Gaffer Goggles's geese know what time o'day it is, neither. Whoop! come along.'

Or you'd like to be quiet and think. Very well. Pussy can sit on the arm of the chair, and purr, and Montmorency will curl himself up on the rug, and blink at the fire, yet keeping one eye on you the while, in case you are seized with any sudden desire in the direction of rats.

And when we bury our face in our hands and wish we had never been born, they don't sit up very straight, and observe that we have brought it all upon ourselves. They don't even hope it will be a warning to us. But they come up softly; and shove their heads against us. If it is a cat, she stands on your shoulder, rumples your hair, and says, 'Lor', I am sorry for you, old man', as plain as words can speak; and if it is a dog, he looks up at you with his big, true eyes, and says with them, 'Well, you've always got me, you know. We ll go through the world together, and always stand by each other, won't we?'

from *Idle Thoughts of an Idle Fellow* (1886)

THE VAIN CAT

Ambrose Bierce (1842–1914)

Remarked a Tortoise to a Cat:
'Your speed's a thing to marvel at!
I saw you as you flitted by,
And wished I were one-half so spry.'
The Cat said, humbly: 'Why, indeed
I was not showing then my speed –
That was a poor performance.' Then
She said exultantly (as when
The condor feels his bosom thrill
Remembering Chimborazo's hill,
And how he soared so high above,
It looked a valley, he a dove):
' 'Twould fire your very carapace
To see me with a dog in chase!'
Its snout in any kind of swill,
Pride, like a pig, will suck its fill.

MOTHER TABBYSKINS

Elizabeth Anna Hart (1822–c.1888)

Sitting at a window
In her cloak and hat,
I saw Mother Tabbyskins,
The *real* old cat!
Very old, very old,
Crumplety and lame;
Teaching kittens how to scold –
Is it not a shame?

Kittens in the garden
Looking in her face,
Learning how to spit and swear –
Oh, what a disgrace!
Very wrong, very wrong,
Very wrong and bad;
Such a subject for our song,
Makes us all too sad.

Old Mother Tabbyskins,
Sticking out her head,
Gave a howl, and then a yowl,
Hobbled off to bed.
Very sick, very sick,
Very savage, too;
Pray send for a doctor quick –
Any one will do!

Doctor Mouse came creeping,
Creeping to her bed;
Lanced her gums and felt her pulse,
Whispered she was dead.
Very sly, very sly,
The *real* old cat
Open kept her weather eye –
Mouse! beware of that!

Old Mother Tabbyskins,
Saying 'Serves him right',
Gobbled up the doctor, with
Infinite delight.
Very fast, very fast,
Very pleasant, too –
'What a pity it can't last!
Bring another, do!'

Doctor Dog comes running,
Just to see her begs;
Round his neck a comforter,
Trousers on his legs.
Very grand, very grand –
Golden-headed cane
Swinging gaily from his hand,
Mischief in his brain!

'Dear Mother Tabbyskins,
And how are you now?
Let me feel your pulse – so, so;
Show your tongue – bow, wow!
Very ill, very ill,
Please attempt to purr;
Will you take a draught or pill?
Which do you prefer?'

Ah, Mother Tabbyskins,
Who is now afraid?
Of poor little Doctor Mouse
You a mouthful made.
Very nice, very nice
Little doctor he;
But for Doctor Dog's advice
You must pay the fee.

Doctor Dog comes nearer,
Says she must be bled;
I heard Mother Tabbyskins
Screaming in her bed.
Very near, very near,
Scuffling out and in;
Doctor Dog looks full and queer –
Where is Tabbyskin?

I will tell the Moral
Without any fuss:
Those who lead the young astray
Always suffer thus.
Very nice, very nice,
Let our conduct be;
For all doctors are not mice,
Some are dogs, you see!

HINSE THE CAT

Washington Irving (1783–1859)

Among the other important and privileged members of the household who figured in attendance at the dinner, was a large grey cat, who I observed was regaled from time to time with tit-bits from the table. This sage grimalkin was a favourite of both master and mistress and slept at night in their room. And Scott laughingly observed that one of the least wise parts of their establishment was, that the window was left open at night for puss to go in and out. The cat assumed a kind of ascendancy among the quadrupeds; sitting in state in Scott's armchair, and occasionally stationing himself on a chair beside the door as if to review his subjects as they passed, giving each dog a cuff beside the ears as he went by. This clapperclawing was always taken in good part; it appeared to be, in fact, a mere act of sovereignty on the part of grimalkin to remind the others of their vassalage; which they acknowledged, by the most perfect acquiescence. A general harmony prevailed between sovereign and subjects, and they would all sleep together in the sunshine.

from 'Abbotsford' in *The Crayon Miscellamy* (1849)

DOG, CATS, BOOKS AND THE AVERAGE MAN

Henry Harland (1861–1905)

I hope you will not suspect me of making a bid for his affection, when I remark that the Average Man loves the Obvious. By consequence (for, like all unthinking creatures, the duffer's logical), by consequence, his attitude towards the Subtle, the Elusive, when not an attitude of mere torpid indifference, is an attitude of positive distrust and dislike.

Of this ignoble fact, pretty nearly everything – from the popularity of beer and skittles, to the popularity of Mr Hall Caine's novels; from the general's distaste for caviar, to the general's neglect of Mr Henry James's tales – pretty nearly everything is a reminder. But, to go no further afield, for the moment, than his own hearthrug, may I ask you to consider a little the relative positions occupied in the Average Man's regard by the Dog and the Cat?

The Average Man ostentatiously loves the Dog.

The Average Man, when he is not torpidly indifferent to that princely animal, positively distrusts and dislikes the Cat.

I have used the epithet 'princely' with intention, in speaking of the near relative of the King of Beasts. The Cat is a Princess of the Blood. Yes, my dear, always a Princess, though the Average Man, with his unerring instinct for the malappropriate word, sometimes names her Thomas. The Cat is always a Princess, because everything nice in this world, everything fine, sensitive, distinguished, everything beautiful, everything worth while, is of essence Feminine, though it may be male by the accident of sex; and that's as true as gospel, let Mr W. E. Henley's lusty young disciples shout their loudest in celebration of the Virile. The Cat is a Princess.

The Dog, on the contrary, is not even a gentleman. Far otherwise: his admirers may do what they will to forget it, the circumstance remains, writ large in every Natural History, that the Dog is sprung from quite the meanest family of the Quadrupeds. That coward thief the wolf is his bastard brother; the carrion hyena is his cousin-german. And in his person, as in his character, bears he not an hundred marks of his base descent? In his rough coat (contrast it with the silken mantle of the Cat); in his harsh, monotonous

voice (contrast it with the flexible organ of the Cat, her versatile mewings, chirpings, and purrings, and their innumerable shades and modulations); in the stiff-jointed clumsiness of his movements (compare them to the inexpressible grace and suppleness of the Cat's); briefly, in the all-pervading plebeian commonness that hangs about him like an atmosphere (compare it to the high-bred reserve and dignity that invest the Cat). The wolf's brother, is the Dog not himself a coward? Watch him when, emulating the ruffian who insults an unprotected lady, he puts a Cat to flight in the streets: watch him when the lady halts and turns. Faugh, the craven! with his wild show of savagery so long as there is not the slightest danger – and his sudden chopfallen drawing back when the lady halts and turns! The hyena's cousin, is he not himself of carrion an impassioned amateur? At Constantinople he serves ('tis a labour of love; he receives no stipend), he serves as Public Scavenger, swallowing with greed the ordures cast by the Turk. Scripture tells us to what he returneth: who has failed to observe that he returneth not to his own alone? And the other day, strolling upon the sands by the illimitable sea, I came upon a friend and her pet terrier. She was holding the little beggar by the scruff of his neck, and giving him repeated sousing in a pool. I stood a pleased spectator of this exercise, for the terrier kicked and spluttered and appeared to be unhappy. 'He found a decaying jellyfish below there, and rolled in it,' my friend pathetically explained. I should like to see the Cat who could be induced to roll in a decaying jellyfish. The Cat's fastidiousness, her meticulous cleanliness, the time and the pains she bestows upon her toilet, and her almost morbid delicacy about certain more private errands, are among the material indications of her patrician nature. It were needless to allude to the vile habits and impudicity of the Dog.

Have you ever met a Dog who wasn't a bounder? Have you ever met a Dog who wasn't a bully, a sycophant, and a snob? Have you ever met a Cat who was? Have you ever met a Cat who would half frighten a timid little girl to death, by rushing at her and barking? Have you ever met a Cat who, left alone with a visitor in your drawing-room, would truculently growl and show her teeth, as often as that visitor ventured to stir in his chair? Have you ever met a Cat who would snarl and snap at the servants, Master's back being turned? Have you ever met a Cat who would cringe to you and fawn to you, and kiss the hand that smote her?

Conscious of her high lineage, the Cat understands and accepts the responsibilities that attach to it. She knows what she owes to herself, to her rank, to the Royal Idea. Therefore, it is you who must be the courtier. The Dog, poor-spirited today, will study your eye to divine your mood, and slavishly adapt his own mood and his behaviour to it. Not so the Cat. As between you and her, it is you who must do the toadying. A guest in the house, never a dependant, she remembers always the courtesy and the consideration that are her due. You must respect her pleasure. Is it her pleasure to slumber, and do you disturb her: note the disdainful melancholy with which she silently comments your rudeness. Is it her pleasure to be grave: tempt her to frolic, you will tempt in vain. It is her pleasure to be cold: nothing in human possibility can win a caress from her. Is it her pleasure to be rid of your presence: only the physical influence of a closed door will persuade her to remain in the room with you. It is you who must be the courtier, and wait upon her desire.

But then!

When, in her own good time, she chooses to unbend, how graciously, how entrancingly, she does it! Oh, the thousand wonderful lovelinesses and surprises of her play! The wit, the humour, the imagination, that inform it! Her ruses, her false leads, her sudden triumphs, her feigned despairs! And the topazes and emeralds that sparkle in her eyes; the satiny lustre of her apparel; the delicious sinuousities of her body! And her parenthetic interruptions of the game: to stride in regal progress round the apartment, flourishing her tail like a banner: or coquettishly to throw herself in some en-ravishing posture at length upon the carpet at your feet: or (if she loves you) to leap upon your shoulder, and press her cheek to yours, and murmur rapturous assurances of her passion! To be loved by a Princess! Whosoever, from the Marquis de Carabas down, has been loved by a Cat, has savoured that felicity. My own particular treasure of a Cat, at this particular moment is lying wreathed about my neck, watching my pen as it moves along the paper, and purring approbation of my views. But when, from time to time, I chance to use a word that doesn't strike her altogether as the fittest, she reaches down her little velvet paw, and dabs it out. I should like to see the Dog who could do that.

But – the Cat is subtle, the Cat is elusive, the Cat is not to be read at

a glance, the Cat is not a simple equation. And so the Average Man, gross mutton-devouring, money-grubbing mechanism that he is, when he doesn't just torpidly tolerate her, distrusts her and dislikes her. A great soul, misappreciated, misunderstood, she sits neglected in his chimney-corner; and the fatuous idgit never guesses how she scorns him.

But – the Dog is obvious. Any fool can grasp the meaning of the Dog. And the Average Man, accordingly, recreant for once to the snobbism which is his religion, hugs the hyena's cousin to his bosom.

What of it?

Only this: that in the Average Man's sentimental attitude towards the Dog and the Cat, we have a formula, a symbol, for his sentimental attitude towards many things, especially for his sentimental attitude towards Books.

Some books, in their uncouthness, their awkwardness, their boisterousness, in their violation of the decencies of art, in their low truckling to the tastes of the purchaser, in their commonness, their vulgarity, in their total lack of suppleness and distinction, are the very Dogs of Bookland. The Average Man loves 'em. Such as they are, they're obvious.

And other books, by reason of their beauties and their virtues, their graces and refinements; because they are considered finished; because they are delicate, distinguished, aristocratic; because their touch is light, their movement deft and fleet; because they proceed by omission, by implication and suggestion; because they employ the *demi-mot* and the *nuance*; because, in fine, they are Subtle – other books are the Cats of Bookland. And the Average Man hates them or ignores them.

from The Yellow Book (1896)

CHATTIE

Mrs Humphry Ward (1851–1920)

Rose sat fanning herself with a portentous hat, which when in its proper place served her, apparently, both as hat and as parasol. She seemed to have been running races with a fine collie, who lay at her feet panting, but studying her with his bright eyes, and evidently ready to be off again at the first indication that his playmate had recovered her wind. Chattie was coming lazily over the lawn, stretching each leg behind her as she walked, tail arched, green eyes flaming in the sun, a model of treacherous beauty.

'Chattie, you fiend, come here!' cried Rose, holding out a hand to her; 'if Miss Barks were ever pretty she must have looked like you at this moment.'

'I won't have Chattie put upon,' said Agnes, establishing herself at the other side of the little tea-table; 'she has done you no harm. Come to me, beastie. I won't compare you to disagreeable old maids.'

The cat looked from one sister to the other, blinking; then with a sudden magnificent spring leaped on to Agnes's lap and curled herself up there.

'Nothing but cupboard love,' said Rose scornfully, in answer to Agnes's laugh; 'she knows you will give her bread and butter and I won't, out of a double regard for my skirts and her morals.'

from *Robert Elsmere* (1888)

DOG AND CAT

William Shakespeare (1564–1616)

I think Crab my dog be the sourest-natured dog that lives: my mother weeping, my father wailing, my sister crying, our maid howling, our cat wringing her hands, and all our house in a great perplexity, yet did not this cruel-hearted cur shed one tear.

from *Two Gentlemen of Verona*, Act 2, Scene 2

CATS AS FAITHFUL AS DOGS?

Jerome K. Jerome (1859–1927)

Cats have the credit of being more worldly wise than dogs – of looking more after their own interests, and being less blindly devoted to those of their friends. And we men and women are naturally shocked at such selfishness. Cats certainly do love a family that has a carpet in the kitchen more than a family that has not; and if there are many children about, they prefer to spend their leisure time next door. But, taken altogether, cats are libelled. Make a friend of one, and she will stick to you through thick and thin. All the cats that I have had have been most firm comrades.

from 'On Cats and Dogs' in *Idle Thoughts of an Idle Fellow* (1886)

MATTHEW ARNOLD'S DOGS AND CATS

Mrs Humphry Ward (1851–1920)

His visits to Russell Square, and our expeditions to Cobham where he lived, in the pretty cottage beside the Mole, are marked in memory with a very white stone. The only drawback to the Cobham visits were the 'dear, dear boys'! – i.e. the dachshunds, Max and Geist, who, however adorable in themselves, had no taste for visitors and no intention of letting such intruding creatures interfere with their possession of their master. One would go down to Cobham, eager to talk to 'Uncle Matt' about a book or an article – covetous at any rate of *some* talk with him undisturbed. And it would all end in a breathless chase after Max, through field after field where the little wretch was harrying either sheep or cows, with the dear poet, hoarse with shouting, at his heels. The dogs were always *in the party*, talked to, caressed, or scolded exactly like spoilt children; and the cat of the house was almost equally dear. Once, at Harrow, the then ruling cat – a tom – broke his leg, and the house was in lamentation. The vet was called in, and hurt him horribly. Then Uncle Matt ran up to town, met Professor Huxley at the Athenaeum, and anxiously consulted him. 'I'll go down with you,' said Huxley. The two travelled back instanter to Harrow, and while Uncle Matt held the cat, Huxley – who had begun life, let it be remembered, as Surgeon to the *Rattlesnake!* – examined him, the two black heads together. There is a rumour that Charles Kingsley was included in the consultation. Finally the limb was put in splints, and left to nature. All went well.

from *A Writer's Recollections* (1918)

THE CAT

Vicomte de Chateaubriand (1768–1848)

I value in the cat the independent and almost ungrateful spirit which prevents her from attaching herself to anyone, the indifference with which she passes from the salon to the housetop. When we caress her, she stretches herself and arches her back responsively; but this is because she feels an agreeable sensation, not because she takes a silly satisfaction, like the dog, in faithfully loving a thankless master. The cat lives alone, has no need of society, obeys only when she pleases, pretends to sleep that she may see the more clearly, and scratches everything on which she can lay her paw.

A SUPERIOR CAT

Sir Walter Scott (1771–1832)

I have added a romantic inmate to my family – a large bloodhound, allowed to be the finest dog of the kind in Scotland, perfectly gentle, affectionate, good-natured, and the darling of all the children. He is between the deer-greyhound and mastiff, with a shaggy mane like a lion, and always sits beside me at dinner, his head as high as the back of my chair; yet it will gratify you to know that a favourite cat keeps him in the

greatest possible order, insists upon all rights of precedence, and scratches with impunity the nose of an animal who would make no bones of a wolf, and pulls down a red deer without fear or difficulty. I heard my friend set up some most piteous howls (and I assure you the noise was no joke), all occasioned by his fear of passing Puss, who had stationed himself on the stairs.

from a letter to Joanna Baillie

MY PETS

Sir Richard Steele (1672–1729)

They both of them sit by my fire every Evening and wait with Impatience; and, at my Entrance, never fail of running up to me, and bidding me Welcome, each of them in its proper Language. As they have been bred up together from Infancy, and have seen no other Company, they have acquired each other's Manners; so that the Dog gives himself the Airs of a Cat, and the Cat, in several of her Motions and Gestures, affects the Behaviour of the little Dog.

from *The Tatler* (1711)

MONTMORENCY'S BAD DAY

Jerome K. Jerome (1859–1927)

We got up tolerably early on the Monday morning at Marlow, and went for a bathe before breakfast; and, coming back, Montmorency made an awful ass of himself. The only subject on which Montmorency and I have any serious difference of opinion is cats. I like cats; Montmorency does not.

When I meet a cat, I say, 'Poor Pussy!' and stoop down and tickle the side of its head; and the cat sticks up its tail in a rigid, cast-iron manner, arches its back, and wipes its nose up against my trousers; and all is gentleness and peace. When Montmorency meets a cat, the whole street knows about it; and there is enough bad language wasted in ten seconds to last an ordinary respectable man all his life, with care.

I do not blame the dog (contenting myself, as a rule, with merely clouting his head or throwing stones at him), because I take it that it is his nature. Fox-terriers are born with about four times as much original sin in them as other dogs are, and it will take years and years of patient effort on the part of us Christians to bring about any appreciable reformation in the rowdiness of the fox-terrier nature . . .

Such is the nature of fox-terriers; and, therefore, I do not blame Montmorency for his tendency to row with cats; but he wished he had not given way to it that morning.

We were, as I have said, returning from a dip, and halfway up the High Street a cat darted out from one of the houses in front of us, and began to trot across the road. Montmorency gave a cry of joy – the cry of a stern warrior who sees his enemy given over to his hands – the sort of cry Cromwell might have uttered when the Scots came down the hill – and flew after his prey.

His victim was a large black tom. I never saw a larger cat, nor a more disreputable-looking cat. It had lost half its tail, one of its ears, and a fairly appreciable proportion of its nose. It was a long, sinewy-looking animal. It had a calm, contented air about it.

Montmorency went for that poor cat at the rate of twenty miles an hour; but the cat did not hurry up – did not seem to have grasped the idea that its life was in danger. It trotted quietly on until its would-be assassin was within a yard of it, and then it turned round and sat down in the middle of the road, and looked at Montmorency with a gentle, inquiring expression, that said: 'Yes! You want me?'

Montmorency does not lack pluck; but there was something about the look of that cat that might have chilled the heart of the boldest dog. He stopped abruptly, and looked back at Tom.

Neither spoke; but the conversation that one could imagine was clearly as follows:

THE CAT: 'Can I do anything for you?'

MONTMORENCY: 'No – no, thanks.'

THE CAT: 'Don't you mind speaking if you really want anything, you know.'

MONTMORENCY (*backing down the High Street*): 'Oh, no – not at all – certainly – don't you trouble. I – I am afraid I've made a mistake. I thought I knew you. Sorry I disturbed you.'

THE CAT: 'Not at all – quite a pleasure. Sure you don't want anything, now?'

MONTMORENCY (*still backing*): 'Not at all, thanks – not at all – very kind of you. Good morning.'

THE CAT: 'Good morning.'

Then the cat rose, and continued his trot; and Montmorency, fitting what he calls his tail carefully into its groove, came back to us, and took up an unimportant position in the rear. To this day, if you say the word 'Cats!' to Montmorency, he will visibly shrink and look up piteously at you, as if to say: 'Please don't.'

from *Three Men in a Boat* (1889)

THE CAT'S PILGRIMAGE

James Anthony Froude (1818–94)

I

'It is all very fine,' said the Cat, yawning, and stretching herself against the fender, 'but it is rather a bore; I don't see the use of it.' She raised herself, and arranging her tail into a ring, and seating herself in the middle of it, with her forepaws in a straight line from her shoulders, at right angles to the hearth rug, she looked pensively at the fire. 'It is very odd,' she went on. 'There is my poor Tom; he is gone. I saw him stretched out in the yard. I spoke to him, and he took no notice of me. He won't, I suppose, ever any more, for they put him under the earth. Nice fellow he was. It is wonderful how little one cares about it. So many jolly evenings we spent together; and now I seem to get on quite as well without him. I wonder what has become of him; and my last children, too, what has become of them. What are we here for? I would ask the men, only they are so conceited and stupid they can't understand what we say. I hear them droning away, teaching their little ones every day; telling them to be good, and to do what they are bid, and all that. Nobody ever tells me to do anything; if they do I don't do it, and I am not very good. I wonder whether I should be any better if I minded more. I'll ask the Dog.

'Dog,' said she, to a little fat spaniel coiled up on a mat, like a lady's muff with a head and tail stuck on to it, 'Dog, what do you make of it all?'

The Dog faintly opened his languid eyes, looked sleepily at the Cat for a moment, and dropped them again.

'Dog,' she said, 'I want to talk to you; don't go to sleep. Can't you answer a civil question?'

'Don't bother me,' said the Dog, 'I am tired. I stood on my hind legs ten minutes this morning before I could get my breakfast, and it hasn't agreed with me.'

'Who told you to do it?' said the Cat.

'Why, the lady I have to take care of me,' replied the Dog.

'Do you feel any better for it, Dog, after you have been standing on your legs?' asked she.

'Haven't I told you, you stupid Cat, that it hasn't agreed with me? Let me go to sleep and don't plague me.'

'But I mean,' persisted the Cat, 'do you feel improved, as the men call it? They tell their children that if they do what they are told they will improve, and grow good and great. Do you feel good and great?'

'What do I know?' said the Dog. 'I eat my breakfast and am happy. Let me alone.'

'Do you never think, O Dog without a soul! Do you never wonder what dogs are, and what this world is?'

The Dog stretched himself, and rolled his eyes lazily round the room. 'I conceive,' he said, 'that the world is for dogs, and men and women are put into it to take care of dogs; women to take care of little dogs like me, and men for the big dogs like those in the yard – and cats, he continued, are to know their place, and not to be troublesome.'

'They beat you sometimes,' said the Cat. 'Why do they do that? They never beat me.'

'If they forget their places, and beat me,' snarled the Dog, 'I bite them, and they don't do it again. I should like to bite you, too, you nasty Cat; you have woken me up.'

'There may be truth in what you say,' said the Cat, calmly; 'but I think your view is limited. If you listened like me you would hear the men say it was all made for them, and you and I were made to amuse them.'

'They don't dare to say so?' said the Dog.

'They do, indeed,' said the Cat. 'I hear many things which you lose by sleeping so much. They think I am asleep, and so they are not afraid to talk before me; but my ears are open when my eyes are shut.'

'You surprise me,' said the Dog. 'I never listen to them, expect when I take notice of them, and then they never talk of anything except of me.'

'I could tell you a thing or two about yourself which you don't know,' said the Cat. 'You have never heard, I dare say, that once upon a time your fathers lived in a temple, and that people prayed to them?'

'Prayed! What is that?'

'Why, they went on their knees to you to ask you to give them good things, just as you stand on your toes to them now to ask for your breakfast. You don't know either that you have got one of those bright things we see up in the air at night called after you?'

'Well, it is just what I said,' answered the Dog. 'I told you it was all made for us. They never did anything of that sort for you.'

'Didn't they? Why, there was a whole city where the people did nothing else, and as soon as we got stiff and couldn't move about any more, instead of being put under the ground like poor Tom, we used to be stuffed full of all sorts of nice things, and kept better than we were when we were alive.'

'You are a very wise Cat,' answered her companion, 'but what good is it knowing all this?'

'Why, don't you see?' said she. 'They don't do it any more. We are going down in the world, we are, and that is why living on this way is such an unsatisfactory sort of thing. I don't mean to complain for myself, and you needn't, Dog; we have a quiet life of it; but a quiet life is not the thing, and if there is nothing to be done except sleep and eat, and eat and sleep, why, as I said before, I don't see the use of it. There is something more in it than that; there was once, and there will be again, and I shan't be happy till I find it out. It is a shame, Dog, I say. The men have been here only a few thousand years, and we – why, we have been here hundreds of thousands. If we are older, we ought to be wiser. I'll go and ask the creatures in the wood.'

'You'll learn more from the men,' said the Dog.

'They are stupid, and they don't know what I say to them; besides, they are so conceited they care for nothing except themselves. No, I shall try what I can do in the woods. I'd as soon go after poor Tom as stay living any longer like this.'

'And where is poor Tom?' yawned the Dog.

'That is just one of the things I want to know,' answered she. 'Poor Tom is lying under the yard, or the skin of him, but whether that is the whole I don't feel so sure. They didn't think so in the city I told you about. It is a beautiful day, Dog; you won't take a trot out with me?' she added wistfully.

'Who? I?' said the Dog. 'Not quite.'

'You may get so wise,' said she.

'Wisdom is good,' said the Dog; 'but so is the hearth rug, thank you!'

'But you may be free,' said she.

'I shall have to hunt for my own dinner,' said he.

'But, Dog, they may pray to you again,' said she.

'But I shan't have a softer mat to sleep upon, Cat, and as I am rather delicate, that is a consideration.'

II

So the Dog wouldn't go, and the Cat set off by herself to learn how to be happy, and to be all that a cat could be. It was a fine sunny morning. She determined to try the meadow first, and, after an hour or two, if she had not succeeded, then to go off to the wood. A Blackbird was piping away on a thornbush as if his heart was running over with happiness. The Cat had breakfasted, and so was able to listen without any mixture of feeling. She didn't sneak. She walked boldly up under the bush, and the bird, seeing she had no bad purpose, sat still and sung on.

'Good morning, Blackbird; you seem to be enjoying yourself this fine day.'

'Good morning, Cat.'

'Blackbird, it is an odd question, perhaps. What ought one to do to be as happy as you?'

'Do your duty, Cat.'

'But what is my duty, Blackbird?'

'Take care of your little ones, Cat.'

'I haven't any,' said she.

'Then sing to your mate,' said the bird.

'Tom is dead,' said she.

'Poor Cat!' said the bird. 'Then sing over his grave. If your song is sad, you will find your heart grow lighter for it.'

Mercy! thought the Cat. I could do a little singing with a living lover, but I never heard of singing for a dead one. 'But you see, bird, it isn't cats' nature. When I am cross, I mew. When I am pleased, I purr; but I must be pleased first. I can't purr myself into happiness.'

'I am afraid there is something the matter with your heart, my Cat. It wants warming; goodbye.'

The Blackbird flew away. The Cat looked sadly after him.

'He thinks I am like him; and he doesn't know that a cat is a cat,' said she. 'As it happens, now, I feel a great deal for a cat. If I hadn't got a heart I shouldn't be unhappy. I won't be angry. I'll try that great fat fellow.'

The Ox lay placidly chewing, with content beaming out of his eyes and playing on his mouth.

'Ox,' she said, 'what is the way to be happy?'

'Do your duty,' said the Ox.

'Bother,' said the Cat, 'duty again. What is it, Ox?'

'Get your dinner,' said the Ox.

'But it is got for me, Ox; and I have nothing to do but to eat it.'

'Well, eat it, then, like me.'

'So I do; but I am not happy for all that.'

'Then you are a very wicked, ungrateful Cat.'

The Ox munched away. A Bee buzzed into a buttercup under the Cat's nose.

'I beg your pardon,' said the Cat, 'it isn't curiosity – what are you doing?'

'Doing my duty; don't stop me, Cat.'

'But, Bee, what is your duty?'

'Making honey,' said the Bee.

'I wish I could make honey,' sighed the Cat.

'Do you mean to say you can't?' said the Bee. 'How stupid you must be. What do you do, then?'

'I do nothing, Bee. I can't get anything to do.'

'You won't get anything to do, you mean, you lazy Cat! You are a good-for-nothing drone. Do you know what we do to our drones? We kill them; and that is all they are fit for.'

'Well, I am sure,' said the Cat, 'they are treating me civilly! I had better have stopped at home at this rate. Stroke my whiskers! Heartless! wicked! good-for-nothing! stupid! and only fit to be killed! This is a pleasant beginning, anyhow. I must look for some wiser creatures than these are. What shall I do? I know. I know where I will go.'

It was in the middle of the wood. The bush was very dark, but she found him by his wonderful eye. Presently, as she got used to the light, she distinguished a sloping roll of feathers, a rounded breast, surmounted by a round head, set close to the body, without an inch of neck intervening. 'How wise he looks!' she said; 'what a brain; what a forehead! His head is not long, but what an expanse! and what a depth of earnestness!'

The Owl sloped his head a little on one side; the Cat slanted hers upon the other. The Owl set it straight again, the Cat did the same. They stood looking in this way for some minutes; at last, in a whispering voice, the Owl said, 'What are you, who presume to look into my repose? Pass on upon your way, and carry elsewhere those prying eyes.'

'O wonderful Owl,' said the Cat, 'you are wise, and I want to be wise; and I am come to you to teach me.'

A film floated backwards and forwards over the Owl's eyes; it was his way of showing that he was pleased.

'I have heard in our schoolroom,' went on the Cat, 'that you sat on the shoulder of Pallas, and she told you all about it.'

'And what would you know, O my daughter?' said the Owl.

'Everything,' said the Cat, 'everything. First of all, how to be happy.'

'Mice content you not, my child, even as they content not me,' said the Owl. 'It is good.'

'Mice indeed!' said the Cat; 'no, parlour cats don't eat mice. I have better than mice, and no trouble to get it; but I want something more.'

'The body's meat is provided. You would now fill your soul?'

'I want to improve,' said the Cat. 'I want something to do. I want to find out what the creatures call my duty.'

'You would learn how to employ those happy hours of your leisure? – rather, how to make them happy by a worthy use? Meditate, O Cat! meditate! meditate!'

'That is the very thing,' said she. 'Meditate! that is what I like above all things. Only I want to know how: I want something to meditate about. Tell me, Owl, and I will bless you every hour of the day as I sit by the parlour fire.'

'I will tell you,' answered the Owl, 'what I have been thinking of ever since the moon changed. You shall take it home with you and think about it too; and the next full moon you shall come again to me: we will compare our conclusions.'

'Delightful! delightful!' said the Cat. 'What is it? I will try this minute.'

'From the beginning,' replied the Owl, 'our race have been considering which first existed, the Owl or the egg. The Owl comes from the egg, but likewise the egg from the Owl.'

'Mercy!' said the Cat.

'From sunrise to sunset I ponder on it, O Cat! When I reflect on the beauty of the complete Owl I think that must have been first, as the cause is greater than the effect. When I remember my own childhood I incline the other way.'

'Well, but how are we going to find out?' said the Cat.

'Find out!' said the Owl. 'We can never find out. The beauty of the question is, that its solution is impossible. What would become of all our delightful reasonings, O unwise Cat, if we were so unhappy as to know?'

'But what in the world is the good of thinking about it, if you can't, O Owl?'

'My child, that is a foolish question. It is good, in order that the thoughts on these things may stimulate wonder. It is in wonder that the Owl is great.'

'Then you don't know anything at all,' said the Cat. 'What did you sit on Pallas's shoulder for? You must have gone to sleep.'

'Your tone is over-flippant, Cat, for philosophy. The highest of all knowledge is to know that we know nothing.'

The Cat made two great arches with her back and her tail.

'Bless the mother that laid you,' said she. 'You were dropped by mistake in a goose nest. You won't do. I don't know much, but I am not such a creature as you, anyhow. A great white thing!'

She straightened her body, stuck her tail up on end, and marched off with much dignity. But, though she respected herself rather more than before, she was not on the way to the end of her difficulties. She tried all the creatures she met without advancing a step. They had all the old story, 'Do your duty.' But each had its own, and no one could tell her what hers was. Only one point they all agreed upon – the duty of getting their dinner when they were hungry. The day wore on, and she began to think she would like hers. Her meals came so regularly at home that she scarcely knew what hunger was; but now the sensation came over her very palpably, and she experienced quite new emotions as the hares and rabbits skipped about her, or as she spied a bird upon a tree. For a moment she thought she would go back and eat the Owl – he was the most useless creature she had seen; but on second thoughts she didn't fancy he would be nice: besides that, his claws were sharp and his beak too. Presently, however, as she sauntered down the path, she came on a little open patch of green, in the middle of which a fine fat Rabbit was sitting. There was no escape. The path ended there, and the bushes were so thick on each side that he couldn't get away except through her paws.

'Really,' said the Cat, 'I don't wish to be troublesome; I wouldn't do it if I could help it; but I am very hungry; I am afraid I must eat you. It is very unpleasant, I assure you, to me as well as to you.'

The poor Rabbit begged for mercy.

'Well,' said she, 'I think it is hard; I do really – and, if the law could be altered, I should be the first to welcome it. But what can a cat do? You eat the grass; I eat you. But, Rabbit, I wish you would do me a favour.'

'Anything to save my life,' said the Rabbit.

'It is not exactly that,' said the Cat; 'but I haven't been used to killing my own food, and it is disagreeable. Couldn't you die? I shall hurt you dreadfully if I kill you.'

'Oh!' said the Rabbit, 'you are a kind Cat; I see it in your eyes, and your whiskers don't curl like those of the cats in the woods. I am sure you will spare me.'

'But, Rabbit, it is a question of principle. I have to do my duty; and the only duty I have, as far as I can make out, is to get my dinner.'

'If you kill me, Cat, to do your duty, I shan't be able to do mine.'

It was a doubtful point, and the Cat was new to casuistry.

'What is your duty?' said she.

'I have seven little ones at home – seven little ones, and they will all die without me. Pray let me go.'

'What! Do you take care of your children?' said the Cat. 'How interesting! I should like to see that; take me.'

'Oh! You would eat them, you would,' said the Rabbit. 'No! Better eat me than them. No, no.'

'Well, well,' said the Cat, 'I don't know; I suppose I couldn't answer for myself. I don't think I am right, for duty is pleasant, and it is very unpleasant to be so hungry; but I suppose you must go. You seem a good Rabbit. Are you happy, Rabbit?'

'Happy! Oh, dear beautiful Cat! If you spare me to my poor babies!'

'Pooh, pooh!' said the Cat, peevishly; 'I don't want fine speeches; I meant whether you thought it worth while to be alive? Of course you do! It don't matter. Go, and keep out of my way; for, if I don't find something to eat, you may not get off another time. Get along, Rabbit.'

III

It was a day in the Fox's cave. The eldest cub had the night before brought home his first goose, and they were just sitting down to it as the Cat came by.

'Ah, my young lady! What, you in the woods? Bad feeding at home, eh? Come out to hunt for yourself?'

The goose smelt excellent; the Cat couldn't help a wistful look. She was only come, she said, to pay her respects to her wild friends.

'Just in time,' said the Fox. 'Sit down and take a bit of meat; I see you want it. Make room, you cubs; place a seat for the lady.'

'Why, thank you,' said the Cat; 'yes; I acknowledge it is not unwelcome. Pray, don't disturb yourselves, young Foxes. I am hungry. I met a rabbit on my way here. I was going to eat him, but he talked so prettily I let him go.'

The cubs looked up from their plates, and burst out laughing.

'For shame, young rascals,' said their father. 'Where are your manners? Mind your business, and don't be rude.'

'Fox,' she said, when it was over, and the cubs were gone to play, 'you are very clever. The other creatures are all stupid.' The Fox bowed. 'Your family were always clever,' she continued. 'I have heard about them in the books they use in our schoolroom. It is many years since your ancestor stole the crow's dinner.'

'Don't say *stole*, Cat; it is not pretty. Obtained by superior ability.'

'I beg your pardon,' said the Cat; 'it is all living with those men. That is not the point. Well, but I want to know whether you are any wiser or any better than Foxes were then.'

'Really,' said the Fox, 'I am what Nature made me. I don't know. I am proud of my ancestors, and do my best to keep up the credit of the family.'

'Well, but, Fox, I mean, do you improve? Do I? Do any of you? The men are always talking about doing their duty, and that, they say, is the way to improve, and to be happy. And as I was not happy I thought that had, perhaps, something to do with it, so I came out to talk to the creatures. They also had the old chant – duty, duty, duty; but none of them could tell me what mine was, or whether I had any.'

The Fox smiled. 'Another leaf out of your schoolroom,' said he. 'Can't they tell you there?'

'Indeed,' she said, 'they are very absurd. They say a great deal about themselves, but they only speak disrespectfully of us. If such creatures as they can do their duty, and improve, and be happy, why can't we?'

'They say they do, do they?' said the Fox. 'What do they say of me?'

The Cat hesitated.

'Don't be afraid of hurting my feelings, Cat. Out with it.'

'They do all justice to your abilities, Fox,' said she; 'but your morality, they say, is not high. They say you are a rogue.'

'Morality!' said the Fox. 'Very moral and good they are. And you really believe all that? What do they mean by calling me a rogue?'

'They mean, you take whatever you can get, without caring whether it is just or not.'

'My dear Cat, it is very well for a man, if he can't bear his own face, to paint a pretty one on a panel and call it a looking glass; but you don't mean that it takes *you* in?'

'Teach me,' said the Cat. 'I fear I am weak.'

'Who get justice from the men unless they can force it? Ask the sheep that are cut into mutton. Ask the horses that draw their ploughs. I don't mean it is wrong of the men to do as they do; but they needn't lie about it.'

'You surprise me,' said the Cat.

'My good Cat, there is but one law in the world. The weakest goes to the wall. The men are sharper-witted than the creatures, and so they get the better of them and use them. They may call it just, if they like; but when a tiger eats a man I guess he has just as much justice on his side as the man when he eats a sheep.'

'And that is the whole of it,' said the Cat. 'Well, it is very sad. What do you do with yourself?'

'My duty, to be sure,' said the Fox; 'use my wits and enjoy myself. My dear friend, you and I are on the lucky side. We eat and are not eaten.'

'Except by the hounds now and then,' said the Cat.

'Yes, by brutes that forget their nature, and sell their freedom to the man,' said the Fox, bitterly. 'In the meantime my wits have kept my skin whole hitherto, and I bless nature for making me a Fox and not a goose.'

'And are you happy, Fox?'

'Happy? Yes, of course. So would you be if you would do like me, and use your wits. My good Cat, I should be as miserable as you if I found my geese every day at the cave's mouth. I have to hunt for them, lie for them, sneak for them, fight for them; cheat those old fat farmers, and bring out what there is inside me; and then I am happy – of course I am. And then, Cat, think of my feelings as a father last night, when my dear boy came home with the very young gosling which was marked for the Michaelmas dinner! Old Reinke himself wasn't more than a match for that young Fox at his years. You know our epic?'

'A little of it, Fox. They don't read it in our schoolroom. They say it is not moral; but I have heard pieces of it. I hope it is not all quite true.'

'Pack of stuff! It is the only true book that ever was written. If it is not, it ought to be. Why, that book is the law of the world – *la carrière aux talents* – and writing it was the honestest thing ever done by a man. That fellow knew a thing or two, and wasn't ashamed of himself when he did know. They are all like him, too, if they would only say so. There never was one of them yet who wasn't more ashamed of being called ugly than of being called a rogue, and of being called stupid than of being called naughty.'

'It has a roughish end, this life of yours, if you keep clear of the hounds, Fox,' said the Cat.

'What! A rope in the yard? Well, it must end some day; and when the farmer catches me I shall be getting old, and my brains will be taking leave of me; so the sooner I go the better, that I may disgrace myself the less. Better be jolly while it lasts, than sit mewing out your life and grumbling at it as a bore.'

'Well,' said the Cat, 'I am very much obliged to you. I suppose I may even get home again. I shall not find a wiser friend than you, and perhaps I shall not find another good-natured enough to entertain me so handsomely. But it is very sad.'

'Think of what I have said,' answered the Fox. 'I'll call at your house some night; you will take me a walk round the yard, and then I'll show you.'

Not quite, thought the Cat, as she trotted off. One good turn deserves another, that is true; and you have given me a dinner. But they have given me many at home, and I mean to take a few more of them; so I think you mustn't go round our yard.

IV

The next morning, when the Dog came down to breakfast, he found his old friend sitting in her usual place on the hearth rug.

'Oh! So you have come back?' said he. 'How d'ye do? You don't look as if you had had a very pleasant journey.'

'I have learnt something,' said the Cat. 'Knowledge is never pleasant.'

'Then it is better to be without it,' said the Dog.

'Especially better to be without knowing how to stand on one's hind legs, Dog,' said the Cat; 'still, you see, you are proud of it; but I have learnt a great deal, Dog. They won't worship you any more, and it is better for you; you wouldn't be any happier. What did you do yesterday?'

'Indeed,' said the Dog, 'I hardly remember. I slept after you went away. In the afternoon I took a drive in the carriage. Then I had my dinner. My maid washed me and put me to bed. There is the difference between you and me; you have to wash yourself and put yourself to bed.'

'And you really don't find it a bore, living like this? Wouldn't you like something to do? Wouldn't you like some children to play with? The Fox seemed to find it very pleasant.'

'Children, indeed!' said the Dog, 'when I have got men and women. Children are well enough for foxes and wild creatures; refined dogs know better; and, for doing – can't I stand on my toes? Can't I dance? At least, couldn't I before I was so fat?'

'Ah! I see everybody likes what he was bred to,' sighed the Cat. 'I was bred to do nothing, and I must like that. Train the cat as the cat should go, and the cat will be happy and ask no questions. Never seek for impossibilities, Dog. That is the secret.'

'And you have spent a day in the woods to learn that?' said he. 'I could have taught you that. Why, Cat, one day when you were sitting scratching your nose before the fire, I thought you looked so pretty that I should have liked to marry you; but I knew I couldn't, so I didn't make myself miserable.'

The Cat looked at him with her odd green eyes. 'I never wished to marry you, Dog; I shouldn't have presumed. But it was wise of you not to fret about it. Listen to me, Dog – listen. I met many creatures in the wood, all sorts of creatures, beasts and birds. They were all happy; they didn't find it a bore. They went about their work, and did it, and enjoyed it, and yet none of them had the same story to tell. Some did one thing, some another; and, except the Fox, each had got a sort of notion of doing its duty. The Fox was a rogue, he said he was; but yet he was not unhappy. His conscience never troubled him. Your work is standing on your toes, and you are happy. I have none, and this is why I am unhappy. When I came to think about it, I found every creature out in the wood had to get its own living. I tried to get mine, but I didn't like it, because I wasn't used to it; and as for knowing, the Fox, who didn't care to know anything except how to cheat greater fools than himself, was the cleverest fellow I came across. Oh! the Owl, Dog – you should have heard the Owl. But I came to this, that it was no use trying to know, and the only way to be jolly was to go about one's own business like a decent Cat. Cats' business seems to be killing rabbits and such-like, and it is not the pleasantest possible; so the sooner one is bred to it the better. As for me, that have been bred to do nothing, why, as I said before, I must try to like that; but I consider myself an unfortunate Cat.'

'So, don't I consider myself an unfortunate Dog?' said her companion.

'Very likely you do not,' said the Cat.

By this time their breakfast was come in. The Cat ate hers, the Dog did penance for his; and if one might judge by the purring on the hearth rug, the Cat, if not the happier of the two, at least was not exceedingly miserable.

7

DEMONIC CATS

Those who'll play with cats must expect to be scratched.

Miguel de Cervantes Saavedra (1547–1616)

THE BLACK CAT

Edgar Allan Poe (1809–49)

For the most wild yet most homely narrative which I am about to pen, I neither expect nor solicit belief. Mad indeed would I be to expect it, in a case where my very senses reject their own evidence. Yet mad am I not – and very surely do I not dream. But tomorrow I die, and today I would unburden my soul. My immediate purpose is to place before the world, plainly, succinctly, and without comment, a series of mere household events. In their consequences, these events have terrified – have tortured – have destroyed me. Yet I will not attempt to expound them. To me, they have presented little but horror – to many they will seem less terrible than *baroques*. Hereafter, perhaps, some intellect may be found which will reduce my phantasm to the commonplace – some intellect more calm, more logical, and far less excitable than my own, which will perceive, in the circumstances I detail with awe, nothing more than an ordinary succession of very natural causes and effects.

From my infancy I was noted for the docility and humanity of my disposition. My tenderness of heart was even so conspicuous as to make me the jest of my companions. I was especially fond of animals, and was indulged by my parents with a great variety of pets. With these I spent most of my time, and never was so happy as when feeding and caressing them. This peculiarity of character grew with my growth, and, in my manhood, I derived from it one of my principal sources of pleasure. To those who have cherished an affection for a faithful and sagacious dog, I need hardly be at the trouble of explaining the nature or the intensity of the gratification thus derivable. There is something in the unselfish and self-sacrificing love of a brute, which goes directly to the heart of him who has had frequent occasion to test the paltry friendship and gossamer fidelity of mere *Man*.

I married early, and was happy to find in my wife a disposition not uncongenial with my own. Observing my partiality for domestic pets, she lost no opportunity of procuring those of the most agreeable kind. We had birds, goldfish, a fine dog, rabbits, a small monkey, and a *cat*.

This latter was a remarkably large and beautiful animal, entirely black, and sagacious to an astonishing degree. In speaking of his intelligence, my wife, who at heart was not a little tinctured with superstition, made frequent allusion to the ancient popular notion, which regarded all black cats as witches in disguise. Not that she was ever *serious* upon this point – and I mention the matter at all for no better reason than that it happens, just now, to be remembered.

Pluto – this was the cat's name – was my favourite pet and playmate. I alone fed him, and he attended me wherever I went about the house. It was even with difficulty that I could prevent him from following me through the streets.

Our friendship lasted, in this manner, for several years, during which my general temperament and character – through the instrumentality of the Fiend Intemperance – had (I blush to confess it) experienced a radical alteration for the worse. I grew, day by day, more moody, more irritable, more regardless of the feelings of others. I suffered myself to use intemperate language to my wife. At length, I even offered her personal violence. My pets, of course, were made to feel the change in my disposition. I not only neglected, but ill-used them. For Pluto, however, I still retained sufficient regard to restrain me from maltreating him, as I made no scruple of maltreating the rabbits, the monkey, or even the dog, when, by accident, or through affection, they came in my way. But my disease grew upon me – for what disease is like Alcohol! – and at length even Pluto, who was now becoming old, and consequently somewhat peevish – even Pluto began to experience the effects of my ill temper.

One night, returning home, much intoxicated, from one of my haunts about town, I fancied that the cat avoided my presence. I seized him; when, in his fright at my violence, he inflicted a slight wound upon my hand with his teeth. The fury of a demon instantly possessed me. I knew myself no longer. My original soul seemed, at once, to take its flight from my body; and a more than fiendish malevolence, gin-nurtured, thrilled every fibre of my frame. I took from my waistcoat pocket a penknife, opened it, grasped the poor beast by the throat, and deliberately cut one of its eyes from the socket! I blush, I burn, I shudder, while I pen the damnable atrocity.

When reason returned with the morning – when I had slept off the fumes of the night's debauch – I experienced a sentiment half of horror, half of remorse, for the crime of which I had been guilty; but it was, at best, a feeble and equivocal feeling, and the soul remained untouched. I again plunged into excess, and soon drowned in wine all memory of the deed.

In the meantime the cat slowly recovered. The socket of the lost eye presented, it is true, a frightful appearance, but he no longer appeared to suffer any pain. He went about the house as usual, but, as might be expected, fled in extreme terror at my approach. I had so much of my old heart left, as to be at first grieved by this evident dislike on the part of a creature which had once so loved me. But this feeling soon gave place to irritation. And then came, as if to my final and irrevocable overthrow, the spirit of *perverseness*. Of this spirit philosophy takes no account. Yet I am not more sure that my soul lives, than I am that perverseness is one of the primitive impulses of the human heart – one of the indivisible primary faculties, or sentiments, which give direction to the character of Man. Who has not, a hundred times, found himself committing a vile or a stupid action, for no other reason than because he knows he should *not*? Have we not a perpetual inclination, in the teeth of our best judgement, to violate that which is Law, merely because we understand it to be such? This spirit of perverseness, I say, came to my final overthrow. It was this unfathomable longing of the soul to *vex itself* – to offer violence to its own nature – to do wrong for the wrong's sake only – that urged me to continue and finally to consummate the injury I had inflicted upon the unoffending brute. One morning, in cold blood, I slipped a noose about its neck and hung it to the limb of a tree – hung it with the tears streaming from my eyes, and with the bitterest remorse at my heart – hung it *because* I knew that it had loved me, and *because* I felt it had given me no reason of offence hung it *because* I knew that in so doing I was committing a sin – a deadly sin that would so jeopardize my immortal soul as to place it – if such a thing were possible – even beyond the reach of the infinite mercy of the Most Merciful and Most Terrible God.

On the night of the day on which this most cruel deed was done, I was aroused from sleep by the cry of fire. The curtains of my bed were in flames. The whole house was blazing. It was with great difficulty that my wife, a servant, and myself, made our escape from the conflagration. The destruction was complete. My entire worldly wealth was swallowed up, and I resigned myself thenceforward to despair.

I am above the weakness of seeking to establish a sequence of cause and effect, between the disaster and the atrocity. But I am detailing a chain of facts – and wish not to leave even a possible link imperfect. On the day succeeding the fire, I visited the ruins. The walls, with one exception, had fallen in. This exception was found in a compartment wall, not very thick, which stood about the middle of the house, and against which had rested the head of my bed. The plastering had here, in great measure, resisted the action of the fire – a fact which I attributed to its having been recently spread. About this wall a dense crowd were collected, and many persons seemed to be examining a particular portion of it with very minute and eager attention. The words 'strange!' 'singular!' and other similar expressions, excited my curiosity. I approached and saw, as if graven in bas-relief upon the white surface, the figure of a gigantic *cat*. The impression was given with an accuracy truly marvellous. There was a rope about the animal's neck.

When I first beheld this apparition – for I could scarcely regard it as less – my wonder and my terror were extreme. But at length reflection came to my aid. The cat, I remembered, had been hung in a garden adjacent to the house. Upon the alarm of fire, this garden had been immediately filled by the crowd – by some one of whom the animal must have been cut from the tree and thrown, through an open window, into my chamber. This had probably been done with the view of arousing me from sleep. The falling of other walls had compressed the victim of my cruelty into the substance of the freshly spread plaster; the lime of which, with the flames, and the ammonia from the carcass, had then accomplished the portraiture as I saw it.

Although I thus readily accounted to my reason, if not altogether to my conscience, for the startling fact just detailed, it did not the less fail to make a deep impression upon my fancy. For months I could not rid myself of the phantasm of the cat; and, during this period, there came back into my spirit a half-sentiment that seemed, but was not, remorse. I went so far as to regret the loss of the animal, and to look about me, among the vile haunts which I now habitually frequented, for another pet of the same species, and of somewhat similar appearance, with which to supply its place.

One night as I sat, half stupefied, in a den of more than infamy, my attention was suddenly drawn to some black object, reposing upon the head of one of the immense hogsheads of gin, or of rum, which constituted the chief furniture of the apartment. I had been looking steadily at the top of this hogshead for some minutes, and what now caused me surprise was the fact that I had not sooner perceived the object thereupon. I approached it, and touched it with my hand. It was a black cat – a very large one – fully as large as Pluto, and closely resembling him in every respect but one. Pluto had not a white hair upon any portion of his body; but this cat had a large, although indefinite splotch of white, covering nearly the whole region of the breast.

Upon my touching him, he immediately arose, purred loudly, rubbed against my hand, and appeared delighted with my notice. This, then, was the very creature of which I was in search. I at once offered to purchase it of the landlord; but this person made no claim to it – knew nothing of it – had never seen it before.

I continued my caresses, and when I prepared to go home, the animal evinced a disposition to accompany me. I permitted it to do so; occasionally stooping and patting it as I proceeded. When it reached the house it domesticated itself at once, and became immediately a great favourite with my wife.

For my own part, I soon found a dislike to it arising within me. This was just the reverse of what I had anticipated; but – I knew not how or why it was – its evident fondness for myself rather disgusted and annoyed me. By slow degrees these feelings of disgust and annoyance rose into the bitterness of hatred. I avoided the creature; a certain sense of shame, and the remembrance of my former deed of cruelty, preventing me from physically abusing it. I did not, for some weeks, strike, or otherwise violently ill use it; but gradually – very gradually – I came to look upon it with unutterable loathing, and to flee silently from its odious presence, as from the breath of a pestilence.

What added, no doubt, to my hatred of the beast, was the discovery, on the morning after I brought it home, that, like Pluto, it also had been deprived of one of its eyes. This circumstance, however, only endeared it to my wife, who, as I have already said, possessed, in a high degree, that humanity of feeling which had once been my distinguishing trait, and the source of many of my simplest and purest pleasures.

With my aversion to this cat, however, its partiality for myself seemed to increase. It followed my footsteps with a pertinacity which it would be difficult to make the reader comprehend. Whenever I sat, it would crouch beneath my chair, or spring upon my knees, covering me with its loathsome caresses. If I arose to walk it would get between my feet and thus nearly throw me down, or, fastening its long and sharp claws in my dress, clamber, in this manner, to my breast. At such times, although I longed to destroy it with a blow, I was yet withheld from so doing, partly by a memory of my former crime, but chiefly – let me confess it at once – by absolute *dread* of the beast.

This dread was not exactly a dread of physical evil – and yet I should be at a loss how otherwise to define it. I am almost ashamed to own – yes, even in this felon's cell, I am almost ashamed to own – that the terror and horror with which the animal inspired me, had been heightened by one of the merest chimeras it would be possible to conceive. My wife had called my attention, more than once, to the character of the mark of white hair, of which I have spoken, and which constituted the sole visible difference between the strange beast and the one I had destroyed. The reader will remember that this mark, although large, had been originally very indefinite; but, by slow degrees – degrees nearly imperceptible, and which for a long time my reason struggled to reject as fanciful – it had, at length, assumed a rigorous distinctness of outline. It was now the representation of an object that I shudder to name – and for this, above all, I loathed, and dreaded, and would have rid myself of the monster *had I dared* – it was now, I say, the image of a hideous – of a ghastly thing – of the *Gallows*! – oh, mournful and terrible engine of Horror and of Crime – of Agony and of Death!

And now was I indeed wretched beyond the wretchedness of mere Humanity. And a *brute beast* – whose fellow I had contemptuously destroyed – *a brute beast* to work out for *me* – for me, a man fashioned in the image of the High God – so much of insufferable woe! Alas! neither by day nor by night knew I the blessing of rest any more! During the former the creature left me no moment alone, and in the latter I started hourly from dreams of unutterable fear to find the hot breath of *the thing* upon my face, and its vast weight – an incarnate nightmare that I had no power to shake off – incumbent eternally upon my *heart*!

Beneath the pressure of torments such as these the feeble remnant of the good within me succumbed. Evil thoughts became my sole intimates – the darkest and most evil of thoughts. The moodiness of my usual temper increased to hatred of all things and of all mankind; while from the sudden, frequent, and ungovernable outbursts of a fury to which I now blindly abandoned myself, my uncomplaining wife, alas, was the most usual and the most patient of sufferers.

One day she accompanied me, upon some household errand, into the cellar of the old building which our poverty compelled us to inhabit. The cat followed me down the steep stairs, and, nearly throwing me headlong, exasperated me to madness. Uplifting an axe, and forgetting in my wrath the childish dread which had hitherto stayed my hand, I aimed a blow at the animal, which, of course, would have proved instantly fatal had it descended as I wished. But this blow was arrested by the hand of my wife. Goaded by the interference into a rage more than demoniacal, I withdrew my arm from her grasp and buried the axe in her brain. She fell dead upon the spot without a groan.

This hideous murder accomplished, I set myself forthwith, and with entire deliberation, to the task of concealing the body. I knew that I could not remove it from the house, either by day or by night, without the risk of being observed by the neighbours. Many projects entered my mind. At one period I thought of cutting the corpse into minute fragments, and destroying them by fire. At another, I resolved to dig a grave for it in the floor of the cellar. Again, I deliberated about casting it in the well in the yard – about packing it in a box, as if merchandise, with the usual arrangements, and so getting a porter to take it from the house. Finally I hit upon what I considered a far better expedient than either of these. I determined to wall it up in the cellar, as the monks of the Middle Ages are recorded to have walled up their victims.

For a purpose such as this the cellar was well adapted. Its walls were loosely constructed, and had lately been plastered throughout with a rough plaster, which the dampness of the atmosphere had prevented from hardening. Moreover, in one of the walls was a projection, caused by a false chimney, or fireplace, that had been filled up and made to resemble the rest of the cellar. I made no doubt that I could readily displace the bricks at this point, insert the corpse, and wall the whole up as before, so that no eye could detect anything suspicious.

And in this calculation I was not deceived. By means of a crowbar I easily dislodged the bricks, and, having carefully deposited the body against the inner wall, I propped it in that position, while with little trouble I relaid the whole structure as it originally stood. Having procured mortar, sand and hair, with every possible precaution, I prepared a plaster which could not be distinguished from the old and with this I very carefully went over the new brickwork. When I had finished, I felt satisfied that all was right. The wall did not present the slightest appearance of having been disturbed. The rubbish on the floor was picked up with the minutest care. I looked around triumphantly, and said to myself: 'Here at least, then, my labour has not been in vain.'

My next step was to look for the beast which had been the cause of so much wretchedness; for I had, at length, firmly resolved to put it to death. Had I been able to meet with it at the moment, there could have been no doubt of its fate; but it appeared that the crafty animal had been alarmed at the violence of my previous anger, and forbore to present itself in my present mood. It is impossible to describe or to imagine the deep, the blissful sense of relief which the absence of the detested creature occasioned in my bosom. It did not make its appearance during the night; and thus for one night, at least, since its introduction into the house, I soundly and tranquilly slept; aye, *slept* even with the burden of murder upon my soul.

The second and the third day passed, and still my tormentor came not. Once again I breathed as a free man. The monster, in terror, had fled the premises for ever! I should behold it no more! My happiness was supreme! The guilt of my dark deed disturbed me but little. Some few inquiries had been made, but these had been readily answered. Even a search had been instituted – but of course nothing was to be discovered. I looked upon my future felicity as secured.

Upon the fourth day of the assassination, a party of the police came, very unexpectedly, into the house, and proceeded again to make rigorous investigation of the premises. Secure, however, in the inscrutability of my place of concealment, I felt no embarrassment whatever. The officers bade me accompany them in their search. They left no nook or corner unexplored. At length, for the third or fourth time, they descended into the cellar. I quivered not in a muscle. My heart beat calmly as that of one who slumbers in innocence. I walked the cellar from end to end. I folded my arms upon my bosom, and roamed easily to and fro. The police were thoroughly satisfied and prepared to depart. The glee at my heart was too strong to be restrained. I burned to say if but one word, by way of triumph, and to render doubly sure their assurance of my guiltlessness.

'Gentlemen,' I said at last, as the party ascended the steps, 'I delight to have allayed your suspicions. I wish you all health and a little more courtesy. By the bye, gentlemen, this – this is a very well-constructed house' (in the rabid desire to say something easily, I scarcely knew what I uttered at all) – 'I may say an *excellently* well-constructed house. These walls – are you going, gentleman? – these walls are solidly put together'; and here, through the mere frenzy of bravado, I rapped heavily with a cane which I held in my hand, upon that very portion of the brickwork behind which stood the corpse of the wife of my bosom.

But may God shield and deliver me from the fangs of the Arch-Fiend! No sooner had the reverberation of my blows sunk into silence, than I was answered by a voice from within the tomb! – by a cry, at first muffled and broken, like the sobbing of a child, and then quickly swelling into one long, loud and continuous scream, utterly anomalous and inhuman – a howl – a wailing shriek, half of horror and half of triumph, such as might have arisen only out of hell, conjointly from the throats of the damned in their agony and of the demons that exult in the damnation.

Of my own thoughts it is folly to speak. Swooning, I staggered to the opposite wall. For one instant the party on the stairs remained motionless, through extremity of terror and awe. In the next a dozen stout arms were toiling at the wall. It fell bodily. The corpse, already greatly decayed and clotted with gore, stood erect before the eyes of the spectators. Upon its head, with red extended mouth and solitary eye of fire, sat the hideous beast whose craft had seduced me into murder, and whose informing voice had consigned me to the hangman. I had walled the monster up within the tomb.

from *Works of Edgar Allan Poe* (1874)

THE VAMPIRE CAT OF NABÉSHIMA

Lord Redesdale (1837–1916)

There is a tradition in the Nabéshima family that, many years ago, the Prince of Hizen was bewitched and cursed by a cat that had been kept by one of his retainers. This prince had in his house a lady of rare beauty, called O Toyo: amongst all his ladies she was the favourite, and there was none who could rival her charms and accomplishments. One day the Prince went out into the garden with O Toyo, and remained enjoying the fragrance of the flowers until sunset, when they returned to the palace, never noticing that they were being followed by a large cat. Having parted with her lord, O Toyo retired to her own room and went to bed. At midnight she awoke with a start, and became aware of a huge cat that crouched watching her; and when she cried out, the beast sprang on her, and, fixing its cruel teeth in her delicate throat, throttled her to death. What a piteous end for so fair a dame, the darling of her prince's heart, to die suddenly, bitten to death by cat! Then the cat, having scratched out a grave under the verandah, buried the corpse of O Toyo, and assuming her form, began to bewitch the Prince.

But my lord the Prince knew nothing of all this, and little thought that the beautiful creature who caressed and fondled him was an impish and foul beast that had slain his mistress and assumed her shape in order to drain out his life's blood. Day by day, as time went on, the Prince's strength dwindled away; the colour of his face was changed, and became pale and livid; and he was as a man suffering from a deadly sickness. Seeing this, his councillors and his wife became greatly alarmed; so they summoned the physicians, who prescribed various remedies for him; but the more medicine he took, the more serious did his illness appear, and no treatment was of any avail. But most of all did he suffer in the night-time, when his sleep would be troubled and disturbed by hideous dreams. In consequence of this, his councillors nightly appointed a hundred of his retainers to sit up and watch over him; but, strange to say, towards ten o'clock on the very first night that the watch was set, the guard were seized with a sudden and unaccountable drowsiness, which they could not resist, until one by one every man had fallen asleep. Then the false O Toyo came in and harassed the Prince until morning. The following night the same thing occurred, and the Prince was subjected to the imp's tyranny, while his guards slept helplessly around him. Night after night this was repeated, until at last three of the Prince's councillors determined themselves to sit up on guard, and see whether they could overcome this mysterious drowsiness; but they fared no better than the others, and by ten o'clock were fast asleep. The next day the three councillors held a solemn conclave, and their chief, one Isahaya Buzen, said –

'This is a marvellous thing, that a guard of a hundred men should thus be overcome by sleep. Of a surety, the spell that is upon my lord and upon his guard must be the work of witchcraft. Now, as all our efforts are of no avail, let us seek out Ruiten, the chief priest of the temple called Miyô In, and beseech him to put up prayers for the recovery of my lord.'

And the other councillors approving what Isahaya Buzen had said, they went to the priest Ruiten and engaged him to recite litanies that the Prince might be restored to health.

So it came to pass that Ruiten, the chief priest of Miyô In, offered up prayers nightly for the Prince. One night, at the ninth hour (midnight), when he had finished his religious exercises and was preparing to lie down to sleep, he fancied that he heard a noise outside in the garden, as if someone were washing himself at the well. Deeming this passing strange, he looked down from the window; and there in the moonlight he saw a handsome young soldier, some twenty-four years of age, washing himself, who, when he had finished cleaning himself and had put on his clothes, stood before the figure of Buddha and prayed fervently for the recovery of my lord the Prince. Ruiten looked on with admiration; and the young man, when he had made an end of his prayer, was going away; but the priest stopped him, calling out to him –

'Sir, I pray you to tarry a little: I have something to say to you.'

'At your reverence's service. What may you please to want?'

'Pray be so good as to step up here, and have a little talk.'

'By your reverence's leave'; and with this he went upstairs. Then Ruiten said –

'Sir, I cannot conceal my admiration that you, being so young a man, should have so loyal a spirit. I am Ruiten, the chief priest of this temple, who am engaged in praying for the recovery of my lord. Pray what is your name?'

'My name, sir, is Itô Sôda, and I am serving in the infantry of Nabéshima. Since my lord has been sick, my one desire has been to assist in nursing him; but, being only a simple soldier, I am not of sufficient rank to come into his presence, so I have no resource but to pray to the gods of the country and to Buddha that my lord may regain his health.'

When Ruiten heard this, he shed tears in admiration of the fidelity of Itô Sôda, and said –

'Your purpose is, indeed, a good one; but what a strange sickness this is that my lord is afflicted with! Every night he suffers from horrible dreams; and the retainers who sit up with him are all seized with a mysterious sleep, so that not one can keep awake. It is very wonderful.'

'Yes,' replied Sôda, after a moment's reflection, 'this certainly must be witchcraft. If I could but obtain leave to sit up one night with the Prince, I would fain see whether I could not resist this drowsiness and detect the goblin.'

At last the priest said, 'I am in relations of friendship with Isahaya Buzen, the chief councillor of the Prince. I will speak to him of you and of your loyalty, and will intercede with him that you may attain your wish.'

'Indeed, sir, I am most thankful. I am not prompted by any vain thought of self-advancement, should I succeed: all I wish for is the recovery of my lord. I commend myself to your kind favour.'

'Well, then, tomorrow night I will take you with me to the councillor's house.'

'Thank you, sir, and farewell.' And so they parted.

On the following evening Itô Sôda returned to the temple Miyô In, and having found Ruiten, accompanied him to the house of Isahaya Buzen: then the priest, leaving Sôda outside, went in to converse with the councillor, and inquire after the Prince's health.

'And pray, sir, how is my lord? Is he in any better condition since I have been offering up prayers for him?'

'Indeed, no; his illness is very severe. We are certain that he must be the victim of some foul sorcery; but as there are no means of keeping a guard awake after ten o'clock, we cannot catch a sight of the goblin, so we are in the greatest trouble.'

'I feel deeply for you: it must be most distressing. However, I have something to tell you. I think that I have found a man who will detect the goblin; and I have brought him with me.'

'Indeed! Who is the man?'

'Well, he is one of my lord's foot-soldiers, named Itô Sôda, a faithful fellow, and I trust that you will grant his request to be permitted to sit up with my lord.'

'Certainly, it is wonderful to find so much loyalty and zeal in a common soldier,' replied Isahaya Buzen, after a moment's reflection; 'still it is impossible to allow a man of such low rank to perform the office of watching over my lord.'

'It is true that he is but a common soldier,' urged the priest; 'but why not raise his rank in consideration of his fidelity, and then let him mount guard?'

'It would be time enough to promote him after my lord's recovery. But come, let me see this Itô Sôda, that I may know what manner of man he is: if he pleases me, I will consult with the other councillors, and perhaps we may grant his request.'

'I will bring him in forthwith,' replied Ruiten, who thereupon went out to fetch the young man.

When he returned, the priest presented Itô Sôda to the councillor, who looked at him attentively, and, being pleased with his comely and gentle appearance, said –

'So I hear that you are anxious to be permitted to mount guard in my lord's room at night. Well, I must consult with the other councillors, and we will see what can be done for you.'

When the young soldier heard this he was greatly elated, and took his leave, after warmly thanking Ruiten, who had helped him to gain his object. The next day the councillors held a meeting, and sent for Itô Sôda, and told him that he might keep watch with the other retainers that very night. So he went his way in high spirits, and at nightfall, having made all his preparations, took his place among the hundred gentlemen who were on duty in the prince's bedroom.

Now the Prince slept in the centre of the room, and the hundred guards around him sat keeping themselves awake with entertaining conversation and pleasant conceits. But, as ten o'clock approached, they began to doze off as they sat; and in spite of all their endeavours to keep one another awake, by degrees they all fell asleep. Itô Sôda all this while felt an irresistible desire to sleep creeping over him, and, though he tried by all sorts of ways to rouse himself, he saw that there was no help for it, but by resorting to an extreme measure, for which he had already made his preparations. Drawing out a piece of oil paper which he had brought with him, and spreading it over the mats, he sat down upon it; then he took the small knife which he carried in the sheath of his dirk, and stuck it into his own thigh. For awhile the pain of the wound kept him awake; but as the slumber by which he was assailed was the work of sorcery, little by little he became drowsy again. Then he twisted the knife round and round in his thigh, so that the pain becoming very violent, he was proof against the feeling of sleepiness, and kept a faithful watch. Now the oil paper which he had spread under his leg was in order to prevent the blood, which might spurt from his wound, from defiling the mats.

So Itô Sôda remained awake, but the rest of the guard slept; and as he watched, suddenly the sliding-doors of the Prince's room were drawn open, and he saw a figure coming in stealthily, and, as it drew nearer, the form was that of a marvellously beautiful woman some twenty-three years of age. Cautiously she looked around her; and when she saw that all the guard were asleep, she smiled an ominous smile, and was going up to the Prince's bedside, when she perceived that in one corner of the room there was a man yet awake. This seemed to startle her, but she went up to Sôda and said –

'I am not used to seeing you here. Who are you?'

'My name is Itô Sôda, and this is the first night that I have been on guard.'

'A troublesome office, truly! Why, here are all the rest of the guard asleep. How is it that you alone are awake? You are a trusty watchman.'

'There is nothing to boast about. I'm asleep myself, fast and sound.'

'What is that wound on your knee? It is all red with blood.'

'Oh! I felt very sleepy; so I stuck my knife into my thigh, and the pain of it has kept me awake.'

'What wondrous loyalty!' said the lady.

'Is it not the duty of a retainer to lay down his life for his master? Is such a scratch as this worth thinking about?'

Then the lady went up to the sleeping Prince and said, 'How fares it with my lord to-night?' But the Prince, worn out with sickness, made no reply. But Sôda was watching her eagerly, and guessed that it was O Toyo, and made up his mind that if she attempted to harass the Prince he would kill her on the spot. The goblin, however, which in the form of O Toyo had been tormenting the Prince every night, and had come again that night for no other purpose, was defeated by the watchfulness of Itô Sôda; for whenever she drew near to the sick man, thinking to put her spells upon him, she would turn and look behind her, and there she saw Itô Sôda glaring at her; so she had no help for it but to go away again, and leave the Prince undisturbed.

At last the day broke, and the other officers, when they awoke and opened their eyes, saw that Itô Sôda had kept awake by stabbing himself in the thigh; and they were greatly ashamed, and went home crestfallen.

That morning Itô Sôda went to the house of Isahaya Buzen, and told him all that had occurred the previous night. The councillors were all loud in their praise of Itô Sôda's behaviour, and ordered him to keep watch again that night. At the same hour, the false O Toyo came and looked all round the room, and all the guard were asleep, excepting Itô Sôda, who was wide awake; and so, being again frustrated, she returned to her own apartments.

Now as since Sôda had been on guard the Prince had passed quiet nights, his sickness began to get better, and there was great joy in the palace, and Sôda was promoted and rewarded with an estate. In the meanwhile O Toyo, seeing that her nightly visits bore no fruits, kept away; and from that time forth the night-guard were no longer subject to fits of drowsiness. This coincidence struck Sôda as very strange, so he went to Isahaya Buzen and told him that of a certainty this O Toyo was no other than a goblin. Isahaya Buzen reflected for a while, and said –

'Well, then, how shall we kill the foul thing?'

'I will go to the creature's room, as if nothing were the matter, and try to kill her; but in case she should try to escape, I will beg you to order eight men to stop outside and lie in wait for her.'

Having agreed upon this plan, Sôda went at nightfall to O Toyo's apartment, pretending to have been sent with a message from the Prince. When she saw him arrive, she said –

'What message have you brought me from my lord?'

'Oh! nothing in particular. Be so good as to look at this letter; and as he spoke, he drew near to her, and suddenly drawing his dirk cut at her; but the goblin, springing back, seized a halberd, and glaring fiercely at Sôda, said –

'How dare you behave like this to one of your lord's ladies? I will have you dismissed'; and she tried to strike Sôda with the halberd. But Sôda fought desperately with his dirk; and the goblin, seeing that she was no match for him, threw away the halberd, and from a beautiful woman became suddenly transformed into a cat, which, springing up the sides of the room, jumped on to the roof. Isahaya Buzen and his eight men who were watching outside shot at the cat, but missed it, and the beast made good its escape.

So the cat fled to the mountains, and did much mischief among the surrounding people, until at last the Prince of Hizen ordered a great hunt, and the beast was killed.

But the Prince recovered from his sickness; and Itô Sôda was richly rewarded.

from Tales of Old Japan (1871)

LADY JANE

Charles Dickens (1812–70)

'Hi, Lady Jane!'

A large grey cat leapt from some neighbouring shelf on his shoulder, and startled us all.

'Hi! Show 'em how you scratch. Hi! Tear, my lady!" said her master.

The cat leaped down, and ripped at a bundle of rags with her tigerish claws, with a sound that it set my teeth on edge to hear.

'She'd do as much for anyone I was to set her on,' said the old man. 'I deal in cat-skins among other general matters, and hers was offered to me. It's a very fine skin, as you may see, but I didn't have it stripped off! *That* warn't like Chancery practice though, says you!'

He had by this time led us across the shop, and now opened a door in the back part of it, leading to the house-entry. As he stood with his hand upon the lock, the little old lady graciously observed to him before passing out: 'That will do, Krook. You mean well, but are tiresome.' [...]

She lived at the top of the house, in a pretty large room, from which she had a glimpse of Lincoln's Inn Hall. [...] She partly drew aside the curtain of the long low garret-window, and called our attention to a number of birdcages hanging there: some, containing several birds. There were larks, linnets, and gold-finches – I should think at least twenty. [...]

We all draw nearer to the cages, feigning to examine the birds.

'I can't allow them to sing much,' said the little old lady, 'for (you'll think this curious) I find my mind confused by the idea that they are singing, while I am following the arguments in Court. And my mind requires to be so very clear, you know! Another time, I'll tell you their names. Not at present. On a day of such good omen, they shall sing as much as they like. In honour of youth,' a smile and curtsey, 'hope', a smile and curtsey, 'and beauty', a smile and curtsey. 'There! We'll let in the full light.'

The birds began to stir and chirp.

'I cannot admit the air freely,' said the little old lady – the room was close, and would have been the better for it – 'because the cat you saw downstairs – called Lady Jane – is greedy for their lives. She crouches on the parapet outside for hours and hours. I have discovered,' whispering mysteriously, 'that her natural cruelty is sharpened by a jealous fear of their regaining their liberty. In consequence of the judgment I expect being shortly given. She is sly, and full of malice. I half believe, sometimes, that she is no cat, but the wolf of the old saying. It is so very difficult to keep her from the door.' [...]

Passing through the shop on our way out, as we had passed through it on our way in, we found the old man storing a quantity of packets of waste paper, in a kind of well in the floor. He seemed to be working hard, with the perspiration standing on his forehead, and had a piece of chalk by him; with which, as he put each separate package or bundle down, he made a crooked mark on the panelling of the wall.

Richard and Ada, and Miss Jellyby, and the little old lady had gone by him, and I was going, when he touched me on the arm to stay me, and chalked the letter J upon the wall – in a very curious manner, beginning with the end of the letter, and shaping it backward. It was a capital letter, not a printed one, but just such a letter as any clerk in Messrs Kenge and Carboy's office would have made.

'Can you read it?' he asked me with a keen glance.

'Surely,' said I. 'It's very plain.'

'What is it?'

'J.'

With another glance at me, and a glance at the door, he rubbed it out, and turned an *a* in its place (not a capital letter this time) and said, 'What's that?'

I told him. He then rubbed that out, and turned the letter r, and asked me the same question. He went on quickly until he had formed, in the same curious manner, beginning at the ends and bottoms of the letters, the word *Jarndyce*, without once leaving two letters on the wall together.

'What does that spell?' he asked me.

When I told him, he laughed. In the same odd way, yet with the same rapidity, he then produced singly, and rubbed out singly, the letters forming the words *Bleak House*. These, in some astonishment, I also read; and he laughed again.

'Hi!' said the old man, laying aside the chalk, 'I have a turn for copying from memory, you see, miss, though I can neither read nor write.'

He looked so disagreeable, and his cat looked so wickedly at me, as if I were a blood-relation of the birds upstairs, that I was quite relieved by Richard's appearing at the door and saying: 'Miss Summerson, I hope you are not bargaining for the sale of your hair. Don't be tempted. Three sacks below are quite enough for Mr Krook!'

I lost no time in wishing Mr Krook good morning, and joining my friends outside, where we parted with the little old lady, who gave us her blessing with great ceremony, and renewed her assurance of yesterday in reference to her intention of settling estates on Ada and me. Before we finally turned out of those lanes, we looked back, and saw Mr Krook standing at his shop-door, in his spectacles, looking after us, with his cat upon his shoulder, and her tail sticking up on one side of his hairy cap, like a tall feather.

from *Bleak House* (1852–3)

THE SEA-CAT

St Brendan (c.484–c.577)

After this they rowed for a while over the ocean in a westerly direction, and found a pleasant little island with a number of fishermen in it. As they were going round it they saw in it a little stone church, in which was an aged man, pale and sorrowful, engaged in prayer. And he had neither flesh nor blood, but merely a thin miserable skin over his hard and yellow bones. Then that elder said: 'Flee, Brendan, with all speed,' said he. 'For there is here now a sea-cat as big as a young ox or a three-year-old horse, which has thriven on the fish of the sea and of this island; beware of it now.'

They betake them to their boat, and row over the ocean with all their might. As they were thus, they saw the monstrous sea-cat swimming after them; each of its two eyes was as big as a cauldron, it had tusks like a boar, sharp-pointed bristles, the maw of a leopard, the strength of a lion, and the rage of a mad dog. Then each of them began to pray to God by reason of the great fear which seized them. Then said Brendan: 'O God Almighty,' said he, 'keep off Thy monsters from us, that they may not reach us.'

Then a great sea-whale rose up between them and the cat-monster, and each of them set to work to try and drown the other in the depths of the sea, and neither of them ever appeared again. Then Brendan and his company gave thanks to God, and turned back again to the place where the elder was. And the elder wept for the greatness of the joy which possessed him, and said: 'I am of the men of Erin,' said he, 'and twelve of us were there when we came on our pilgrimage, and we brought that bestial sea-cat with us, and we were very fond of it; and it grew afterwards enormously, but it never hurt any of us. And now of our original company eleven have died, and I am left alone, waiting for thee to give me the body and blood of Christ, that therewith I may go to heaven.'

He revealed to them afterwards the little country which they were seeking, that is the *Land of Promise*. And after receiving the body and blood of Christ, the elder went to heaven. He was buried there beside his brethren with great reverence, and with psalms and hymns, in the name of the Father, and of the Son, and of the Holy Ghost.

from *The Voyage of St Brendan*

THE DEMON CAT

Lady Wilde (1826–96)

There was a woman in Connemara, the wife of a fisherman; as he had always good luck, she had plenty of fish at all times stored away in the house ready for market. But, to her great annoyance, she found that a great cat used to come in at night and devour all the best and finest fish. So she kept a big stick by her, and determined to watch.

One day, as she and a woman were spinning together, the house suddenly became quite dark; and the door was burst open as if by the blast of the tempest, when in walked a huge black cat, who went straight up to the fire, then turned round and growled at them.

'Why, surely this is the devil,' said a young girl, who was by, sorting fish.

'I'll teach you how to call me names,' said the cat; and, jumping at her, he scratched her arm till the blood came. 'There, now,' he said, 'you will be more civil another time when a gentleman comes to see you.' And with that he walked over to the door and shut it close, to prevent any of them going out, for the poor young girl, while crying loudly from fright and pain, had made a desperate rush to get away.

Just then a man was going by, and hearing the cries, he pushed open the door and tried to get in; but the cat stood on the threshold, and would let no one pass. On this the man attacked him with his stick, and gave him a sound blow; the cat, however, was more than a match in the fight, for it flew at him and tore his face and hands so badly that the man at last took to his heels and ran away as fast as he could.

'Now, it's time for my dinner,' said the cat, going up to examine the fish that was laid out on the tables. 'I hope the fish is good today. Now, don't disturb me, nor make a fuss; I can help myself.' With that he jumped up, and began to devour all the best fish, while he growled at the woman.

'Away, out of this, you wicked beast,' she cried, giving it a blow with the tongs that would have broken its back, only it was a devil; 'out of this; no fish shall you have today.'

But the cat only grinned at her, and went on tearing and spoiling and devouring the fish, evidently not a bit the worse for the blow. On this, both the women attacked it with sticks, and struck hard blows enough to kill it, on which the cat glared at them, and spit fire; then making a leap, it tore their heads and arms till the blood came, and the frightened women rushed shrieking from the house.

But presently the mistress returned, carrying with her a bottle of holy water; and, looking in, she saw the cat still devouring the fish, and not minding. So she crept over quietly and threw holy water on it without a word. No sooner was this done than a dense black smoke filled the place, through which nothing was seen but the two red eyes of the cat, burning like coals of fire. Then the smoke gradually cleared away, and she saw the body of the creature burning slowly till it became shrivelled and black like a cinder, and finally disappeared. And from that time the fish remained untouched and safe from harm, for the power of the evil one was broken, and the demon cat was seen no more.

THE SQUAW

Bram Stoker (1847–1912)

Nurnberg at the time was not so much exploited as it has been since then. Irving had not been playing *Faust*, and the very name of the old town was hardly known to the great bulk of the travelling public. My wife and I being in the second week of our honeymoon, naturally wanted someone else to join our party, so that when the cheery stranger, Elias P. Hutcheson, hailing from Isthmian City, Bleeding Gulch, Maple Tree County, Nebraska, turned up at the station at Frankfurt, and casually remarked that he was going on to see the most all-fired old Methuselah of a town in Yurrup, and that he guessed that so much travelling alone was enough to send an intelligent, active citizen into the melancholy ward of a daft house, we took the pretty broad hint and suggested that we should join forces. We found, on comparing notes afterwards, that we had each intended to speak with some diffidence or hesitation so as not to appear too eager, such not being a good compliment to the success of our married life; but the effect was entirely marred by our both beginning to speak at the same instant – stopping simultaneously and then going on together again. Anyhow, no matter how, it was done; and Elias P. Hutcheson became one of our party. Straightway Amelia and I found the pleasant benefit; instead of quarrelling, as we had been doing, we found that the restraining influence of a third party was such that we now took every opportunity of spooning in odd corners. Amelia declares that ever since she has, as the result of that experience, advised all her friends to take a friend on the honeymoon. Well, we 'did' Nurnberg together, and much enjoyed the racy remarks of our Transatlantic friend, who, from his quaint speech and his wonderful stock of adventures, might have stepped out of a novel. We kept for the last object of interest in the city to be visited the Burg, and on the day appointed for the visit strolled round the outer wall of the city by the eastern side.

The Burg is seated on a rock dominating the town, and an immensely deep fosse guards it on the northern side. Nurnberg has been happy in that it was never sacked: had it been it would certainly not be so spick and span perfect as it is at present. The ditch has not been used for centuries, and now its base is spread with tea-gardens and orchards, of which some of the trees are of quite respectable growth. As we wandered round the wall, dawdling in the hot July sunshine, we often paused to admire the views spread before us, and in especial the great plain covered with towns and villages and bounded with a blue line of hills, like a landscape of Claude Lorraine. From this we always turned with new delight to the city itself, with its myriad quaint old gables and acre-wide red roofs dotted with dormer windows, tier upon tier. A little to our right rose the towers of the Burg, and nearer still, standing grim, the Torture Tower, which was, and is, perhaps, the most interesting place in the city. For centuries the tradition of the Iron Virgin of Nurnberg has been handed down as an instance of the horrors of cruelty of which man is capable; we had long looked forward to seeing it; and here at last was its home.

In one of our pauses we leaned over the wall of the moat and looked down. The garden seemed quite fifty or sixty feet below us, and the sun pouring into it with an intense, moveless heat like that of an oven. Beyond rose the grey, grim wall seemingly of endless height, and losing itself right and left in the angles of bastion and counterscarp. Trees and bushes crowned the wall, and above again towered the lofty houses on whose massive beauty Time has only set the hand of approval. The sun was hot and we were lazy; time was our own, and we lingered, leaning on the wall. Just below us was a pretty sight – a great black cat lying stretched in the sun, whilst round her gambolled prettily a tiny black kitten. The mother would wave her tail for the kitten to play with, or would raise her feet and push away the little one as an encouragement to further play. They were just at the foot of the wall, and Elias P. Hutcheson, in order to help the play, stooped and took from the walk a moderate-sized pebble.

'See!' he said, 'I will drop it near the kitten, and they will both wonder where it came from.'

'Oh, be careful,' said my wife; 'you might hit the dear little thing!'

'Not me, ma'am,' said Elias P. 'Why, I'm as tender as a Maine cherry-tree. Lor, bless ye, I wouldn't hurt the poor pooty little critter more'n I'd scalp a baby. An' you may bet your variegated socks on that! See, I'll drop it fur away on the outside so's not to go near her!' Thus saying, he leaned over and held his arm out at full length and dropped the stone. It may be that there is some attractive force which draws lesser matters to greater; or more probably that the wall was not plumb but sloped to its base – we not noticing the inclination from above; but the stone fell with a sickening thud that came up to us through the hot air, right on the kitten's head, and shattered out its little brains then and there. The black cat cast a swift upward glance, and we saw her eyes like green fire fixed an instant on Elias P. Hutcheson; and then her attention was given to the kitten, which lay still with just a quiver of her tiny limbs, whilst a thin red stream trickled from a gaping wound. With a muffled cry, such as a human being might give, she bent over the kitten, licking its wound and moaning. Suddenly she seemed to realize that it was dead, and again threw her eyes up at us. I shall never forget the sight, for she looked the perfect incarnation of hate. Her green eyes blazed with lurid fire, and the white, sharp teeth seemed to almost shine through the blood which dabbled her mouth and whiskers. She gnashed her teeth, and her claws stood out stark and at full length on every paw. Then she made a wild rush up the wall as if to reach us, but when the momentum ended fell back, and further added to her horrible appearance for she fell on the kitten, and rose with her back fur smeared with its brains and blood. Amelia turned quite faint, and I had to lift her back from the wall.

There was a seat close by in shade of a spreading plane-tree, and here I placed her whilst she composed herself. Then I went back to Hutcheson, who stood without moving, looking down on the angry cat below.

As I joined him, he said: 'Wall, I guess that air the savagest beast I ever see – 'cept once when an Apache squaw had an edge on a half-breed what they nicknamed "Splinters" 'cos of the way he fixed up her papoose which he stole on a raid just to show that he appreciated the way they had given his mother the fire torture. She got that kinder look so set on her face that it just seemed to grow there. She followed Splinters more'n three year till at last the braves got him and handed him over to her. They did say that no man, white or Injun, had ever been so long a-dying under the tortures of the Apaches. The only time I ever see her smile was when I wiped her out. I kem on the camp just in time to see Splinters pass in his checks, and he wasn't sorry to go either. He was a hard citizen, and though I never could shake with him after that papoose business – for it was bitter bad, and he should have been a white man, for he looked like one – I see he had got paid out in full. Durn me, but I took a piece of his hide from one of his skinnin' posts an had it made into a pocket-book. It's here now!' and he slapped the breast pocket of his coat.

Whilst he was speaking the cat was continuing her frantic efforts to get up the wall. She would take a run back and then charge up, sometimes reaching an incredible height. She did not seem to mind the heavy fall which she got each time but started with renewed vigour; and at every tumble her appearance became more horrible. Hutcheson was a kind-hearted man – my wife and I had both noticed little acts of kindness to animals as well as to persons – and he seemed concerned at the state of fury to which the cat had wrought herself.

'Wall now!' he said, 'I du declare that that poor critter seems quite desperate. There! there! poor thing, it was all an accident – though that won't bring back your little one to you. Say! I wouldn't have had such a thing happen for a thousand! Just shows what a clumsy fool of a man can do when he tries to play! Seems I'm too darned slipperhanded to even play with a cat. Say, Colonel!' – it was a pleasant way he had to bestow titles freely – 'I hope your wife don't hold no grudge against me on account of this unpleasantness? Why, I wouldn't have had it occur on no account.'

He came over to Amelia and apologized profusely, and she with her usual kindness of heart hastened to assure him that she quite understood that it was an accident. Then we all went again to the wall and looked over.

The cat, missing Hutcheson's face, had drawn back across the moat, and was sitting on her haunches as though ready to spring. Indeed, the very instant she saw him she did spring, and with a blind unreasoning fury, which would have been grotesque, only that it was so frightfully real. She did not try to run up the wall, but simply launched herself at him as though hate and fury could lend her wings to pass straight through the great distance between them. Amelia, womanlike, got quite concerned, and said to Elias P. in a warning voice: 'Oh! you must be very careful. That animal would try to kill you if she were here; her eyes look like positive murder.'

He laughed out jovially. 'Excuse me, ma'am,' he said, 'but I can't help laughin'. Fancy a man that has fought grizzlies an' Injuns bein' careful of bein' murdered by a cat!'

When the cat heard him laugh, her whole demeanour seemed to change. She no longer tried to jump or run up the wall, but went quietly over, and sitting again beside the dead kitten began to lick and fondle it as though it were alive.

'See!' said I, 'the effect of a really strong man. Even that animal in the midst of her fury recognizes the voice of a master, and bows to him!'

'Like a squaw!' was the only comment of Elias P. Hutcheson, as we moved on our way round the city fosse. Every now and then we looked over the wall and each time saw the cat following us. At first she had kept going back to the dead kitten, and then as the distance grew greater took it in her mouth and so followed. After a while, however, she abandoned this, for we saw her following all alone; she had evidently hidden the body somewhere. Amelia's alarm grew at the cat's persistence, and more than once she repeated her warning; but the American always laughed with amusement, till finally, seeing that she was beginning to be worried, he said: 'I say, ma'am, you needn't be skeered over that cat. I go heeled, I du!' Here he slapped his pistol pocket at the back of his lumbar region. 'Why, sooner'n have you worried, I'll shoot the critter, right here, an risk the police interferin' with a citizen of the United States for carryin' arms contrairy to reg'lations!' As he spoke he looked over the wall, but the cat, on seeing him, retreated, with a growl, into a bed of tall flowers, and was hidden. He went on: 'Blest if that ar critter ain't got more sense of what's good for her than most Christians. I guess we've seen the last of her! You bet, she'll go back now to that busted kitten and have a private funeral of it, all to herself!'

Amelia did not like to say more, lest he might, in mistaken kindness to her, fulfil his threat of shooting the cat: and so we went on and crossed the little wooden bridge leading to the gateway whence ran the steep paved roadway between the Burg and the pentagonal Torture Tower. As we crossed the bridge we saw the cat again down below us. When she saw us her fury seemed to return, and she made frantic efforts to get up the steep wall. Hutcheson laughed as he looked down at her, and said:

'Goodbye, old girl. Sorry I injured your feelin's, but you'll get over it in time! So long!' And then we passed through the long, dim archway and came to the gate of the Burg.

When we came out again after our survey of this most beautiful old place which not even the well-intended efforts of the Gothic restorers of forty years ago have been able to spoil – though their restoration was then glaring white – we seemed to have quite forgotten the unpleasant episode of the morning. The old lime tree with its great trunk gnarled with the passing of nearly nine centuries, the deep well cut through the heart of the rock by those captives of old, and the lovely view from the city wall whence we heard, spread over almost a full quarter of an hour, the multitudinous chimes of the city, had all helped to wipe out from our minds the incident of the slain kitten.

We were the only visitors who had entered the Torture Tower that morning – so at least said the old custodian – and as we had the place all to ourselves were able to make a minute and more satisfactory survey than would have otherwise been possible. The custodian, looking to us as the sole source of his gains for the day, was willing to meet our wishes in any way. The Torture Tower is truly a grim place, even now when many thousands of visitors have sent a stream of life, and the joy that follows life, into the place; but at the time I mention it wore its grimmest and most gruesome aspect. The dust of ages seemed to have settled on it, and the darkness and the horror of its memories seemed to have become sentient in a way that would have satisfied the Pantheistic souls of Philo or Spinoza. The lower chamber where we entered was seemingly, in its normal state, filled with incarnate darkness; even the hot sunlight streaming in through the door seemed to be lost in the vast thickness of the walls, and only showed the masonry rough as when the builder's scaffolding had come down, but coated with dust and marked here and there with patches of dark stain which, if walls could speak, could have given their own dread memories of fear and pain. We were glad to pass up the dusty wooden staircase, the custodian leaving the outer door open to light us somewhat on our way; for to our eyes the one long-wick'd, evil-smelling candle stuck in a sconce on the wall gave an inadequate light. When we came up through the open trap in the corner of the chamber overhead, Amelia held on to me so tightly that I could actually feel her heart beat. I must say for my own part that I was not surprised at her fear, for this room was even more gruesome than that below. Here there was certainly more light, but only just sufficient to realize the horrible surroundings of the place. The builders of the tower had evidently intended that only they who should gain the top should have any of the joys of light and prospect. There, as we had noticed from below, were ranges of windows, albeit of medieval smallness, but elsewhere in the tower were only a very few narrow slits such as were habitual in places of medieval defence. A few of these only lit the chamber, and these so high up in the wall that from no part could the sky be seen through the thickness of the walls. In racks, and leaning in disorder against the walls, were a number of headmen's swords, great double-handed weapons with broad blade and keen edge. Hard by were several blocks whereon the necks of the victims had lain, with here and there deep notches where the steel had bitten through the guard of flesh and shored into the wood. Round the chamber, placed in all sorts of irregular ways, were many implements of torture which made one's heart ache to see – chairs full of spikes which gave instant and excruciating pain; chairs and couches with dull knobs whose torture was seemingly less, but which, though slower, were equally efficacious; racks, belts, boots, gloves, collars, all made for compressing at will; steel baskets in which the head could be slowly crushed into a pulp if necessary; watchmen's hooks with long handle and knife that cut at resistance – this a speciality of the old Nurnberg police system; and many, many other devices for man's injury to man. Amelia grew quite pale with the horror of the things, but fortunately did not faint, for being a little overcome she sat down on a torture chair, but jumped up again with a shriek, all tendency to faint gone. We both pretended that it was the injury done to her dress by the dust of the chair, and the rusty spikes which had upset her, and Mr Hutcheson acquiesced in accepting the explanation with a kind-hearted laugh.

But the central object in the whole of this chamber of horrors was the engine known as the Iron Virgin, which stood near the centre of the room. It was a rudely shaped figure of a woman, something of the bell order, or, to make a closer comparison, of the figure of Mrs Noah in the children's Ark, but without that slimness of waist and perfect *rondeur* of hip which marks the aesthetic type of the Noah family. One would hardly have recognized it as intended for a human figure at all, had not the founder shaped on the forehead a rude semblance of a woman's face. This machine was coated with rust without, and covered with dust; a rope was fastened to a ring in the front of the figure, about where the waist should have been, and was drawn through a pulley, fastened on the wooden pillar which sustained the flooring above. The custodian pulling this rope showed that a section of the front was hinged like a door at one side; we then saw that the engine was of considerable thickness, leaving just room enough inside for a man to be placed. The door was of equal thickness and of great weight, for it took the custodian all his strength, aided though he was by the contrivance of the pulley, to open it. This weight was partly due to the fact that the door was of manifest purpose hung so as to throw its weight downwards, so that it might shut of its own accord when the strain was released. The inside was honey-combed with rust – nay more, the rust alone that comes through time would hardly have eaten so deep into the iron walls; the rust of the cruel stains was deep indeed! It was only, however, when we came to look at the inside of the door that the diabolical intention was manifest to the full. Here were several long spikes, square and massive, broad at the base and sharp at the points, placed in such a position that when the door should close the upper ones would pierce the eyes of the victim, and the lower ones his heart and vitals. The sight was too much for poor Amelia, and this time she fainted dead off, and I had to carry her down the stairs, and place her on a bench outside till she recovered. That she felt it to the quick was afterwards shown by the fact that my eldest son bears to this day a rude birthmark on his breast, which has, by family consent, been accepted as representing the Nurnberg Virgin.

When we got back to the chamber we found Hutcheson still opposite the Iron Virgin; he had been evidently philosophizing, and now gave us the benefit of his thought in the shape of a sort of exordium.

'Wall, I guess I've been learnin' somethin' here while madam has been gettin' over her faint. 'Pears to me that we're a long way behind the times on our side of the big drink. We uster think out on the plains that the Injun could give us points in tryin' to make a man oncomfortable; but I guess your old medieval law-and-order party could raise him every time. Splinters was pretty good in his bluff on the squaw, but this here young miss held a straight flush all high on him. The points of them spikes air sharp enough still, though even the edges air eaten out by what uster be on them. It'd be a good thing for our Indian section to get some specimens of this here play-toy to send round to the Reservations jest to knock the stuffin' out of the bucks, and the squaws too, by showing them as how old civilization lays over them at their best. Guess but I'll get in that box a minute jest to see how it feels!'

'Oh no! no!' said Amelia. 'It is too terrible!'

'Guess, ma'am, nothin's too terrible to the explorin' mind. I've been in some queer places in my time. Spent a night inside a dead horse while a prairie fire swept over me in Montana Territory – an' another time slept inside a dead buffler when the Comanches was on the war path an' I didn't keer to leave my kyard on them. I've been two days in a caved-in tunnel in the Billy Broncho gold mine in New Mexico, an' was one of the four shut up for three parts of a day in the caisson what slid over on her side when we was settin' the foundations of the Buffalo Bridge. I've not funked an odd experience yet, an' I don't propose to begin now!'

We saw that he was set on the experiment, so I said: 'Well, hurry up, old man, and get through it quick?'

'All right, General,' said he, 'but I calculate we ain't quite ready yet. The gentlemen, my predecessors, what stood in that thar canister, didn't volunteer for the office – not much! And I guess there was some ornamental tyin' up before the big stroke was made. I want to go into this thing fair and square, so I must get fixed up proper first. I dare say this old galoot can rise some string and tie me up accordin' to sample?'

This was said interrogatively to the old custodian, but the latter, who understood the drift of his speech, though perhaps not appreciating to the full the niceties of dialect and imagery, shook his head. His protest was, however, only formal and made to be overcome. The American thrust a gold piece into his hand, saying, 'Take it, pard! it's your pot; and don't be skeer'd. This ain't no necktie party that you're asked to assist in!' He produced some thin frayed rope and proceeded to bind our companion, with sufficient strictness for the purpose. When the upper part of his body was bound, Hutcheson said: 'Hold on a moment, Judge. Guess I'm too heavy for you to tote into the canister. You jest let me walk in, and then you can wash up regardin' my legs!'

Whilst speaking he had backed himself into the opening which was just enough to hold him. It was a close fit and no mistake. Amelia looked on with fear in her eyes, but she evidently did not like to say anything. Then the custodian completed his task by tying the American's feet together so that he was now absolutely helpless and fixed in his voluntary prison. He seemed to really enjoy it, and the incipient smile which was habitual to his face blossomed into actuality as he said: 'Guess this here Eve was made out of the rib of a dwarf! There ain't much room for a full-grown citizen of the United States to hustle. We uster make our coffins more roomier in Idaho territory. Now, Judge, you just begin to let this door down, slow, on to me. I want to feel the same pleasure as the other jays had when those spikes began to move toward their eyes!'

'Oh no! no! no!' broke in Amelia hysterically. 'It is too terrible ! I can't bear to see it! – I can't! I can't!'

But the American was obdurate. 'Say, Colonel,' said he, 'why not take Madame for a little promenade? I wouldn't hurt her feelin's for the world; but now that I am here, havin' kem eight thousand miles, wouldn't it be too hard to give up the very experience I've been pinin' an' pantin' fur? A man can't get to feel like canned goods every time! Me and the Judge here'll fix up this thing in no time, an' then you'll come back, an' we'll all laugh together!'

Once more the resolution that is born of curiosity triumphed, and Amelia stayed holding tight to my arm and shivering whilst the custodian began to slacken slowly inch by inch the rope that held back the iron door. Hutcheson's face was positively radiant as his eyes followed the first movement of the spikes.

'Wall!' he said, 'I guess I've not had enjoyment like this since I left Noo York. Bar a scrap with a French sailor at Wapping – an' that warn't much of a picnic neither – I've not had a show fur real pleasure in this dod-rotted

Continent, where there ain't no b'ars nor no Injuns, an' wheer nary man goes heeled. Slow there, Judge! Don't you rush this business! I want a show for my money this game – I du!'

The custodian must have had in him some of the blood of his predecessors in that ghastly tower, for he worked the engine with a deliberate and excruciating slowness which after five minutes, in which the outer edge of the door had not moved half as many inches, began to overcome Amelia. I saw her lips whiten, and felt her hold upon my arm relax. I looked around an instant for a place whereon to lay her, and when I looked at her again found that her eye had become fixed on the side of the Virgin. Following its direction I saw the black cat crouching out of sight. Her green eyes shone like danger lamps in the gloom of the place, and their colour was heightened by the blood which still smeared her coat and reddened her mouth. I cried out: 'The cat! Look out for the cat!' for even then she sprang out before the engine. At this moment she looked like a triumphant demon. Her eyes blazed with ferocity, her hair bristled out till she seemed twice her normal size, and her tail lashed about as does a tiger's when the quarry is before it.

Elias P. Hutcheson when he saw her was amused, and his eyes positively sparkled with fun as he said: 'Darned if the squaw hain't got on all her war paint! Jest give her a shove off if she comes any of her tricks on me, for I'm so fixed everlastingly by the boss, that durn my skin if I can keep my eyes from her if she wants them! Easy there, Judge! Don't you slack that ar rope or I'm euchered!'

At this moment Amelia completed her faint, and I had to clutch hold of her round the waist or she would have fallen to the floor. Whilst attending to her I saw the black cat crouching for a spring, and jumped up to turn the creature out.

But at that instant, with a sort of hellish scream, she hurled herself, not as we expected at Hutcheson, but straight at the face of the custodian. Her claws seemed to be tearing wildly as one sees in the Chinese drawings of the dragon rampant, and as I looked I saw one of them light on the poor man's eye, and actually tear through it and down his cheek, leaving a wide band of red where the blood seemed to spurt from every vein.

With a yell of sheer terror which came quicker than even his sense of pain, the man leaped back, dropping as he did so the rope which held back the iron door. I jumped for it, but was too late, for the cord ran like lightning through the pulley-block, and the heavy mass fell forward from its own weight. As the door closed I caught a glimpse of our poor companion's face. He seemed frozen with terror. His eyes stared with a horrible anguish as if dazed, and no sound came from his lips. And then the spikes did their work. Happily the end was quick, for when I wrenched open the door they had pierced so deep that they had locked in the bones of the skull through which they had crushed, and actually tore him – it – out of his iron prison till, bound as he was, he fell at full length with a sickly thud upon the floor, the face turning upward as he fell. I rushed to my wife, lifted her up and carried her out, for I feared for her very reason if she should wake from her faint to such a scene. I laid her on the bench outside and ran back. Leaning against the wooden column was the custodian moaning in pain whilst he held his reddening handkerchief to his eyes. And sitting on the head of the poor American was the cat, purring loudly as she licked the blood which trickled through the gashed sockets of his eyes.

I think no one will call me cruel because I seized one of the old executioner's swords and shore her in two as she sat.

from *Dracula's Guest and Other Weird Stories* (1914)

8

A CLOWDER OF CATS

A house without a cat, and a well-fed, well-petted and
properly revered cat, may be a perfect home, perhaps,
but how can it prove its title?

Mark Twain (1835–1910)

THE YOUNG CATS' CLUB FOR POETRY-MUSIC

Heinrich Heine (1797–1856)

The philharmonic young cats' club
    Upon the roof was collected
Tonight, but not for sensual joys,
    No wrong could there be detected.

No summer night's wedding dream there was dreamt,
    No song of love did they utter
In the winter season, in frost and snow,
    For frozen was every gutter.

A newborn spirit hath recently
    Come over the whole cat-nation,
But chiefly the young, and the young cat feels
    More earnest with inspiration.

The frivolous generation of old
    Is extinct, and a newborn yearning,
A pussy-springtime of poetry
    In art and in life they're learning.

The philharmonic young cats' club
    Is now returning to artless
And primitive music, and naiveté,
    From modern fashions all heartless.

It seeks in music for poetry,
    Roulades with the quavers omitted;
It seeks for poetry, music-void,
    For voice and instrument fitted.

It seeks for genius's sovereign sway,
    Which often bungles truly,
Yet oft in art unconsciously
    Attains the highest stage duly.

It honours the genius which prefers
    Dame Nature to keep at a distance,
And will not show off its learning – in fact
    Its learning not having existence.

This is the programme of our cat club,
    And with these intentions elated,
It holds its first winter concert tonight
    On the roof, as before I have stated.

Yet sad was the execution, alas,
    Of this great idea so splendid;
I'm sorry, my dear friend Berlioz,
    That by thee it wasn't attended.

It was a charivari, as though
    With brandy elated greatly,
Three dozen pipers struck up the tune
    That the poor cow died of lately.

It was an utter medley, as though
    In Noah's ark were beginning
The whole of the beasts in unison
    The Deluge to tell of in singing.

O what a croaking, snarling, and noise!
    O what a mewing and yelling!
And even the chimneys all join'd in,
    The wonderful chorus swelling.

And loudest of all was heard a voice
    Which sounded languid and shrieking
As Sontag's voice became at the last,
    When utterly broken and squeaking.

The whimsical concert! Methinks that they
    A grand Te Deum were chanting,
To honour the triumph o'er reason obtain'd
    By commonest frenzy and canting.

Perchance moreover the young cats' club
    The open grand were essaying
That the greatest pianist of Hungary*
    Composed for Charenton's playing.

It was not till the break of day
    That an end was put to the party;
A cook was in consequence brought to bed,
    Who before had seem'd well and hearty.

The lying-in woman lost her wits,
    Her memory, too, was affected,
And who was the father of her child
    No longer she recollected.

Say, was it Peter? Say, was it Paul?
    Say who is the father, Eliza!
'O Liszt, thou heavenly cat!' she said,
    And simper'd and look'd the wiser.

*Liszt

from *The Poems of Heine* (1861), translated by E. A. Bowring

THE PARSON AND THE CAT

William Cowper Junior (1784–1872)

Let Cowper's ease and merry vein,
    In every verse appear,
And soon shall Nimrod's cassock'd train
    To Gilpin tune the ear.

'Twas at a time when scent was keen,
    What dog his nose could blame?
A Vicar paced the sylvan scene,
    In hot pursuit of game.

Only more strong the burning scent,
    When livings were in view;
The fleece possess'd – he lived content,
    Though vacant every pew.

More fragrant far such scent inhaled,
    Than incense upward borne,
No psalmody his ears assailed,
    Like clang of huntsman's horn.

Dearer to him the pack's full cry,
    Than Sabbath-bell's deep tone;
Not half so sweet the sinner's sigh,
    As Reynard's dying groan.

He saw a swain as forth he hied,
    Advancing to a brook,
Whose cat beneath his arm was tied,
    With wildness in her look.

'And whither,' asked the buckskin priest,
    'Say, whither dost thou go?
If silent here, relate at least,
    Why bind Miss Pussey so?'

'Why,' said John, 'may't please your honour,
    I go this cat to drown.'
'Why not set the dogs upon her?
    They soon will hunt her down.'

To please his heavenly minded guide,
    Of tenderness composed,
He took poor pussey from his side,
    By hungry dogs enclosed.

And soon he snapp'd her hempen fetters,
    For sport prepared the way –
Sport, so fitting men of letters,
    Returned to childhood's day.

Full joyous was the priest as pack,
    When John threw down the cat,
The tide of early life roll'd back,
    In spite of wig and hat.

Tho' paid for preaching, 'twas his choice
    To whisper out the truth:
But now he stretch'd his stentor voice,
    More loud than any youth.

The dogs who knew their patron's shout,
    Nor did his flock so well,
Fired with parsonic zeal throughout,
    Made echo every dell.

Poor puss, in fright, for mercy begs,
    Nor tree nor mercy near,
She fastens on the horse's legs,
    And mounts him by the rear.

The steed unused to such a guest,
    Still less to spurs behind,
Snorted, and kicked, and onward press'd,
    A resting place to find.

Nor were her fangs the less employed,
    Her safety to complete;
'Twas through their grasp she still enjoyed,
    Her elevated seat.

The angry pack in dread array,
    With widened jaws and throats,
Leaped round and round the prancing bay,
    Howling their hideous notes.

Through raising fear and lengthened pain,
    The horse still raged the more,
And now, to sit, and guide the rein,
    The rider deemed were o'er.

Off went the parson with his mate,
    The hounds in full pursuit;
Transferr'd to him was her dread fate,
    He now, alas! was mute.

A change of scene effected thus;
    The priest appeared the game;
The triumph seemed to rest with puss,
    Till near the trackers came.

At length the ardour of the steed,
    Was checked by strength of arm;
The dog closed in which took the lead,
    And puss was all alarm.

Afraid lest some rude hound should reach,
    And drag her through the pack,
She left the horse's goaded breech,
    And scaled the parson's back.

Around his neck, in apish mood,
    Her foremost limbs she twined,
And from each cheek she drew the blood,
    As erst from steed behind.

Thus author-like, fair EXTRACTS made,
    Not ELEGANT, 'tis true,
But cutting as the sharpest blade,
    And flowing to the view.

Such Extracts from a work so rare –
    A Sportsman and Divine,
Must surely make the reader stare,
    Be doomed for aye to shine.

Himself he could not disengage,
    From pussey's fond embrace;
'Twas toil enough to calm the rage,
    And check the horse's pace.

The howling dogs now thickened round
    All thirsting for the cat;
The hunter made a sudden bound,
    And off flew wig and hat.

Away went priest – away went he,
    Like Gilpin fam'd of yore
The villagers came out to see,
    The dogs kept up the roar.

Both old and young their voices raised,
    'Our Parson!' was the cry;
To see such game they stood amazed,
    And rent with shouts the sky.

Not long before they saw him borne,
    Full stately to the sight,
But little dreamt so swift return,
    And in such piteous plight.

His cheeks were like the damask rose,
    But not with morning air;
Miss Pussey, with the tint that glows,
    Had placed her pencil there.

All mingled in the merry chase,
    The greatest and the least,
The village cur e'en shewed his face,
    To kennel up the priest.

As forth, the hound and human pack,
    Poured like a stream along
Some joined, like minor rills, their track,
    And sang the jocund song.

Again the rider checked his horse,
    And hoped for parish aid,
But noisy crowds made matters worse,
    The steed was more afraid.

Away went priest – away went he,
    Like Gilpin famed of yore;
'Twas laughable Miss Puss to see,
As high as heretofore.

The seat of learning she had gained,
    Which spoke superior sense,
And though unroofed, she still maintained
    It should not drive her thence.

The time was once – but then had fled,
    When easy had it been,
To deck, with frizzled roof, her head,
    Enlivening thus the scene.

For, in her fear, she might have placed,
    Her head beneath the wig,
And, forcing upward, might in haste,
    Have run another rig.

One sudden spring, when on the rise,
    Had borne it off complete;
With hat and wig – how wondrous wise!
    So near to learning's seat.

Ah, luckless wight, he should have been,
    Within his study walls,
Where seldom such as he are seen,
    Though loud the church's calls.

He brought from college his degree,
    But studious habits left;
The scholar's shadow you might see,
    Of substance he was reft.

Preferment's goal he long had gained,
　　And fattened on the spoil;
The present goal unseen remained –
　　For this he still must toil.

Miss Pussey like the parson rode,
　　And like him kept her hold,
And while she o'er his Reverence strode,
　　Each twitch she gave him told.

Her form between his shoulders lay,
　　Her head behind his own,
Her foremost limbs were free to play,
　　And straight before her thrown.

Her limbs – the rein, her claws – the bit,
　　Like tenter hooks to view,
And while she held as seemed her fit,
　　His cheeks she backward drew.

The more she drew as moved by fear;
　　If fancy speak the truth,
She nearly stretched from ear to ear,
　　His Reverence's mouth.

The neighbouring swains who met him straight,
　　Would deem him catching flies,
But soon he passed – they saw his fate,
　　When pussey caught their eyes.

Ah! luckless wight, had he but been,
　　Intent upon his call
He had not now beheld this scene,
　　Nor thus been jeered by all.

But still though greatly out of place,
    For safety he must strive,
Once more he checked his horse's pace,
    To every fear alive.

The roar of dogs and swains was heard,
    And nearer as they came,
More desperate still the steed appeared,
    Nor skill his rage could tame.

Away went priest – away went he,
    Like Gilpin famed of yore,
The fence-crushed farmer said with glee,
    'We ne'er shall see him more.'

Others, anon as loudly cried,
    'No fear of him today;
Far better he is skill'd to ride,
    Than skill'd to preach and pray.'

Let him, some wags might next have said,
    Nor limb nor cranium break,
The goal by him must soon be made,
    Or puss will tithe his cheek.

And why not pay like those around,
    For pleasures thus received?
It matters not how harsh the sound,
    The tithed are always grieved;

And grieved the more, as tithes are given,
    To those, whom all declare,
Nor either seek the road to heaven,
    Nor point their hearers there.

These are the Church's greatest foes,
 And not the different sects;
From these she feels the heaviest blows,
 On these the muse reflects.

And yet, than drunkards, and the gay,
 Dancers, and stage offenders;
Few talk of 'DANGER' more than they,
 Or plume themselves defenders.

Not on the good, in heaven's pursuit,
 Who toil with all their power;
But grubs who only eat the fruit,
 Would satire's vengeance shower.

In virtue's cause – whate'er the name,
 The muse would e'er assume,
The two-edged sword – a sword of flame,
 Her enemies to consume.

But stay, while wandering from my tale,
 Wide as the priest from sport,
The painted claws his cheeks assail,
 His features still distort.

The pars'nage-house at length was gained,
 Without a broken limb,
But ne'er was he so tightly reined,
 Nor caught in such a trim.

The house-dog heard the horse's feet,
 And hastened to the door,
His master's reverend eye to meet,
 And greet him as before.

How much surprised to see his lord,
    With mouth so widely stretched!
Though grinning – not an angry word,
    No hand to him was reach'd.

The mastiff knew – for wise was he,
    That he had done no harm,
Nor sooner did Miss Pussey see,
    Than he began to warm.

Forward he dashed in bristled mood,
    The horse again took fright,
But ere he drew a drop of blood,
    The pack was full in sight.

And who his gruffness could gainsay,
    Though with the hounds he fought?
He wished a snack as well as they,
    For this he sternly sought.

Tremendous was the fray indeed,
    And madly did they strive;
The priest, in poor Miss Pussey's stead,
    Was next to flayed alive.

Fancy would sketch another scene,
    For farming priests abound,
And shew the stack-yard, and the green,
    In motion all around.

The chuckling hens and cackling geese,
    United with the dogs,
Cows, calves and sheep, who sought their peace,
    Fled with the grunting hogs.

Fear, ire, and mirth, prevailed throughout,
    Though slight indeed the cause,
For all were moved or put to rout,
    By touch of pussey's claws.

With Hogarth's genius brought to bear,
    On villagers and beasts,
On poultry flying through the air,
    On chief of hunting priests;

Soon would a new creation rise,
    With cat and scampering crowd,
The clerk, to lead, with leering eyes,
    The choristers so loud.

The parson, more than satisfied,
    With leave, we now dismount,
And place both mirth and wounded pride,
    To pussey's just account.

But what can inmates say or do,
    Returning in such haste?
He carries game – Miss Puss, 'tis true –
    But not to suit the taste.

Enough of her to stay his fast,
    For one fair mornin's meal;
He gladly hoped 'twould be the last,
    His appetite should feel.

'Tis but to guess how pussey fared,
    Though guiltless more than he;
For cruel intent, *he* was not spared,
    His friends must e'en agree.

But all may know how he was heard,
    And heard with what applause,
When in the rostrum, he appeared,
    With scars in such a cause.

What merriment would Paul inspire,
    Religion how much slur,
Clothed with huntsman's red attire,
    In boots, and cap, and spur!

How strange to Christian ears the sound,
    To come from Peter's lip,
'Hark, hark to cover,' to the hound,
    And see him crack his whip!

In other language than to bless,
    It were outrageous quite;
In other than the priestly dress,
    Unseemly to the sight.

As strange it were to see a pig,
    Come bolting from the stye,
With three-cocked hat, and powdered wig,
    Laced coat, and buskins high.

Oh! worse than swine, more useless far,
    And still more out of place,
No more in Christ's right hand, a star,
    A blot on Zion's face –

Yes, worse – whose fate we here rehearse,
    And may he stand alone!
May priests no longer shine in verse,
    Where knaves and fools are shown.

Repent, reform, and imitate
    Those clergymen of fame –
True pillars of the Church and State,
    Of EVANGELIC name;

Those men, whose piety and zeal,
    Put sportsmen to the blush,
Who only toil for Zion's weal,
    And scorn to beat the bush.

This, for the tuneful organ calls,
    To draw the thoughtless crowd,
And *that*, to warm the church's walls,
    For blazing fires is loud.

Thus wide the good man never roves;
    For these ne'er opes his mouth;
He warms his church with living stoves,
    He draws by force of TRUTH.

Let every pulpit once be fill'd,
    With EVANGELIC men,
Soon shall the voice of foes be still'd,
    And useless be their pen.

May glorious days the church await!
    Such glories meet our eyes!
When every pile shall prove too straight,
    And new ones towering rise.

And now we sign God save the King,
    And Church from selfish ends;
Pray for ever, Lord deliver,
    From Nimrod's cassock'd friends!

THE WIDOW'S CAT

Anne Brontë (1820–49)

I took the opportunity of repairing to the widow's cottage, where I found her in some anxiety about her cat, which had been absent all day. I comforted her with as many anecdotes of that animal's roving propensities as I could recollect. 'I'm feared o' th' gamekeepers,' said she, 'that's all 'at I think on. If th' young gentlemen had been at home, I should a' thought they'd been setting their dogs at her, an' worried her, poor thing, as they did many a poor thing's cat; but I haven't that to be feared on now.' Nancy's eyes were better, but still far from well: she had been trying to make a Sunday shirt for her son, but told me she could only bear to do a little bit at it now and then, so that it progressed but slowly, though the poor lad wanted it sadly. So I proposed to help her a little, after I had read to her, for I had plenty of time that evening, and need not return till dusk. She thankfully accepted the offer.

'An you'll be a bit o' company for me too, miss,' said she; 'I like as I feel lonesome without my cat.' But when I had finished reading, and done the half of a seam, with Nancy's capacious brass thimble fitted on to my finger by means of a roll of paper, I was disturbed by the entrance of Mr Weston, with the identical cat in his arms. I now saw that he could smile, and very pleasantly too.

'I've done you a piece of good service, Nancy,' he began: then seeing me, he acknowledged my presence by a slight bow. I should have been invisible to Hatfield, or any other gentleman of those parts. 'I've delivered your cat,' he continued, 'from the hands, or rather the gun, of Mr Murray's gamekeeper.'

'God bless you, sir!' cried the grateful old woman, ready to weep for joy as she received her favourite from his arms.

'Take care of it,' said he, 'and don't let it go near the rabbit warren, for the gamekeeper swears he'll shoot it if he sees it there again: he would have done so today, if I had not been in time to stop him. I believe it is raining, Miss Grey,' added he, more quietly, observing that I had put aside my work, and was preparing to depart. 'Don't let me disturb you – I shan't stay two minutes.'

'You'll *both* stay while this shower gets 'owered,' said Nancy, as she stirred the fire, and placed another chair beside it; 'what! there's room for all.'

'I can see better here, thank you, Nancy,' replied I, taking my work to the window, where she had the goodness to suffer me to remain unmolested, while she got a brush to remove the cat's hairs from Mr Weston's coat, carefully wiped the rain from his hat, and gave the cat its supper, busily talking all the time: now thanking her clerical friend for what he had done; now wondering how the cat had found out the warren; and now lamenting the probable consequences of such a discovery. He listened with a quiet, good-natured smile, and at length took a seat in compliance with her pressing invitations, but repeated that he did not mean to stay.

'I have another place to go to,' said he, 'and I see' (glancing at the book on the table) 'someone else has been reading to you.'

'Yes, sir; Miss Grey has been as kind as read me a chapter; an' now she's helping me with a shirt for our Bill – but I'm feared she'll be cold there. Won't you come to th' fire, miss?'

'No, thank you, Nancy, I'm quite warm. I must go as soon as this shower is over.'

'Oh, miss! You said you could stop while dusk!' cried the provoking old woman, and Mr Weston seized his hat.

'Nay, sir,' exclaimed she, 'pray don't go now, while it rains so fast.'

'But it strikes me I'm keeping your visitor away from the fire.'

'No, you're not, Mr Weston,' replied I, hoping there was no harm in a falsehood of that description.

'No, sure!' cried Nancy. 'What, there's lots o' room!'

'Miss Grey,' said he, half-jestingly, as if he felt it necessary to change the present subject, whether he had anything particular to say or not, 'I wish you would make my peace with the squire when you see him. He was by when I rescued Nancy's cat, and did not quite approve of the deed. I told him I thought he might better spare all his rabbits than she her cat, for which audacious assertion he treated me to some rather ungentlemanly language; and I fear I retorted a trifle too warmly.'

'Oh, lawful sir! I hope you didn't fall out wi' th' maister for sake o' my cat! he cannot bide answering again – can th' maister.'

'Oh! it's no matter, Nancy: I don't care about it, really; I said nothing *very* uncivil; and I suppose Mr Murray is accustomed to use rather strong language when he's heated.'

from Agnes Grey (1847)

HODGE

James Boswell (1740–95)

Nor would it be just under this head, to omit the fondness which he shewed for animals which he had taken under his protection. I never shall forget the indulgence with which he treated Hodge, his cat; for whom he himself used to go out and buy oysters, lest the servants, having that trouble, should take a dislike to the poor creature. I am, unluckily, one of those who have an antipathy to a cat, so that I am uneasy when in the room with one; and I own, I frequently suffered a good deal from the presence of this same Hodge. I recollect him one day scrambling up Dr Johnson's breast, apparently with much satisfaction, while my friend smiling and half-whistling, rubbed down his back, and pulled him by the tail; and when I observed he was a fine cat, saying 'Why, yes, Sir, but I have had cats whom I liked better than this'; and then as if perceiving Hodge to be out of countenance, adding, 'but he is a very fine cat, a very fine cat indeed.'

This reminds me of the ludicrous account which he gave Mr Langton, of the despicable state of a young gentleman of good family. 'Sir, when I heard of him last, he was running about town shooting cats.' And then in a sort of kindly reverie, he bethought himself of his own favourite cat, and said, 'But Hodge shan't be shot: no, no, Hodge shall not be shot.'

from The Life of Dr Johnson (1783)

THE CAT

Geroffrey Chaucer (c.1343–1400)

The cat, if you but singe her tabby skin,
The chimney keeps, and sits content within:
But once grown sleek, will from her corner run,
Sport with her tail and wanton in the sun:
She licks her fair round face, and frisks abroad
To show her fur, and to be catterwaw'd.

from the Prologue to 'The Wife of Bath's Tale'
in *Canterbury Tales* (c.1387)

FLAVISO

Frederick Rolfe (1860–1913)

He rose and went to the window. The yellow cat deliberately stretched himself, yawned, and followed; and proceeded to carry out a wonderful scheme of feints and ambuscades in regard to a ping-pong ball which was kept for his proper diversion. The man looked on almost lovingly. Flavio at length captured the ball, took it between his forepaws, and posed with all the majesty of a lion of Trafalgar Square. Anon he uttered a little low gurgle of endearment, fixing the great eloquent mystery of amber and black and velvet eyes, tardy, grave, upon his human friend. No notice was vouchsafed. Flavio got up; and gently rubbed his head against the nearest hand.

'My boy!' the man murmured; and he lifted the little cat on to his shoulder.

From *Hadrian the Seventh* (1904)

THE DIMINUTIVE LYON

William Salmon (1644–1713)

I. It is called in Hebrew, כטול, מחגד, *Catul*, *Schanar*; in Chaldean, חתול, *pl.* חתוליז, *Chatul*, *pl. Chatulin*; in Greek, Κατλης, αιλουρος; in Latin, *Catus*, *felis*; in English, *the Cat*, but the wild Cat is supposed to be called in Hebrew, אייס, *Jim. Isa.* 13, 22, and 34, 14. for so *Arius Montanus* translates it; as for *Kat* or *Cat*, it is the most usual name that almost all Nations call it by.

II. It is bred and is an Inhabitant of almost all Countries in the World, all Cats were at first wild, but were at length tamed by the industry of Mankind; it is a Beast of prey, even the tame one, more especially the wild, it being in the opinion of many nothing but a diminutive Lyon.

III. It is now said to be of three kinds, 1. *The tame Cat*. 2. *The wild wood Cat*. 3. *The Cat of Mountain*, all which are of one nature, and agree much in one Shape, save as to their magnitude, the *wild Cat* being larger much than the *tame*, and the *Cat of Mountain* much larger than the *wild Cat*.

IV. It has a broad Face almost like a Lyon, short Ears, large Whiskers, shining Eyes, short smooth Hair, long Tail, rough Tongue, and armed on its Feet with Claws, being a crafty, subtle watchful Creature, very loving and familiar with Mankind, the mortal enemy to the Rat, Mouse, and all sorts of Birds, which it seizes on as its prey. As to its Eyes, Authors say that they shine in the Night, and see better at the full, and more dimly at the change of the Moon; as also that the Cat doth vary his Eyes with the Sun, the Apple of its Eye being long at Sunrise, round towards Noon, and not to be seen at all at night, but the whole Eye shining in the night. These appearances of the Cats Eyes I am sure are true, but whether they answer to the times of the day, I never observed.

V. It is a neat and cleanly creature, often licking itself, to keep it fair and clean, and washing its Face with its forefeet; the best are such as are of a fair and large kind, and of an exquisite Tabby colour, called *Cyprus* Cats. They usually generate in the winter Season, making a great noise, go 56 Days or

8 weeks with young, and bring forth 2, 3, 4, 5, 6, or more at a time, they cover their excrements, and love to keep their old habitations.

VI. *Its Flesh* is not usually eaten, yet in some Countries it is accounted an excellent Dish, but the Brain is said to be poisonous, causing madness, stupidity, and loss of memory, which is cured only by vomiting, and taking musk in Wine.

From The Compleat English Physician (1693)

VERSES ON A CAT

Percy Bysshe Shelley (1792–1822)

A cat in distress,
Nothing more, nor less;
Good folks, I must faithfully tell ye,
As I am a sinner,
It waits for some dinner
To stuff out its own little belly.

You would not easily guess
All the modes of distress
Which torture the tenants of earth;
And the various evils,
Which like so many devils,
Attend the poor souls from their birth.

Some a living require,
And others desire
An old fellow out of the way:
And which is the best
I leave to be guessed,
For I cannot pretend to say.

One wants society,
Another variety,
Others a tranquil life;
Some want food,
Others, as good,
Only want a wife.

But this poor little cat
Only wanted a rat,
To stuff out its own little maw;
And it were as good
Some people had such food,
To make them *hold their jaw*!

THE GENTLEMAN FARMER AND HIS ELEVEN CATS

W.H. Hudson (1841–1922)

One of my old shepherd's stories about strange or eccentric persons he had known during his long life was of a gentleman farmer, an old bachelor, in the parish of Winterbourne Bishop, who had (for a man) an excessive fondness for cats and who always kept eleven of these animals as pets. For some mysterious reason that number was religiously adhered to. The farmer was fond of riding on the downs, and was invariably attended by a groom in livery – a crusty old fellow; and one of this man's duties was to attend to his master's eleven cats. They had to be fed at their proper time, in their own dining-room, eating their meals from a row of eleven plates on a long, low table made expressly for them. They were taught to go each one to his own place and plate, and not to get on to the table, but to eat like Christians, without quarrelling or interfering with their neighbours on either side. And, as a rule, they all behaved properly, except one big tom-cat, who developed so greedy, spiteful, and tyrannical a disposition that there was never a meal but he upset the harmony and brought it to a disorderly end, with spittings, snarlings, and scratchings. Day after day the old groom went to his master with a long, dolorous plaint of this cat's intolerable behaviour, but the farmer would not consent to its removal, or to any strong measures being taken; kindness combined with patience and firmness, he maintained, would at last win even this troublesome animal to a better mind. But in the end he, too, grew tired of this incorrigible cat, who was now making the others spiteful and quarrelsome by his example; and one day, hearing a worse account than usual, he got into a passion, and taking a loaded gun handed it to the groom with orders to shoot the cat on the spot on the very next occasion of its misbehaving, so that not only would they be rid of it but its death in that way would serve as a warning to the others. At the very next meal the bad cat got up the usual row, and by and by they were all fighting and tearing each other on the table, and the groom, seizing the gun, sent a charge of shot into the thickest of the fight, shooting three of the cats dead. But the author of all the mischief escaped without so much as a pellet! The farmer was in a great rage at this disastrous blundering, and gave notice to his groom on the spot; but the man was an old and valued servant, and by and by he forgave him, and the quarrelsome animal having been got rid of, and four fresh cats obtained to fill up the gaps, peace was restored.

from *A Shepherd's Life* (1910)

THE MONKEY AND THE CAT

Jean de la Fontaine (1621–95)

Sly Bertrand and Ratto in company sat,
(The one was a monkey, the other a cat)
Co-servants and lodgers:
More mischievous codgers
Ne'er mess'd from a platter, since platters were flat.
Was anything wrong in the house or about it,
The neighbours were blameless – no mortal could doubt it;

For Bertrand was thievish, and Ratto so nice,
More attentive to cheese than he was to the mice.
One day the two plunderers sat by the fire,
Where chestnuts were roasting, with looks of desire.
To steal them would be a right noble affair.
A double inducement our heroes drew there –
'Twould benefit them, could they swallow their fill,
And then 'twould occasion to somebody ill.
Said Bertrand to Ratto, 'My brother, today
Exhibit your powers in a masterly way,
And take me these chestnuts, I pray.
Which were I but otherwise fitted
(As I am ingeniously witted)
For pulling things out of the flame,
Would stand but a pitiful game.'
' 'Tis done,' replied Ratto, all prompt to obey;
And thrust out his paw in a delicate way.
First giving the ashes a scratch,
He open'd the coveted batch;
Then lightly and quickly impinging,
He drew out, in spite of the singeing,
One after another, the chestnuts at last –
While Bertrand contrived to devour them as fast.
A servant girl enters. Adieu to the fun.
Our Ratto was hardly contented, says one.

No more are the princes, by flattery paid
For furnishing help in a different trade,
And burning their fingers to bring
More power to some mightier king.

from *The Fables* (1842), translated by Elizur Wright

THE HEN AND THE CAT

Aesop (6th century BC)

All the barnyard knew that the hen was indisposed. So one day the cat decided to pay her a visit of condolence. Creeping up to her nest, the cat in his most sympathetic voice said: 'How are you, my dear friend? I was so sorry to hear of your illness. Isn't there something that I can bring you to cheer you up and to help you feel like yourself again?'

'Thank you,' said the hen. 'Please be good enough to leave me in peace, and I have no fear but I shall soon be well.'

MORAL

Uninvited guests are often most welcome when they are gone.

from *Fables*

TYBERT THE CAT

Anonymous

Then the King said: 'Sir Tybert, ye shall now go to Reynard, and say to him this second time that he come to Court unto the plea for to answer; for, though he be fell to other beasts, he trusteth you well and will do by your counsel. And tell [him], if he come not, he shall have the third warning and be summoned, and, if he then come not, we shall proceed by law against him and all his lineage without mercy.'

Tybert spake: 'My Lord the King, they that this counselled you were not my friends. What shall I do there? He will not for me neither come ne abide. I beseech you, dear King, send some other to him. I am little and feeble. Bruin the Bear, which was so great and strong, could not bring him: how should I then take it on hand?'

'Nay,' said the King, 'Sir Tybert, ye are wise and well learned. Though ye be not great, there lieth not much in that. Many do more with skill and knowledge than with might and strength.'

Then said the Cat: 'Sith it must needs be done, I must then take it upon me. God give grace that I may well achieve it, for my heart is heavy, and evil-willed thereto.'

Tybert made him soon ready toward Maleperduys. And he saw from far come flying one of Saint Martin's birds; then cried he [a]loud and said: 'All hail, gentle bird, turn thy wings hitherward, and fly on my right side.' The bird flew forth upon a tree which stood on the left side of the Cat. Then was Tybert woe; for he thought it was a sinister token and a sign of harm. For, if the bird had flown on his right side, he had been merry and glad; but now he was anxious lest his journey should turn to misfortune. Nevertheless, he did as many do, and gave to himself better hope than his heart said. He went and ran toward Maleperduys, and there he found the Fox alone standing before his house.

Tybert said: 'The rich God give you good even, Reynard! The King hath menaced you for to take your life from you if ye come not now with me to the Court.'

The Fox then spake and said: 'Tybert, my dear cousin, ye be right welcome! I would well truly that ye had much good luck.' What hurted [it] the Fox to speak fair? Though he said well, his heart thought it not; and that shall be seen ere they depart.

Reynard said: 'Shall we this night be together? I will make you good cheer, and tomorrow early in the dawning we will together go to the Court. Good nephew, let us so do: I have none of my kin that I trust so much to as to you. Here was Bruin the Bear – the traitor! He looked so knavishly on me, and methought he was so strong, that I would not for a thousand mark have gone with him; but, cousin, I will tomorrow early go with you.'

Tybert said: 'It is best that we now go, for the moon shineth all so light as it were day: I never saw fairer weather.'

'Nay, dear cousin, such might meet us by daytime that would make us good cheer and by night peradventure might do us harm. It is suspicious to walk by night. Therefore abide this night here by me.'

Tybert said: 'What should we eat if we abode here?' Reynard said: 'Here is but little to eat. Ye may well have an honeycomb, good and sweet. What say ye, Tybert, will ye any thereof?'

Tybert answered: 'I set naught thereby. Have ye nothing else? If ye gave me a good fat mouse, I should be better pleased.'

'A fat mouse!' said Reynard. 'Dear cousin, what say ye? Hereby dwelleth a Priest and hath a barn by his house; therein are so many mice that a man could not lead them away upon a wain. I have heard the Priest many times complain that they did him much harm.'

'Oh, dear Reynard, lead me thither for all that I may do for you!'

'Yea, Tybert, say ye me truth? Love ye well mice?'

'If I love them well?' said the Cat. 'I love mice better than anything that men give me! Know ye not that mice savour better than game – yea, than pancakes or pasties? Will ye well do, so lead me thither where the mice are, and then shall ye win my love, yea, although ye had slain my father, mother, and all my kin.'

Reynard said: 'Ye mock and jest therewith!'

The Cat said: 'So help me God, I do not!'

'Tybert,' said the Fox, 'wist I that verily, I would yet this night make that ye should be full of mice.'

'Reynard!' quoth he, 'Full? That were many.'

'Tybert, ye jest!'

'Reynard,' quoth he, 'in truth I do not. If I had a fat mouse, I would not give it for a golden noble.'

'Let us go, then, Tybert' quoth the Fox; 'I will bring you to the place ere I go from you.'

'Reynard,' quoth the Cat, 'upon your safe-conduct I would well go with you to Montpellier.'

'Let us then go,' said the Fox; 'we tarry all too long.'

Thus went they forth, without hindrance to the place where they would be, to the Priest's barn, which was fast walled about with a mud wall. And the night before the Fox had broken in, and had stolen from the Priest a good fat hen; and the Priest, all angry, had set a snare before the hole to avenge him; for he would fain have taken the Fox. This knew well the fell thief, the Fox, and said: 'Sir Tybert, cousin, creep into this hole, and ye shall not long tarry but that ye shall catch mice by great heaps. Hark how they pipe! When ye be full, come again; I will tarry here after you before this hole. We will tomorrow go together to the Court. Tybert, why tarry ye thus long? Come off, and so may we return soon to my wife which waiteth for us, and shall make us good cheer.'

Tybert said: 'Reynard, cousin, is it then your counsel that I go into this hole? These Priests are so wily and shrewish I dread to take harm.'

'Oh, ho, Tybert!' said the Fox, 'I saw you never so sore afraid! What aileth you?'

The Cat was ashamed, and sprang into the hole. And anon he was caught in the snare by the neck, ere he wist. Thus deceived Reynard his guest and cousin.

As Tybert was ware of the snare, he was afraid and sprang forth – the snare went to. Then he began to shout, for he was almost strangled. He called, he cried, and made a villainous noise.

Reynard stood before the hole and heard all, and was well satisfied, and said: 'Tybert, love ye well mice? Be they fat and good? Knew the Priest hereof, or Mertynet, they be so gentle that they would bring you sauce. Tybert, ye sing and eat – is that the custom of the Court? Lord God, if Isegrim were there by you, in such rest as ye now be, then should I be glad; for oft he hath done me damage and harm.'

Tybert could not go away; but he mewed and cried out so loud, that Mertynet sprang up, and cried [a]loud: 'God be thanked, my snare hath taken the thief that hath stolen our hens. Arise up; we will reward him!'

With these words arose the Priest in an evil time; and waked all them that were in the house, and cried with a loud voice:

'The Fox is taken!'

There leapt and ran all that there was. The Priest himself ran, all mother-naked. Mertynet was the first that came to Tybert. The Priest took to Julocke his wife an offering-candle, and bade her light it at the fire; and he smote Tybert with a great staff. There received Tybert many a great stroke over all his body. Mertynet was so angry that he smote the Cat an eye out. The naked Priest lifted up and should have given a great stroke to Tybert, but Tybert, that saw that he must die, sprang between the Priest's legs with his claws and with his teeth that he tore out his right colyon or balock-stone. That leap became ill to the Priest, and to his great shame.

This thing fell down upon the floor. When Dame Julocke knew that, she sware by her father's soul, that she would [rather] it had cost her all the offering of a whole year [than] that the Priest should have had that harm, hurt, and shame and that it had not happened; and said: 'In the Devil's name was the snare there set! See Mertynet, dear son, this is thy father's harness. This is a great shame and to me a great hurt, for, though he be healed thereof, he is but a lost man to me, and also shall never be able to do that sweet play and game.' The Fox stood without, before the hole, and heard all these words, and laughed so sore that he scarcely could stand. He spake thus all softly: 'Dame Julocke, be all still, and your great sorrow sink. Although hath the Priest lost one of his stones, it shall not hinder him: he shall do with you well enough. There is in the world many a chapel in which is rung but one bell.' Thus scorned and mocked the Fox the Priest's wife, Dame Julocke, that was full of sorrow.

The Priest fell down a-swoon. They took him up, and brought him again to bed. Then went the Fox again in towards his burrow and left Tybert the Cat in great dread and jeopardy, for the Fox wist none other but that the Cat was nigh dead. But, when Tybert the Cat saw them all busy about the Priest, then began he to bite and gnaw the snare in the middle asunder and sprang out of the hole, and went rolling and rolling towards the King's Court. Ere he came thither it was fair day, and the sun began to rise. And he came to the Court as a poor wight. He had caught harm at the Priest's house by the help and counsel of the Fox. His body was all beaten to pieces, and blind on the one eye. When the King wist this, that Tybert was thus arrayed, he was sore angry, and menaced Reynard the thief sore; and anon gathered his Council to know what they would advise him how he might bring the Fox to the law, and how he should be fetched.

Then spake Sir Grymbart, which was the Fox's sister's son, and said: 'Ye Lords, though my uncle were twice so bad and knavish, yet is there remedy enough. Let him be done to as to a free man. When he shall be judged, he must be warned the third time for all; and, if he come not then, he is then guilty in all the trespasses that are laid against him and his, or complained on.'

'Grymbart, who would ye that should go and summon him to come? Who will adventure for him his ears, his eye, or his life – which is so fell a beast? I trow there is none here so much a fool.'

Grymbart spake: 'So help me God, I am so much a fool that I will do this message myself to Reynard, if ye will command me.'

from *History of Reynard the Fox* (1481)

BREAKFAST AND PUSS

Anonymous

Here's my baby's bread and milk,
For her lips as soft as silk;
Here's the basin clean and neat,
Here's the spoon of silver sweet,
Here's the stool, and here's the chair,
For my little lady fair.

No, you must not spill it out,
And drop the bread and milk about;
But let it stand before you flat,
And pray remember pussy-cat:
Poor old pussy-cat that purrs
All so patiently for hers.

True, she runs about the house,
Catching now and then a mouse;
But, though she thinks it very nice,
That only makes a tiny slice:
So don't forget that you should stop
And leave poor puss a little drop.

from *Rhymes for the Nursery* (new edition, 1839)

BORODIN'S CATS

N.A. Rimsky-Korsakov (1844–1908)

Their whole home life was one unending disorder. Dinner-time and other meal-times were most indefinite. Once I came to their house at eleven in the evening and found them at dinner. Leaving out of account the girls, their protégées, of whom their house had never any lack, their apartment was often used as shelter or a night's lodging by various poor (or 'visiting') relations, who picked that place to fall ill or even lose their minds. Borodin had his hands full of them, doctored them, took them to hospitals, and then visited them there. In the four rooms of his apartment there often slept several strange persons of this sort; sofas and floors were turned into beds. Frequently it proved impossible to play the piano, because someone lay asleep in the adjoining room. At dinner and at tea, too, great disorder prevailed. Several tom-cats that found a home in Borodin's apartment paraded across the dinner-table, sticking their noses into plates, unceremoniously leaping to the diners' backs. These tom-cats basked in Yekatyerina Sergeyevna's protection; various details of their biography were related. One tabby was called *Rybolov* ('Fisherman'), because, in the winter, he contrived to catch small fish with his paw through the ice-holes; the other was called *Dlinyenki* ('Longy') and he was in the habit of fetching homeless kittens by the neck to Borodin's apartment; these the Borodins would harbour, later finding homes for them. Then there were other, and less remarkable specimens of the genus *Felis*. You might sit at their tea-table – and behold! Tommy marches along the board and makes for your plate; you shoo him off, but Yekatyerina Sergeyevna invariably takes his part and tells some incident from his biography. Meantime, zip! another cat has bounded at Alyeksandr Porfiryevich's neck and, twining himself about it, has fallen to warming that neck without pity. 'Listen, dear Sir, this is too much of a good thing!' says Borodin, but without stirring; and the cat lolls blissfully on.

from *My Musical Life* (1924)

CAT QUOTATIONS

Cat: A soft indestructible automaton provided by nature to be kicked when things go wrong in the domestic circle.

Ambrose Bierce (1842–c.1914)

Everything that moves seems to interest and amuse a cat.

Paradis de Moncrif (1687–1770)

Of all God's creatures there is only one that cannot be made the slave of the lash. That one is the cat. If man could be crossed with the cat it would improve man, but it would deteriorate the cat.

Mark Twain (1835–1910)

Cats, by the way, rarely suffer from excess of adulation. A cat possesses a very fair sense of the ridiculous, and will put her paw down kindly but firmly upon any nonsense of this kind.

Jerome K. Jerome (1859–1927)

Far in the stillness a cat languishes loudly.

W.E. Henley (1849–1903)

OF JEOFFRY, HIS CAT

Christopher Smart (1722–71)

For I will consider my Cat Jeoffry.

For he is the servant of the Living God, duly and daily serving him.

For at the first glance of the glory of God in the East he worships in his way.

For is this done by wreathing his body seven times round with elegant quickness.

For then he leaps up to catch the musk, which is the blessing of God upon his prayer.

For he rolls upon prank to work it in.

For having done duty and received blessing he begins to consider himself.

For this he performs in ten degrees.

For first he looks upon his forepaws to see if they are clean.

For secondly he kicks up behind to clear away there.

For thirdly he works it upon stretch with the forepaws extended.

For fourthly he sharpens his paws by wood.

For fifthly he washes himself.

For sixthly he rolls upon wash.

For seventhly he fleas himself, that he may not be interrupted upon the beat.

For eighthly he rubs himself against a post.

For ninthly he looks up for his instructions.

For tenthly he goes in quest of food.

For having consider'd God and himself he will consider his neighbour.

For if he meets another cat he will kiss her in kindness.

For when he takes his prey he plays with it to give it chance.

For one mouse in seven escapes by his dallying.

For when his day's work is done his business more properly begins.

For [he] keeps the Lord's watch in the night against the adversary.

For he counteracts the powers of darkness by his electrical skin and glaring eyes.

For he counteracts the Devil, who is death, by brisking about the life.

For in his morning orisons he loves the sun and the sun loves him.

For he is of the tribe of Tiger.

For the Cherub Cat is a term of the Angel Tiger.

For he has the subtlety and hissing of a serpent, which in goodness he suppresses.

For he will not do destruction, if he is well-fed, neither will he spit without provocation.

For he purrs in thankfulness, when God tells him he's a good Cat.

For he is an instrument for the children to learn benevolence upon.

For every house is incompleat without him and a blessing is lacking in the spirit.

For the Lord commanded Moses concerning the cats at the departure of the Children of Israel from Egypt.

For every family had one cat at least in the bag.

For the English Cats are the best in Europe.

For he is the cleanest in the use of his forepaws of any quadrupede.

For the dexterity of his defence is an instance of the love of God to him exceedingly.

For he is the quickest to his mark of any creature.

For he is tenacious of his point.

For he is a mixture of gravity and waggery.

For he knows that God is his Saviour.

For there is nothing sweeter than his peace when at rest.

For there is nothing brisker than his life when in motion.

For he is of the Lord's poor and so indeed is he called by benevolence perpetually – Poor Jeoffry! poor Jeoffry! the rat has bit thy throat.

For I bless the name of the Lord Jesus that Jeoffry is better.

For the divine spirit comes about his body to sustain it in compleat cat.

For his tongue is exceeding pure so that it has in purity what it wants in musick.

For he is docile and can learn certain things.

For he can set up with gravity which is patience upon approbation.

For he can fetch and carry, which is patience in employment.

For he can jump over a stick which is patience upon proof positive.

For he can spraggle upon waggle at the word of command.

For he can jump from an eminence into his master's bosom.

For he can catch the cork and toss it again.

For he is hated by the hypocrite and miser.

For the former is afraid of detection.

For the latter refuses the charge.

For he camels his back to bear the first notion of business.

For he is good to think on; if a man would express himself neatly.

For he made a great figure in Egypt for his signal services.

For he killed the Ichneumon-rat very pernicious by land.

For his ears are so acute that they sting again.

For from this proceeds the passing quickness of his attention.

For by stroaking of him I have found out electricity.

For I perceived God's light about him both wax and fire.

For the Electrical fire is the spiritual substance, which God sends from
    heaven to sustain the bodies both of man and beast.

For God has blessed him in the variety of his movements.

For, tho he cannot fly, he is an excellent clamberer.

For his motions upon the face of the earth are more than any other
    quadrupede.

For he can tread to all the measures upon the musick.

For he can swim for life.

For he can creep.

from *Jubilate Agno* (1759–63)

ENJOLRAS AND GAVROCHE

Théophile Gautier (1811–72)

Just at that time Victor Hugo's *Misérables* was in great vogue, and the names of the characters in the novel were on everyone's lips. I called the two male kittens Enjolras and Gavroche, while the little female received the name of Eponine.

They were perfectly charming in their youth. I trained them like dogs to fetch and carry a bit of paper crumpled into a ball, which I threw for them. In time they learnt to fetch it from the tops of cupboards, from behind chests or from the bottom of tall vases, out of which they would pull it very cleverly with their paws. When they grew up they disdained such frivolous games, and acquired that calm philosophic temperament which is the true nature of cats.

To people landing in America in a slave colony all negroes are negroes, and indistinguishable from one another. In the same way, to careless eyes, three black cats are three black cats; but attentive observers make no such mistake. Animal physiognomy varies as much as that of men, and I could distinguish perfectly between those faces, all three as black as Harlequin's mask, and illuminated by emerald discs shot with gold.

Enjolras was by far the handsomest of the three. He was remarkable for his great leonine head and big ruff, his powerful shoulders, long back and splendid feathery tail. There was something theatrical about him, and he seemed to be always posing like a popular actor who knows he is being admired. His movements were slow, undulating and majestic. He put each foot down with as much circumspection as if he were walking on a table covered with Chinese bric-à-brac or Venetian glass. As to his character, he was by no means a stoic, and he showed a love of eating which that virtuous and sober young man, his namesake, would certainly have disapproved. Enjolras would undoubtedly have said to him, like the angel to Swedenborg:

'You eat too much.'

I humoured this gluttony, which was as amusing as a gastronomic monkey's, and Enjolras attained a size and weight seldom reached by the domestic cat. It occurred to me to have him shaved poodle-fashion, so as to give the finishing touch to his resemblance to a lion.

We left him his mane and a big tuft at the end of his tail, and I would not swear that we did not give him mutton-chop whiskers on his haunches like those Munito wore. Thus tricked out, it must be confessed he was much more like a Japanese monster than an African lion. Never was a more fantastic whim carved out of a living animal. His shaven skin took odd blue tints, which contrasted strangely with his black mane.

Gavroche, as though desirous of calling to mind his namesake in the novel, was a cat with an arch and crafty expression of countenance. He was smaller than Enjolras, and his movements were comically quick and brusque. In him absurd capers and ludicrous postures took the place of the banter and slang of the Parisian gamin. It must be confessed that Gavroche had vulgar tastes. He seized every possible occasion to leave the drawing-room in order to go and make up parties in the back yard, or even in the street, with stray cats, 'De naissance quelconque et de sang peu prouvé', in which doubtful company he completely forgot his dignity as cat of Havana, son of Don Pierrot de Navarre, grandee of Spain of the first order, and of the aristocratic and haughty Doña Seraphita.

Sometimes in his truant wanderings he picked up emaciated comrades, lean with hunger, and brought them to his plate of food to give them a treat in his good-natured, lordly way. The poor creatures, with ears laid back and watchful side-glances, in fear of being interrupted in their free meal by the broom of the housemaid, swallowed double, triple, and quadruple mouth-fuls, and, like the famous dog Siete-Aguas (seven waters) of Spanish posadas (inns), they licked the plate as clean as if it had been washed and polished by one of Gerard Dow's or Mieris's Dutch housewives.

Seeing Gavroche's friends reminded me of a phrase which illustrates one of Gavarni's drawings, 'Ils sont jolis les amis dont vous êtes susceptible d'aller avec!' ('Pretty kind of friends you like to associate with!')

But that only proved what a good heart Gavroche had, for he could easily have eaten all the food himself.

from 'The White and Black Dynasties'
in La Ménagerie Intime, translated by Lady Chance

THE GRINNING CAT

Lewis Carroll (1832–98)

The door led right into a large kitchen, which was full of smoke from one end to the other: the Duchess was sitting on a three-legged stool in the middle, nursing a baby; the cook was leaning over the fire, stirring a large cauldron which seemed to be full of soup.

'There's certainly too much pepper in that soup!' Alice said to herself, as well as she could for sneezing.

There was certainly too much of it in the *air*. Even the Duchess sneezed occasionally; and as for the baby, it was sneezing and howling alternately without a moment's pause. The only two creatures in the kitchen that did *not* sneeze were the cook, and a large cat which was lying on the hearth and grinning from ear to ear.

'Please would you tell me,' said Alice a little timidly, for she was not quite sure whether it was good manners for her to speak first, 'why your cat grins like that?'

'It's a Cheshire cat,' said the Duchess, 'and that's why. Pig!' She said the last word with such sudden violence that Alice quite jumped; but she saw in another moment that it was addressed to the baby, and not to her, so she took courage, and went on again: 'I didn't know that Cheshire cats always grinned; in fact, I didn't know that cats could grin.'

'They all can,' said the Duchess; 'and most of 'em do.'

'I don't know of any that do,' Alice said very politely, feeling quite pleased to have got into conversation.

'You don't know much,' said the Duchess; 'and that's a fact.'

from *Alice's Adventures in Wonderland* (1865)

DICK BAKER'S CAT

Mark Twain (1835–1910)

One of my comrades there – another of those victims of eighteen years of unrequited toil and blighted hopes – was one of the gentlest spirits that ever bore its patient cross in a weary exile; grave and simple Dick Baker, pocket miner of Dead-Horse Gulch. He was forty-six, grey as a rat, earnest, thoughtful, slenderly educated, slouchily dressed, and clay-soiled, but his heart was finer metal than any gold his shovel ever brought to light – than any, indeed, that ever was mined or minted.

Whenever he was out of luck and a little downhearted, he would fall to mourning over the loss of a wonderful cat he used to own (for where women and children are not, men of kindly impulses take up with pets, for they must love something). And he always spoke of the strange sagacity of that cat with the air of a man who believed in his secret heart that there was something human about it – maybe even supernatural.

I heard him talking about this animal once. He said: 'Gentlemen, I used to have a cat here, by the name of Tom Quartz, which you'd 'a' took an interest in, I reckon – most anybody would. I had him here eight year – and he was the remarkablest cat I ever see. He was a large grey one of the Tom specie, an' he had more hard, natchral sense than any man in this camp – 'n' a *power* of dignity – he wouldn't let the Gov'ner of Californy be familiar with him. He never ketched a rat in his life – 'peared to be above it. He never cared for nothing but mining. He knowed more about mining, that cat did, than any man I ever, ever see. You couldn't tell him noth'n' 'bout placer-diggin's – 'n 'as for pocket mining, why he was just born for it. He would dig out after me an' Jim when we went over the hills prospect'n' , and he would trot along behind us for as much as five mile, if we went so fur. 'An he had the best judgment about mining ground – why, you never see anything like it. When we went to work, he'd scatter a glance round, 'n' if he didn't think much of the indications, he would give a look as much as to say, 'Well, I'll have to get you to excuse me' – 'n' without another word he'd hyste his nose in the air 'n' shove for home. But if the ground suited him, he would lay low 'n' keep dark till the first pan was washed, 'n' then he would sidle

up 'n' take a look, 'an if there was about six or seven grains of gold *he* was satisfied – he didn't want no better prospect 'n' that – 'n' then he would lay down on our coats and snore like a steamboat till we'd struck the pocket, an' then get up 'n' superintend. He was nearly lightnin' on superintending.

'Well, by an' by, up comes this yer quartz excitement. Everybody was into it – everybody was pick'n' 'n' blast'n instead of shovellin' dirt on the hillside – everybody was putt'n down a shaft instead of scrapin' the surface. Noth'n' would do Jim, but *we* must tackle the ledges, too, 'n' so we did. We commenced putt'n down a shaft, 'n' Tom Quartz he begin to wonder what in the dickens it was all about. He hadn't ever seen any mining like that before, 'n' he was all upset, as you may say – he couldn't come to a right understanding of it no way – it was too many for *him*. He was down on it too, you bet you – he was down on it powerful – 'n' always appeared to consider it the cussedest foolishness out. But that cat, you know, was *always* agin' newfangled arrangements – somehow he never could abide 'em. You know how it is with old habits. But by and by Tom Quartz begin to git sort of reconciled a little though he never *could* altogether understand that eternal sinkin' of a shaft 'an never pannin' out anything. At last he got to comin' down in the shaft, hisself, to try to cipher it out. An' when he'd git the blues, 'n' feel kind o' scruffy, 'n' aggravated 'n' disgusted – knowin' as he did, that the bills was runnin' up all the time an' we warn't makin' a cent – he would curl up on a gunnysack in the corner an' go to sleep. Well, one day when the shaft was down about eight foot, the rock got so hard that we had to put in a blast – the first blast'n' we'd ever done since Tom Quartz was born. An' then we lit the fuse 'n' clumb out 'n' got off 'bout fifty yards – 'n' forgot 'n' left Tom Quartz sound asleep on the gunnysack. In 'bout a minute we seen a puff of smoke bust up out of the hole, 'n' then everything let go with an awful crash 'n' about four million ton of rocks 'n' dirt 'n' smoke 'n' splinters shot up 'bout a mile an' a half into the air, an' by George, right in the dead centre of it was old Tom Quartz a-goin' end over end, an' a-snortin' an' a-sneezin', an' a-clawin' an' a-reach'n' for things like all possessed. But it warn't no use, you know, it warn't no use. An' that was the last we see of *him* for about two minutes 'n' a half, an' then all of a sudden it begin to rain rocks and rubbage an' directly he come down ker-whoop about ten foot off f'm where we stood. Well, I reckon he was p'r'aps the orneriest-lookin' beast you ever see. One ear was sot back on his neck, 'n' his tail was stove up, 'n' his eye-winkers was singed off, 'n' he was all blacked up with powder an' smoke, an' all sloppy with mud 'n' slush f'm one end to the other. Well, sir, it warn't no use to try to apologize – we couldn't say a word. He took a sort of disgusted look at himself, 'n' then he looked at us – an' it was just exactly the same as if he had said – "Gents, maybe *you* think it's smart to take advantage of a cat that ain't had no experience of quartz minin', but I think different" – an' then he turned on his heel 'n' marched off home without ever saying another word.

'That was jest his style. An' maybe you won't believe it, but after that you never see a cat so prejudiced agin' quartz mining as what he was. An' by an' by when he *did* get to goin' down in the shaft agin', you'd 'a' been astonished at his sagacity. The minute we'd tetch off a blast 'n' the fuse'd begin to sizzle, he'd give a look as much as to say, "Well, I'll have to git you to excuse *me*," an' it was surpris'n' the way he'd shin out of that hole 'n' go f'r a tree. Sagacity? It ain't no name for it. 'Twas inspiration!'

I said, 'Well, Mr Baker, his prejudice against quartz mining *was* remarkable, considering how he came by it. Couldn't you ever cure him of it?'

'*Cure him!* No! When Tom Quartz was sot once, he was *always* sot – and you might a blowed him up as much as three million times 'n' you'd never a broken him of his cussed prejudice agin' quartz mining.'

THE GREAT CAT

Anonymous (c.1700 BC)

Praise be to thee, O Ra, exalted Lion-god, thou art the Great Cat, the Avenger of the Gods and the Judge of Words, the President of the Sovereign Chiefs and the Governor of the Holy Circle; thou art indeed the bodies of the Great Cat.

from *The Seventy-five Praises of Ra*

ARSINOË'S CATS

Graham Tomson (1863–1911)

Arsinoë the fair, the amber-tressed,
    Is mine no more;
Cold as the unsunned snows are, is her breast,
    And closed her door.
No more her ivory feet and tresses braided
    Make glad mine eyes;
Snapt are my viol strings, my flowers are faded;
    My love-lamp dies.

Yet, once for dewy myrtle-buds and roses,
    All summer long,
We searched the twilight-haunted garden closes
    With jest and song.
Ay, all is over now – my heart hath changèd
    Its heaven for hell;
And that ill chance which all our love estrangèd
    In this wise fell:

A little lion, small and dainty sweet
    (For such there be!),
With sea-grey eyes and softly stepping feet,
    She prayed of me.
For this through lands Egyptian far away
    She bade me pass;
But, in an evil hour, I said her nay –
    And now, alas!
Far-travelled Nicias hath wooed and won
    Arsinoë,
With gifts of furry creatures white and dun
    From over-sea.

ON CATS

Edward Topsell (c.1572–1625)

Cats are of divers colours, but for the most part gryseld, like to congealed yse, which cometh from the condition of her meate: her head is like unto the head of a Lyon, except in her sharpe eares: her flesh is soft and smooth: her eyes glitter above measure especially when a man cometh to see a Cat on the sudden, and in the night, they can hardly be endured, for their flaming aspect. Wherefor Democritus describing the Persian smaradge saith that it is not transparent but filleth the eye with pleasant brightnesse, such as in the eyes of Panthers and Cats, for they cast forth beames in the shadow and darkness, but in the sunshine they have no such clearness and therefore Alexander Aphrodise giveth this reason, both for the sight of Cattes and Battes, that they have by nature a most sharp spirit of seeing.

Albertus compareth their eyesight to carbuncles in dark places, because in the night, they can see perfectly to kill Rattes and Myce: the roote of the herbe Valerian (commonly called Phu) is very like to the eye of a Cat, and wherefore it groweth if cats come thereunto, they instantly dig it up, for the love thereof, as I myself have seene in mine owne Garden, and not once onely, but often, even then when I had caused it to be hedged or compassed round about with thornes, for it smelleth marveilous like to a cat.

The Egyptians hath observed in the eyes of a Cat, the encrease of the Moonlight, for with the Moone, they shine more fully at the ful, and more dimly in the change and wain, and the male Cat doth also vary his eyes with the sunne; for when the sunne ariseth, the apple of his eye is long; towards noone it is round, and at the evening it cannot be seene at all, but the whole eye sheweth alike.

The tongue of a Cat is very attractive, and forcible like a file, attenuating by licking the flesh of a man, for which cause, when she is come neere to the blood, so that her own spittle be mingled there with, she falleth mad. Her teeth are like a saw, and if the long haires growing about her mouth (which some call Granons) be cut away, she looseth her courage. Her nailes sheathed like the nailes of a Lyon, striking with her fore-feete, both Dogs and other things, as a man doth with his hand.

The beast is wonderful nimble, setting upon her prey like the Lyon, by leaping: and therefore she hunteth both Rats, all kinds of Myce, and Birds, eating not only them, but also Fish, wherewith all she is best pleased. It is a neat and cleanely creature, oftentimes licking her own body to keepe it smoothe and faire, having naturally a flexible backe for this purpose, and washing her face with her fore-feete, but some observe that if she put her feete beyond the crowne of her head, that it is a presage of raine, and if the backe of a Cat be thinne, the beast is of no courage or value.

It is needlesse to spend any time about her loving nature to man, how she flattereth by rubbing her skinne against one's Legges, how she whurleth with her voyce, having as many tunes as turnes, for she hath one voyce to beg and complain, another to testify her delight and pleasure, another among her own kind by flattering, by hissing, by puffing, by spitting, insomuch as some have thought that they have a peculiar intelligible language among themselves. Therefore how she beggeth, playeth, leapeth, looketh, catcheth, tosseth with her foote, riseth up to strings held over her head, sometimes creeping, sometimes lying on the back, playing with one foot, sometimes on the bely, snatching, now with the mouth, and anon with foot, apprehending greedily anything save the hand of a man with divers such gestical actions, it is needelesse to stand upon; insomuch as Cœlus was wont to say, that being free from his Studies and more urgent weighty affairs, he was not ashamed to play and sport himself with his Cat, and verily it might well be called an idle man's pastime . . .

from *The Historie of Foure-Footed Beastes* (1658)

OLD TOM-CAT INTO DAMSEL GAY

Paul Scarron (1610–60)

In strictest secrecy I've heard
And promised not to say a word
About a certain Lady's age,
Her name and face and parentage;
This Lady had a Cat whom she
Adored quite immoderately;
For his amusement once, her whim
Invented a disguise for him.
With tresses cleverly attached,
And precious earrings nicely matched,
The Cat's head she adorned, then she
Regarded him admiringly:
About his neck she hung fine pearls
Larger than the eyes of Merles;
A fine, white, laundered, linen shirt,
A little jacket and a skirt,
A collar and a neckerchief
Made, with the help of her belief,
Old Tom-cat into Damsel gay.
Not quite a beauty,
But adequate, at least, to stir
The Dame who'd decorated her.
Then up before a looking-glass
The Lady held this darling lass:
This Cat who showed no evidence
Of being surprised, or of pretence
At joy for being by fool caressed,
Or seeing himself an Idol dressed.
Whatever happened then took place
Because she failed to embrace
Her Cat as closely as she might.

Without considering wrong or right,
The good Cat gained the stair,
And then the attic, and from there
Out upon the tiles he strayed;
Loudly crying, the Lady prayed
Her servants instantly to be
Out after him assiduously:

But in the country of the tiles
Wary Tom-cats show their wiles.
They searched for him until they tired,
And the next day they inquired
Of the neighbours; some averred
They couldn't credit what they heard,
Others their belief asserted;
All were very much diverted;
And all the while the Cat uncaged
Never returned; the Lady raged
Less for the necklace's expense
Than for her Tom-cat vanished thence.

A CAT

Robert Herrick (1591–1674)

A Cat
I keep, that plays about my House,
Grown fat
With eating many a miching Mouse.

CURED BY A CAT

Revd James Woodforde (1740–1803)

The Stiony on my right Eye-lid still swelled and inflamed very much. As it is commonly said that the Eye-lid being rubbed by the tail of a black Cat would do it much good if not entirely cure it, and having a black Cat, a little before dinner I made a trial of it, and very soon after dinner I found my Eye-lid much abated of the swelling and almost free from Pain. I cannot therefore but conclude it to be of the greatest service to a Stiony of the Eye-lid. Any other Cat's Tail may have the above effect in all probability – but I did my Eye-lid with my own black Tom Cat's Tail.

from *The Diary of a County Parson*, 11 March 1791

A DIGNIFIED CAT

Andrew Lang (1844–1912)

A regretted friend of my own, a black cat with a great deal of retenue, never went near another cat's dish; while, if another cat approached his dish, he instantly retired. More food, he seemed to say, is not worth a wrangle. He withdrew from all forms of competition, like a dignified Royal cat in exile. On the other hand, many cats, and one of mine in particular, always desert their own platter (however tempting) for that of their neighbour.

LISY'S PARTING WITH HER CAT

James Thomson (1834–82)

The dreadful hour with leaden pace approached,
Lashed fiercely on by unrelenting fate,
When Lisy and her bosom Cat must part:
For now, to school and pensive needle doomed,
She's banished from her childhood's undashed joy,
And all the pleasing intercourse she kept
With her grey comrade, which has often soothed
Her tender moments, while the world around
Glowed with ambition, business, and vice.
Or lay dissolved in sleep's delicious arms:
And from their dewy orbs the conscious stars
Shed on their friendship influence benign.
But see where mournful Puss, advancing, stood
With outstretched tail, casts looks of anxious woe
On melting Lisy, in whose eye the tear
Stood tremulous, and thus would fain have said,
If nature had not tied her struggling tongue:
'Unkind, Oh! who shall now with fattening milk,
With flesh, with bread, and fish beloved, and meat,
Regale my taste? and at the cheerful fire,
Ah, who shall bask me in their downy lap?
Who shall invite me to the bed, and throw
The bedclothes o'er me in the winter night,
When Eurus roars? Beneath whose soothing hand
Soft shall I purr? But now, when Lisy's gone,
What is the dull officious world to me?
I loathe the thoughts of life': thus plained the Cat,
While Lisy felt, by sympathetic touch,
These anxious thoughts that in her mind revolved,
And casting on her a desponding look,
She snatched her in her arms with eager grief,

And mewing, thus began: 'O Cat beloved!
Thou dear companion of my tender years!
Joy of my youth! that oft hast licked my hands
With velvet tongue ne'er stained by mouse's blood.
Oh, gentle Cat! how shall I part with thee?
How dead and heavy will the moments pass
When you are not in my delighted eye,
With Cubi playing, or your flying tail.
How harshly will the softest muslin feel,
And all the silk of schools, while I no more
Have your sleek skin to soothe my softened sense?
How shall I eat while you are not beside
To share the bit? How shall I ever sleep
While I no more your lulling murmurs hear?
Yet we must part – so rigid fate decrees –
But never shall your loved idea, dear,
Part from my soul, and when I first can mark
The embroidered figure on the snowy lawn,
Your image shall my needle keen employ.
Hark! now I'm called away! Oh direful sound!
I come – I come, but first I charge you all –
You – you – and you, particularly you,
O Mary, Mary, feed her with the best,
Repose her nightly in the warmest couch,
And be a Lisy to her!' Having said,
She sat her down, and with her head across,
Rushed to the evil which she could not shun,
While a sad mew went knelling to her heart!

THE ROYAL CAT WAGER

Charles H. Ross (1835–97)

It is stated in a Japanese book that the tip of a Cat's nose is always cold, except on the day corresponding with our Midsummer-day. This is a question I cannot say I have gone into very deeply. I know, however, that Cats always have a warm nose when they awaken from sleep. All Cats are fond of warmth. I knew one which used to open an oven door after the kitchen fire was out; and creep into the oven. One day the servant shut the door, not noticing the cat was inside, and lighted the fire. For a long while she could not make out whence came the sounds of its crying and scratching, but fortunately made the discovery in time to save its life. A Cat's love of the sunshine is well known, and perhaps this story may not be unfamiliar to the reader:

One broiling hot summer's day Charles James Fox and the Prince of Wales were lounging up St James's Street, and Fox laid the Prince a wager that he would see more Cats than his Royal Highness during their promenade, although the Prince might choose which side of the street he thought fit. On reaching Piccadilly, it turned out that Fox had seen thirteen Cats and the Prince none. The Prince asked for an explanation of this apparent miracle.

'Your Royal Highness,' said Fox, 'chose, of course, the shady side of the way as most agreeable. I knew that the sunny side would be left for me, and that Cats prefer the sunshine.'

from *The Book of Cats* (1868)

THAT LITTLE BLACK CAT

D'Arcy Wentworth Thompson (1829–1902)

Who's that ringing at our door-bell?
    'I'm a little black cat and I'm not very well.'
    'Then rub your little nose with a little mutton fat,
       And that's the best cure for a little pussy-cat.'

ALL CATS TOGETHER

Andrew Lang (1844–1912)

Other cats came, with kind inquiries, to visit a puss whose leg had been hurt in a rabbit trap. One of them, having paid her visit, went out, caught a rabbit, and brought it back to the sufferer. What sportsman could do more?

C

Edward Lear (1812–88)

C was Papa's grey Cat,
    Who caught a squeaky Mouse;
She pulled him by his twirly tail
    All about the house.

from *Nonsense Songs, Stories, Botany and Alphabets* (1871)

MEMOIR OF THE CATS OF GRETA HALL

Robert Southey (1774–1843)

For as much, most excellent Edith May [Southey's daughter], as you must always feel a natural and becoming concern in whatever relates to the house wherein you were born, and in which the first part of your life has thus far so happily been spent, I have for your instruction and delight composed these Memoirs of the Cats of Greta Hall: to the end that the memory of such worthy animals may not perish, but be held in deserved honour by my children, and those who shall come after them. And let me not be supposed unmindful of Beelzebub of Bath, and Senhor Thomas de Lisboa, that I have not gone back to an earlier period, and included them in my design. Far be it from me to intend any injury or disrespect to their shades! Opportunity of doing justice to their virtues will not be wanting at some future time, but for the present I must confine myself within the limits of these precincts.

In the autumn of the year 1803, when I entered upon this place of abode, I found the hearth in possession of two cats, whom my nephew Hartley Coleridge (then in the seventh year of his age) had named Lord Nelson, and Bona Marietta. The former, as the name implies, was of the worthier gender: it is as decidedly so in Cats, as in Grammar and in law. He was an ugly specimen of the streaked-carroty, or Judas-coloured kind; which is one of the ugliest varieties. But *nimium ne crede colori*. In spite of his complexion, there was nothing treacherous about him. He was altogether a good Cat, affectionate, vigilant and brave; and for services performed against the Rats was deservedly raised in succession to the rank of Baron, Viscount and Earl. He lived to a good old age; and then, being quite helpless and miserable, was in mercy thrown into the river. I had more than once interfered to save him from this fate; but it became at length plainly an act of compassion to consent to it. And here let me observe that in a world wherein death is necessary, the law of nature by which one creature preys upon another is a law of mercy, not only because death is thus made instrumental to life, and more life exists in consequence, but also because it is better for the creatures themselves to be cut off suddenly, than to perish by disease or hunger – for these are the only alternatives.

There are still some of Lord Nelson's descendants in the town of Keswick. Two of the family were handsomer than I should have supposed any Cats of this complexion could have been; but their fur was fine, the colour a rich carrot, and the striping like that of the finest tyger or tabby kind. I named one of them William Rufus; the other Danayr le Roux, after a personage in the Romance of Gyron le Courtoys. […]

For a considerable time afterwards, an evil fortune attended all our attempts at re-establishing a Cattery. Ovid disappeared and Virgil died of some miserable distemper. You and your cousin are answerable for these names: the reasons which I could find for them were, in the former case the satisfactory one that the same Ovid might be presumed to be a master in the Art of Love; and in the latter, the probable one that something like Maro might be detected in the said Virgil's notes of courtship.

There was poor Othello: most properly named, for black he was, and jealous undoubtedly he would have been, but he in his kittenship followed Miss Wilbraham into the street, and there in all likelihood came to an untimely end. There was the Zombi – (I leave the Commentators to explain that title, and refer them to my History of Brazil to do it) – his marvellous story was recorded in a letter to Bedford – and after that adventure he vanished. There was Prester John, who turned out not to be of John's gender, and therefore had the name altered to Pope Joan. The Pope I am afraid came to a death of which other Popes have died. I suspect that some poison which the rats had turned out of their holes, proved fatal to their enemy. For some time I feared we were at the end of our Cat-a-logue: but at last Fortune as if to make amends for her late severity sent us two at once – the never-to-be-enough-praised Rumpelstilzchen, and the equally-to-be-admired Hurlyburlybuss.

And 'first for the first of these' as my huge favourite and almost namesake Robert South, says in his Sermons.

When the Midgeleys went away from the next house, they left this creature to our hospitality, cats being the least movable of all animals because of their strong local predilections; they are indeed in a domesticated state the serfs of the animal creation, and properly attached to the soil. The change was gradually and therefore easily brought about,

for he was already acquainted with the children and with me; and having the same precincts to prowl in was hardly sensible of any other difference in his condition than that of obtaining a name; for when he was consigned to us he was an anonymous cat; and I having just related at breakfast with universal applause the story of Rumpelstilzchen from a German tale in Grimms' Collection, gave him that strange and magnisonant appellation; to which upon its being ascertained that he came when a kitten from a bailiff's house, I added the patronymic of Macbum. Such is his history, his character may with most propriety be introduced after the manner of Plutarch's parallels when I shall have given some previous account of his great compeer and rival Hurlyburlybuss – that name also is of Germanic and Grimmish extraction.

Whence Hurlyburlybuss came was a mystery when you departed from the Land of Lakes, and a mystery it long remained. He appeared here, as Mango Gapac did in Peru, and Quetzalcohuatl among the Aztecas, no one knew from whence. He made himself acquainted with all the philofelists of the family – attaching himself more particularly to Mrs Lovell, but he never attempted to enter the house, frequently disappeared for days, and once since my return for so long a time that he was actually believed to be dead and veritably lamented as such. The wonder was whither did he retire at such times – and to whom did he belong; for neither I in my daily walks, nor the children, nor any of the servants ever by any chance saw him anywhere except in our own domain, There was something so mysterious in this, that in old times it might have excited strong suspicion, and he would have been in danger of passing for a Witch in disguise, or a familiar. The mystery however was solved about four weeks ago, when as we were returning from a walk up the Greta, Isabel saw him on his transit across the road and the wall from Shulicrow in a direction towards the Hill. But to this day we are ignorant who has the honour to be his owner in the eye of the law; and the owner is equally ignorant of the high honour in which Hurlyburlybuss is held, of the heroic name which he has obtained, and that his fame has extended far and wide – even unto Norwich in the East, and Escott and Crediton and Kellerton in the West, yea – that with Rumpelstilzchen he has been celebrated in song, by some hitherto undiscovered poet, and that his glory will go down to future generations.

The strong enmity which unhappily subsists between these otherwise gentle and most amiable cats, is not unknown to you. Let it be imputed, as in justice it ought, not to their individual characters (for Cats have characters – and for the benefit of philosophy, as well as felisophy, this truth ought generally to be known) but to the constitution of Cat nature – an original sin, or an original necessity, which may be only another mode of expressing the same thing:

> Two stars keep not their motion in one sphere,
> Nor can one purlieu brook a double reign
> Of Hurlyburlybuss and Rumpelstilzchen.

When you left us, the result of many a fierce conflict was that Hurly remained master of the green and garden, and the whole of the out of door premises, Rumpel always upon the appearance of his victorious enemy retiring into the house as a citadel or sanctuary. The conqueror was perhaps in part indebted for this superiority to his hardier habits of life, living always in the open air, and providing for himself; while Rumpel (who though born under a bum-bailiff's roof was nevertheless kittened with a silver spoon in his mouth) passed his hours in luxurious repose beside the fire, and looked for his meals as punctually as any two-legged member of the family. Yet I believe that the advantage on Hurly's side is in a great degree constitutional also, and that his superior courage arises from a confidence in his superior strength, which as you well know is visible in his make. What Benito and Maria Rosa used to say of my poor Thomaz, that he was *muito hidalgo*, is true of Rumpelstilzchen, his countenance, deportment and behaviour being such that he is truly a gentleman-like tom-cat. Far be it from me to praise him beyond his deserts – he is not beautiful, the mixture, tabby and white, is not good (except under very favourable combinations) and the tabby is not good of its kind. Nevertheless he is a fine cat, handsome enough for his sex, large, well-made, with good features, and an intelligent countenance, and carrying a splendid tail, which in Cats and Dogs is undoubtedly the seat of honour. His eyes which are soft and expressive are of a hue between chrysolite and emerald. Hurlyburlybuss's are between chrysolite and topaz. Which may be the more esteemed shade for the *olho de gato* I am not lapidary enough to decide. You should ask my Uncle. But both are of the finest water. In all his other features Hurly must yield the palm, and in form also; he has no pretensions to elegance, his size is ordinary and his figure bad: but the character of his face and neck is so masculine, that the Chinese, who use the word 'bull' as synonymous with 'male', and call a boy a bull-child, might with great propriety denominate him a bull-cat. His make evinces such decided marks of strength and courage that if cat-fighting were as fashionable as cock-fighting, no cat would stand a fairer chance of winning a Welsh main. He would become as famous as the Dog Billy himself, whom I look upon as the most distinguished character that has appeared since Buonaparte.

Some weeks ago Hurlyburlybuss was manifestly emaciated and enfeebled by ill health, and Rumpelstilzchen with great magnanimity made overtures of peace. The whole progress of the treaty was seen from the parlour window. The caution with which Rumpel made his advances, the sullen dignity with which they were received, their mutual uneasiness when Rumpel, after a slow and wary approach, seated himself whisker-to-whisker with his rival, the mutual fear which restrained not only teeth and claws, but even all tones of defiance, the mutual agitation of their tails which, though they did not expand with anger, could not be kept still for suspense, and lastly the manner in which Hurly retreated, like Ajax still keeping his face towards his old antagonist, were worthy to have been represented by that painter who was called the Rafaelle of Cats. The overture I fear was not accepted as generously as it was made; for no sooner had Hurlyburlybuss recovered strength than hostilities were recommenced with greater violence than ever, Rumple who had not abused his superiority while he possessed it, had acquired meantime a confidence which made him keep the field. Dreadful were the combats which ensued, as their ears, faces and legs bore witness. Rumpel had a wound which went through one of his feet. The result had been so far in his favour that he no longer seeks to avoid his enemy, and we are often compelled to interfere and separate them. Oh it is awful to hear the 'dreadful note of preparation' with which they prelude their encounters! – the long low growl slowly rises and swells till it becomes a high sharp yowl – and then it is snapt short by a sound which seems as if they were spitting fire and venom at each other. I could half persuade myself that the word 'felonious' is derived from the feline temper as displayed at such times. All means of reconciling them and making them understand how goodly a thing it is for cats to dwell together in peace, and what fools they are to quarrel and tear each other, are in vain. The proceedings of the Society for the Abolition of War are not more utterly ineffectual and hopeless.

All we can do is to act more impartially than the Gods did between Achilles and Hector, and continue to treat both with equal regard.

written for his daughter, 18 June 1824

EDWARDS LEAR'S FOSS

Henry Strachey (1863–1940)

When staying at Cannes at Christmas, 1882, I was invited by Mr Lear to go over to San Remo to spend a few days with him. Mr Lear's villa was large, and the second he had built; the first became unbearable to him from a large hotel having been planted in front of it. So he put his new house in a place by the sea, where, as he said, nothing could interrupt his light unless the fishes built. The second house was exactly like the first. This, Mr Lear explained to me, was necessary or else Foss, his cat, might not have approved of the new villa. At breakfast the morning after I arrived, this much-thought of, though semi-tailed, cat jumped in at the window and ate a piece of toast from my hand. This, I found, was considered an event; when visitors stayed at the Villa Tennyson, Foss generally hid himself in the back regions; but his recognition of me was a sort of guinea stamp which seemed to please Mr Lear greatly, and assured him of my fitness to receive the constant acts of kindness he was showing me [. . .] He took from a place in his bureau a number of carefully cut-out backs of old envelopes, and on these he drew, to send to my sister, then eight years old, the delightful series of heraldic pictures of his cat. After he had done seven he said it was a great shame to caricature Foss, and laid aside the pen.

quoted in Sir Edward Stanley's Introduction to Lear's *Nonsense Songs and Stories*, 1895

NURSERY RHYMES

Anonymous (19th century)

Pussy-cat, Pussy-cat, Where Are You Going?

Pussy-cat, Pussy-cat, where are you going?
'Into the meadow to see the men mowing.'
If you go there you are sure to be shot,
Put in a pudding, and boiled in a pot.

Pussy-cat Mew

Pussy-cat Mew jumped over a coal,
And in her best petticoat burnt a great hole.
Pussy-cat Mew shall have no more milk
Till she has mended her gown of silk.

Ten Little Mice

Ten little mice sat down to spin;
Pussy passed by, and just looked in,
'What are you doing, my jolly ten?'
'We're making coats for gentlemen.'
'Shall I come in and cut your threads?'
'No! No! Mistress Pussy – you'd bite off our heads.'

Fanny and Her Cat

Come here, little Puss,
　　And I'll make you quite smart,
You shall wear this gold chain,
　　And I'll wear this fine heart;
And when we are drest,
　　My dear Aunty shall see
Who then will look best,
　　Little Pussy or me.

'Pussy-cat, Pussy-cat, Where Have You Been?'
'Pussy cat, pussy cat, where have you been?'
'I've been to London to look at the queen'.
'Pussy cat, pussy cat, what did you there?'
'I frightened a little mouse under her chair.'

MONSIGNORE CAPELECATRO AND HIS CAT

Walter Savage Landor (1775–1864)

Taranto now has lost her guide,
A prelate without prelate's pride.
On that Parthenopean coast,
Incredulous of fog or frost.
His Persian puss he smiles to see
Leap boldly on a stranger's knee,
And stretch out flat and lick his fur,
And switch his tail, and gape and purr.
Oh my two friends! may, many a day,
Both think of me when far away.

9

REQUIESCAT

O heaven will not ever heaven be
Unless my cats are there to welcome me.

Epitaph in a pet cemetery

LAST WORDS TO A DUMB FRIEND

Thomas Hardy (1840–1928)

Pet was never mourned as you
Purrer of the spotless hue,
Plumy tail, and wistful gaze
While you humoured our queer ways,
Or outshrilled your morning call
Up the stairs and through the hall –
Foot suspended in its fall –
While expectant, you would stand
Arched to meet the stroking hand;
Till your way you chose to wend
Yonder, to your tragic end.

Never another pet for me!
Let your place all vacant be;
Better blankness day by day
Than companion torn away.
Better bid his memory fade,
Better blot each mark he made,
Selfishly escape distress
By contrived forgetfulness,
Than preserve his prints to make
Every morn and eve an ache.

From the chair whereon he sat
Sweep his fur, nor wince thereat;
Rake his little pathways out
Mid the bushes roundabout;
Smooth away his talons' mark
From the claw-worn pine-tree bark,
Where he climbed as dusk embrowned,
Waiting us who loitered round.

Strange it is this speechless thing,
Subject to our mastering,
Subject for his life and food
To our gift, and time, and mood;
Timid pensioner of us Powers,
His existence ruled by ours,
Should – by crossing at a breath
Into safe and shielded death,
By the merely taking hence
Of his insignificance –
Loom as largened to the sense,
Shape as part, above man's will,
Of the Imperturbable.

As a prisoner, flight debarred,
Exercising in a yard,
Still retain I, troubled, shaken,
Mean estate, by him forsaken;
And this home, which scarcely took
Impress from his little look,
By his faring to the Dim
Grows all eloquent of him.

Housemate, I can think you still
Bounding to the window-sill,
Over which I vaguely see
Your small mound beneath the tree,
Showing in the autumn shade
That you moulder where you played.

CALVIN, THE CAT

Charles Dudley Warner (1829–1900)

Calvin is dead. His life, long to him, but short for the rest of us, was not marked by startling adventures, but his character was so uncommon and his qualities were so worthy of imitation that I have been asked by those who personally knew him to set down my recollections of his career.

His origin and ancestry were shrouded in mystery; even his age was a matter of pure conjecture. Although he was of the Maltese race, I have reason to suppose that he was American by birth as he certainly was in sympathy. Calvin was given to me eight years ago by Mrs Stowe, but she knew nothing of his age or origin. He walked into her house one day out of the great unknown and became at once at home, as if he had been always a friend of the family. He appeared to have artistic and literary tastes, and it was as if he had inquired at the door if that was the residence of the author of *Uncle Tom's Cabin*, and, upon being assured that it was, had decided to dwell there. This is, of course, fanciful, for his antecedents were wholly unknown, but in his time he could hardly have been in any household where he would not have heard *Uncle Tom's Cabin* talked about. When he came to Mrs Stowe, he was as large as he ever was, and apparently as old as he ever became. Yet there was in him no appearance of age; he was in the happy maturity of all his powers, and you would rather have said in that maturity he had found the secret of perpetual youth. And it was as difficult to believe that he would ever be aged as it was to imagine that he had ever been in immature youth. There was in him a mysterious perpetuity.

After some years, when Mrs Stowe made her winter home in Florida, Calvin came to live with us. From the first moment, he fell into the ways of the house and assumed a recognized position in the family – I say recognized, because after he became known he was always inquired for by visitors, and in the letters to the other members of the family he always received a message. Although the least obtrusive of beings, his individuality always made itself felt.

His personal appearance had much to do with this, for he was of royal mould, and had an air of high breeding. He was large, but he had nothing of the fat grossness of the celebrated Angora family; though powerful, he was exquisitely proportioned, and as graceful in every movement as a young leopard. When he stood up to open a door – he opened all the doors with old-fashioned latches – he was portentously tall, and when he stretched on the rug before the fire he seemed too long for this world – as indeed he was. His coat was the finest and softest I have ever seen, a shade of quiet Maltese; and from his throat downward, underneath, to the white tips of his feet, he wore the whitest and most delicate ermine; and no person was ever more fastidiously neat. In his finely formed head you saw something of his aristocratic character; the ears were small and cleanly cut, there was a tinge of pink in the nostrils, his face was handsome, and the expression of his countenance exceedingly intelligent – I should call it even a sweet expression if the term were not inconsistent with his look of alertness and sagacity.

It is difficult to convey a just idea of his gaiety in connection with his dignity and gravity, which his name expressed. As we know nothing of his family, of course it will be understood that Calvin was his Christian name. He had times of relaxation into utter playfulness, delighting in a ball of yarn, catching sportively at stray ribbons when his mistress was at her toilet, and pursuing his own tail, with hilarity, for lack of anything better. He could amuse himself by the hour, and he did not care for children; perhaps something in his past was present to his memory. He had absolutely no bad habits, and his disposition was perfect. I never saw him exactly angry, though I have seen his tail grow to an enormous size when a strange cat appeared upon his lawn. He disliked cats, evidently regarding them as feline and treacherous, and he had no association with them. Occasionally there would be heard a night concert in the shrubbery. Calvin would ask to have the door opened, and then you would hear a rush and a 'Pestzt', and the concert would explode, and Calvin would quietly come in and resume his seat on the hearth. There was no trace of anger in his manner, but he wouldn't have any of that about the house. He had the rare virtue of magnanimity. Although he had fixed notions about his own rights, and extraordinary persistency in getting them, he never showed temper at a repulse; he simply and firmly persisted till he had what he wanted. His diet was one point; his idea was that of the scholars about dictionaries – to get the best. He knew as well as anyone what was in the house, and would refuse beef if turkey was to be had; and if there were oysters, he would wait over the turkey to see if the oysters would not be forthcoming. And yet he was not a gross gourmand; he would eat bread if he saw me eating it, and thought he was not being imposed on. His habits of feeding, also, were refined; he never used a knife, and he would put up his hand and draw the fork down to his mouth as gracefully as a grown person. Unless necessity compelled, he would not eat in the kitchen, but insisted upon his meals in the dining-room, and would wait patiently, unless a stranger were present; and then he was sure to importune the visitor, hoping that the latter was ignorant of the rule of the house, and would give him something. They used to say that he preferred as his tablecloth on the floor a certain well-known Church journal; but this was said by an Episcopalian. So far as I know, he had no religious prejudices, except that he did not like the association with Romanists. He tolerated the servants, because they belonged to the house, and would sometimes linger by the kitchen stove; but the moment visitors came in he arose, opened the door, and marched into the drawing-room. Yet he enjoyed the company of his equals, and never withdrew, no matter how many callers – whom he recognized as of his society – might come into the drawing-room. Calvin was fond of company, but he wanted to choose it; and I have no doubt that his was an aristocratic fastidiousness rather than one of faith. It was so with most people.

The intelligence of Calvin was something phenomenal, in his rank of life. He established a method of communicating his wants, and even some of his sentiments; and he could help himself in many things. There was a furnace register in a retired room, where he used to go when he wished to be alone, that he always opened when he desired more heat; but never shut it, any more than he shut the door after himself. He could do almost everything but speak; and you would declare sometimes that you could see a pathetic longing to do that in his intelligent face. I have no desire to overdraw his qualities, but if there was one thing in him more noticeable than another, it was his fondness for nature. He could content himself for hours at a low window, looking into the ravine and at the great trees, noting the smallest stir there; he delighted, above all things, to accompany me walking about the garden, hearing the birds, getting the smell of the fresh earth, and rejoicing in the sunshine. He followed me and gambolled like a dog, rolling over on the turf and exhibiting his delight in a hundred ways. If I worked, he sat and watched me, or looked off over the bank, and kept his ear open to the twitter in the cherry trees. When it stormed, he was sure to sit at the window, keenly watching the rain or the snow, glancing up and down at its falling; and a winter tempest always delighted him. [...]

I hesitate to speak of his capacity for friendship and the affectionateness of his nature, for I know from his own reserve that he would not care to have it much talked about. We understood each other perfectly, but we never made any fuss about it; when I spoke his name and snapped my fingers, he came to me; when I returned home at night, he was pretty sure to be waiting for me near the gate, and would rise and saunter along the walk, as if his being there were purely accidental – so shy was he commonly of showing feeling; and when I opened the door he never rushed in, like a cat, but loitered, and lounged, as if he had had no intention of going in, but he would condescend to. And yet, the fact was, he knew dinner was ready, and he was bound to be there. He kept the run of dinner-time. It happened sometimes, during our absence in the summer, that dinner would be early, and Calvin, walking about the grounds, missed it and came in late. But he never made a mistake the second day. There was one thing he never did – he never rushed through an open doorway. He never forgot his dignity. If he had asked to have the door opened, and was eager to go out, he always went deliberately; I can see him now, standing on the sill, looking about at the sky as if he was thinking whether it were worthwhile to take an umbrella, until he was near having his tail shut in.

His friendship was rather constant than demonstrative. When we returned from an absence of nearly two years, Calvin welcomed us with evident pleasure, but showed his satisfaction rather by tranquil happiness than by fuming about. He had the faculty of making us glad to get home. It was his constancy that was so attractive. He liked companionship, but he wouldn't be petted, or fussed over, or sit in anyone's lap a moment; he always extricated himself from such familiarity with dignity and with no show of temper. If there was any petting to be done, however, he chose to do it. Often he would sit looking at me, and then, moved by a delicate affection, come and pull at my coat and sleeve until he could touch my face with his nose, and then go away contented. He had a habit of coming to my study in the morning, sitting quietly by my side or on the table for hours, watching the pen run over the paper, occasionally swinging his tail round for a blotter, and then going to sleep among the papers by the inkstand. Or, more rarely, he would watch the writing from a perch on my shoulder. Writing always interested him, and, until he understood it, he wanted to hold the pen.

He always held himself in a kind of reserve with his friend, as if he had said, 'Let us respect our personality, and not make a "mess" of friendship.' He saw, with Emerson, the risk of degrading it to trivial conveniency. 'Why insist on rash personal relations with your friends? Leave this touching and clawing.' Yet I would not give an unfair notion of his aloofness, his fine sense of the sacredness of the me and the not-me. And, at the risk of not being believed, I will relate an incident, which was often repeated. Calvin had the practice of passing a portion of the night in the contemplation of its beauties, and would come into our chamber over the roof of the conservatory through the open window, summer and winter, and go to sleep at the foot of my bed. He would do this always exactly in this way; he never was content to stay in the chamber if we compelled him to go upstairs and through the door. He had the obstinacy of General Grant. But this is by the way. In the morning he performed his toilet and went down to breakfast with the rest of the family. Now, when the mistress was absent from home, and at no other time, Calvin would come in the morning, when the bell rang, to the head of the bed, put up his feet and look into my face, follow me about when I rose, 'assist' at the dressing, and in many purring ways show his fondness, as if he had plainly said, 'I know that she has gone away, but I am here.' Such was Calvin in rare moments. He had his limitations. Whatever passion he had for nature, he had no conception of art. There was sent to him once a fine and very expressive cat's head in bronze, by Frémiet. I placed it on the floor. He regarded it intently, approached it cautiously and crouchingly, touched it with his nose, perceived the fraud, turned away abruptly, and never would notice it afterward. On the whole, his life was not only a successful one, but a happy one. He never had but one fear, so far as I know: he had a mortal and a reasonable terror of plumbers. He would never stay in the house when they were here. No coaxing could quiet him. Of course, he didn't share our fear about their charges, but he must have had some dreadful experience with them in that portion of his life which is unknown to us. A plumber was to him the devil, and I have no doubt that, in his scheme, plumbers were foreordained to do him mischief.

In speaking of his worth, it has never occurred to me to estimate Calvin by the worldly standard. I know that it is customary now, when anyone dies, to ask how much he was worth, and that no obituary in the newspapers is considered complete without such an estimate. The plumbers in our house were one day overheard to say that, 'They say that *she* says that *he* says that he wouldn't take a hundred dollars for him.' It is unnecessary to say that I never made such a remark, and that, so far as Calvin was concerned, there was no purchase in money. As I look back upon it, Calvin's life seems to me a fortunate one, for it was natural and unforced. He ate when he was hungry, slept when he was sleepy, and enjoyed existence to the very tips of his toes and the end of his expressive and slow-moving tail. He delighted to roam about the garden, and stroll among the trees, and to lie on the green grass and luxuriate in all the sweet influences of summer. You could never accuse him of idleness, and yet he knew the secret of repose. The poet who wrote so prettily of him that his little life was rounded with a sleep, understated his felicity; it was rounded with a good many. His conscience never seemed to interfere with his slumbers. In fact, he had good habits and a contented mind. I can see him now walk in at the study door, sit down by my chair, bring his tail artistically about his feet, and look up at me with unspeakable happiness in his handsome face. I often thought that he felt the dumb limitation which denied him the power of language. But since he was denied speech, he scorned the inarticulate mouthings of the lower animals. The vulgar mewing and yowling of the cat species was beneath him; he sometimes uttered a sort of articulate and well-bred ejaculation when he wished to call attention to something that he considered remarkable or to some want of his, but he never went whining about. He would sit for hours at a closed window, when he desired to enter, without a murmur, and when it was opened he never admitted that he had been impatient by bolting in. Though speech he had not, and the unpleasant kind of utterance given to his race he would not use, he had a mighty power of purr to express his measureless content with congenial society. There was in him a musical organ with stops of varied power and expression, upon which I have no doubt he could have performed Scarlatti's celebrated cat's fugue. Whether Calvin died of old age, or was carried off by one of the diseases incident to youth, it is impossible to say; for his departure was as quiet as his advent was mysterious. I only know that he appeared to us in this world in his perfect stature and beauty, and that after a time, like Lohengrin, he withdrew. In his illness there was nothing more to be regretted than in all his blameless life. I suppose there never was an illness that had more dignity and sweetness and resignation in it. It came on gradually, in a kind of listlessness and want of appetite. An alarming symptom was his preference for the warmth of a furnace register to the lively sparkle of the open wood fire. Whatever pain he suffered, he bore it in silence, and seemed only anxious not to obtrude his malady. We tempted him with the delicacies of the season, but it soon became impossible for him to eat, and for two weeks he ate or drank scarcely anything. Sometimes he made an effort to take something, but it was evident that he made the effort to please us. The neighbours – and I am convinced that the advice of neighbours is never good for anything – suggested catnip. He wouldn't even smell it. We had the attendance of an amateur practitioner of medicine, whose real office was the cure of souls, but nothing touched his case. He took what was offered, but it was with the air of one to whom the time for pellets was past. He sat or lay day after day almost motionless, never once making a display of those vulgar convulsions or contortions of pain which are so disagreeable to society. His favourite place was on the brightest spot of a Smyrna rug by the conservatory, where the sunlight fell and he could hear the fountain play. If we went to him and exhibited our interest in his condition, he always purred in recognition of our sympathy. And when I spoke his name, he looked up with an expression that said, 'I understand it, old fellow, but it's no use.' He was to all who came to visit him a model of calmness and patience in affliction.

I was absent from home at the last, but heard by daily postal card of his failing condition; and never again saw him alive. One sunny morning he rose from his rug, went into the conservatory (he was very thin then), walked around it deliberately, looking at all the plants he knew, and then went to the bay window in the dining room, and stood a long time looking out upon the little field, now brown and sere, and towards the garden, where perhaps the happiest hours of his life had been spent. It was a last look. He turned and walked away, laid himself down upon the bright spot in the rug, and quietly died. It is not too much to say that a little shock went through the neighbourhood when it was known that Calvin was dead, so marked was his individuality; and his friends, one after another, came in to see him. There was no sentimental nonsense about his obsequies; it was felt that any parade would have been distasteful to him. John, who acted as undertaker, prepared a candlebox for him, and I believe assumed a professional decorum; but there may have been the usual levity underneath, for I heard that he remarked in the kitchen that it was the driest wake he ever attended. Everybody, however, felt a fondness for Calvin, and regarded him with a certain respect. Between him and Bertha there existed a great friendship, and she apprehended his nature; she used to say that sometimes she was afraid of him, he looked at her so intelligently; she was never certain that he was what he appeared to be.

When I returned, they had laid Calvin on a table in an upper chamber by an open window. It was February. He reposed in a candlebox, lined about the edge with evergreen, and at his head stood a little wineglass with flowers. He lay with his head tucked down in his arms – a favourite position of his before the fire – as if asleep in the comfort of his soft and exquisite fur. It was the involuntary exclamation of those who saw him, 'How natural he looks!' As for myself, I said nothing. John buried him under the twin hawthorn trees – one white and the other pink – in a spot where Calvin was fond of lying and listening to the hum of summer insects and the twitter of birds.

Perhaps I have failed to make appear the individuality of character that was so evident to those who knew him. At any rate, I have set down nothing concerning him but the literal truth. He was always a mystery. I did not know whence he came; I do not know whither he has gone. I would not weave one spray of falsehood in the wreath I lay upon his grave.

from *My Summer in a Garden* (1882)

ATOSSA

Matthew Arnold (1822–88)

Poor Matthias! Wouldst thou have
More than pity? claim'st a stave?
– Friends more near us than a bird
We dismiss'd without a word.
Rover, with the good brown head,
Great Atossa, they are dead;
Dead, and neither prose nor rhyme
Tells the praises of their prime.
Thou didst know them old and grey,
Know them in their sad decay.
Thou hast seen Atossa sage
Sit for hours beside thy cage;
Thou wouldst chirp, thou foolish bird,
Flutter, chirp – she never stirr'd!
What were now these toys to her?
Down she sank amid her fur;
Eyed thee with a soul resign'd –
And thou deemedst cats were kind!
– Cruel, but composed and bland,
Dumb, inscrutable and grand,
So Tiberius might have sat,
Had Tiberius been a cat.

from 'Poor Matthias'

EGYPTIAN CATS

Herodotus (c.480–c.425 BC)

And when a fire breaks out very strange things happen to the cats. The Egyptians stand round in a broken line, thinking more of the cats than of quenching the burning; but the cats slip through or leap over the men and spring into the fire. When this happens, there is great mourning in Egypt. Dwellers in a house where a cat has died a natural death shave their eyebrows and no more; where a dog has so died, the head and the whole body are shaven.

Dead cats are taken away into sacred buildings, where they are embalmed and buried, in the town of Bubastis; bitches are buried in sacred coffins by the townsmen, in their several towns; and the like is done with ichneumons. Shrewmice and hawks are taken away to Buto, ibises to the city of Hermes. There are but few bears, and the wolves are little bigger than foxes; both these are buried wherever they are found lying.

CAT HYPNOSIS

W.H. Hudson (1841–1922)

I must now return to the subject of [...] Bawcombe's cat at Doveton, who had the habit of sitting on a rail of the line which runs through the vale, and was eventually killed by a train. So strange a story – for how strange it seems that an animal of so cautious and well-balanced a mind, so capable above all others of saving itself in difficult and dangerous emergencies, should have met its end in such a way! – might very well have suggested something behind the mere fact, some mysterious weakness in the animal similar to that which Herodotus relates of the Egyptian cat in its propensity of rushing into the fire when a house was burning and thus destroying itself. Yet no such idea came into my mind: it was just a strange fact, an accident in the life of an individual, and after telling it I passed on, thinking no more about the subject, only to find long months afterwards, by the merest chance, that I had been very near to a discovery of the greatest significance and interest in the life-history of the animal.

It came about in the following way. I was on the platform of a station on the South-Western line from Salisbury to Yeovil, waiting for my train, when a pretty little kitten came out of the stationmaster's house at the end of the platform, and I picked it up. Then a child, a wee girlie of about five, came out to claim her pet, and we got into a talk about the kitten. She was pleased at its being admired, and saying she would show me the other one, ran in and came out with a black kitten in her arms. I duly admired this one too. 'But,' I said, 'they won't let you keep both, because then there would be too many cats.'

'No – only two,' she returned.

'Three, with their mother.'

'No, they haven't got a mother – she was killed on the line.'

I remembered the shepherd's cat, and by and by finding the stationmaster I questioned him about the cat that had been killed.

'Oh, yes,' he said, 'cats are always getting killed on the line – we can never keep one long. I don't know if they try to cross the line or how it is. One of the porters saw the last one get killed and will tell you just how it happened.'

I found the porter, and his account was that he saw the cat on the line, standing with its forepaws on a rail when an express train was coming. He called to the cat two or three times, then yelled at it to frighten it off, but it never moved; it stared as if dazed at the coming train, and was struck on the head and knocked dead.

This story set me making inquiries at other village stations, and at other villages where there are no stations, but close to which the line runs in the Wylye vale and where there is a pointsman. I was told that cats are very often found killed on the line, in some instances crushed as if they had been lying or sitting on a rail when the train went over them. They got dazed, the men said, and could not save themselves.

I was also told that rabbits were sometimes killed and, more frequently, hares. 'I've had several hares from the line,' one man told me. He said that he had seen a hare running before a train, and thought that in most cases the hare kept straight on until it was run down and killed. But not in every case, as he had actually seen one hare killed, and in this case the hare sat up and remained staring at the coming train until it was struck. It cannot be doubted, I think, that the cat is subject to this strange weakness. It is not a case of 'losing its head' like a cyclist amidst the traffic in a thoroughfare, or of miscalculating the speed of a coming train and attempting too late to cross the line. The sight of the coming train paralyzes its will, or hypnotizes it, and it cannot save itself.

Now the dog, a less well-balanced animal than the cat and inferior in many ways, has no such failing, and is killed by a train purely through blundering. While engaged in making these inquiries, a Wiltshire woman told me of an adventure she had with her dog, a fox-terrier. She had just got over the line at a level crossing when the gates swung to, and looking for her dog she saw him absorbed in a smell he had discovered on the other side of the line. An express train was just coming, and screaming to her dog she saw him make a dash to get across just as the engine came abreast of her. The dog had vanished from sight, but when the whole train had passed up he jumped from between the rails where he had been crouching and bounded across to her, quite unhurt. He had dived under the train behind the engine, and waited there till it had gone by!

It is, however, a fact that not all the cats killed on the line have been hypnotized or dazed at the sight of the coming train; undoubtedly some do meet their death through attempting to cross the line before a coming train. At all events, I heard of one such case from a person who had witnessed it. It was at a spot where a small group of workmen's cottages stands close to the line at a village; here I was told that several cats got killed on the line every year, and as the man who gave me the information had seen a cat running across the line before a train and getting killed, it was assumed by the cottagers that it was so in all cases.

from *A Shepherd's Life* (1910)

ON THE DEATH OF A FAVOURITE CAT, DROWNED IN A TUB OF GOLD FISHES

Thomas Gray (1716–71)

'Twas on a lofty vase's side,
Where China's gayest art had dy'd
    The azure flowers that blow;
Demurest of the tabby kind,
The pensive Selima, reclin'd,
    Gaz'd on the lake below.

Her conscious tail her joy declar'd;
The fair round face, the snowy beard,
    The velvet of her paws,
Her coat, that with the tortoise vies,
Her ears of jet, and emerald eyes,
    She saw; and purr'd applause.

Still had she gaz'd; but midst the tide
Two angel forms were seen to glide,
    The Genii of the stream:
Their scaly armour's Tyrian hue
Thro' richest purple to the view
    Betray'd a golden gleam.

The hapless Nymph with wonder saw:
A whisker first, and then a claw,
    With many an ardent wish,
She stretch'd in vain to reach the prize.
What female heart can gold despise?
    What Cat's averse to fish?

Presumptuous Maid! with looks intent
Again she stretch'd, again she bent,

Nor knew the gulf between.
(Malignant Fate sat by, and smil'd.)
The slipp'ry verge her feet beguil'd,
    She tumbled headlong in.

Eight times emerging from the flood
She mew'd to ev'ry wat'ry God,
    Some speedy aid to send.
No Dolphin came, no Nereid stirr'd:
Nor cruel *Tom*, nor *Susan* heard.
    A Fav'rite has no friend!

From hence, ye Beauties, undeceiv'd,
Know, one false step is ne'er retriev'd,
    And be with caution bold.
Not all that tempts your wand'ring eyes
And heedless hearts, is lawful prize;
    Nor all that glisters, gold.

DON PIERROT DE NAVARRE

Théophile Gautier (1811–72)

A cat brought from Havana by Mademoiselle Aita de la Penuela, a young Spanish artist whose studies of white angoras may still be seen gracing the printsellers' windows, produced the daintiest little kitten imaginable. It was just like a swan's-down powder-puff, and on account of its immaculate whiteness it received the name of Pierrot. When it grew big this was lengthened to Don Pierrot de Navarre as being more grandiose and majestic.

Don Pierrot, like all animals which are spoiled and made much of, developed a charming amiability of character. He shared the life of the household with all the pleasure which cats find in the intimacy of the domestic hearth. Seated in his usual place near the fire, he really appeared to understand what was being said, and to take an interest in it.

His eyes followed the speakers, and from time to time he would utter little sounds, as though he too wanted to make remarks and give his opinion on literature, which was our usual topic of conversation. He was very fond of books, and when he found one open on a table he would lie on it, look at the page attentively, and turn over the leaves with his paw; then he would end by going to sleep, for all the world as if he were reading a fashionable novel.

Directly I took up a pen he would jump on my writing-desk and with deep attention watch the steel nib tracing black spider-legs on the expanse of white paper, and his head would turn each time I began a new line. Sometimes he tried to take part in the work, and would attempt to pull the pen out of my hand, no doubt in order to write himself, for he was an aesthetic cat, like Hoffman's Murr, and I strongly suspect him of having scribbled his memoirs at night on some house-top by the light of his phosphorescent eyes. Unfortunately these lucubrations have been lost.

Don Pierrot never went to bed until I came in. He waited for me inside the door, and as I entered the hall he would rub himself against my legs and arch his back, purring joyfully all the time. Then he proceeded to walk in front of me like a page, and if I had asked him, he would certainly have carried the candle for me. In this fashion he escorted me to my room and waited while I undressed; then he would jump on the bed, put his paws round my neck, rub noses with me, and lick me with his rasping little pink tongue, while giving vent to soft inarticulate cries, which clearly expressed how pleased he was to see me again. Then when his transports of affection had subsided, and the hour for repose had come, he would balance himself on the rail of the bedstead and sleep there like a bird perched on a bough. When I woke in the morning he would come and lie near me until it was time to get up. Twelve o'clock was the hour at which I was supposed to come in. On this subject Pierrot had all the notions of a concierge.

At that time we had instituted little evening gatherings among a few friends, and had formed a small society, which we called the Four Candles Club, the room in which we met being, as it happened, lit by four candles in silver candlesticks, which were placed at the corners of the table.

Sometimes the conversation became so lively that I forgot the time, at the risk of finding, like Cinderella, my carriage turned into a pumpkin and my coachman into a rat.

Pierrot waited for me several times until two o'clock in the morning, but in the end my conduct displeased him, and he went to bed without me. This mute protest against my innocent dissipation touched me so much that ever after I came home regularly at midnight. But it was a long time before Pierrot forgave me. He wanted to be sure that it was not a sham repentance; but when he was convinced of the sincerity of my conversion, he deigned to take me into favour again, and he resumed his nightly post in the entrance-hall. [...]

Don Pierrot de Navarre, being a native of Havana, needed a hot-house temperature. This he found indoors, but the house was surrounded by large gardens, divided up by palings through which a cat could easily slip, and planted with big trees in which hosts of birds twittered and sang; and sometimes Pierrot, taking advantage of an open door, would go out hunting of an evening and run over the dewy grass and flowers. He would then have to wait till morning to be let in again, for although he might come mewing under the windows, his appeal did not always wake the sleepers inside.

He had a delicate chest, and one colder night than usual he took a chill which soon developed into consumption. Poor Pierrot, after a year of coughing, became wasted and thin, and his coat, which formerly boasted such a snowy gloss, now put one in mind of the lustreless white of a shroud. His great limpid eyes looked enormous in his attenuated face. His pink nose had grown pale, and he would walk sadly along the sunny wall with slow steps, and watch the yellow autumn leaves whirling up in spirals. He looked as though he were reciting Millevoye's elegy.

There is nothing more touching than a sick animal; it submits to suffering with such gentle, pathetic resignation.

Everything possible was done to try and save Pierrot. He had a very clever doctor who sounded him and felt his pulse. He ordered him asses' milk, which the poor creature drank willingly enough out of his little china saucer. He lay for hours on my knee like the ghost of a sphinx, and I could feel the bones of his spine like the beads of a rosary under my fingers. He tried to respond to my caresses with a feeble purr which was like a death rattle.

When he was dying he lay panting on his side, but with a supreme effort he raised himself and came to me with dilated eyes in which there was a look of intense supplication. This look seemed to say: 'Cannot you save me, you who are a man?' Then he staggered a short way with eyes already glazing, and fell down with such a lamentable cry, so full of despair and anguish, that I was pierced with silent horror.

He was buried at the bottom of the garden under a white rosebush which still marks his grave.

from 'The White and Black Dynasties'
in *La Ménagerie Intime*, translated by Lady Chance

IN MEMORIAM MRS SNOWBALL PAT PAW

Louisa M. Alcott (1832–88)

THE PUBLIC BEREAVEMENT

It is our painful duty to record the sudden and mysterious disappearance of our cherished friend, Mrs Snowball Pat Paw. This lovely and beloved cat was the pet of a large circle of warm and admiring friends; for her beauty attracted all eyes, her graces and virtues, endeared her to all hearts, and her loss is deeply felt by the whole community.

When last seen, she was sitting at the gate, watching the butcher's cart; and it is feared that some villain, tempted by her charms, basely stole her. Weeks have passed, but no trace of her has been discovered; and we relinquish all hope, tie a black ribbon to her basket, set aside her dish, and weep for her as one lost to us for ever.

A Lament

For S. B. Pat Paw

We mourn the loss of our little pet,
    And sigh o'er her hapless fate.
For never more by the fire she'll sit,
    Nor play by the old green gate.

The little grave where her infant sleeps,
    Is 'neath the chestnut tree;
But o'er *her* grave we may not weep,
    We know not where it may be.

Her empty bed, her idle ball,
    Will never see her more;
No gentle tap, no loving purr
    Is heard at the parlour door.

Another cat comes after her mice,
    A cat with a dirty face;
But she does not hunt as our darling did,
    Nor play with her airy grace.

Her stealthy paws tread the very hall
    Where Snowball used to play,
But she only spits at the dogs our pet
    So gallantly drove away.

She is useful and mild, and does her best,
    But she is not fair to see;
And we cannot give her your place, dear,
    Nor worship her as we worship thee.

from *Little Women* (1868–9)

A FAVOURITE CAT'S DYING SOLILOQUY ADDRESSED TO MRS PATTON OF LICHFIELD

Anna Seward (1747–1809)

Long years beheld me *Patton*'s mansion grace,
The gentlest, fondest of the feline race;
Before her frisking thro' the garden glade,
Or at her feet, in quite slumber, laid;
Prais'd for my glossy back, of tortoise streak,
And the warm smoothness of my snowy neck;
Soft paws, that sheath'd for her the clawing nails,
The shining whisker, and meand'ring tail.
Now feeble age each glazing eye-ball dims,
And pain has stiffen'd these once supple limbs;
Fate of eight lives the forfeit gasp obtains,
And e'en the ninth creeps languid thro' my veins.

Much, sure, of good the future has in store,
When Lucy basks on *Patton*'s hearth no more,
In those blest climes where fishes oft forsake
The winding river and the glassy lake;
There as our silent-footed race behold
The spots of crimson and the fins of gold,
Venturing beyond the shielding waves to stray,
They gasp on shelving banks, our easy prey;
While birds unwing'd hop careless o'er the ground,
And the plump mouse incessant trots around,
Near wells of cream, which mortals never skim,
Warm marum creeping round their shallow brim;
Where green valerian tufts, luxuriant spread,
Cleanse the sleek hide, and form the fragrant bed.

Yet, stern dispenser of the final blow,
Before thou lay'st an aged Grimalkin low,

Bend to her last request a gracious ear,
Some days, some few short days to linger here!
So, to the guardian of her earthly weal
Shall softest purs these tender truths reveal:
Ne'er shall thy now expiring Puss forget
To thy kind cares her long-enduring debt;
Nor shall the joys that painless realms decree,
Efface the comforts once bestow'd by thee;
To countless mice thy chicken bones preferr'd,
Thy toast to golden fish and wingless bird:
O'er marum border and valerian bed
Thy Lucy shall decline her moping head;
Sigh that she climbs no more, with grateful glee,
Thy downy sofa and thy cradling knee;
Nay, e'en by walls of cream shall sullen swear,
Since *Patton*, her lov'd mistress, is not there.

MORE EGYPTIAN CATS

Diodorus of Sicily (1st century BC)

When one of these animals dies they wrap it in fine linen and then, wailing and beating their breasts, carry it off to be embalmed; and after it has been treated with cedar oil and such spices as have the quality of imparting a pleasant odour and of preserving the body for a long time, they lay it away in a consecrated tomb. And whoever intentionally kills one of these animals is put to death, unless it be a cat or an ibis that he kills; but if he kills one of these, whether intentionally or unintentionally, he is certainly put to death, for the common people gather in crowds and deal with the perpetrator most cruelly, sometimes doing this without waiting for a trial. And because of their fear of such a punishment any who have caught sight of one of these animals lying dead withdraw to a great distance and shout with lamentations and protestations that they found the animal already dead. So deeply implanted also in the hearts of the common people is their superstitious regard for these animals and so unalterable are the emotions cherished by every man regarding the honour due to them that once, at the time when Ptolemy their king had not as yet been given by the Romans the appellation of 'friend' and the people were exercising all zeal in courting the favour of the embassy from Italy which was then visiting Egypt and, in their fear, were intent upon giving no cause for complaint or war, when one of the Romans killed a cat and the multitude rushed in a crowd to his house, neither the officials sent by the king to beg the man off nor the fear of Rome which all the people felt were enough to save the man from punishment, even though his act had been an accident. And this incident we relate, not from hearsay, but we saw it with our own eyes on the occasion of the visit we made to Egypt.

THE DEATH OF RUMPELSTILTZCHEN

Robert Southey (1774–1843)

Alas, Grosvenor, this day died poor old Rumpel, after as long and happy a life as cat could wish for, if cats form wishes on that subject. His full titles were: 'The most Noble the Archduke Rumpelstiltzchen, Marquis Macbum, Earl Tomlemagne, Baron Raticide, Waowhler, and Skaratch.'
There should be a court mourning in Catland, and if the Dragon [Bedford's cat] wear a black ribbon round his neck, or a band of crape, *à la militaire*, on one of his forelegs, it will be but a becoming mark of respect.

As we have no catacombs here, he is to be decently interred in the orchard, and catmint planted on his grave. Poor creature, it is well that he has thus come to his end, since he had grown to be an object of pity. I believe we are, each and all, servants included, more sorry for his loss, or rather more affected by it, than any one of us would like to confess.

from a letter to Grosvenor C. Bedford

DEDICATION

Graham R. Tomson (1863–1911)

Dear Furry Shade! in regions of the Dead,
On pleasant plains, by murmurous waters, led;
What placid joys your brindled bosom swell!
While smiling virgins crowned with asphodel
Bring brimming bowls of milk in sacrifice,
And, passing plump and sleek, th' Elysian mice
Sport round your feet, and frisk, and glide away,
Captured at last – a not too facile prey.
Yet, with each earthly care and tremor stilled,
With every wish of cat-hood well fulfilled,
Still sometimes turn, with retrospective gaze,
To count the sweets of less luxurious days,
When you were wont to take your simple ease
Couched at my feet or stretched along my knees:
When never cloud our loving-kindness knew
(Though now and then, alas! I punished you),
Still were you fain, conciliating, bland,
With velvet cheek to chafe th' avenging hand.
Still would you watch, did I but chance to roam,
Supine upon the threshold of our home
Until, my brief-paced aberrations o'er,
With purrings deep you welcomed me once more.
O dearly-loved! Untimely lost! – today
An offering at your phantom feet I lay:
Purr fond applause, and take in gracious kind
This little wreath of various verses twined;
Nor, though Persephone's own Puss you be,
Let Orcus breed oblivion – of me.

JEREMY BENTHAM'S CAT

Dr John Bowring (1792–1872)

Bentham was very fond of animals, particularly 'pussies', as he called them, when they had domestic virtues, but he had no particular affection for the common race of cats. He had one, however, of which he used to boast that he had made a man of him, and whom he was wont to invite to eat macaroni at his own table. This puss got knighted, and rejoiced in the name of Sir John Langbourne. In his early days he was a frisky, inconsiderate, and, to say the truth, somewhat profligate gentleman; and had, according to the report of his patron, the habit of seducing light and giddy young ladies, of his own race, into the garden of Queen's Square Place: but tired at last, like Solomon, of pleasures and vanities, he became sedate and thoughtful – took to the church, laid down his knightly title, and was installed as the Reverend John Langbourne. He gradually obtained a great reputation for sanctity and learning, and a Doctor's degree was conferred upon him. When I knew him, in his declining days, he bore no other name than the Reverend Doctor John Langbourne: and he was alike conspicuous for his gravity and philosophy. Great respect was invariably shown his reverence: and it was supposed that he was not far off from a mitre, when old age interfered with his hopes and honours. He departed amidst the regrets of his many friends, and was gathered to his fathers, and to eternal rest, in a cemetery in Milton's garden.

UPON A FRIEND'S PET CAT, BEING SICK

John Winstanley (1678–1751)

How fickle's Health! when sickness thus
So sharp, so sudden visits *Puss*!
A warning fair, and Instance good,
To show how frail are Flesh and Blood,
That Fate has Mortals at a Call,
Men, Women, Children – Cats and all.
Nor should we fear, despair, or sorrow,
If well today, and ill tomorrow,
Grief being but a Med'cine vain,
For griping Gut, or aching Brain,
And Patience the best Cure for Pain.
How brisk and well, last Week, was *Puss*!
How sleek, and plump, as one of us:
Yet now, alack! and well-a-day!
How dull, how rough, and fall'n away.
How feintly creeps about the House!
Regardless or of Play, or Mouse;
Nor stomach has, to drink, or eat,
Of sweetest Milk, or daintiest Meat;
A grievous this, and sore Disaster
To all the House, but most his Master,
Who sadly takes it thus to heart,
As in his Pains he bore a part.
And, what increases yet his Grief,
Is, nought can cure, or give Relief,
No Doctor caring to prescribe,
Or Med'cine give, for Love, or Bribe,
Nor other Course, but to petition
Dame Nature, oft the best Physician,
The readiest too, and cheapest sure,
Since she ne'er asks a Fee for Cure

Nor ever takes a single Shilling,
As many basely do for killing.
So, for a while, snug let him lie,
As Fates decree, to live or die,
While I, in dismal dog'rel Verse,
His Beauties and his Fame rehearse.
Poor *Bob*! how have I smiled to see
Thee sitting on thy Master's Knee?
While, pleased to stroke thy Tabby-coat,
Sweet Purrings warbling in thy Throat,
He would with rapturous Hug declare,
No Voice more sweet, or Maid more fair.
No prating Poll, or Monkey bold,
Was more caress'd by Woman old,
Nor flutt'ring Fop, with Am'rous Tongue,
So much admir'd by Virgin Young.
Miss *Betty's* Bed-fellow, and Pet
(Too young to have another yet),
At Dinner, he'd beside her sit,
Fed from her Mouth with sweetest Bit;
Not Mrs L——'s so charming *Philly*
Was more familiar, fond, or silly,
Nor Mrs C——'s ugly Cur
Made more a foustre, or more stir.
Oft tir'd, and cloy'd, with being petted,
Or else by *Molly* beaten, fretted,
He'd out into the Garden run,
To sleep in th' Shade, or bask in th' Sun;
Sometimes about the Walks he'd ramble,
Or on the verdant Green would amble,
Or under the hedges sculking sit,
To catch the unwary *Wren*, or *Tit*,
Or *Sparrows* young, which Sun-beams hot
Had forc'd to quit their mansion Pot,
Then murther with relentless Claws.

Now, cruel Death, so fierce and grim,
With gaping jaws does threaten him,
While pining, he, with Sickness sore,
Oppress'd and griev'd, can hunt no more.

Now joyful Mice skip, frisk, and play,
And safely revel, Night and Day.
The Garrets, Kitchens, Stairs, and Entry,
Unguarded by that dreadful Sentry.

The Pantry now is open set,
No fear for *Puss* therein to get,
With Chicken cold to run away,
Or sip the Cream set by for Tea;
Jenny now need not watch the Door,
Or for lost Meat repine no more,
Nor *Molly* many a scolding dread
For slamming him from off the Bed;
Poor harmless Animal! now lies
As who can say, he lives or dies.
Tho' I have heard a saying that
Some three times three Lives has a Cat;
Should Death then now the Conquest gain,
And feeble *Bob*, with struggle vain,
To his resistless Fate give way,
Yet come to Life, another Day,
How will Time scratch his old bald Pate,
To see himself so *Bobb'd*, so Bit,
To find that *Bob* has eight Lives more
To lose, e'er he can him secure.
Should he however, this Bout dye,
What Pen should write his Elegy?
No living Bard is fit, not One;
Since *Addison*, and Parnel's gone;
Or such another Pen, as that
Which wrote so fine on Mountaign's Cat.

THE CHURCH CAT

George Borrow (1803–81)

As I and my family sat at tea in our parlour, an hour or two after we had taken possession of our lodgings, the door of the room and that of the entrance of the house being open, on account of the fineness of the weather, a poor black cat entered hastily, sat down on the carpet by the table, looked up towards us, and mewed piteously. I never had seen so wretched a looking creature. It was dreadfully attenuated, being little more than skin and bone, and was sorely afflicted with an eruptive malady. And here I may as well relate the history of this cat previous to our arrival which I subsequently learned by bits and snatches. It had belonged to a previous vicar of Llangollen, and had been left behind at his departure. His successor brought with him dogs and cats, who, conceiving that the late vicar's cat had no business at the vicarage, drove it forth to seek another home, which, however, it could not find. Almost all the people of the suburb were Dissenters, as indeed were the generality of the people at Llangollen, and knowing the cat to be a church cat, not only would not harbour it, but did all they could to make it miserable; whilst the few who were not Dissenters, would not receive it into their houses, either because they had cats of their own, or dogs, or did not want a cat, so that the cat had no home and was dreadfully persecuted by nine-tenths of the suburb. Oh, there never was a cat so persecuted as that poor Church of England animal, and solely on account of the opinions which it was supposed to have imbibed in the house of its late master, for I never could learn that the Dissenters of the suburb, nor indeed of Llangollen in general, were in the habit of persecuting other cats; the cat was a Church of England cat, and that was enough: stone it, hang it, drown it! were the cries of almost everybody. If the workmen of the flannel factory, all of whom were Calvinistic Methodists, chanced to get a glimpse of it in the road from the windows of the building, they would sally forth in a body, and with sticks, stones, or for want of other weapons, with clots of horse-dung, of which there was always plenty on the road, would chase it up the high bank or perhaps over the Camlas – the inhabitants of a small street between our house and the factory leading from the road to the river, all of whom were Dissenters, if they saw it moving about the perllan, into which their back windows looked, would shriek and hoot at it, and fling anything of no value, which came easily to hand, at the head or body of the ecclesiastical cat. The good woman of the house, who though a very excellent person, was a bitter Dissenter, whenever she saw it upon her ground or heard it was there, would make after it, frequently attended by her maid Margaret, and her young son, a boy about nine years of age, both of whom hated the cat, and were always ready to attack it, either alone or in company, and no wonder, the maid being not only a Dissenter, but a class teacher, and the boy not only a Dissenter, but intended for the Dissenting ministry. Where it got its food, and food it sometimes must have got, for even a cat, an animal known to have nine lives, cannot live without food, was only known to itself, as was the place where it lay, for even a cat must lie down sometimes; though a labouring man who occasionally dug in the garden told me he believed that in the springtime it ate freshets, and the woman of the house once said that she believed it sometimes slept in the hedge, which hedge, by the bye, divided our perllan from the vicarage grounds, which were very extensive. Well might the cat having led this kind of life for better than two years look mere skin and bone when it made its appearance in our apartment, and have an eruptive malady, and also a bronchitic cough, for I remember it had both. How it came to make its appearance there is a mystery, for it had never entered the house before, even when there were lodgers; that it should not visit the woman, who was its declared enemy, was natural enough, but why, if it did not visit her other lodgers, did it visit us? Did instinct keep it aloof from them? Did instinct draw it towards us?

We gave it some bread-and-butter, and a little tea with milk and sugar. It ate and drank and soon began to purr. The good woman of the house was horrified when on coming in to remove the things she saw the church cat on her carpet. 'What impudence!' she exclaimed, and made towards it, but on our telling her that we did not expect that it should be disturbed, she let it alone. A very remarkable circumstance was, that though the cat had hitherto been in the habit of flying not only from her face, but the very echo of her voice, it now looked her in the face with perfect composure, as much as to say, 'I don't fear you, for I know that I am now safe and with my own people.' It stayed with us two hours and then went away. The next morning it returned. To be short, though it went away every night, it became our own cat, and one of our family. I gave it something which cured it of its eruption, and through good treatment it soon lost its other ailments and began to look sleek and bonny.

We were at first in some perplexity with respect to the disposal of the ecclesiastical cat; it would of course not do to leave it in the garden to the tender mercies of the Calvinistic Methodists of the neighbourhood, more especially those of the flannel manufactory, and my wife and daughter could hardly carry it with them. At length we thought of applying to a young woman of sound church principles who was lately married and lived over the water on the way to the railway station, with whom we were slightly acquainted, to take charge of the animal, and she on the first intimation of our wish willingly acceded to it. So with her poor puss was left along with a trifle for its milk-money, and with her, as we subsequently learned, it continued in peace and comfort till one morning it sprang suddenly from the hearth into the air, gave a mew and died. So much for the ecclesiastical cat.

from *Wild Wales* (1862)

BATHSHEBA

John Greenleaf Whittier (1807–92)

To whom none ever said scat,
No worthier cat
Ever sat on a mat
Or caught a rat:
Requies – cat.

EPITAPH

Revd John Jortin (1698–1770)

Worn out with age and dire disease, a cat,
Friendly to all save wicked mouse and rat,
I'm sent at last to ford the Stygian lake,
And to the infernal coast a voyage make.
Me Proserpine received, and smiling said:
'Be blessed within these mansions of the dead.
Enjoy among thy velvet-footed loves,
Elysian's sunny banks, and shady groves!'
'But if I've well deserved (O gracious Queen),
If patient under sufferings I have been,
Grant me at least one night to visit home again,
Once more to see my home and mistress dear,
And purr these grateful accents in her ear:
"Thy faithful cat, thy poor departed slave
Still loves her mistress, e'en beyond the grave."'

ELEGY ON DE MARSAY

J.K. Stephen (1859–92)

Come cats and kittens everywhere,
　　What'er of cat the world contains,
From Tabby on the kitchen stair
To Tiger burning in his lair
　　Unite your melancholy strains;

Weep, likewise, kindred dogs, and weep
　　Domestic fowls and pigs and goats;
Weep horses, oxen, poultry, sheep,
Weep finny monsters of the deep,
　　Weep foxes, badgers, weasels, stoats.

Weep more than all, exalted man
　　And hardly less exalted maid;
Out-weep creation if you can
Which never yet, since time began,
　　Such creditable grief displayed.

It little profiteth that we
　　Go proudly up and down the land,
And drive our ships across the sea,
And babble of Eternity,
　　And hold the Universe in hand;

If, when our pride is at its height,
　　And glory sits upon our head,
A sudden mist can dim the light,
A voice be heard in pride's despite,
　　A voice which cries: 'De Marsay's dead.'

De Marsay dead! and never more
    Shall I behold that silky form
Lie curled upon the conscious floor
With sinuous limbs and placid snore,
    As one who sleeps through calm and storm?

De Marsay dead! De Marsay dead!
    And are you dead, de Marsay, you?
The sun is shining overhead
With glory undiminished,
    And you are dead; let me die too!

The birds, and beasts, and fishes come,
    And people come, of all degrees;
Beat, sadly beat the funeral drum,
And let the gloomy organ hum
    With dark mysterious melodies.

And (when we've adequately moaned),
    For all the world to wonder at,
Let this great sentence be intoned:
No cat so sweet a mistress owned;
    No mistress owned so sweet a cat.

from *Lapsus Calami* (1891)

ON THE DEATH OF A CAT, A FRIEND OF MINE, AGED TEN YEARS AND A HALF

Christina Rossetti (1830–94)

Who shall tell the lady's grief
When her Cat was past relief?
Who shall number the hot tears
Shed o'er her, beloved for years?
Who shall say the dark dismay
Which her dying caused that day?

Come, ye Muses, one and all,
Come obedient to my call.
Come and mourn, with tuneful breath,
Each one for a separate death;
And while you in numbers sigh,
I will sing her elegy.

Of a noble race she came,
And Grimalkin was her name.
Young and old full many a mouse
Felt the prowess of her house:
Weak and strong full many a rat
Cowered beneath her crushing pat:
And the birds around the place
Shrank from her too close embrace.
But one night, reft of her strength,
She laid down and died at length:
Lay a kitten by her side,
In whose life the mother died.
Spare her line and lineage,
Guard her kitten's tender age,

And that kitten's name as wide
Shall be known as hers that died.

And whoever passes by
The poor grave where Puss doth lie,
Softly, softly let him tread,
Nor disturb her narrow bed.

from *Verses* (1847)

Mark Bryant has written/compiled a number of books on cats and pets including *The Church Cat: Clerical Cats in Stories and Verse*; *Cat Tales for Christmas*; *The Artful Cat: A Tribute with 60 Portraits*; *The World's Greatest Cat Cartoons*; *The Complete Lexicat: A Cat Name Companion*; *It's a Dog's Life: A Canine Cartoon Collection* (Foreword by Jilly Cooper) and *Casanova's Parrot and Other Tales of the Famous and Their Pets*. In addition, he is the author of *Constable: A Brief History of Britain's Oldest Independent Publisher* and other books. He lives in London with his wife and their black-and-white rescue cat, Lucky.